# GRAVE ERRORS

**Books by Carol J. Perry**

*Grave Errors*

*Murder Go Round*

*Look Both Ways*

*Tails, You Lose*

*Caught Dead Handed*

**Available from Kensington Publishing Corp.**

# GRAVE ERRORS

Carol J. Perry



KENSINGTON PUBLISHING CORP.
http://www.kensingtonbooks.com

KENSINGTON BOOKS are published by

Kensington Publishing Corp.
119 West 40th Street
New York, NY 10018



ISBN-13: 978-1-4967-0717-8
ISBN-10: 1-4967-0717-6
First Kensington Mass Market Edition: September 2017

eISBN-13: 978-1-4967-0718-5
eISBN-10: 1-4967-0718-4
First Kensington Electronic Edition: September 2017

10 9 8 7 6 5 4 3 2 1

Printed in the United States of America

*For Dan*
*My husband and best friend.*

*"Three may keep a secret, if two are dead."*

—Benjamin Franklin

# CHAPTER 1

If you've ever been to my hometown of Salem, Massachusetts, during the month of October, you know how crazy it can be—and the closer you get to Halloween, the nuttier it becomes. The following week though, is the exact opposite—kind of like a deflated balloon. The empty candy wrappers have been swept from the streets, the carved pumpkins have gone soft, their jagged-toothed smiles sagging crookedly, and most of the visiting witches and witch wannabes have left town.

I'm Lee Barrett, née Maralee Kowolski, thirty-two, red-haired and Salem-born. I was orphaned early, married once and widowed young. I teach a course in Television Production at the Tabitha Trumbull Academy of the Arts—Salem's newest school. We call it "the Tabby." The sprawling building was once Trumbull's Department Store, back in the 1960s before the shopping malls came. Tabitha Trumbull, the school's namesake, was the founder's wife.

I've worked in television, mostly in front of the camera, ever since graduating from Emerson College, but this was just my second year as a teacher. My lesson plan called for special emphasis on interview skills and investigative reporting. I'd been boning up on those topics myself, with the aid of a shelf full of textbooks and some real-life investigation advice from my police detective boyfriend, Pete Mondello.

Today, one of my students thought of a way to spice up the annual let-down that invariably follows Halloween and to, at the same time, fulfill our annual class assignment—producing a video involving some aspect of Salem's history. Hilda Mendez thought it might be fun to get the city involved in celebrating *Dia de los Muertos*—Day of the Dead—the traditional Mexican celebration that takes place at the beginning of November.

"It's a happier holiday than Halloween," she said. "It celebrates all the cool stuff people enjoyed when they were alive—food and drink and fancy clothes and parties. There are sugar skulls and paper skeletons and flowers at the gravesides and everybody has a good time." Hilda's enthusiasm was contagious. "Salem has such wicked cool cemeteries. Think about it! Close-ups of those really creepy headstones—the ones with the winged skeleton faces and the weird inscriptions. What great video!"

Therese Della Monica, a returning student (and a novice witch-in-training), chimed in. "I'm sure at least one of the old cemeteries is haunted. Maybe all of them!"

"I like it," I said. "Those cemeteries are historical sites for sure, and the whole celebration seems like a perfect fit for Salem. What do the rest of you think?"

I glanced around my classroom which was located in what had been the mezzanine shoe department of the old Trumbull's Department Store. Now a giant flat screen TV, assorted monitors, news desk, green screen and cameras—both rolling and stationary—shared space with vintage Thonet chairs, a lithographed cutout of Buster Brown and his dog Tige, a neon macaw advertising Poll Parrot shoes and a large half-model of a black patent leather pump.

Two men and four women had signed up for the course. Therese was back for more behind-the-camera training. Hilda and the others were new faces. The arts courses offered at the Tabby held attraction for people of all ages who'd always wanted to act or paint or dance or write or—as in the case of my classes—to be involved in the world of television, either behind or in front of the camera.

My oldest students were a pair of over sixty-five identical twins—retired Boston police officers named Roger and Ray Temple, with aspirations of investigative reporting. The two not only dressed alike, but often spoke in unison and/or finished each other's sentences. Quite disconcerting until you got used to it.

"Well," began Roger, "gotta go by the book here, y'know. Pull the right permits. Involve city hall."

"By the book," echoed Ray. "Can't just go around stomping through cemeteries, violating ordinances."

Shannon Dumas paused in mid-application of lip gloss to a perfect pout. "Anybody can visit the graveyards. They even have tours you can go on." Shannon, at nineteen, was the youngest of the group and planned on a career as a television anchor. "Can we wear those great off-the-shoulder Mexican dresses? With all the gorgeous embroidery?"

The twins gave synchronized headshakes and arm foldings. Hilda nodded and Therese looked thoughtful. The remaining woman in the class, Dorothy Alden, spoke up softly—too softly for the on-camera investigative reporting role she seemed to be envisioning, but we were working on that. I leaned forward to catch her words.

"Maybe we could go on one of those tours Shannon was talking about?"

The suggestion was met with "yeahs," and "good ideas," and a simultaneous nod between the twins.

"I know one of the best guides," Therese said. "Want me to see if we can get a reservation for a private tour? Just us? No tourists?"

"A reservation is probably a good idea," I said. "The summer visitors have pretty much left, but the leaf-peepers are here now, and in a few weeks the Halloween mob will start showing up."

"It doesn't give us much time to plan if we're going to pull this off in November," said Hilda, "but it's not a super complicated event. We should be able to do it."

"Maybe we can involve the Art Department," Therese offered. "Maybe Costumes and Makeup too."

"Of course we'll need Mr. Pennington's approval," I said. "I'm sure he'll like the idea though."

Rupert Pennington was the director of the Tabby, and since last year's video project had scored the school a substantial federal grant, I was confident he'd okay the plan. Besides that, Mr. Pennington was dating my sixty-something ball-of-fire aunt, Isobel Russell. Aunt Ibby was the one who'd raised me after my parents died in a plane accident when I was five.

"How many cemeteries are there in Salem anyway?" Shannon asked. "We ought to check them all out to be sure we pick the best one."

Hilda held up her smart phone. "There are ten," she said. "I already checked."

"We should probably narrow it down to the really old ones." Dorothy spoke a little louder this time.

Hilda nodded. "Yeah. The ones with the really creepy headstones."

"It's the Howard Street Cemetery then, for sure." Therese's

tone was firm. "It has the creepy headstones *and* it's definitely haunted."

"Haunted? Really?" Shannon's already wide eyes grew even bigger.

The twins snorted in unison. "Nonsense," said Ray. "No such thing," Roger sputtered.

Therese smiled. "You'll see. Old Giles Corey is still there . . . floating around . . . touching people with his cold, dead hands." She waved her arms in the air, fixing the twins with a blue-eyed stare. "And it was the sheriff who tortured him to death. Piled rocks on the poor old man's chest until he suffocated, just because he wouldn't admit to being a witch." She dropped her voice to a whisper, still smiling. "Hey, you guys weren't sheriffs by any chance, were you?"

That brought firm headshakes of denial from the two.

Hilda snapped her fingers. "Hey! The cemetery covers the history angle and we can probably get some interviews from people who think they've been groped by a ghost."

"Then we can investigate the dumb ghost story," Ray said, "and debunk the whole thing."

Roger nodded. "That's real investigative reporting. Right, Ms. Barrett?"

"That's one way to look at it," I agreed. "It's a short ride over to Howard Street. What do you say we take a little field trip? Then we'll put together a proposal for Mr. Pennington."

The idea of a field trip, of spending time outside of a school building, is just as attractive to adult students as it is to little kids. Car pooling arrangements were hastily made. The twins would take Shannon with them in their Ford Crown Victoria, Hilda and Therese would ride in Hilda's Jeep and Dorothy would come with me in my almost new two-seater Corvette Stingray.

Since second-year student Therese had the most experience with camcorders, I entrusted her with one of the Tabby's new Panasonic shoulder-mounted models. "Therese, put on your director's hat. You're in charge." I could tell by her shy smile that she was pleased with the responsibility. "The rest of us can use our phones or personal cameras," I said. "This is just a preliminary exercise. A little 'show and tell' for Mr. Pennington."

In a more or less orderly fashion we trooped from the classroom area to the mezzanine landing where a life-size portrait of the old store's founder, Oliver Wendel Trumbull, gazed benignly across the main floor of his once-upon-a-time retail kingdom. Together we clattered down the broad stairway, across the polished hardwood floor and through the glass doors onto Essex Street.

At the entrance to the Tabby's parking lot we separated, each of us heading for his or her designated ride. I motioned for Dorothy to follow me to the Laguna blue 'vette, glad for the opportunity to spend a few one-on-one minutes with the soft-spoken young woman. She'd told us that she'd come to Salem from Alaska, but other than answering a few general questions about cold weather, northern lights, ice fishing and the presence of bears in her backyard, she'd shared very little information about herself.

"What a beautiful car." She gave the sweet curve of a rear fender a gentle pat and I noticed that her fingernails were bitten down to the quick. "Bet it's fast too," she murmured.

"Sure is," I said. "My late husband, Johnny Barrett, was a NASCAR driver. Got my love for big, speedy American cars from him."

She climbed into the passenger seat and I took my place behind the wheel.

"I'm sorry," she said, "about your husband. I know what it's like to lose someone you love."

I waited for her to continue—to tell me about her own loss. But she'd lapsed into silence, turning away from me, seemingly intent on the passing scenery. It had been three years since Johnny's death but I still didn't like talking about it, so I could understand her not opening up. I searched for another topic as we approached the fenced-in green expanse of the Salem Common before she spoke again.

"It seems to me there ought to be sheep in there, enjoying all that nice grass."

"A few hundred years ago, I guess there were. But the only livestock on the Common these days are the squirrels and, of course, dogs chasing Frisbees."

"Do you have a dog?"

"Nope. No dog. Just a big yellow cat. Do you?" I smiled, thinking of O'Ryan, the very special cat who shared the big house on Winter Street with Aunt Ibby and me. O'Ryan is far from being an ordinary housecat. He once belonged to a witch—her "familiar," some say. In Salem, a witch's familiar is to be respected—and sometimes feared.

"I have several dogs, back in Alaska," she said. "They're quite necessary for transportation."

"Transportation?" Surprise showed in my voice. "You mean like dog sleds? Mush? Like that?"

She ran her fingers through short brown hair and smiled. "I guess I didn't mention that I've been living 'off the grid,' as they say, for several years."

"Wow." I was seriously impressed. "I've never met anyone who did that before. No TV? No indoor plumbing? No electricity?"

"That's about it," she said as we turned onto Howard Street and moved slowly downhill toward the cemetery.

She leaned forward in her seat as staggered rows of tombstones came into view. "And as soon as I've learned what you can teach me about conducting an investigation, I'll be heading back to Alaska."

"I'll do my best," I said. "I think you'll find the course useful. Are you planning a TV reporting career up there?"

Again, the soft laugh. "Hell, no. I just think your class might save me some time in figuring out who murdered my sister."

# CHAPTER 2

Before I'd had time to react to that little bombshell we'd reached the parking lot between the cemetery and the old Salem jail. I parked beside the Crown Vic and, with a smile, Dorothy climbed out and joined her classmates at the cemetery entrance.

"Come on, Ms. Barrett," Shannon called. "Therese is going to get a shot of us going in."

"Try not to get any ghosts in the picture, okay Therese?" Hilda said, with a sidelong glance at the twins. "I've heard that they can ruin a whole photo shoot with those darned floating white orbs."

"Lot of graves in there," Ray said, peering over the wrought iron fence.

"Whole lot of graves," Roger echoed.

"Over three hundred," Hilda said. "I looked it up."

Following Dorothy, I joined the group as Ray pushed the gate open. Roger stood to the side waving us onto the grassy surface one by one. The two men hesitated, still standing outside the burial ground. Therese waved an impatient hand. "Come on, you guys. Group shot. Inside the gate. Smile, everybody."

Once assembled to the photographer's satisfaction, we dutifully trooped up the incline to the top of one of the family crypts cut into the side of a hill. Therese focused on a memorial plaque for a moment, then directed us to walk around, look at tombstones, take pictures with our own cameras and phones. I tried to stay with Dorothy, hoping to hear more about the dead sister—*Had she said "murdered"*?—but Dorothy had scampered away, following Hilda along a narrow path bordering Howard Street. The cemetery stretches uphill along almost the entire length of the street and the two were quickly out of sight.

Shannon and the twins stood together watching a young man who knelt in front of an ancient looking stone, one of those with the winged death's heads at the top. I moved closer, looking over the man's shoulder. *He's making a gravestone rubbing*, I thought, and moved closer to get a better look at the process.

"He's a grave rubber," Ray whispered. "I think that's against Massachusetts law."

"No, he's not a grave rubber. See? He's not touching the gravestone at all. Besides, at least he's not a grave *robber.*" Roger snickered at his own joke. "Get it?"

On closer inspection I saw that Roger was right. The man wasn't touching the stone. He was working at an easel and the death's head was taking shape on paper. Wishing I'd worn flats as the heels of my boots sunk into damp, uneven ground, I headed up a small hill in the direction Dorothy and Hilda had taken and caught up with them at the back part of the cemetery. Therese approached from the opposite direction and the four of us met beneath an oak tree, its leaves tinged with gold. Therese aimed the camcorder toward jagged remnants of the turreted roof of the old prison. "They're making the place into condos over there," she said. "Nice ones, I heard."

"Haunted?" Hilda wanted to know.

Therese shrugged. "Could be. Even if they *aren't* haunted, with a cemetery view and right next door to where they squooshed old Giles Corey to death, people will say there are ghosts in there anyway."

Dorothy smiled. "In Salem that's probably a good selling point."

"Sure. The place will be on all the ghost tours." Hilda moved closer to the fence separating us from the old jail property. "You believe in ghosts, Ms. Barrett?"

It wasn't a question I'd expected and I wasn't quite sure how I should answer it. Actually, I have good reason to believe in ghosts, but it wasn't anything I cared to discuss with my students. I decided to treat it lightly. "I guess I have to," I said. "Didn't you know the top floor of the Tabby is supposed to be haunted by Tabitha Trumbull?"

Dorothy interrupted, saving me from any further conjecture about Salem's ghost population. "Is this really the place where they crushed that old man to death? Right here?"

"It wasn't a cemetery back then," Therese said. "Just a big open field next to the dungeon where they kept the witches before the trials." She adjusted the Panasonic on her shoulder and started down the hill. "I'm going back to check out the front row grave stones. Those look like the oldest ones. Need to get close-ups of the creepy inscriptions."

Dorothy pointed to an obelisk-shaped stone. "They all look pretty old. They don't still bury people in here, do they?"

"Nope." Hilda held up her phone. "Not since the 1930s. I looked it up."

Dorothy fell into step beside me, facing the back rows of markers while Hilda gave us a brief wave and—alone—

followed the path beside the wrought iron fence surrounding the old cemetery.

Dorothy pulled her phone from a vest pocket, knelt on the grass and took several shots of a tall headstone with a carved weeping willow at the top. "Look. Poor Dorcas Sims. Only thirty-six years old. Bummer."

"It's a sad place," I agreed. "The children's headstones get to me. People died way too young in those days."

"People die too young these days too," she pointed out. "Your Johnny. My sister. Poor Emily—she was only twenty-five."

I watched her face. Her expression hadn't changed. She adjusted the zoom on her camera, focused on another headstone. The rhythmic sound of a jackhammer echoed from the condo construction site next door, a jarring sound. "You said she was murdered. Is it . . . can you . . . do you want to talk about it? I understand if you don't."

"I can talk about it." She'd dropped her voice again. I leaned close to catch her words. "You probably won't believe me though. Nobody does."

"Try me." We continued walking, moving carefully among the headstones—large and small—pausing to photograph an epitaph here, a winged head there, an occasional long shot of orderly rows of aged, sun-bleached monuments.

"Her name was Emily Alden and she was murdered," Dorothy said, her voice growing stronger. "Right here in Salem."

I frowned. "When did it happen?" Not that Salem is crime-free, but murder still makes the front pages around here and the name Emily Alden didn't ring any bells for me.

"Two months ago. I wasn't even here, you know. It took a while for word to reach me. I live far away from everything." She shook her head. "My stepmother, Paula, tried to contact me. Emily's boss says he did too." She spread her hands in a helpless gesture. "There's a price to pay for choosing to live the way I do, far away from everything . . . and everybody."

"I'm so sorry," I said. "Were you and Emily close?"

"Very. We were raised together. My own mother ran off when I was little. I don't even remember her. Dad married Paula and when I was around four they had Emily. She's always been my baby sister." Her voice broke. She paused for a moment, then, cupping her ear, looked toward the jail. "Listen. The construction noise has stopped."

I nodded. "Probably lunch time." We stood there among the headstones in relative silence as I waited for her to go on with her story. The muffled hum of traffic drifted up from Bridge Street, and a brief whistle-toot signaled an MBTA train coming or going from Salem's nearby new commuter station.

Another sound. I reached into my pocket for my phone. "Oops, sorry," I said. "Meant to turn this off." Pete's name showed on the screen. "I'll just tell him to call back later."

"No, please," Dorothy held up one hand in protest. "Take your call. I'm going to catch up with Hilda." Before I could reply, she'd sprinted off toward the path Hilda had taken.

"Hi Pete," I said, watching Dorothy's retreating back. "Guess where I am."

"I know you're not in your classroom at the Tabby." I could hear the smile in his voice. "That's where I am. Came to take you to lunch."

"Oh. Pete. I'm sorry." I really was sorry too. Pete's schedule as a police detective is so erratic, lunches together are rare. "I should be back to the school pretty soon. Can you wait?"

"Can't do it, babe. Just happened to be in the area. But you have me wondering, where are you anyway?"

"Howard Street Cemetery."

"Charming place. Um . . . do I dare to ask why?"

I could understand Pete's questioning tone. When it comes to topics on the spooky side—like ghosts, witches, spirits and, yes, cemeteries—I've given him good reason to wonder about me. I learned fairly recently that I'm a scryer. My best friend River North calls me a "gazer." (She's a Tarot card reader, a late-night TV show host and a practicing Salem witch. River knows a lot about things paranormal.) Somehow I've acquired the not-altogether-welcome ability to see things in reflective surfaces that other people can't see. Unfortunately, this "gift" often shows me visions I wish *I* couldn't see either, and it's not something Pete and I talk about very often.

I was quick to let him know that there was nothing at all vision related about the cemetery visit, invited him to share a pizza at my apartment when his shift was over, then asked the question that was nagging me. "Pete," I said. "Do you know anything about the death of a young woman named Emily Alden?"

"Sure," he said. "Sad case. Accidentally OD'd on pills. Gotta go. See you tonight."

Pete hung up and Dorothy disappeared behind rows of tombstones. A cool breeze came up and it felt as though the temperature had suddenly dropped about ten degrees. It was broad daylight—high noon—in the heart of a busy city but at that moment I felt quite alone. I headed downhill and, sliding on the damp grass, I careened into a tilted tombstone, its shattered edge raking my thigh.

"Damn," I looked down at the jagged tear in almost-new Michael Kors jeans and wanted nothing more than to round up my group and get out of this place.

# CHAPTER 3

Back at the Tabby, Therese got to work editing her video while the rest of us compared photos, selecting thirty of the best for a slide show. Incorporating Hilda's information on *Dia de los Muertos* along with some Googled photos of sugar skulls and festively decorated gravesides, we collaborated on a script for a voice-over and by five o'clock had our pitch ready to present to Rupert Pennington the following morning. I dismissed my class with sincere praise for a job well done, and headed for the school parking lot.

Still wondering about Dorothy's insistence that her sister had been murdered, and about Pete's statement that Emily Alden's death had been accidental, I offered her a ride home, hoping to learn more.

"Thanks anyway. I can walk. I live just over there." Waving in the general direction of Washington Street, she hurried away. I shrugged and aimed the Corvette toward home with a vague feeling of relief that this day was almost over.

With my car safely garaged behind our house, I cut through Aunt Ibby's garden where a few hardy sunflowers still nodded among late-blooming orange marigolds. I climbed the granite steps to our back door which opens into the downstairs hall leading to my aunt's kitchen, our shared laundry room and a narrow stairway to my third-floor apartment. I knew that our cat, O'Ryan, would be waiting inside to greet me.

I turned my key, pushing the door open, and was welcomed with purrs and "mrrows" and much joyous ankle-rubbing. I lifted the big yellow cat in my arms, and with a free hand knocked on the kitchen door. "You home, Aunt Ibby?"

"Come in, come in. It's open."

The bright kitchen smelled wonderful. I put the cat down and sniffed fragrant air. "Apples?"

"Apple pie. The Macintoshes are gorgeous this fall. Perfect for pie. I made two. Thought you and Pete might like one."

Aunt Ibby is, among many other things, a fabulous cook. She's also a semiretired reference librarian, computer genius and whiz at all things technical. A slim and attractive sixty-something, her hair is almost as red as mine. (She admits to the "occasional touch-up.")

"Fabulous. Thanks. Pete'll be coming by later. You know how he loves your pies."

She hung her red-and-white striped apron on a hook beside the pantry door and gestured toward the round oak table. "Do you have time for coffee before you go upstairs? Sit down. Tell me about your day." Not waiting for an answer, she poured that life-giving fluid into my favorite mug—a souvenir of my first trip to Walt Disney World when I was eight. (Yes, I was allowed to drink coffee, heavily milk-diluted, even at that early age.)

O'Ryan had already hopped up onto one of the captain's

chairs. I took the one opposite his. "It's been quite a day. This may take a while."

"Good. I have plenty of time." She put the cream pitcher and sugar bowl on the table along with a plateful of the round little cinnamon rolls she always makes from left-over pie crust. Smiling, she sat down beside O'Ryan. "Don't leave anything out."

I began with Hilda's idea about a Salem celebration of Day of the Dead. "She thinks it will cover our history project and appeal to tourists at the same time."

"A grand idea," my aunt said. "We have such wonderful cemeteries. Old Burying Point on Charter Street and the Howard Street Cemetery." She clapped her hands together. "I can just see it now! Those dear old tombstones decorated for *Dia de los Muertos.* Rupert must be pleased."

"I took the whole class on a field trip to Howard Street today. We put together a presentation for Mr. Pennington. We plan to show it to him tomorrow." I described the slide show and video and recited some of the planned narration. "You think he'll approve?"

"I'm sure of it." She tilted her head to one side. "You said you'd had quite a day, but you frowned just a bit when you said it. What are you leaving out?"

"I'm getting to it," I said. "I really want your thoughts on something one of my students told me." I paused, thinking about Dorothy's words. *"Her name was Emily Alden and she was murdered."*

I repeated as closely as I could the brief, interrupted conversations I'd had with Dorothy. "She seems to be convinced that her sister Emily was murdered here in Salem just a couple of months ago. I don't remember hearing anything about a woman's murder. Do you?"

She shook her head. "Can't say I do. Did you ask Pete about it?"

"I did. He says that Emily Alden died from an accidental overdose of pills."

She picked up her cup and stood. "Come on." She motioned for me to follow and we headed for her office. The furnishings in most of the rooms in the house on Winter Street are on the traditional side with a judicious sprinkling of antiques, but Aunt Ibby's office is something else. An MIT professor or a NASA official would undoubtedly be at home with the state-of-the-art computer, copier, printer, fax machine, laminator and wall full of other gadgets whose functions I can only guess at. My aunt sat at her desk and turned on the Mac. I pulled up a chair beside her.

"Emily Alden, you said? Good old New England name." She tapped in the information at her usual blinding speed—attributable, she claims, to a summer course at Katie Gibbs when she was in high school. The name popped up immediately in a *Salem News* obituary.

> ALDEN, Emily J., 25, passed away suddenly at her home in Salem.
>
> She is survived by her mother, Paula Alden of Gainesville, Georgia, and a sister, Dorothy Alden of False Pass, Alaska. A memorial service will be held at the Murphy Funeral Home on Federal Street on Saturday from six to eight P.M. For those who wish to make a contribution in her memory, a donation can be made to the Massachusetts Earth Day Foundation.

"That's it?" I said, surprised by the brevity of the piece.

"Apparently." Aunt Ibby scrolled up and down the page. "That's it. Pete said she died from an accidental overdose?"

"Yes. That's all he had time to tell me. I'll ask him about it tonight though."

"In a sad case like that, I'm sure they usually omit the details out of courtesy to the family."

"I imagine they do. Well, I have to get changed and order that pizza. Look. My new jeans got torn at the cemetery." I stood and pointed to the damaged fabric.

"That's a shame. What happened?"

"Tripped over a broken headstone." I winked. "Or maybe old Giles Corey pushed me."

We returned to the kitchen where I picked up my still-warm apple pie and a couple of the cinnamon treats, kissed my aunt's cheek, then passed through her dining room and living room to the front hall foyer. With the cat scampering ahead of me, I climbed the curving mahogany staircase to my apartment.

O'Ryan had scooted through the cat door and was already perched on the windowsill when I entered my kitchen. Aunt Ibby had surprised me with the thoroughly renovated space after a fire destroyed much of the two upper stories of our house. Shiny stainless steel appliances—which I'm sure had been meant to encourage my meager cooking skills—blended nicely with my 1970s Lucite table and chairs, the open cabinet display of Russel Wright pastel china and green Jadeite bowls, and the vintage google-eyed Kit Kat clock on the wall.

I hurried to my bedroom and surveyed the damage to my jeans in the antique oval mirror. Within seconds, the twinkling lights and swirling colors that always precede a vision appeared on the glass.

I tried to look away.

Too late.

The woman, sightless brown eyes staring straight up, lay surrounded by pink-streaked bubbles in an old-fashioned, claw-footed bathtub. A wineglass, broken at the stem, lay on the tile floor.

# CHAPTER 4

Once again my so called "gift" offered a scene of death. I didn't recognize the woman or her surroundings. Squeezing my eyes shut, I willed the picture in the mirror to go away. After a moment I dared to look at the glass again. She was still there. Still in the bathtub. Still, I supposed, dead.

By then O'Ryan had joined me in the bedroom. Hopping up onto the foot of the bed he crept as close as he could get to the mirror. Could the cat see what I was seeing? By his rapt attention and tense muscled position, I had to believe that he could.

"What is it, boy? *Who* is it?" I whispered. I didn't expect an answer of course. At least not a *verbal* one. He is, after all, a cat. But O'Ryan seems to *know* things, *understand* things, even *do* things your ordinary housecat cannot. His previous owner was a witch called Ariel Constellation and some say O'Ryan was her "familiar." According to my friend River North, also a witch, but a much nicer one than Ariel was—a familiar can be a powerful ally—or enemy.

The image began to fade and once again my own reflection—a tall redhead with a puzzled expression and ripped jeans—looked back at me. The cat, apparently no longer interested in me or the woman in the bathtub, headed back to his windowsill bird-watching position.

The only dead woman I'd heard about lately was, of course, Dorothy Alden's recently deceased sister Emily. But no one—including Dorothy, Pete and the *Salem News*—had said anything about a bathtub. I tried to shake away the unpleasant image and began to carefully peel off my poor ruined pants, wondering if they could be mended somehow.

"Ouch," I said aloud, realizing for the first time that there'd been a little blood involved in the cemetery mishap. Mine. The edges of the denim threads had stuck to a thin red streak issuing from a long scrape along my thigh. It wasn't much of a wound—barely a scratch, really. But when I thought about where it had come from—a crumbling, maybe moldy, old chunk of somebody's gravestone—I lost no time in heading for the bathroom medicine cabinet. I used about half a bottle of peroxide in the wound-cleaning process, took a longer than necessary shower and changed into comfy old faded jeans and a 2013 World Series T-shirt.

A glance at the Kit Kat clock told me that I'd better get my order for pizza in pretty soon if Pete and I were to eat something besides apple pie—not that there'd be anything wrong with that. I speed dialed the Pizza Pirate, arranging for the seven-thirty delivery of our extra large pepperoni with extra cheese and two liters of Pepsi. I looked around the kitchen, realizing that I was searching for something to do—something to keep me busy—something to make the image of the dead woman in the bathtub go away.

I sat in the Lucite chair closest to the window where O'Ryan crouched, facing the glass, his long whiskers twitching. Sundown had passed and the neighborhood birds should have been asleep in their nests, so what was the big yellow cat seeing out there? I moved a little closer. The windowpane showed a reflection of . . . a fuzzy cat-face.

I laughed. "Admiring your handsome self, cat? I don't blame you. You are a gorgeous animal, no doubt about it." I stood up and looked away, then turned back toward the still immobile cat. Was it possible that—like me—O'Ryan could see things in reflective surfaces? Things that others might not see?

The thought was disturbing.

The buzzing of my phone was a welcome interruption. Caller ID showed River North.

"Hi River. I'm glad you called."

"Hi Lee, Listen. Do you still have any of those outfits you wore on the *Nightshades* show?"

"I'm sure I do. Why?" The show River was talking about was a rather forgettable late show program on WICH-TV where I'd pretended to be Crystal Moon, a psychic. Between scary old movies I'd taken phone calls from viewers and tried my best to solve problems, find lost dogs and generally fake people out. *Nightshades* was mercifully canceled after a series of very bad happenings and had been replaced by *Tarot Time with River North*. River is an expert with the Tarot and her show was a big hit from the start.

"We're showing *The Hunchback of Notre Dame* tomorrow night. I thought maybe I'd dress up like Esmeralda if you'd saved any of your low-necked blouses and junk jewelry."

"Sure. They're all packed away in the attic. Which *Hunchback* are you showing?"

"Nineteen thirty-nine. Charles Laughton and Maureen O'Hara."

"The best one of all," I said. "I'll dig out the costumes. Do you want to come over here or should I drop them off at the station?"

"Well, if I wouldn't be interrupting anything, I could come over to your place on my way to the station tonight." She paused. "Around ten maybe?"

"Pete's coming over for pizza. Why not come now and join us? I ordered extra large."

"Really? If you think Pete won't mind I'd love to."

"Of course he won't mind. You're practically family." I thought about the vision in the mirror. "And I wanted to talk to you about . . . something."

River knows me pretty well. "A gazing thing?"

"Uh-huh."

River, Aunt Ibby and Pete are the only ones who know about my scrying ability. Pete avoids the topic as much as possible, Aunt Ibby accepts it because she loves me. River, though, more than anyone else, understands it. "It happened just a little while ago," I said. "I'm trying to figure it out."

"I'll be right over. Bringing the cards."

I smiled. "You always do."

As it turned out, everybody arrived at once. Pete and River came up the back stairway—Pete has a key to the door—while the Pizza Pirate delivery guy rang the front doorbell on the Winter Street side of the house. I dashed down the two flights to the front door, paid for the pizza, tipped the man, then hurried back upstairs. Pete and River were already sitting at the table, hiding smiles, pretending they'd been waiting for hours. Pete, his dark hair still wet from a shower, looked as handsome as ever in white shirt and khaki slacks. River was already dressed for her show, glamourous in silver lamé, trademark silver stars and moons sparkling in her long black braid. "If one of you two goofs will grab some glasses and pour the soda," I said, "I'll serve the main course."

Within minutes we three had put a healthy dent in the extra-large pizza while O'Ryan lurked watchfully under the table, hoping for scraps of pepperoni. Conversation was casual and at that point no one had mentioned cemeteries, murder or even the *Hunchback of Notre Dame*. I decided to simply say what was on my mind. Why not? I was with my best friend and the man I loved.

"I had a vision today," I began, "and I think it may have something to do with that woman I asked you about, Pete. Emily Alden."

"Really?" Pete frowned. "That was a couple of months ago. Young woman. Took a couple too many prescription sleeping pills with alcohol." He shrugged. "It happens."

"Who's Emily Alden?" River wanted to know.

"She was the younger sister of one of my students."

"You didn't tell me that," Pete said. "I knew there was a sister but I thought she lived in Hawaii or someplace."

"Alaska," I said. "But she's here now." I watched Pete's face. "She's trying to find out who murdered her sister."

"What about the vision?" River interrupted.

"Her sister wasn't murdered." Pete spoke in what I've learned to recognize as his cop voice. "It was an accident. I told you that."

I took a deep breath. "Did she die in a bathtub? An old-fashioned bathtub with claw feet?"

He nodded, stern cop face in place. "She did."

"Wow." River sounded breathless. "That's what you saw in the vision? A body in a bathtub? Wow. Shall I read you now?" She reached for her denim handbag, incongruous with the glittering gown. "I brought the cards."

"Not yet, River." Pete held up one hand. "What makes her sister think she was murdered, Lee?"

"I don't know. Dorothy told me that she wanted to learn about investigative reporting because it would help her figure out who murdered her sister. That's what she said."

"That's all?"

"Pretty much. She was Emily's half sister. Dorothy is about four years older."

Pete reached for his jacket on the back of the chair and pulled his ever-present notebook and pencil from the inside pocket. "I'll check into it but I'm sure there was no indication of foul play. Nothing there at all. You got a phone number for this Dorothy?"

"Not offhand. I'm sure the school has it. I'll get it tomorrow. Thanks for checking."

"Speaking of tomorrow," River said. "Can we check out the attic costume stash?"

"Sure. And don't forget we have Aunt Ibby's famous apple pie for dessert. Pete, want to make coffee while we run upstairs and get a couple of things?"

"No problem. Hurry back."

I put the pie into the warming oven while Pete measured out coffee, and River and I went out the kitchen door into the third floor front hall. I was glad she was with me. Even O'Ryan stayed behind and I don't like going up into that attic alone.

# CHAPTER 5

I paused in front of the door that opened onto the staircase to the attic. Of course, none of it looks the way it did before the fire. The third floor with my sparkling new apartment and the top floor attic had been completely rebuilt since that awful night of flames and danger. I pulled the door open, pressed the light switch and started up the stairs—slowly.

The smell of smoke was long gone. The place now had the pleasant aroma of new wood. Not as crowded with old furniture, trunks and boxes as it had once been, the well-lit space held a long garment rack, a couple of unpainted, undistinguished but sturdy and serviceable bureaus, some spare dining room chairs and a few cardboard cartons.

*Nothing here to be afraid of.*

I squared my shoulders and stepped onto the wide boards of the attic floor. River was right behind me. "Neat place," she said, looking around the long room "It's so organized. Good feng shui."

"Glad to hear it," I said. "Come on. Let's find some of those *Nightshades* outfits. I think the skirts are in garment bags on the rack and the blouses and jewelry are in the bureau drawers."

It didn't take long to put together a couple of Esmeralda-suitable combinations along with plenty of clunky, colorful costume jewelry. River sat in one of the dining room chairs.

"I don't see any books up here," she said, her voice dropping to a whisper. "Was that one . . . the one you gave to me . . . the only one that didn't get burned up?"

The book she was talking about had once belonged to Ariel Constellation and for a long time I'd thought it had been destroyed in the flames. In fact, I'd hoped it had. It was an ancient witch's spell book, dated 1692, and when I'd found it still intact—not even singed—I'd realized that it was quite likely that the damned thing couldn't be destroyed. I thought that maybe a witch would know what to do with it so I gave it to River. "That was the only one," I said. I'd never asked her what she'd done with it. Maybe I didn't want to know.

"It's in a safe place," she whispered. "No one knows about it except you and me."

"Good," I said, not knowing whether it was or not. I looked over my shoulder. "Shall we go downstairs and have some of that pie?"

"Okay." She gathered up the clothes and headed for the stairway. "Let's go. This place gives me the creeps. Maybe the feng shui here isn't so hot after all."

No argument from me on that. She was first down the stairs with me close behind.

Happily back in the cozy comfort of my own kitchen, warm with the smells of good coffee and perfect apple pie, I gave Pete a quick kiss and sat at the table.

"There's time for a quick reading," River said, pulling a fat deck of cards from the denim handbag. "Maybe we can figure out what the lady in the bathtub means."

"Mind if I sit in?" Pete's question surprised me. He usually tries to avoid what he calls "River's hocus-pocus."

"No problem," River said. "Pull up a chair." But I knew she was surprised too. "You have a question you want to ask, Lee?"

"Yes. What can you tell me about the woman in the bathtub?"

Three humans and one cat gathered around the table. I shuffled and cut the cards at River's direction. She placed the Queen of Wands—the card she always chooses to represent me—in the center of the table. (The red-haired queen sits on a throne with golden lions forming the arms. She holds a staff in one hand, a sunflower in the other and a black cat sits in the foreground.) In rapid succession, River placed nine other cards facedown in a pattern I'd seen many times before, then began to turn them over, one at a time.

"Here's the Page of Wands," she said. "He's a young man, possibly a messenger. You haven't met him yet." She turned another card. "The six of swords."

I peered closely at the card. It showed a man ferrying a dejected looking woman and a child across water. River tapped the card. "The woman was worried when she stepped into the water in the tub. She planned to ask someone for help with a problem." She turned over the next card in the pattern. "Look, here's the seven of swords. It shows a man stealing five swords, leaving two in the ground. See it?"

"I see," I said.

Pete frowned. "What's that supposed to mean?"

"It means dishonesty. A failed plan. Even spying. Could someone have been spying on the woman, Pete?"

He shrugged. "I don't know why anybody would be. Nice ordinary girl. Low level job with a good company."

River smiled. "I can only tell you what the cards signify

to me. Sometimes I'm wrong." She turned another card. "Look. Here's the King of Wands."

"What does he mean?" I asked. "He looks nice."

"He comes from good family. He's blond. Probably married. He holds a scepter and also a magician's rod. He's powerful. He can use the earth's forces for profit."

"Is that good?" Pete leaned forward and touched the card.

"Usually. Sometimes he makes rash decisions though." River glanced at the clock. "I still have to get to the station and do my makeup."

"Maybe we can finish another time," I said

River shook her head. "No. I'm going to race through the last five." She flipped the remaining cards over, one after the other. "Interesting. The eight of swords. Did you shuffle these well, Lee? That's six, seven and eight of the same suit."

"I'm sure I did. What does the eight mean? Looks like a blindfolded woman. Is she standing in water?"

"Uh-huh. She's in a situation she's afraid to move out of. Not good." River tapped the next card. "The four of pentacles. This is the miser, hanging onto his gold. But the card is reversed. He might be about to lose his earthly possessions. Okay. We're down to the last three. Here goes."

She stood, running her forefinger across the three cards. "Three of swords. Separation and quarrels. Not for you. For the woman you asked about. The nine of pentacles. A project is canceled, and finally the Temperance card. Interesting. Even though she's dead, what she thought might happen is going to happen anyway." She gathered up the cards and put them into the denim bag. "Sorry to eat, read and run. Thanks for the costumes, Lee. Be sure to watch the show tomorrow night."

"You don't have time for pie?" I asked.

She patted her tummy. "One more calorie and I'll pop the seams of this shiny dress." She gathered up the pile of skirts and blouses, popped the jewelry into her bag, gave me a hug and headed for the back hall. "I'll let myself out. Bye, Pete. How'd you like the reading?"

Pete stood. "It was okay. Thanks, River."

O'Ryan followed River down the short hall toward the living room as I retrieved the pie from the warming oven and put it on the table. Pete was silent as he poured coffee into our matching mugs marked NEW HAMPSHIRE SPEEDWAY, souvenirs of the first weekend we'd ever spent together.

"You're awfully quiet," I said. "Did the card reading bother you?"

"Huh? Oh, no, that's just River's hocus-pocus. I was thinking about what you saw in that vision." He reached for my hand. "That must be so awful for you. I have to see bad stuff. It's my job. But it's just not fair that *you* have to—you know—see things."

"This was one of the worst ones yet, Pete," I admitted. "I keep trying to put it out of my mind, to just forget about it. You'd think I'd get used to it by now. I mean seeing things I don't want to see." I sliced a couple of neat triangles from the pie and handed Pete the plate with the biggest one. "I can't seem to erase this one—or really, any of them." I felt a quick rush of tears.

Pete reached for my hand and squeezed it. "I never get used to it babe, and maybe you can't either. I'm so sorry."

# CHAPTER 6

I left for school a little earlier than usual, allowing time for coffee in the Tabby's fifties-style diner. The popular restaurant was attached to the school, but the chrome-trimmed front door opened onto Essex Street and the reasonably priced food and vintage décor had made it one of Salem's most popular eateries.

Therese Della Monica waved to me from one of the red vinyl–upholstered booths. "Come sit with us," she called, moving over to make room for me at the gray marble–patterned Formica tabletop. Shannon and Hilda sat across from Therese and I noticed the twins sitting together on stools at the long lunch counter.

*The gang's all here. Almost.*

I slid into the booth and ordered coffee and a small cheese Danish. "Everybody ready for our presentation?"

Nodded heads all around. "I'm sure Mr. Pennington's going to like it," Hilda said. "How could he not? We've covered all the bases." She counted on her fingers. "Salem history, videography, tourism promotion, interview skills."

"I've edited my video of the cemetery," Therese said, "and put together a little slide show of the shots everybody took with their phones along with a couple of YouTube pictures of Mexican celebrations. Nothing fancy but it looks good enough I think."

"I'm sure it'll be fine," I said. "Of course we haven't really had a chance to practice our interview skills yet, but we'll get to that soon enough."

"Shannon practiced hers," Hilda said, with what could only be described as a smirk.

"She sure did," Therese agreed. "Did you get his phone number, Shannon?"

Shannon colored slightly and twisted a strand of long brunette hair. "No I didn't. But if I'd asked for it I bet he would have given it to me."

I looked around the table, from one smiling face to another. "What am I missing? Is anyone going to let the teacher in on it?"

"The hot guy drawing the tombstone thing," Hilda said. "You mean you didn't notice him?"

"OMG. Those eyes," Therese said. "Gorgeous."

"I saw him, but only from the back," I said. "What did I miss?"

"Well," Therese leaned forward, resting her chin on both fists. "When I took Costume Design last year we had a color theory class. They showed us some paintings by a guy named Maxfield Parrish. Ever hear of him?"

"Sure. I took the same class at Emerson."

"He used some special kind of blue paint," Therese said. "Cerulean, they call it. Anyway, the grave rubbing man has cerulean blue eyes."

"So, what did you talk to the blue-eyed gravestone rubber about, Shannon?" I teased. "Want to share?"

Shannon shrugged, a dainty lift of one shoulder. "He's an artist. He doesn't really rub the gravestones you know. That's against the law. I just asked him what he was doing and he rattled off a whole bunch of stuff about how he copies what's on the stone. He uses special paper—rice paper he calls it—and a really soft black pencil. Underneath the rice paper he has a big sheet of some kind of rough sandpaper, so that when he draws it makes the surface look rough. You know. Like the real gravestone is. Anyway, when he's done, he cuts the edges off the paper, puts it in a frame and sells it to tourists. It's not the real thing of course but the tourists don't care. They like it that he doesn't harm the old gravestones by messing around with them." Another pretty shrug. "Beats me why anybody wants a picture of a dead person's tombstone hanging on the wall anyhow."

Hilda held up her smart phone. "I just Googled cerulean blue. His eyes are much prettier than the Sherwin Williams paint sample."

"Maybe we can interview him next time we go to the cemetery," I said. "Meanwhile, first we have to get Mr. Pennington's blessing on this whole project. See you all in class." I paid for my coffee and waved to the twins as I left the diner via the side door leading to the school.

I climbed the stairs to the mezzanine floor where my classroom dominated the space that once housed Trumbull's shoe department. (Aunt Ibby loved getting her back-to-school shoes there when she was a kid.) No shoppers filled the sales floor any more, and at that moment I was all alone. The click-click of my heels echoed in the expanse of hardwood floor and high ceilings. My classroom area was carpeted though, and a dropped section of foam insulation over our simulated news desk, giant screen and wall full of TV monitors masked sound to some extent. For serious recording and filming work we used the new studio in the basement.

I hurried to my desk, tucked my handbag into a bottom

drawer and turned on my computer. Pulling up my recently begun file on Salem cemeteries, I swiveled the chair around so that I could reach the row of history books in the bookcase behind me. I knew there were some pretty famous people buried in Salem and it wouldn't hurt our project to drop a few names. As I reached for my copy of *Who Was Who in Salem and Where Are They Now?* I caught a flash of light—of color—just above the bookcase. Hanging on that wall was the giant half-model of a black patent leather pump.

Mr. Pennington had insisted from the beginning that the Tabby would preserve as much of the flavor—the ambiance—of the old Trumbull's department store as possible. School trophies and memorabilia are displayed in old glass-topped display counters. There's a giant portrait of the founder, Oliver Wendell Trumbull, on the main landing of the giant staircase. The elevators still bear the old floor designations . . . hosiery, furniture, domestics. In the one-time shoe department we still have the vintage signs, the original chairs, and, on the wall, the half model of the patent leather shoe. It's a highly reflective surface, one which I deliberately keep behind my back when I'm at my desk. It has, in the past, shown me scenes I didn't want to see.

The flash of light, the swoosh of color told me that I was about to see something in that damned shoe and it would undoubtedly be something else that I didn't want to see. The sound of voices, the clatter of feet sounded from the stairway. My class—minus Dorothy—had arrived right on time. I turned to face them—but not fast enough to avoid the quick glimpse of a picture forming on that gleaming patent leather surface before it blinked away. A picture of . . . what?

I tried to process what I'd just viewed and to, at the same

time, smile, greet the five students and pretend that I hadn't just had a puzzling vision. It had only lasted for a fraction of a second, but I was quite sure I'd seen a hand holding a small green-handled trowel filled with dirt.

This wasn't the first time I'd had to pretend that all was normal in my world, that I didn't have strange pictures popping up here and there—pictures no one else could see. I shook away the image of somebody's backyard garden—or whatever it was. I'd deal with it later.

"Everybody ready for our big pitch?" I said. "Mr. Pennington will be here at about nine-thirty." I looked at the round clock over the ninety-inch flat screen. "That gives us twenty minutes. Any questions?"

"Will you do the talking, Ms. Barrett?" Hilda wanted to know.

"I'll introduce the topic, yes," I agreed, "but you all need to be prepared to answer questions. Hilda, you're our resident expert on Day of the Dead, so I think you can give a brief rundown on the history of the event. And Therese, you'll narrate your PowerPoint presentation. Nothing elaborate. This is just to give him a general idea of where we're going with this."

"Can I tell him about that ghost?" Shannon asked. "The old man who touches people?"

"Giles Corey," I said. "Sure. Why not? Ghost stories seem appropriate for the occasion."

"No such thing as ghosts," Ray sputtered.

"No such thing," said Roger.

"Maybe he'll touch you guys," Hilda said, extending her arms and wiggling her fingers. "Then you'll believe."

The comment caused some good natured laughter and gentle kidding, which covered the sound of Dorothy's tardy entrance. She gave an apologetic shrug and a soft "I'm sorry," and slid into her accustomed seat.

"That's okay," I said. "We're just doing some last minute prep for our pitch. Any suggestions?"

"Since this is Salem," she said, "you might call it pitch-craft."

"Good one, Dot," Therese said, gathering up her materials and moving to a tall stool behind the news desk. "Everybody ready?"

Rupert Pennington stepped from the elevator at precisely 9:30. The school director was impeccably—if somewhat theatrically—dressed, as usual. On this particular day Mr. Pennington favored an old-school kind of British look, complete with an apricot-colored ascot tie and black-and-white herringbone tweed jacket. All of the students stood as he approached—just as I'd instructed them to do. "Well then, ladies and gentlemen," he intoned. "Ms. Barrett has told me a bit about the class project you've envisioned and I must say it sounds exciting." He rubbed his hands together and took the front row armchair seat I indicated. "Let's get on with your presentation, shall we?" He gave a dramatic wave of one hand. "Please be seated."

I introduced the class members, each by name, and announced that we'd like to propose a special city celebration of *Dia de los Muertos*, then turned the program over to Therese.

The twins had surprised us all by preparing a small brochure describing the project and incorporating a few of their own creative cemetery photos. Ray presented one to Mr. Pennington while Roger passed them out to the rest of us. Therese had not only carefully edited the graveyard footage, but had integrated appropriately mournful music to accompany the shots of individual stones. She gave a well-organized recitation of the history of Salem's cemeteries and emphasized the possibility of extending the city's important month-long Halloween tourism bonanza for yet another week. The funereal music merged neatly with a happy fiesta tune as the screen displayed some authentic Mexican *Dia de los Muertos* scenes and Hilda picked up the narrative, explaining the holiday customs. The slide show moved quickly, with photos of winged skulls, weeping willows and the tower of the nearby jail as Shannon gave a brief rundown of the Giles Corey saga. There was a good picture of the grave rubbing man, but his back was to the camera so the highly praised blue eyes were not displayed. The show ended with a close-up of a memorial stone bearing the name Giles Corey.

I was pretty sure all had gone well, and waited for the director's reaction. There was a brief pause—a dramatic one—then he stood, clapped his hands together and cried, "Bravo! Well done! Please proceed with the project."

We were all pleased, of course, but waited until the elevator doors had closed behind him for the high-fives and self-congratulatory comments.

"Okay. Now we begin the real work," I said, returning to my desk. "We're going to have to let the Chamber of Commerce and the VCB know what we're doing and it's important that we get the witch shops involved."

"We can print up some more brochures," Ray offered. "Maybe we can take them around to the shops and talk it up."

"Talk it up," Roger said. "The witch shops will need to order those candy skulls and Mexican costumes."

"Good idea," I said, turning to pick up the brochures I'd left on my desk, again facing the wall. The shiny black shoe. The swirling colors and flashing lights.

It was still there. A small, green-handled garden trowel partly submerged in rich brown soil.

# CHAPTER 7

Once again, I managed to cover my surprise—confusion—horror—whatever mixed feelings the vision presented—and continued with the day's lesson plan. "Keep calm and carry on," like the old British war poster says. I was getting pretty good at it.

"Now that we have the official go-ahead," I said, "I think the formation of a few key committees is in order. How about this? Hilda and Therese seem to me to be well qualified to handle the historical aspects of the holiday and its relevance to Salem." The two women smiled and nodded to each other. "Ray and Roger clearly have a talent for publicity." I picked up the brochure. "I'm sure we can arrange for a printing and advertising budget if you two agree."

"Agreed," said Roger.

"Absolutely," said Ray.

"Dorothy and Shannon, I'd like you to work together on the interviewing aspects of the project. We'll need to talk with city officials—especially the people who oversee the cemeteries and maybe the Hispanic American Society over at Salem State would like to be involved. Okay?"

With agreements all around, preliminary work on the project was soon under way. Some of the class members worked on the school-provided desktop computers, some chose to use their personal smart phones or tablets. The room was so quiet we could hear a muffled thump-thump from the dance class in the studio above us.

As the niece of a reference librarian, I still maintain great confidence in the printed word, not so much in Wikipedia. I texted Aunt Ibby. Need much *Dia de los Muertos* info. Interlibrary request?

Her response was almost immediate. Done.

I knew there'd be a hefty stack of books at our disposal within days. There was a lot to learn, and a short time to learn it. If we were going to top last year's project, we'd better be good.

At noon, most of us returned to the diner for lunch and a note-comparing session. Six of us crowded into the widest booth at the far end of the diner. Dorothy excused herself, saying that she had to run home for an appointment with the super of her apartment building.

"Problems?" I asked.

"Not exactly," she said. "I'm renewing my sister's lease on the place and I guess there are papers to sign. I'll be back as soon as I can."

*Her sister's place? Wait a minute. What does that mean?*

But Dorothy was gone. The woman had a disturbing way of disappearing and leaving unanswered questions trailing in her wake.

We ordered our meals, and began a review of the morning's efforts. Hilda, who was beginning to remind me a lot of my tech-savvy Aunt Ibby, had already found and contacted a local photographer who'd spent the previous Day of the Dead in Mexico and had a huge file of photos. Therese had a friend who taught Spanish at Salem High and she'd arranged for him to help with any translation problems that might arise. The twins, it turned out, had both served as information officers during the Vietnam War, and still had contacts within the Boston press. Shannon and Dorothy had downloaded the directory of Salem city officials and had begun to put together a list of people who seemed relevant to our mission. I was impressed by the group's industry and told them so.

"Great job, all of you," I said. "It's going to take a lot of work to pull this off, both artistically and logistically, but you've already convinced me that we can do it."

"Going to have to involve the police department," Ray said. "And you'll need plenty of security in the old cemetery."

"Can't just have people running around in there willy-nilly," Roger sounded serious. "And there's an ordinance says nobody can be in there at night you know."

"Roger's right," Hilda said. "I Googled it. All the cemeteries are closed after dark."

"That's okay," I said. "Most people don't want to be in a cemetery in the dark anyway."

"You've got that right," Shannon said. "I sure don't. You, Therese?"

"I don't think I'd be scared," the young witch-in-training said. "Witches like to meet after dark, but it's usually in somebody's yard or in a big field or on the beach."

"Witches!" Ray snapped his fingers. "That reminds me. Somebody needs to contact the Ghost Tour people. Want us to do that?"

"Yes. Please do. That would definitely come under publicity," I told him. "We'd better exchange lists of what we're doing so we won't be duplicating each other," I said, pausing as our meals were delivered. "And I'll post progress reports every day."

"I'm going to interview the grave rubbing guy then," said Shannon. "Put me on the list for that before somebody else decides to do it."

"Did you get his phone number already?" Hilda teased.

"Not yet, but I'll have it this afternoon." Shannon looked smug.

"Really? How come you're so sure?" Hilda giggled. "We don't even have his name yet. Just his eye color."

"Dorothy said she'd get it for me. She knows him."

*Dorothy knows the gravestone rubbing guy?*

Hilda echoed my unspoken thought. "Dorothy knows the blue-eyed hottie?"

Shannon took a bite of her cheeseburger and nodded. "Yep. Ray, would you please pass the ketchup?"

For the remainder of the lunch hour the conversation veered from publicity ideas to how best to transition from the ghoulish craziness of a Salem Halloween to the happy noise and family friendliness of the Mexican *Dia de los Muertos.*

We returned to the classroom with a general feeling of accomplishment. In my case, the feeling was accompanied by confusion and curiosity—mostly about Dorothy—along with an extra large helping of wondering what the green-handled trowel was all about.

Dorothy rejoined the group in the classroom at one o'clock. She immediately took the seat beside Shannon and the two huddled over a shared computer, leaving no opportunity for my questions about things which were probably none of my business anyway. The twins were headed to the second floor art studio in search of a commercial art student who might come up with a suitably attractive logo for the event and Hilda was on speaker phone with a representative of the Salem Cemetery Commission, while Therese busily took notes.

*So far, so good.*

I opened a package of colored markers and began preparing a to-do chart on a large white board, trying to remember all of the varied duties we'd discussed. There were enough items to nearly fill the board. I paused after printing "Contact Ghost Tours," and sat there staring at the list, unable to think of even one more thing to add.

I turned on my computer and checked my e-mail. I know. I know. Shouldn't do it on company time. A brief note from River said thanks for the pizza, sorry she missed the pie, and reminded me to watch that night's show to see how the costume turned out. It was unusual to see a message from Aunt Ibby. "Been thinking of Emily," it read. "Look at this." Attached was a copy of the police notes from the *Salem News* dated several days before the obituary we'd read earlier. "Woman found dead in Bathtub. A 25-year-old woman was found unresponsive in a bathtub at her apartment. She was transported to Salem Hospital where she was pronounced dead, police said. Her family has not yet been notified. A toxicology report is pending."

*Toxicology?* Would that have something to do with whatever had been in the wineglass? Had Pete said something about pills? *Found unresponsive?* Found? Who found her? More questions. I looked toward the desks where Dorothy and Shannon now sorted through a stack of copy paper printouts. I planned to make a point of having at least a few words with Dorothy before she could manage another disappearing act.

*Is she dodging me on purpose?*

Another question. But no, that didn't seem likely. After all, she'd signed up for this class because she wanted my help, and she'd been forthcoming with information about her sister so far.

At five o'clock the sound of an old-fashioned school

bell rang—Mr. Pennington liked to keep things vintage wherever possible—and this time Dorothy didn't disappear. Smiling, she approached my desk. "Is that offer of a ride home still good?" She pointed to her feet. "Wearing a pair of my sister's shoes. I'm not used to heels and besides, these are too small. They hurt."

"Of course," I said, gathering up books and papers and putting them into the appropriate drawers and folders. "Be right with you."

She gestured toward the giant black pump. "My feet feel so swollen right now I probably need a pair that size."

Naturally, I didn't look at the big shoe. I'd already seen quite enough of it for one day. We took the elevator down to the first floor—out of sympathy for her sore feet—and crossed Essex Street to the Tabby's parking lot.

Dorothy again expressed admiration for my car—which always makes points with me—and climbed into the passenger seat. "Okay, where to?" I aimed the 'vette for the lot exit.

"Not far," she said, indicating that I should turn right. "Just take Washington Street down to Norman. Ordinarily I'd walk." She made a wry face and pointed once again to her feet. "Guess I've spent too many years stamping around in boots and Mukluks." She glanced over at my own Arturo Chiang three-inch platform sandals. "How do you do it?" She didn't wait for an answer. Good thing. I didn't have one. "Emily must have worn heels every day. Even weekends." There was a note of wonderment in her voice. "She had a whole closet full. Every color. Oh, and one pair of beat-up hiking boots in a plastic bag."

"I take mine off as soon as I get home," I admitted, "and usually wear sneakers all weekend."

"Turn here," Dorothy instructed, and we pulled in behind a four-story apartment house. It was one of Salem's many rehabbed old homes. "You can park in any space marked 'Visitor.' Want to come up for a minute?"

"I'd like that," I said. "Maybe you can fill me in on what makes you think Emily was murdered." I glanced around the parking lot. There were a few cars in the reserved spaces, none in the visitor's slots. "Didn't your sister have a car?"

"She did. A little VW I think. Paula drove it back to Georgia. Didn't want to just abandon it here. Anyway, I think she bought it for Emily in the first place." She motioned for me to follow her to a side door of the building, and tapped a few numbers into a security pad. The door slid open, admitting us to a spacious and attractive foyer. We took an elevator to the fourth floor of the place, stepped out into a carpeted hall and arrived in front of a plain walnut door bearing the number 4-12.

Dorothy used both a key and a pad number on this door and pushed it open, allowing me to enter first. It was a pleasant place, muted earth-toned décor and furniture with modern lines. A few paintings of the interior-decorator-selected variety adorned beige walls. Dorothy waved one hand toward a French door. "The rooms here are tiny, but there's a cute little balcony. My sister put some plants out there and she liked to sit and watch the birds."

The open floor plan gave me a good view of a well-equipped kitchen where black appliances complemented pecan cabinets. "Coffee?" Dorothy asked, kicking off her shoes. "I haven't figured out all the domestic devices yet but I can operate the coffeemaker."

"Yes, thanks. I'd love some." I sat on one of the stools surrounding a granite-topped island and watched her careful coffee preparations. After she'd pressed the "ON" button, she turned and faced me. "I suppose you want to see it, don't you?"

"See what?"

"The bathtub. Where she died."

"Not especially," I said. "Unless you think it's important for me to see it."

"I don't know whether it is or not. But since I'm asking for your help. . . ." She spread her hands apart. "Maybe there's something there they missed. I haven't changed anything. You don't have to look at it if you don't want to."

I didn't want to. I'd already seen it.

"No problem," I lied.

# CHAPTER 8

Dorothy picked up the discarded shoes, and holding them gingerly by their narrow straps, walked across the off-white carpet and opened a door. "I'll just put these away," she said. "Then we can talk about what's important and what's not." She shrugged. "I don't know the difference yet." Seconds later she returned, smiling and still barefoot.

I sipped my coffee and waited, not speaking, hoping she'd answer some of the many questions that had been spinning around in my brain since our conversation on the trip to the cemetery.

She pulled up a stool on the opposite side of the counter and faced me. "Coffee okay?"

"It's fine," I said.

"Back home in False Pass I make it in an old percolator over a wood stove."

"Uh-huh." *Come on Dorothy. Enough small talk. Get to the point.*

"Look, I know the police said it was accidental. Maybe she took too many sleeping pills. Maybe she washed them down with too much wine. Maybe she fell asleep in the tub and just died. Maybe maybe maybe." She put her cup down hard enough to splash coffee onto the granite surface. "I don't think so."

"What makes you think it wasn't an accident?"

"Mostly because I knew my sister. She rarely took a drink. I've never known her to take pills. And there was something . . . something odd about the letters."

"Letters?"

"Yes. We corresponded the old-fashioned way. Wrote letters. Internet is pretty near useless up there except locally. I used to call long distance once in a while from one of the fish house stores, but they close down for part of the year, so letters have been just about it."

"That's why you didn't hear about her death sooner."

"Right. Paula sent a telegram, but the only way to get to False Pass from the mainland is by boat or plane"—she shrugged—"so I didn't get the message until after Emily had been cremated and my stepmother had already gone home to Georgia. I came right away of course. I knew there was something wrong. I was pretty sure it wasn't an accident." She stopped speaking, her eyes misty.

"The letters," I prodded. "You said something about her letters."

"Her letters. Right, here's the thing. I think she had some kind of a problem going on at her work."

"Where did she work?" I asked. "The paper didn't say anything about her job."

"She was kind of a secretary I guess," Dorothy said. "For a real estate business. Happy Shores Real Estate. Kind of a goofy name for Salem, huh? Sounds more like Florida or Hawaii, doesn't it? Happy Shores."

"I don't know. Maybe. We do have shores, you know. North Shore. South Shore. Do you want to tell me about the letters?" I realized that I was beginning to sound impatient and tried to soften my tone. "Take your time, Dorothy. I know this is hard for you to talk about."

"It is," she said. "The letters are in the bedroom. Come on and take a look at the bathroom and her bedroom and then we can sit down and read the letters. Maybe you'll see why I don't think she died by accident."

Going into Emily's—now Dorothy's—bathroom was strange. I'd seen it before in the oval mirror in my own bedroom. Of course the tub was empty now. No body. No bubbles. No wineglass. A black-and-white striped shower curtain hung from circular tubing above the tub, matching the black-and-white tiled floor. I looked around the room. A pedestal sink, a toilet, a towel rack with two fluffy white bath towels, a white wicker shelf displaying folded white hand towels, a bottle of spray cleaner, a soap dish holding a new cake of Ivory soap and a bevel-edged mirror. It struck me as a simple, efficient, almost Spartan environment. I wondered where she'd kept her makeup, hairspray and perfume.

I glanced at Dorothy. She didn't use makeup and perhaps her sister hadn't either.

*None of my business.*

"Very—um—neat," I said. "My bathroom seems a little messy in comparison."

"It seems luxurious to me." Dorothy smiled. "My place in Alaska doesn't even have a bathroom."

"Can't even imagine it," I said. "What do you do there for work up there?" I asked.

"I'm a commercial fisherman," she said. "Have my own boat. Just me and one crew. I sell the catch to one of the fish houses. It's a pretty good living. Off season I do a little hunting." We'd entered a small bedroom, the walls painted the same beige as the living room. A single bed, a nightstand and a long, low bureau dominated the space. She opened one of the top bureau drawers and withdrew a package of letters, tied with white ribbon. "Here they are," she said. "I'm so glad I saved them. I almost didn't."

She headed back to the living room and I followed. We sat together on a chocolate brown microfiber couch. Dorothy turned on a fat, white, round ceramic lamp, then untied the ribbon on the packet of letters.

She unfolded the first one, smoothed the paper gently and held it where I could see it as she read aloud. "Dear Dot," she began. The handwriting was rounded, the letters neatly formed. The stationery was delicate looking, an almost translucent white with scalloped edges all around.

"I guess I told you a little about my new job at Happy Shores Real Estate. The big boss is Mr. Shores. His wife is named Trudy. She's very nice and she more or less runs everything and seems to like me. My work is easy. I do stuff like typing up agreements and making appointments for some of the agents, buying balloons and cupcakes for open houses. I wish I had a little more responsibility though. When are you going to come to Salem? I miss you. Love, Em."

She refolded the letter carefully, placed it on the lamp table, and picked up another. This one was written on the same kind of paper, but had jagged edges as though it had been trimmed with pinking shears.

"Dearest Dot," Dorothy read. "Well, today was kind of fun at work. You would have liked it. I learned something new. It wasn't really part of my job. It was my afternoon off actually, and one of the real estate agents invited me to go with him to get a soil sample from a big piece of property Trudy and Happy own. (The boss's real name is Harold, but everybody calls him "Happy." I don't of course because I'm only a secretary. I call him Mr. Shores.) Anyway, the soil sampling is nothing official. All the testing on the property has already been done, but he wanted to show me how they do it. He's really smart. Has a degree in that sort of thing he says. It was sort of a date I guess. I don't know many of the agents. He's a nice guy. Everybody here calls him J.D. He even brought me a pair of boots to wear because the ground was muddy. Ugly things. You'd probably like them."

Dorothy looked up from the letter. "She drew a little smile face there," she said, brushing a hand across her eyes, then continued reading. "It was interesting, digging holes, putting the dirt in plastic bags and writing on the labels. J.D. is sending our samples to a lab for testing. I think that's exciting! You know how I always liked chemistry and science and all those subjects. Anyway, maybe next time J.D. asks me out it will be for dinner and I won't have to wear ugly boots. Love you. Miss you. Em."

Dorothy folded the letter, gave it a little pat, and put it on the table. The next one was written on a long, narrow sheet of the same paper, this one with wavy edges. "Dear Dot," she read. "I'm writing this early in the morning. Couldn't sleep. Too much on my mind. I wish you were here. Remember when we used to stay up all night just talking sometimes? I miss that. I need someone to talk to. When that fish store opens again, telephone me, will you? Love, Em."

"Did you call her?" I asked. "That one sounded urgent."

"I did, of course. The fish house was still closed so I hitched a ride on a seaplane and phoned from the mainland."

"And did she tell you what was wrong?"

"Yes. And, no." She added the letter to the pile and sighed. "There were no more letters after this one. She told me on the phone that her new friend, the one who'd taken her on the soil sample project, had suddenly quit or maybe even been fired. She'd overheard him and Trudy Shores talking. Then he'd come out of Trudy's office, stopped at Emily's desk and told her he'd call her soon, that he had something important to tell her. He never called. She looked in the employee files for his number but his file was missing. She asked Mr. Shores about him and was told that he'd left town for a better job."

Dorothy paused, folding her arms. "Emily didn't believe him. Now I don't think I do either."

"Did Emily tell you this man J.D.'s full name?"

"At the time I didn't bother to ask. I thought she was just feeling hurt, you know. About this guy not calling." She waved one hand in the air. "We all know what that's like."

I nodded agreement. The thought was interrupted by a sudden, muted burst of music.

At my questioning look, Dorothy smiled. "Next door neighbors. Just moved in last weekend. Other than a little country and western once in a while, they're pretty quiet."

"Does it bother you?"

"A little. I guess when they turned the place into apartments they didn't worry much about insulation. Some of the walls are so thin you could probably hear a mouse fart next door."

I laughed, then returned to the more serious subject of Emily's letter. "So what did you tell Emily about her new friend not calling?"

"I'm afraid I wasn't much help. I told her he'd probably call when he got settled, wherever he'd gone. That he wasn't worth worrying about." She shook her head. "I totally missed the point. She didn't believe he'd left town without calling her. She was actually worried about *him*."

"And you think all this has something to do with Emily's

death?" I was confused, and said so. "I don't get it. Have you talked to the Shores couple?"

"I have. I went to see them as soon as I got to Salem. They were nice as pie. Said how much they missed her, what a good worker she was, how terribly upset they were about what had happened." Dorothy frowned. "Mrs. Shores even had tears in her eyes, said she felt a little bit responsible because they'd had a party at their house that night and maybe—that's what she said—*maybe* Emily had a *teensy bit* too much to drink—that's what she said—a teensy bit too much to drink. She said she'd followed Emily back here in her car that night, just to be sure she got home safely."

"Did you ask about the missing agent? The man Emily was expecting to call her?"

"Sure I did. They said he just wasn't quite right for Salem. Just didn't fit in with their way of selling. Claimed he used high pressure tactics and they thought he was better suited to a different market."

"But did you get his name from them?"

"Not exactly." She frowned. "Mrs. Shores started to tell me. She said he always went by his initials, J.D., but that his name was James . . . she started to say his last name . . . it sounded like 'Dow.' But then Mr. Shores interrupted and said it wouldn't be proper for them to give out private information on employees. Then he told me to have a nice day, handed me a bag full of advertising stuff, held the door open for me and practically pushed me out of the office."

She reached behind the table and pulled out a canvas bag like the ones Aunt Ibby uses for shopping, only this one had a stylized H.S. monogram on it. "Here"—she said, shoving it toward me—"you might be able to use it. I really don't have any use for it."

"Okay then," I said, tucking the bag under my arm. "We can always use an extra grocery bag. Thanks, and listen. Don't worry. I'm sure we can get J.D.'s name. I'll call and pretend to be one of his customers. Someone in that office will let it slip out, maybe even tell me where he went. But meanwhile, have you checked Emily's computer?"

"I tried. I don't know her password."

"Keep trying. It may be the name of a childhood pet, or a street you used to live on."

"Okay. I'll do it tonight."

"Good. Speaking of mystery men, Shannon says that you know the blue-eyed artist who makes the fake grave rubbings."

"Sure do, Dakota Berman. He's the super of this building. Nice guy. He knew Emily."

# CHAPTER 9

"Small world," I said, marveling because it really is. "I didn't notice you talking to him when we were at the cemetery."

"We kind of waved to one another," she said, retying the letters with the white ribbon. "He's really shy. Not much for conversation. Keeps to himself. He lives in the basement here."

"Shannon wants to interview him for the project. Think he'll talk to her?"

Dorothy returned the letters to the bureau drawer. "He might, because she's so pretty. She may as well try. I think he might enjoy talking about his work. He's a pretty good artist, besides the tombstone thing."

Together we walked back to the living room. "Have you talked to him about Emily at all?"

"I've tried to, but I don't think they actually spent any time together. He doesn't gossip. Minds his own business. Good traits for a building superintendent."

I had to agree. "I should think so. I'd like to meet him sometime."

*Maybe I can brush up on my interview skills.*

"I'm sure we'll run into him again at the cemetery," she said. "I'll introduce you if you like."

"Thanks," I said, "and thanks for sharing the letters. I understand why you feel that you need to find out all you can about Emily's death." At that moment I wanted to reach out and hug her, or at least to take her hand, but held back. "I'll help where I can," I said, "but please be prepared to accept that it's entirely possible—even likely—that it was, after all, a terrible accident."

She gave the slightest negative shake of her head, but smiled at the same time. "I understand. Thanks for coming over . . . and for taking pity on my poor sore big feet."

I returned the smile. "Feel free to wear your Mukluks to class if you like. See you tomorrow."

We said our good-byes and I took the elevator down to the foyer and stepped out into the late afternoon sunshine. I walked to my car, then looked back toward the apartment house. I noticed the row of balconies along the top floor and wondered if the one with a profusion of plants was Emily's. A few horizontal narrow windows dotted the base of the building.

*You'd think an artist would need to have more light than that.*

It was just a little past six, not too late for a real estate office to be open. I reached for my phone, called 411 and got the number for Happy Shores. An automated voice told me what button to push. After an interim of classical music—Bach I think—a human answered.

"Happy day from Happy Shores," chirped a female voice. "How can I make your day an even happier one?"

I grimaced and wondered how anyone could maintain that cheery tone of voice while repeating that inane message over and over. "May I speak with James please?" I said.

"He told me to call as soon as I got my cash down payment together. I hope the property is still available."

*Cash probably trumps confidentiality at Happy Shores.*

There was a long pause before the cheery voice resumed. "I'm sorry. There is no one called James connected to the agency." She sounded as though she was reading a script. "May I direct your call to another member of our happy professional staff?"

"No thanks, I really need to talk to James. Can you tell me where I could reach him?"

Again a pause, and the relentlessly cheerful voice. "I'm sorry. There is no agent by that name connected with this agency. May I direct your call to another member of our happy professional staff?"

"Sometimes he goes by J.D." I persisted.

Another pause. More script reading, but this time the chirp had a little edge to it. "I'm sorry. There is no one called J.D. connected with the agency. May I direct your call to another member of our happy professional staff?"

I knew when I was being stonewalled. "Thanks anyway," I said. "Have a happy day." I hung up and headed home. I knew that Pete could get the missing James's name somehow but that it would involve miles of paperwork. Anyway he'd need a reason beyond the possibility that the guy had stood Emily up.

Time to call in the big guns. I'd put Aunt Ibby on it. No problem. Once she had the name, I'd turn it over to Pete—who'd probably tell me that the company had every right to keep employee information confidential.

I'd looked forward to a quiet evening. Aunt Ibby had made plans with Mr. Pennington to attend a lecture on Chinese porcelain at the Peabody Museum and Pete had to work the three to eleven p.m. shift. "Looks like it'll be just you and me, O'Ryan," I told the cat as I put a frozen chicken pot pie into the microwave for me and opened one of those tiny cans of gourmet cat food for him. I turned on the kitchen TV and caught the tail end of the evening news on WICH-TV. Phil Archer reminded viewers to watch the Sox-Yankees game at eight. Wanda the Weather Girl reported on a low pressure area in the Gulf of Mexico. The refrigerator vegetable drawer yielded part of a head of lettuce, a nice tomato from Aunt Ibby's garden and a couple of carrots. Good enough for a salad of sorts with a dab of mayo.

O'Ryan made short work of his *White Meat Chicken Florentine with Garden Greens in Delicate Sauce.* Maybe I should have put it into one of those footed crystal dishes like they show on TV. Scooping the last bite of crust from the bottom of the cardboard pot pie container, then polishing off the better than expected salad, I rinsed our dishes and started a pot of coffee. It would be a while before the start of the game, so I switched channels and watched TMZ for a few minutes, then remembered my promise to Dorothy to do a little checking myself on James D. Why not? Maybe some of my aunt's research skills had rubbed off.

I retrieved my laptop from the bedroom and poured myself a cup of nice fresh coffee. O'Ryan hopped up onto the counter and lay down, paws curled up under his chin so that he had a good view of the screen. I tried the obvious first. Googled James Dow. I found one person by that name—a sixty-five-year-old house painter in Connecticut. I was pretty sure he wasn't the one I was looking for. Tried Jim Dow, Jimmy Dow, J. Dow. Facebook had the housepainter and seventeen-year-old Jimmy. O'Ryan moved closer to the screen, switched his tail against it once or twice and I was back to screen saver—a nice view of Rockport Harbor in winter.

"I guess you figure this is a waste of time," I said, looking directly into those golden eyes.

He didn't blink. "Meh," he said, and headed for his windowsill perch. I decided that he was probably right—he so often is—closed up the laptop, topped off my cup and joined him at the window.

The sun had set and a rising pale moon gave just enough wan light to turn our backyard into a strangely unfamiliar place. A tall row of alien beings with round heads and grasping, misshapen arms reached for one another. At their feet a long, dark sprawling mass undulated in the evening breeze like a fat serpent and, atop the weathered fence separating our yard from the neighbors', a lone gray cat crouched in stalking posture. Nearby, an owl hooted. At the sound, the cat leapt to the ground activating solar motion detector lamps. The aliens once again became sunflowers and the fearsome snake turned into Aunt Ibby's kitchen garden of basil, rosemary and cilantro. The cat, no longer gray, but white, disappeared over the fence.

O'Ryan gave my elbow a friendly lick, cocked his head to one side and fixed me with that golden-eyed stare once again. "I suppose you're telling me there's a deeper meaning here," I said. Another lick. "Things aren't always what they appear to be. Right?" A bob of the fuzzy head. "Aliens and snakes can be your friends?"

He closed his eyes, stuck out his tongue and said, "Meh."

"Okay," I said, thinking of the white cat. "How about a quote from Ben Franklin—'When all candles be out, all cats be gray'?"

He seemed to like that one, rewarded me with another lick, then apparently through with the subject, hopped down and headed for his water bowl. I didn't bother to explain that Franklin was talking about bedding older women.

The idea that things aren't always what they appear to be

wasn't a new concept for me. The reflections—the visions—whatever they are and wherever the damned things come from—very often show me conflicting scenes. Somehow those scenes eventually turn on some kind of mental solar lighting and begin to make sense.

*The stupid green-handled trowel is one of those I guess. Along with the dead woman in the bathtub.*

I didn't want to think about either one just then. Anyway, it was time for the baseball game. Opting for more comfortable seating and a much bigger screen, O'Ryan and I headed down the short hall to the living room. I plumped up a couple of throw pillows and got settled on the couch while the cat curled up on the seat of the zebra print wing chair. I know O'Ryan likes watching baseball but I've never been sure whether he's a Sox fan or not.

One thing about watching a Red Sox game, especially a home game, especially when playing the Yankees, is that it's rarely boring. This one was no exception. Tied three to three at the end of nine, by eleven o'clock the game went into extra innings.

My phone rang.

Not taking my eyes from the screen, I answered. "Hello?"

"You watching this?" Pete asked.

"Yep."

"Mind if I come over after the game?"

*Silly question!*

"I don't mind one bit. Bring some ice cream. We'll celebrate when the Sox win."

He didn't question the assumption of the home team win. "Chocolate?"

What a guy. I knew he preferred vanilla, but chocolate is my favorite. "How about we compromise with fudge ripple?"

"Perfect. See you in a few."

Pedroia quickly settled the Red Sox–Yankees question with a home run for the Sox in the tenth and within twenty minutes Pete arrived with the promised ice cream. I'd already put a pair of vintage tulip-shaped ice cream dishes on the kitchen table along with a plate of Aunt Ibby's version of Tabitha Trumbull's "Cowboy Cookies"—oatmeal cookies with a chocolate chip twist—and started a fresh pot of coffee.

We shared a prolonged kiss—but stopped the action there—just short of risking melted ice cream. I scooped the lovely stuff into the footed containers, added some hot fudge sauce and a hefty squirt of Reddi Wip while Pete poured the coffee. We faced one another across the Lucite table, clicked our mugs in a silent toast, enjoying the moment. O'Ryan had returned to his window seat, so we were *almost* alone.

"How was your day?" he asked. "Any more cemetery trips?"

I smiled. "Not yet, but I'm sure there'll be plenty more before this project gets finished. Yours?"

"Nothing much out of the ordinary," he said. "Oh. I did a little more checking into that case you were asking about. The girl in the bathtub."

I put down my spoon. "Really? Learn anything new?"

"Not really. The pills in her stomach matched the pills in a bottle in her bedroom. A bottle with her name on it."

"Do you know what kind of pills they were? Did you talk to her doctor?"

He picked up a cookie. "These are great. Tabitha's?"

I nodded. "Yeah. Go on."

"A pretty common sleeping pill. One of the kind you see on TV. You know, 'ask your doctor if blah blah medicine would be good for you.' I didn't talk to her doctor but the M.E. did. Her doc had prescribed them because she complained that she wasn't sleeping well. No big deal."

"No big deal? The woman is dead."

"You know what I mean. Anyway, she hadn't taken a lot of them. But she was a small person and if you're not used to that kind of drug, mixing it with booze is a bad idea."

"Was she drunk? Her boss's wife said that she followed Emily home in her own car that night because she was worried about her driving."

Pete frowned. "Who told you that?"

"Her sister. Dorothy Alden."

"Did you get Dorothy's number for me? I'd like to talk to her."

"I did." I reached for my phone and he reached for his notebook. I read off the number and Pete copied it down. It occurred to me that I've been watching Pete write things in a little brown notebook for a couple of years now. It couldn't be the same notebook.

"You must have a lot of those little notebooks full of notes and numbers. Do you save them all?"

He colored slightly. "I do. They're all in a bottom drawer in my desk at the station. Guess I'm kind of a packrat that way."

"Do you ever refer back to any of them?"

"Once in a while I do," he admitted. "Not very often. But," he added, frowning, "I think I might check back a couple of months after I talk to your Dorothy."

"Back to when you found Emily in the bathtub?"

"Yup. As far as the department is concerned, it's a closed case—an accident—and I agree. But you're uneasy about it so I'll check into it. Okay?" He reached for my hand. "Got any more of that ice cream?"

# CHAPTER 10

In the morning my refrigerator yielded nothing the least bit interesting so I invited Pete to join me at the Tabby Diner for breakfast.

"Good idea," he said. "Do you think Dorothy will be there?"

"Wouldn't be surprised. Are you going to ask her about Emily's boss's wife following her home that night?"

"Maybe. I'd like to meet her anyway, and the rest of the class too. Sounds like an interesting group."

"So far they seem to mesh well. Four girls and two guys. Ages from nineteen to over sixty."

"Over sixty? Your class last year was a lot younger."

"The girls are all younger than me. The old-timers are the twins. A pair of ex-Boston cops, Ray and Roger Temple."

"Cops, huh? Can't stay away from 'em, can you?" He laughed.

I gave him a punch in the arm and we started down the back stairs. "I'm going to leave Aunt Ibby a note," I said, picking up the pencil-on-a-string hanging from the wooden "leave-a-note" pad next to her kitchen door.

"Gone to breakfast with Pete," I scribbled. "See what you can dig up on a James Dow or Downey or Dow-something. He may be in real estate."

I followed Pete to the backyard where he'd parked his unmarked Crown Vic. "The twins drive a car just like yours too," I said. "But I have to admit, you're a little bit better looking than they are."

"Glad you think so." Smiling, Pete climbed into his car and I opened the garage and backed the 'vette out onto Oliver Street. It's one-way so he followed me down to Bridge Street. I slowed down a little as we passed the Howard Street Cemetery. I'd driven past it hundreds, maybe thousands of times during the years I'd lived in Salem, but now I looked at the place with new eyes. Three hundred graves?

*Three hundred stories.*

I tried to stop thinking about dead people, touched the gas pedal and turned up Washington Street to the Tabby's parking lot, with Pete close behind me. I parked in my designated staff spot. Pete wheeled into a space at the far corner of the lot and we entered the diner together through the Essex Street front door.

I looked around the long room. The others hadn't arrived yet so we sat at the counter and ordered coffee rather than take up a whole booth during the busy breakfast hours. The twins were the first of my group to appear. They joined us at the counter and I introduced them to Pete. As might be expected, there was an instant rapport evident between them. Some kind of cop brotherhood thing I guessed.

Therese showed up next, via the door connecting the diner to the school. Therese lived in the Tabby's dorm during the school year and spent vacations with her parents in Boston. "Hi Lee, Pete," she said. "I got up at sunrise and got some cemetery shots. Had to jump the fence to get in, but there was this real nice early morning mist hanging over all the graves. Spooky!"

"Good for you, Therese." I said. "You probably should have waited for the gates to be open, but you're getting to be quite the expert with the camera."

"Thanks. I think I've found my 'career path.' My parents are ecstatic. They credit you with my newfound ambition. Of course they don't know about that other thing yet."

(The "other thing" was their daughter's involvement in witchcraft and I certainly didn't take any credit for that.)

"Hilda and Shannon are right behind me," she said, "and I saw Dorothy walking down the street a little way. I'm going to grab that big back booth for us. Come and join us if you want to." She tapped Roger's shoulder. "You too, guys."

Pete lifted his cup. "You go ahead with Therese. I'll pay for our coffees and be right behind you."

I reached the back booth just as Dorothy entered through the front door. I'd never thought about it before, but gray suede Mukluk boots with cable knitted tops look great with tight jeans and a white turtleneck on a cool fall morning. With her straight brown hair and scrubbed clean complexion Dorothy looked really pretty. I waved to her. "Come join us," I called and she slid into the seat opposite me.

Hilda and Shannon came in through the side door and within minutes we were all seated except for the twins, who chose to remain at the counter—Ray reading the *Boston Globe* and Roger studying *The Wall Street Journal.*

Pete was the last to reach our booth and he took the seat next to Dorothy. I introduced him to the group and there were greetings and handshakes all around. He turned to Dorothy and spoke softly—not in his cop voice at all. "I'm sorry about your sister," he said. "I guess Lee must have told you that I was one of the investigators on the case."

Dorothy's eyes widened, puzzled. I probably looked surprised too. It hadn't even occurred to me to mention Pete's job to her.

She did not look pleased. "No. She didn't."

"I'm sorry," I said. "We haven't had much opportunity to discuss each other's—um—relationships."

"That's okay," Dorothy held up one hand. "I understand." She faced Pete. "Has she talked to you about Emily?"

The others had stopped talking among themselves and Dorothy's question sort of hung there in the air, becoming the focus of attention at the table. The appearance of our waitress with her order pad ready was a welcome diversion, as Shannon, Hilda and Therese made their choices. I stuck with the small cheese Danish and more coffee.

Pete's cop voice was activated. "Actually there are a few loose ends I'd like to tie up if you'd be willing to talk to me about it."

Dorothy ordered bacon, scrambled eggs and hash browns before she answered. "Okay. When and where?"

"I'll call you," he said, and ordered pancakes and sausage.

Therese glanced back and forth between Dorothy, Pete and me, cocked her head to one side and asked, "Who's Emily?"

I hadn't thought about it until that moment, but it was evident that Dorothy hadn't talked about her dead sister to anyone in the class except me. The newspaper report weeks ago was vague enough, ordinary enough, and the name "Alden" common enough, to have gone unnoticed. It certainly had slipped past me.

Pete looked confused. "Uh-oh," he said. "Sorry if I spoke out of turn. I thought . . ."

"It's okay." Dorothy shook her head. "My fault. I probably should have said something. But when your sister dies . . . like that . . . you don't want to talk about it." She shrugged. "And I don't know any of you really well yet." The brown eyes were misty.

Shannon brought both hands to her mouth. "Your sister died? Oh my God, Dorothy. That's terrible. What happened?"

Hilda reached over and touched Dorothy's arm. "You don't have to say anything at all. Maybe later you'll want to. Just know please that we're all your friends."

"That's right," Therese echoed, frowning in Shannon's direction. "Let's talk about something else. Did everybody watch the game last night?"

Not everybody had, but it was enough of a subject change to clear the air. Our breakfasts arrived quickly and the normal before-class topics of conversation proceeded as though death—outside of the Howard Street Cemetery—had not been mentioned.

Pete had to leave before the rest of us had finished our meals. He excused himself from the table, said good-bye to the group, told Dorothy he'd be in touch, whispered to me, "I'm off tonight. Call you later, babe," paused at the counter for a word with the twins and left the diner.

Shannon watched Pete's departing back, then turned to me. "Wow, Ms. Barrett—can I call you Lee? He's so cute. Is he your boyfriend?"

I laughed. "Yes, to both questions."

"Speaking of cute guys, Shannon," Hilda teased, "did you talk to Blue-Eyes yet?"

"Not yet, but his first name is Dakota. Isn't that sexy?"

Everyone agreed that Dakota was a suitable name for such a handsome specimen.

We finished our food and, together, entered the Tabby through the side door. Roger and Ray were already in the classroom, sitting in their accustomed seats, watching the WICH-TV morning news on the monitor behind the news desk. Carefully avoiding looking at the black shoe, I sat at my desk and shuffled through the stack of notes I'd accumulated on cemeteries, ghosts, sugar skulls and more.

I'd never assigned specific seats, pretty much letting everyone sit wherever they felt comfortable. Therese liked sitting behind the news desk and Shannon, Hilda and Dorothy had chosen desks behind the twins, facing the giant screen. Scott Palmer, the station's field reporter, was doing a stand-up from what appeared to be a clearing in some sort of forest. There were several other people behind him in the shot. I'd worked with him back when I was doing the late show at WICH-TV, but he wasn't one of my favorite people. Scott was using what I used to call his "big network" voice so this must be something significant.

"Want to turn the sound up a tad, Roger?" I asked. "That looks like the mayor there on the right. Let's see what's going on."

Roger obliged.

"The Salem Wildwood Plaza promises to be one of the North Shore's most modern, most beautiful shopping malls," Scott intoned. "And it will surely be one of the largest."

"Oh boy!" Shannon said. "A new mall right here in Salem. Awesome!"

"Where is he broadcasting from?" Hilda squinted at the screen. "Is that the big section of woods over near the Beverly Bridge? I always thought it was some kind of national park or bird sanctuary or something like that. Nobody ever goes in there."

"No real roads," I said. "Just trails. I think hunters and bird watchers use it. Not many lights around there, so the road that runs beside it has always been 'lover's lane' at night for Salem kids with cars. My aunt took me on a nature walk there one day when I was a kid. A bee stung me and I got poison oak." I frowned at the memory. "Never went back."

"Who's the woman with the mayor?" Therese asked.

"Don't know." I moved to a seat beside Ray and looked closely at the screen. "Palmer's probably going to introduce both of them though."

I was right about that. Scott introduced the mayor first and she gave a glowing description of the wonder of modern merchandising soon to come from the area that generations of Salem kids had called "the wild woods." Hence the name Wildwood Plaza I assumed.

I looked up when Dorothy slid into the seat beside me.

"That's her," she whispered hoarsely. "I only met her once but I'm sure that's her."

"Who?"

"That woman with the mayor. It's her. Trudy."

The name didn't register at once. "Trudy?"

"Trudy Shores. Emily's boss's wife."

*The female side of Happy Shores Real Estate.*

"Big project," Ray interrupted my thought. "Huge project. Lot of trees to clear."

"Roads to grade. Buildings to construct. Big project," Roger declared.

The mayor stepped aside and Scott held a hand microphone in front of the woman Dorothy had just identified as Trudy Shores. She was a tall, full-figured woman with a wide smile. "This is Mrs. Shores of the Happy Shores Real

Estate firm, the Salem company which has worked long and hard to complete the sale of this amazing property. Tell us a little about the coming mall, Mrs. Shores."

"Oh, please call me Trudy, Scott." The woman beamed "It's all so exciting, isn't it? The mall is going to be absolutely stunning. I can hardly wait to show you the drawings of how it will look when its finished. The entire Happy Shores organization has worked for nearly two years to pull it all together. I wish my dear husband, Happy, could be here today to share this moment." She blew a kiss toward the camera. "Love you Happy! He is the genius who has made it all happen. He's been traveling the country for weeks, negotiating with retailers who've expressed interest in opening stores here at Wildwood Plaza."

Scott looked into the camera and smiled. "Thank you Mrs. Shores. I mean Trudy. Thank you. I'm sure all of Salem will be looking forward to seeing this exciting project take shape. Now, back to the studio."

The ever-smiling, always gorgeous Wanda the Weather Girl appeared on screen, with the usual background of isobars and radar images and foreground of plunging neckline. She gave current temperatures and rain probabilities, and cheerfully reminded viewers that she was keeping a careful eye on that pesky tropical depression down south.

"Okay, everybody, time to get to work," I said. "Roger, want to turn the TV off please?"

He did, perhaps with some reluctance, as Wanda performed one of her trademark forward leaning poses.

"That mall is a good idea," Shannon offered. "Will it be finished in time for our cemetery thing?"

"Not a chance," Ray scoffed. "Thing like that takes

years. Permits. Paperwork. Regulations up to here." He waved his hand above his head.

Roger nodded agreement. "Years. Maybe never gets done at all."

"Well, we're going to get our project done on time, I'm sure," I said. "We're off to a great start. I know Mr. Pennington was very impressed. Therese, you said something about getting us a guided tour. Can you get in touch with your guide friend? I'd like to do it as soon as possible."

"Sure. Kelsey Roehl is one of the best ghost tour guides in Salem. Knows lots of history and has more ghost stories than anyone else I know. I'll text her right now."

"A ghost tour guide?" Shannon asked. "Are we going on a real ghost tour?"

Therese shrugged. "We're going to be walking around in a haunted cemetery. What else would you call it?"

Made sense to me. I turned to the twins. "How are you guys coming on the brochure?"

Roger answered. "We're thinking of something a little fancier than the cheap and dirty one we did before. Need some artwork for it. Make it look professional."

"Artwork," Ray echoed. "Real pro stuff."

"I know an artist," Dorothy spoke softly. "Sort of."

"She means Dakota!" Shannon was clearly pleased. "Don't you, Dot?"

Dorothy nodded. "I do. But I don't really know him. He's just an acquaintance."

"Smokin' hot acquaintance, if you ask me," Hilda said. "Let's see if he'll do it."

"I'll ask him," Shannon offered.

"Perhaps it would be best if Roger or Ray did it," I suggested. "Since they're in charge of the brochure."

The men agreed. Dorothy looked relieved. Shannon pouted prettily, but handed Ray the artist's phone number and Hilda Googled copyright-free illustrations in case the artist idea didn't work out. Therese reported that her guide friend was available that afternoon after four for about an hour. Things were moving along swimmingly. I dared to feel confident.

"Everybody ready for another field trip this afternoon? Four o'clock? Howard Street Cemetery again?" There were no objections. Therese gave a thumbs up and booked the tour.

# CHAPTER 11

The sun was low in the sky and shadows were lengthening when we gathered once again at the Howard Street Cemetery. Therese's friend, the ghost tour guide, Kelsey Roehl, waited for us at the Bridge Street entrance.

"Welcome, welcome," Kelsey called as we approached. She was a petite, dark-eyed young woman, wearing a simple thigh-length black dress and old-fashioned high-buttoned boots. The hood of her gray cape didn't entirely disguise a mass of long blond curls. "Therese has told me that some of you have an interest in the spirit of Giles Corey so I think it would be a good idea to begin our journey under his special tree."

The special tree was news to me, but I noticed Therese nodding as though she knew what the woman was talking about. Hilda frowned and consulted her phone with Shannon looking over her shoulder. Dorothy appeared to be focused on the guide's words, while Ray and Roger gave simultaneous head shakes and eye-rolls.

Following Kelsey, we trudged uphill. I'd worn flat heeled shoes on the off chance that a trip like this might come about, and a quick glance at the footwear of the others revealed that all of them must have had similar thoughts. Dorothy's Mukluks looked better every minute. The guide directed us along a grave-studded ridge, down a steep incline and past a large tomb, half buried on the side of a hill. She paused, pointing to the name on the tomb. *Richard Manning.* "Nathaniel Hawthorne's grandfather. His mother and sisters are in there too."

I'd barely digested that little-known fact when Kelsey pointed again. "There it is."

The tree was taller than most of the others dotting the cemetery and appeared to be a member of the pine family, with limbs and boughs tightly twisted around the trunk. Kelsey's voice dropped, taking on a spectral tone. "It's just a local legend of course, but they say that the very spot where poor Giles Corey was tortured, crushed to death with thirty-two boulders and rocks on his chest, is right here. Beside this tree." Long pause. "The old man lingered in anguish for two days and finally died. His last words were 'More weight!'" She paused, looking from one of us to the other. "The date was September 19, 1692."

"OMG!" Shannon was first to make the connection. "That's today!"

A buzz of excited conversation followed. None of my students seemed to be spooked by the coincidence, but rather found it interesting. Phones and cameras were aimed at the tree, and more than a few "haunted tree" selfies would undoubtedly soon show up on Facebook. Even the twins drew closer to the spot the guide indicated. Ray bent and examined the ground there, while Roger gazed, frowning, toward the old jail property on the other side of the nearby fence.

Making a mental note to be sure a few lines about the legendary tree would be included in our Day of the Dead publicity, along with information about the final resting place of Hawthorne's mother and siblings, I stepped into line behind our guide. I was second to last in the single file queue, with Dorothy close behind me.

I'd just brushed past the upward sweeping limbs of the tree when I heard Dorothy's sharp intake of breath followed by a nervous giggle. "I thought for a minute there that the ghost had grabbed me," she said. "It was just a branch brushing through my hair."

Kelsey Roehl seemed to be blessed with extraordinary hearing as well as knowledge of things ghostly. She turned and faced in our direction. "Did you say old Giles pulled somebody's hair?"

"Just a branch," Dorothy answered. "No harm done."

"Don't be too sure about that." The guide smiled. "He does it to me sometimes too. That's why I wear my hood up when I'm in here."

"Maybe we should have brought flowers or something for him." Shannon spoke softly. "To leave under his tree, you know. Because of the date."

"What a sweet kid!" Hilda said, throwing an arm across Shannon's shoulders. "That's a really nice idea. We'll be sure to do something special for the old man when we have the *Dia de los Muertos* celebration here. Okay?"

"Okay," Shannon agreed.

"Is that what this is about?" Kelsey wanted to know. "Are you guys going to do a Day of the Dead party here? Therese, you didn't tell me about that."

"Sorry. We put this together in kind of a hurry." Therese frowned. "Why? Is there a problem with it?"

"It's a great idea! Keep Halloween going for a little while. Great for my business. Can I help with anything?"

"What do you think, Lee?" Therese turned toward me. "Can Kelsey get involved?"

"Absolutely," I said. "An expert on Salem ghosts who

knows her way around the cemeteries is exactly what we need."

"Maybe she can help with the permitting process," Ray said. "City regulations. Cemetery protocol."

"Gotta go by the book," Roger agreed. "Regulations. Permits. She can help."

"No problem," Kelsey said. "Now let's continue with *this* tour, shall we?"

So we did. And a worthwhile tour it was. We learned about a few more Salem dignitaries who reposed there. She told us too about some underground rooms and tunnels below the grassy surface of the place, and about the times the riding mower had broken into the ceilings of the mysterious chambers. Howard Street had actually needed reinforcement a couple of times because of what was under it.

Dorothy sounded incredulous. "You mean there are tunnels and rooms under here somewhere? That's hard to believe."

"Believe it," I said. "I *know* there are tunnels and rooms under Salem."

Questioning looks came from several of the students. "It's true," Kelsey said. "Some guides even do tunnel tours." She shuddered. "Not me. Too dark and scary."

"Me either," I said, meaning it. "Been there. Done that."

We returned to the classroom where everyone seemed to be in an upbeat frame of mind. Therese gave an impromptu PowerPoint showing of her early morning "cemetery in the misty dawn" photos. It was probably due to our recent field trip that several of us thought we saw strange floating white orbs over some of the graves.

"Let's show some of the shots we took of the ghost tree," Hilda said. "If there are orbs anywhere, that's where they should be."

The positive vibes remained and even Ray and Roger were among the first to volunteer to share their own tree pictures, including their selfies. There was good-natured kidding all around as we viewed a slide show of various angles of the twisted old tree. There was a hush in the room though, when Roger's shot of the tree taken with the tower of the old jail in the background appeared on the big screen.

Therese broke the silence. "Well, there's your orb. No doubt about it."

There couldn't be much doubt about what we were seeing. Beside the tree, maybe three-quarters of the way up the trunk, and just over the fence separating the cemetery from the old jail property was a wavy edged oval white shape. Not exactly an orb. More like half of a person.

"Dust mote," Ray insisted. "Or else Roger had his thumb over the lens."

"That's probably it," Roger agreed. "Sure ain't a ghost! No such thing."

"I think it's just the glare from the sun," Hilda offered. "It was getting low in the sky. See? It's a reflection from the windows of the building over there."

"Sure, that's what it is," Shannon giggled. "You guys had me going for a second there."

Heads nodded all around, and everyone seemed to like Hilda's theory. I liked it a lot better than the half-a-ghost blob myself.

The school bell announced five o'clock so class was dismissed. I was nearly ready to head for the exit when my phone buzzed. It was Aunt Ibby.

"Guess what?" she said. "I think I've found your James. His complete name is Henry James Dowgin. I have an app that completes possible name endings. Holds four hundred eighty-five names beginning with Dow. Besides that, some folks use their middle name because they prefer it. I just started with A. James Dow, B. James Dow, and so on. H. James Dowgin turned up. Found him listed with a real estate agents' organization. I'm pretty sure it's the man you're looking for."

"You're a wonder," I told her, not for the first time. "Where is he?"

"He's in Florida," she said. "But unfortunately, he's probably dead."

# CHAPTER 12

I sat in stunned silence on my end.

"Listen," she said. "You come on home and I'll show you all I've found on it. I could be wrong."

"But you're probably not." I found my voice. "I'm on my way."

According to the reports my aunt had found, a man presumed to be Dowgin had died a month earlier while fishing for largemouth bass in one of the many canals adjacent to the Everglades. Dowgin, who was alone at the time, was believed to have slipped on a muddy embankment and fallen into the murky, alligator-infested water. An associate from the real estate office where Dowgin worked, unable to reach him via phone, went to search for him and found his automobile parked on a nearby road. One of Dowgin's boots and his tackle box were near shore. His cell phone and wallet were missing. A search of the area had produced the sleeve of a shirt, identified as part of the shirt Dowgin had been wearing, but no body. Authorities concluded that the man, unfamiliar with his surroundings, had ventured too close to the edge of the canal and had been attacked by one of the thousands of alligators known to inhabit the area.

"What a sad story."

My aunt made a "harrumph" noise. "He should have known better. Poor soul had no business wandering around the 'glades by himself."

Something about this sad story just didn't add up. "Do you think you could learn a little more about this? Like the name of the real estate agency where he worked?"

"I expect that I could. Might take a while. I'll get on it first thing tomorrow. I have a library board meeting this evening." She looked at the clock. "I'd better get dressed. Want to come with me? Should be interesting. We're planning a book signing event for authors of Salem histories."

"I'd like to but thanks, no," I said. "Pete has tonight off and he said he'd call me. I think he has plans for the evening."

"Suit yourself," she said with a smile. "I shouldn't be too late."

"Have fun." I kissed her cheek and headed up the front stairs to my apartment, O'Ryan bounding ahead of me.

I took a welcome shower, tossed my clothes into the laundry chute and dressed in soft, faded blue jeans and a lavender cotton sweater. Pulling my hair up into a messy top-knot, I gave a rueful look at my shoes. A cemetery tour can sure mess up plain old leather flats. I carried them out to the kitchen, spread a sheet of newspaper on the counter and began brushing caked dirt from the soles and sides. A good scrubbing with saddle soap and I judged them clean enough for another wearing. They were a little bit damp, so I lifted the kitchen window and parked them outside on the fire escape to dry.

O'Ryan had watched the entire process with cat-interest. He took his favored place on the sill, appearing to stand guard over shoes while I checked messages on my cell. One from Pete. Must have called while I was in the shower.

"Hi," I said. "You rang?"

"Sure did. Want to go out for a romantic dinner at your choice of fast food emporiums and a moonlight stroll along Deveraux Beach?"

"Sounds good. When?"

"In about ten minutes. I'm on my way."

"Pretty sure I'd be here, huh?"

"If you weren't I'd just watch TV with O'Ryan and wait for you to get home."

"See you in a few," I told him and headed for the bedroom mirror to check my outfit and try to do something about my hair. I decided that the jeans and sweater were okay for burgers and beach. I'd add a jacket against the evening chill. I brushed my hair, which was still a mess, and opted for a baseball cap to cover the damage.

Pete's key clicked in the back door lock and O'Ryan streaked across the kitchen to meet him. I took one last turn in front of the mirror to check my appearance. Big mistake. The swirling colors parted quickly and revealed . . . shoes.

It was almost like the home shopping shows I used to do in Florida. A smiling pitchman stood behind a counter with shoes on it. First I saw a shoebox containing a pair of black patent leather pumps like the one behind my desk at the Tabby. Then came a boxed pair of Mukluks like Dorothy's. Next, my leather flats, which I'd set out to dry on the fire escape. The last picture, a pair of scruffy work boots in a neat new box, looked oddly familiar. It was bad enough to have these damned visions intruding on my life, but did they have to be so maddeningly vague?

I sat on the edge of the bed, willing the shoe show to go away. What did it mean? The pictures in the mirror faded away. The work boot image blinked out just as Pete and O'Ryan appeared in the kitchen.

"You okay?" Pete raised one eyebrow the way he does when he's trying to figure something out. "You look . . . funny." He glanced at the mirror. "Uh-oh. You been seeing things?"

"Yeah. One that doesn't make the slightest bit of sense." I stood up and gave him a quick hug. "But at least there were no dead bodies in it."

He still looked worried. "Want to tell me about it?" He took my hand, leading me to the chair next to the still-open window. O'Ryan followed.

"I guess. But I told you," I said, "it doesn't make sense."

"Try me."

"Shoes."

"Shoes?"

"Right. First I saw a pair like the big black display shoe from the Tabby. Then I saw Dorothy's Mukluks. Then the shoes I wore today and last a pair of dirty old work boots." I folded my arms and watched his face. "Make sense to you?"

He leaned back in his chair. "What's a Mukluk?"

I laughed. "The boots Dorothy had on today. Did you notice them?"

"I did. You should get some of those."

"You like them?"

"Yeah. They look nice. You say you saw the big black shoe. The one that's showed you things before, right?"

"Right."

"Showed you anything lately? Anything you haven't mentioned to me?"

"One little thing," I admitted. "It doesn't make any sense either."

"What was it?"

"A garden trowel. Like the one Aunt Ibby uses, but hers

is old, with worn-off black paint on the handle. The one I saw in the shoe is new looking, with a green handle."

He reached for his notebook. "That was it? Just a trowel? What's the background? A workbench? A garden? Where do you think this trowel was?"

I closed my eyes. Brought the picture back to memory. "No background to speak of. It's just stuck in some dirt."

"Sandy dirt? Muddy dirt? Rich dirt?"

Pete's attention to tiny details is so specific sometimes I find it hard not to smile, let alone laugh outright. But with a straight face I said, "Brown dirt. Maybe what you'd call rich brown dirt."

"A green handle."

"Right."

Pete was quiet then, just scribbling in the notebook. He flipped back a few pages, then a few more. He put the notebook down and looked up. "Well, you about ready for our big dinner date?"

"Sure. Just need a jacket." I stood and headed back to my bedroom. "Aren't you going to tell me what that was all about? All the note taking?"

He grinned and shook his head. "That? That was nothing. You should see me take notes when I'm really serious about something."

I put on my favorite NASCAR jacket and jammed on a matching cap. "Okay. I guess you'll tell me eventually anyway."

"Probably will. I think I need to be more careful about what I say though. Was my letting the cat out of the bag this morning about Dorothy's sister really awkward for you?" O'Ryan looked up at Pete on hearing the word "cat," and, acknowledging the look, Pete bent and patted the big cat's head. "Was Dorothy as annoyed as she sounded?"

"Not really. She seemed surprised about you being a

detective, but after all, on such short acquaintance and within the student-teacher relationship—it really isn't any of her business who I'm dating, is it?"

"Guess not. Good night, O'Ryan. We're off on our wildly exciting date. Take care of things."

I turned off the kitchen light and Pete and I left the apartment through the living room and down the back stairs. We passed Aunt Ibby's kitchen door and Pete paused. "Think your aunt would like to come with us?"

"Not home. Library Board meeting. She keeps busy."

"She's amazing. Hell of a researcher."

"I know. I've been keeping her busy working on finding the guy who took Emily on a soil-sample collecting assignment."

We'd just stepped outside when the proverbial lightbulb went on over my head. I stopped short just outside the garden fence. "I've got it. Soil samples. Shoes. Work boots."

Pete had stopped walking at the same time I had. "What soil samples? What guy? What are you talking about?"

"Dorothy has letters from her sister. She showed them to me. Emily was working with a real estate agent who took her on some kind of soil sample dig. She wore boots. The ones in my vision."

"Letters from her sister, huh? Think she'd let us take a look at them?"

"Are you thinking she could be right about Emily's death? That maybe it wasn't an accident?"

We stopped at a traffic light. "Which way?" Pete asked. "Do you feel like burgers, chicken strips or fish sandwiches?"

"Chicken, I guess. Are you going to reopen the case?"

We headed for dinner with the Colonel, my questions unanswered.

# CHAPTER 13

We brought our chicken strips with us to the nearby city of Marblehead's justly famous Deveraux Beach. We'd passed on the Colonel's soft drink menu, opting instead for the beach restaurant's famous lime rickeys. (It's a New England thing.) The parking lot there closes at ten o'clock, so when we'd finished our dinners that left us a leisurely hour for our moonlight walk. There was just a sliver of moon, but the clear sky was bright with stars.

We walked the crunchy sand in companionable silence, arms around each other's waists, listening to slow rolling waves making their rhythmic landings. Pete spoke first. "Did you get his name?"

I knew who he meant. I'd been thinking about H. James Dowgin too, quite likely dead in a Florida swamp. "Henry James Dowgin," I said. "Only he goes by James or J.D. Dorothy asked the Shoreses about him and all she got was James Dow-something. Seems Mr. Shores interrupted his wife and said that they didn't give information about employees. I tried too, with a phone call, and they wouldn't tell me either. Anyway Aunt Ibby figured it out and located him in Florida—but he's probably dead."

He stopped short. "You're full of surprises today. Dead how?"

"Accident. Another stupid accident. They say he disappeared while he was bass fishing near the Everglades. Police down there say most likely a gator got him. There were a lot of them around." I'd stopped walking too, and stepped back so that I could face him. "Seems like a weird coincidence, doesn't it? A guy who worked for Happy Shores Real Estate dying accidentally in water. His friend Emily, who also worked for Happy Shores, dying accidentally in water. Oh, but you don't believe in coincidences, do you?"

He didn't answer right away, just stood there quietly on the sand as the waves rolled in and the stars sparkled. "Okay," he said. "I'll do a little checking. I'll talk to Dorothy. Maybe drop in at the Shores agency." He put both hands on my shoulders. "I'll check around and you'll keep your pretty little nose out of it. Promise?"

"So you agree with me? That there's something fishy about Emily's death?"

"Nope." We began walking again. "I agree with the chief and the medical examiner that accidents happen. I just want you and your aunt to stop snooping around. Somehow you two wind up getting into trouble whenever you play girl detective."

"I agreed to help Dorothy find out what happened to her sister, so I can't just drop the matter," I said. "How's this? I'll tell you every little thing I learn. And everything Aunt Ibby learns too. You said yourself she's a great researcher. If there's nothing there, she'll know it soon enough."

"You'll tell me about those visions too, if you have any more? Even if you think they don't make sense?"

I hesitated. Pete is really uncomfortable about my "seeing things." It had taken me a long time to tell him about my being a scryer at all, let alone going into detail about the things I see. I don't even always tell Aunt Ibby about them. I thought about things the visions have shown me, and wished I could erase the memory of some of them.

"I'll try to," I said finally. "I'll honestly try to do that, Pete."

He pulled me close and tipped my face up for a long kiss. "That's good enough. Just please be careful. Now let's head back to the parking lot before they tow my car away. Want to run?"

So that's what we did. We ran all the way back to the restaurant. It felt wonderful to breathe that good salt air, to feel my feet pounding across the hard-packed sand, to cleanse my brain of visions of the dead woman in the bathtub, the muddy boots, the green trowel, the tree-bound cemetery orb, and of poor H. James Dowgin, all alone in a faraway gator-infested swamp.

We didn't talk about Emily or Dorothy or letters or visions or any of those disturbing topics on our way home to Winter Street. Pete turned on the radio and rolled down the windows. We rode through darkened streets, sometimes humming along with the music, sometimes laughing about remembered good times we'd shared, sometimes just quietly enjoying being together. All in all, it had been a good date.

Pete dropped me off in front of the house with a quick kiss and a promise to call the next day. I let myself in, patted O'Ryan who'd been waiting just inside the door as usual, and paused at the entrance to Aunt Ibby's living room. The lights were out and all was quiet so I assumed she'd either gone to bed or was still out with Mr. Pennington. I followed the cat up the two flights to my apartment.

It was still too early to go to bed, so I turned on the kitchen TV, made a pot of hazelnut decaf and put on flannel pajama bottoms and an old race week T-shirt of Johnny's. I put a handful of kitty treats into O'Ryan's bowl, filled a mug with coffee, put a couple of cowboy cookies on a paper napkin and sat down at the table to watch the late news.

The program was already under way and Scott Palmer was at the anchor desk. That was a surprise. Scott usually broadcast from off site—either sports or news stories. I wondered if he'd received a promotion or if he was filling in for the regular announcer. The station manager, Bruce Doan, likes to get as much work as humanly possible from every employee.

Whichever it was, it seemed to have been a pretty slow news day in Salem. Once he'd finished reading from the national wire service—which was largely political and largely pretty boring—he told the WICH-TV audience about a puppy being rescued from a storm drain, a local man shooting a hole-in-one at the Salem Country Club and showed a video of a shouting match between a couple of city councilors at their weekly meeting. O'Ryan hopped up onto the chair across from mine and, putting his paws on the edge of the table, focused golden eyes on the TV screen. He's not really very fond of Scott, so I knew there must be something of interest to him in the newscast.

"What is it, big boy?" I asked, and turned the sound up a tad. "Want to hear the commotion at City Hall?"

Some of the words had been bleeped out, but the general gist of the argument between the two seemed to center on some land acquisition. Ho-hum. But when I heard the words "Wildwood Plaza" the late news had my full attention too.

Apparently there was some question about the paperwork

the land owners had filed with the city, and after the short clip ended, Scott announced that the attorney for the property owners had promised to "clear the matter up quickly."

"Drawings of the proposed mall are nearly complete," Scott said, "and here's a look at one of the preliminary sketches, released today especially for the viewers of WICH-TV, courtesy of Mr. Harold Shores."

*Must be back from his cross country search for retail stores for the new mall.*

A smiling Happy, aka Harold, wearing a plaid sport jacket, gestured to a drawing board where a picture of a row of stores with a sort of Tudor architecture look was displayed. He was a well-built man, a good head taller than Scott, with blond hair worn Donald Trump style. I thought of the blond man holding a scepter who'd shown up in my Tarot reading. "Notice the trees bordering the parking lot," he said. "We plan to preserve as many of the lovely old trees as possible, and the paving of the central parking lot will begin just as soon as permitting is complete."

Scott thanked the man, reminded viewers to stay tuned for the weather and sports, to be followed by *Tarot Time with River North* where the feature film would be *The Wolf Man.* I remembered showing that classic horror film back when I was hosting *Nightshades.* I realized that River must still be working the mystic theme. Maria Ouspenskaya was fabulous in that movie as the fortune-teller.

"Shall we watch River, O'Ryan? Let's see how my costume looks on her tonight."

The cat seemed agreeable to that idea. He hopped down from the chair and headed for the bedroom. I watched for a few more minutes before following him. Wanda the Weather Girl forecast a cool day, with a thirty percent chance of showers and gave the coordinates of the growing tropical storm which she said didn't yet threaten the U.S. mainland.

I turned off the kitchen TV, turned off the light and joined O'Ryan in bed. Before turning on the wall-hung screen over my bureau, I checked my voice mail. There was a call from Dorothy which must have come when Pete and I were walking the beach and I'd left my handbag in his car.

"Hi. Lee? Something happened. I got another letter today. It's from Emily. My house sitter forwarded it and I guess I told you everything takes forever in False Pass. Anyway, Emily wrote this letter before she died." Nervous giggle. "I mean of course it was before she died. Anyway, that guy . . . James . . . the guy who took her on that soil sample thing . . . he did get in touch with her after all. She was happy about it. They had a date and it looks to me as though it could have been for the night she died. I'll bring the letter to class tomorrow so you can tell me what you think I should do about it. Call me. Bye."

I looked at the clock. It was far too late to call her—to call anyone. I pulled up the covers, hugged my cat and listened to the intro music for *Tarot Time*.

*Danse macabre.* The dance of death.

# CHAPTER 14

I fell asleep before *The Wolf Man* had found his first victim and missed River's card readings entirely. I did catch a glimpse of my friend wearing my late mother's off-shoulder embroidered blouse, Aunt Ibby's vintage-red broomstick skirt and plenty of beads, rings and bracelets. The TV was still on when I woke at six o'clock the next morning. Turning it off, I looked around the room for O'Ryan. He was absent. I was sure he'd be downstairs with my early-rising aunt. By now she'd be halfway through the *Globe* crossword and he'd be halfway through a big bowl of kitty kibble.

Yawning, I padded down the hall to my bathroom. I splashed cold water on my face, brushed my teeth and thought about last night's message from Dorothy. So Emily had made a date with James—and it may have been for the night she died. Pete will want to know about that.

I thought about Emily, happy that she'd heard from James after all, getting ready for her date. I took a good hard look at my surroundings, and thought about the pristine, uncluttered space I'd seen so recently at Dorothy's apartment. No cabinet under the pedestal sink, no vanity with commodious drawers. Where did they put their bathroom stuff? Unless there was a secret stash somewhere of hair-spray, perfumes, nail polish, day cream, night cream and all the other innumerable helpers women use, I couldn't figure out how Emily—and now Dorothy—managed in that cool, barren, black-and-white space.

My own collection of mascara wands, eyebrow pencils, lip, lid and blusher brushes were stored on the lavender vanity top in an antique sun-purpled Victorian glass spoon holder. Like Dorothy/Emily, I favored fluffy white towels. Two of them hung on a chrome bar and the rest were displayed in a narrow glass-fronted linen closet. Hairdryer, razor and other electrical devices are hidden along with toilet tissue, personal products and paper towels in the cabinet under the sink. Combs and brushes were in one drawer and a few of Pete's necessities are in another. The everyday stuff was arranged, more or less neatly, on a couple of blue glass shelves. Pretty darned normal, I'd say.

I took a shower, washed my hair, plugged in the dryer and combed and teased the curly mass into a semblance of order. Since jeans had so far been the daily choice of all of the women in my class, I pulled a pair of Guess low-rise black ones from the closet, paired them with a yellow silk blouse and black leather booties. The breakfast options in my kitchen hadn't improved any since the previous day, so I headed down the back stairs to where I knew there'd be a full larder.

I knocked on Aunt Ibby's kitchen door with visions of cinnamon buns and eggs benedict and vanilla French toast dancing in my head—and effectively chasing away any lingering unpleasant thoughts. Aunt Ibby called "Come in, Maralee. You're here at the right time! I have popovers in the oven!"

The welcome aroma of coffee drifted into the hall the

moment the door swung open. My aunt, potholder in hand, stood in front of the stove, watching the flashing numerals on the oven timer counting down. O'Ryan, by her side, watched too. Within minutes I was seated at the old, round oak kitchen table with a mug of coffee, two perfectly browned, steaming hot, high-hatted, crusty, hollow-inside popovers with butter melting into homemade raspberry jam. I sighed with pleasure. "It just doesn't get much better than this," I mumbled, mouth full.

"I'm so glad you like them. Haven't made any in years." She spread apple butter onto hers. "This is Tabitha's recipe."

"I'd like to surprise Pete by making these some morning." I paused, thinking of the conversation we'd had on the beach. "But I promised I'd try not to surprise him with—other stuff."

"They're easy. I'll show you how. What kind of other stuff?"

"About Dorothy and her sister. I promised I'd tell him everything you and I found out about it . . . even though he doesn't like us snooping around at all, you know. I told him what you'd learned about James Dowgin, and I've learned something new about him too."

"About James?"

I told her what the message from Dorothy had said about the long-delayed letter. "I'll see it today at school. What do you think?"

"Have you told Pete about it?"

"Not yet. It was really late when I played the voice mail."

"I think it could be quite important. It would put this James person at the scene of the crime, wouldn't it?" she said. "If there was a crime, I mean."

"It would," I agreed. "If there was a crime. And there's

another thing. Pete asked me to tell him about any . . . um . . . visions I might see."

"Uh-oh. What did you say to that? I know you're timid about that topic where he's concerned."

"I told him I'd try. That's the best I could do. It's hard enough to talk to you and River about them."

"I'm sure he understands. More coffee?" She poured the lovely stuff into my mug as she spoke. "I do think though that perhaps you should tell him exactly what's contained in the letter Dorothy told you about."

"I will," I promised.

When I joined the group at the diner they were all crowded into the back booth, even the twins. Therese had enlarged Roger's photo of the cemetery ghost tree and made an eight by ten–inch print. The resulting image of a milky, filmy blob was the object of much excitement. Ray moved over, making room for me.

"It's all nonsense, of course," he said. "But it sure is strange looking." He turned the picture toward me so that the tree was right side up. "What do you think?"

I squinted at the whitish thing and shrugged. "I don't know. Maybe the Michelin Tire man?"

"I was thinking Pillsbury Dough Boy," Shannon added with a giggle.

"No, look." Therese used a spoon handle to outline the shape. "See? There's his head. See the ears? And he has a high collar. Here's his shoulders and one arm. See it?"

Hilda thought maybe it looked a little like a flower. Dorothy tipped her head from side to side, inspecting the photo but didn't comment. I still didn't see a resemblance to anything human. We gave the waitress our orders—just coffee for me—and the conversation turned to our next official cemetery visit with ghost tour guide Kelsey.

Back in the classroom we pooled our notes on the Howard Street excursion. Hilda was fastest on the keyboard, so she began the compilation of information. There was a lot about Giles Corey, and some good notes about the Richard Manning tomb that housed the late Hawthorne siblings. The twins had collaborated on a description of the ghost tree which was so good—darn near poetic—that it drew applause from the class. They'd also made a phone call to Dakota Berman, who'd turned down their request to submit a drawing for their brochure, pleading time constraints. They'd decided to go with a photo instead.

I was anxious to get a moment alone with Dorothy—and to get a look at that letter. The moment didn't happen until noon, when we were ready to break for lunch. When the others stampeded to the stairway heading back to the diner, I motioned for her to stay behind. "Can I speak to you for a moment, Dorothy?"

"Sure thing." She nodded and returned to her desk. I took the seat next to her.

"Did you bring it?"

She reached into her purse, slowly withdrawing the white oblong. "Here it is." She pulled a folded single sheet from the envelope, put it on the desk and smoothed it with both hands. She pushed it toward me. "It isn't very long. She sounded so happy, Lee. So pleased that she was going to see James again."

"I wonder if he ever showed up," I said, almost to myself, and picked up the letter. It was written in the same, round handwriting, on the same delicate paper with fancy cut edges.

*Dear Dot, Good news. Remember I was a little bit upset when I wrote to you about that guy who said he'd call me and then didn't? Well he did. Call me I mean.*

*His name is James and he's very good looking. And single. Well anyway, I have to go to a company party tonight. I'd skip it except it's kind of for me. I asked him to go with me but he said he can't go but that I should call him when I get home no matter what time it is and we'd go have a nice late dinner somewhere. I can hardly wait! I'll write again and let you know how it goes!* ☺

*Love,*
*Your Em*

I looked up. "Well, what do you think about it?"

"Oh, I think he showed up all right," she said, her face stern. "What if he was the one who killed her?"

# CHAPTER 15

I folded the letter slowly, carefully, picked up the envelope and tried to process her words. How did the fairly casual acquaintance of her sister's move from a man whose name Dorothy didn't know until yesterday to murder suspect?

"May I ask what makes you think so? What if he stood her up again? Couldn't that have prompted her to take the sleeping pills?"

She shook her head. "She didn't take those pills voluntarily. I'm sure of it. He probably slipped them into a drink. That's how they do it on TV." She stuck out her chin in a defiant gesture. "She didn't take them. I'm sure."

"I don't mean to disagree with you," I said. "I'm just playing devil's advocate here, but you haven't actually seen Emily, spent time with her, for months. Maybe years." She looked down and her head bobbed in a tiny affirmative nod. "Okay," I continued, "She could have felt the need for the pills. Maybe she was losing sleep because of her job. That happens. Sometimes things keep me awake nights too."

*They certainly do.*

"Me too. Try sleeping when you hear a wolf howling right under your window. But I don't take pills. Do you?"

I had to admit that I didn't although that howling wolf scenario might cause me to pop a few. "Even so," I said, "what kind of motive would this James have? She barely knew him."

She shrugged. "Em didn't always tell me everything, you know. Any more than I told her everything about my life. Maybe she knew him better than she'd let on."

I had to agree with the logic in that. "Would you let me show this letter, or a copy of it, to Pete?"

"I guess it would be okay."

"He might ask you to let him see the other letters too."

Her expression brightened. "Does that mean he's interested in finding out who killed her?"

"No. It means he's willing to look into her death a little more. He doesn't think she was murdered. He agrees with the medical examiner. Accidental overdose."

"But at least he's interested."

"Yes. I'm sure he is."

"You think it's just because you asked him to look into it?"

"Maybe. But what does it matter as long as he does it?"

"You're right. Do we still have time to grab some lunch?"

The diner was packed but we found a couple of seats at the counter. A crowded lunch counter, sitting side by side with strangers, is not a good place to talk of murder. We chatted about Roger's ghost tree picture and even that topic earned us a few questioning looks. But this was Salem after all, and talk of ghosts and witches wasn't as unusual as it might be in another city.

The class reconvened with full tummies and good spirits and got right down to work. Within the next few hours,

Therese surprised us with a short video she intended to offer to WICH-TV. Shannon, in keeping with her interest in fashion, had compiled a collection of Mexican-inspired outfits for men, women and children, culled from national mail order catalogs. Hilda and Dorothy had consulted online catalogs too, and found wholesale price listings for sugar skulls, paper skeletons, sugar coffins and altar decorations. Hilda consulted the Internet and informed us that sugar skull art is called *calavera*. This was turning out to be a true learning experience for all of us and things were moving faster and better than I'd anticipated. Before long we'd be ready to involve some of the city officials we'd need to contact to get approval for our plan.

On the other hand, I'd produced little of value to the project. Instead, I realized, I'd been concentrating on Dorothy and Emily and James. I tried to push the intrusive thoughts to the back of my brain. "Therese," I whispered, "do we have a list of city officials? I think I'll make a preliminary call or two to City Hall."

Ever efficient, Therese handed me a sheet of names with several highlighted in yellow. "Those are the ones with the most clout I think," she said.

I carried my phone to the far side of the mezzanine so that my conversation wouldn't interrupt the others. I recognized the first name on the list. I'd worked with Marcia Monagle on a Halloween Witches Ball project back when I was at WICH-TV. I called Marcia and gave her a brief rundown on what we had in mind for Day of the Dead. She remembered me and agreed to walk me through the permitting process. "It's not too complicated," she said. "I'll get to it as soon as I can, but things have been a little bit hairy around here since the big brawl."

I drew a blank for a moment. "Oh sure," I said, recalling

the brief clip I'd seen on the late news. "Have the warring councilors kissed and made up yet?"

"Far from it. They're promising to sue one another. They're both lawyers you know."

"Afraid I haven't been paying much attention to local politics. What's it all about, anyway?"

"Land use. Environmental impact studies. Endangered species. Nothing for you to worry about. Your request is comparatively simple. Of course your school director will probably have to meet with the cemetery board, arrange for security, cleanup crews. It's a one-day event, you say?"

"Yes. Just the one day. I'm thinking it won't be a lot different from Memorial Day in the cemeteries. Just quite a bit more colorful."

"And noisier," Marcia said. "I went to *Dia de los Muertos* in Louisiana once."

"I think Salem will like it," I said. "My class is working hard on the idea."

Long sigh on her end. "Hope so. We thought everybody would like that other idea too, but now it's all snarled up."

"That other idea?"

"Yes. The one the fight was about. The new mall. Wildwood."

"What's the problem there anyway?" I asked. "I only caught a little bit of it on the news."

"Oh, boy, Lee," she said. "You have no idea. At first it seemed so simple. Good taxpaying use of land that's been sitting there forever producing nothing. The client owns the land and a few old empty buildings outright. Clean it up, clear it out. Build a mall. Everybody's happy. Right?"

"Sounds like a good plan to me," I agreed.

"We thought it was a done deal," she said. "Council has already approved most everything. Some top-flight stores are ready to sign leases, then—wham!"

"Wham?"

"All of a sudden the wildlife people are in a snit about squirrels and birds. The City Planner's office is questioning the blueprints. Citizens are calling my office with questions about water runoff and land contouring. Meanwhile Shores has a grader and cement trucks, at no small expense, standing by ready to put in a five-acre parking lot in the middle of the place, while everything is stalled because of all the objections coming out of the woodwork. Out of the Wildwood work you might say." She gave a short, rueful laugh. "Oh well, I'm sure it'll all pan out. Eventually."

"I'm sure it will."

"I'll get to work on your event, Lee. Shouldn't have any problems there."

"Hope not. Thanks, Marcia." I walked back to where my students waited, glad I hadn't opted for a career in city government.

Roger and Ray stood side by side next to my desk. "What's up, gentlemen?" I asked.

"Want to take a look at this rough of our brochure?" Ray said.

Roger placed two sheets of paper on my desk—one for each side of the proposed ad. "Take a look," he said, "at the art and the copy."

Their experience as information officers must have included layout and copywriting. The artwork on the cover of the piece included a Halloween pumpkin and a sugar skull. The words Day of the Dead and the date of the event were rendered in old-fashioned lettering on a tombstone where the name of the deceased would ordinarily appear. The copy they'd prepared cleverly combined history, humor and hard facts. I couldn't find a darned thing wrong with it.

"It's wonderful, you two," I said. "Did you guys learn to do this when you were in the service?"

"Some of it," Ray said.

Roger nodded. "Yep. Some."

"I think we can get a better photo though." Roger sounded undecided.

"I think so too," Ray agreed.

"Looks fine to me," I said. "What did you do when you were on the Boston police force?"

"Worked our way up from patrolmen." Ray tapped his chest. "I worked the North end."

"Southie for me," Roger said. "Walked a beat."

"I wound up on the missing persons detail. Investigations." Ray picked up the brochure. "But this is more fun."

*Missing persons, huh? Maybe Ray would know how to trace Emily's mystery man. . .figure out what happened to him between here and Florida.*

"They put me on CSI," Roger offered. "And no, it's nothing like the TV show."

*CSI. Wow! Roger's knowledge could be useful . . . if there really was a crime scene.*

"If you're aiming for TV jobs as investigative reporters, I'd say you have a good start."

"That's what we're aiming for all right, Ms. Barrett."

"You can call me Lee," I said. "All the others do."

"Yes, ma'am. Thanks." Smiling identical broad smiles, the men returned to their desks.

With Marcia's assurance that our journey through the permitting process would be comparatively uncomplicated, I allowed my thoughts to drift back to the Emily-Dorothy conundrum. Of course Pete had asked me to "stop snooping around," but satisfying a healthy curiosity and keeping a promise to a student isn't exactly snooping. I'd consider it more on the order of analyzing available information.

Anyway, I'd promised to tell him about anything I—or Aunt Ibby—learned about the case. I smiled as soon as I thought about calling this thing a "case." If Pete heard me say it out loud he'd call me Nancy. But then, I rationalized, he's the one who convinced me to take an online course in criminology, in which I was making A's on a regular basis. But in this matter, so far, there was no criminal to analyze.

I fully intended to be very careful, but at the same time I intended to learn as much as I could about Emily Alden's last days—especially her last hours. I thought then about Pete's method of keeping clues in order when he's working a case—the ever-present notebooks. Most recently I've been a big believer in the index card method of keeping track of things. Write each fact or question on a separate index card, then shuffle them around until they make sense. Effective perhaps, but the ever-growing stacks of cards were bulky, unwieldy and invariably wound up in the recycling bin when I was through with them. Maybe a less obvious way would be a nice little, discreet notebook—one which would fit neatly into a bureau drawer in the event that I ever decided to take another look at it.

One thing a school setting can guarantee is a *wealth* of paper goods. I unlocked the supply cabinet and surveyed the contents. Plenty of spiral bound notebooks, black-and-white marbled composition books, but nothing small enough to fit into purse or pocket. I squinted at the pile of school supplies and remembered exactly where I'd seen the perfect notebook.

"Everybody," I said, closing and relocking the cabinet. "I need to run out to my car for a minute. Be right back. Carry on."

I dashed down the stairs and out the front door. The swag bag from Happy Shores was still under the passenger seat. I grabbed it, hurried back to the classroom and dumped the contents onto my desk. *Calendar with photos of Happy and Trudy. A thick brochure advertising apartments for rent. A ballpoint pen, half-a-dozen refrigerator magnets, a copy of* Finding Your Dream Home *by Happy Shores*. The last thing to fall out of the canvas bag was the notebook I was looking for. A neat little leather-bound book with lined pages and an H.S. stylized monogram on the cover. Stashing all of the Shores swag back into the bag, I made a mental note to give it all to Aunt Ibby who'd surely find a use for some or all of it. I gathered papers with notes on Salem's cemeteries, prints of tombstone photos and ghost tour literature and put them in one neat stack. I opened the notebook and stared at the blank lined pages.

*Okay. Where do I start? Wish I'd looked over Pete's shoulder once in a while.*

I thought about my old index card system which was a kind of "stream of consciousness" method. Good enough.

Emily was found dead in her bathtub.

Q. Who found her? The newspaper account didn't say. Neither did Pete.

The M.E. says she had sleeping pills and alcohol in her system. The prescription is in her name.

Q. Has anyone checked with her doctor?

Emily had been to a party at the Shoreses' house.

Q. Who else was at the party?

Trudy Shores followed her home to be sure she got home safely.

Q. Did Trudy actually see Emily go inside?

Emily had arranged a "late date" with H. James Dowgin.

Q. Did anyone see him in Salem that night?

Hilda must have said my name more than once before I looked up from my note taking. "Yes, Hilda?"

"I just found a recipe for sugar skull cookies. They're really cute. I was thinking, since you know people at the TV station—maybe we could do a video cookie making demonstration."

She held up a magazine spread showing the smiling skulls. "Aren't they cute? It would promote our Day of the Dead and give some of us real TV credits. What do you think? Would the station let us do it?"

"I'm not sure, but do any of you know how to cook?"

She hesitated, then smiled. "I've baked a birthday cake before—from a mix. Shannon says she used to make Christmas cookies with her grandmother. How hard can it be? Therese says she doesn't cook and doesn't want to, but if we can find a nice kitchen to use she can write, direct and produce the video."

"I have a practically new kitchen," I said. "and I'm not proud to say the oven has barely been used." I closed the notebook and slipped it into my purse. "I'll check with the TV station and my friend River North will talk it up on her show too, I'm sure."

"River North from *Tarot Time*? I love those old movies she shows."

"I'm pretty sure she can find some about Day of the Dead," I said. "I'll ask her."

All in all, it had been a really productive day at the Tabby. And by the time the closing message played I'd become confident that this class project would be a piece of cake—or cookie.

*Fat chance.*

# CHAPTER 16

The day had gone well and the evening promised to be the same. O'Ryan greeted me at the back steps with purrs, mrows and ankle rubbings. Aunt Ibby had posted a note on my door telling me that she had some more information on James Dowgin. Pete called and said he was bringing over a big pan of his sister Marie's lasagna for dinner and River texted that she'd read my cards again and it was all good news.

I changed into comfy sweats—not my old gray ones but a new pink set—opened a bag of pre-made salad greens and added a beautiful ripe tomato, a cucumber and a couple of radishes, all from the backyard garden. When Pete said a BIG pan of lasagna, he wasn't kidding. It was huge. We invited Aunt Ibby to come upstairs and join us and I texted River to come over if she had time before she had to go to the station.

It turned out to be quite a party. Good food and good friends. Aunt Ibby came upstairs immediately, whispered that she'd tell me about Dowgin later. River showed up right behind her with a bottle of sangria. Aunt Ibby had brought dessert of course, so by the time we'd cleared the table, and poured the after-dinner coffee, everyone was relaxed, full and happy. River put her stack of Tarot cards on the top of the table. "Reading, anyone? Pete? How about you? I haven't read you in a long time. I did Lee's yesterday and hers was all good. Love, money, job, the whole works."

I was surprised when he said, "Okay. Why not?"

Within a few minutes he must have wished he'd given his usual "no thanks." A reversed Page of Cups suggested deception, obstacles and unpleasant news. Next up was the Five of Cups, an unpleasant looking card at best, promising sorrow and loss. Pretty much the whole reading was like that. Just about the only good cards were the seven of wands and the nine of pentacles. The seven of wands, which River said meant victory through courage, showed a man defending his position on top of a hill with his wand.

"Look," Pete said. "How come his shoes don't match?" I studied the card. Pete was correct. One of the character's shoes was buckled. The other one laced.

"Petruchio," said Aunt Ibby. "From *The Taming of the Shrew.* Am I right?"

"You are," River said. "And the nine of pentacles tells us of material well-being for you, Pete, with an accent on home and gardens. Kind of a 'green thumb' card."

"That must mean you, Miss Russell," Pete told my aunt. "Sure isn't me."

"Not me either," I said, but in my mind's eye the nine of pentacles was a green-handled trowel partly submerged in rich brown soil and the seven of wands with its mismatched shoes was a pair of muddy boots.

The last card she turned was one I really don't like to see. It's called the Tower and it looks too much like 9/11 in New York. There are even bodies falling from a jagged-toothed battlement. River sighed and said, "Sorry, Pete. Looks like some change, conflict at your job. An old idea will be upset." At that point, O'Ryan leaped up onto the table, scattering the cards, then climbed into Pete's lap, reached up and gave his face a lick.

"O'Ryan didn't like your reading," I said, "but he loves Pete."

"Good thing I don't have any faith in your hocus-pocus, River," Pete said with a smile, "or I'd be spooked by all that."

I knew Pete was sincere about not believing in the cards, so I wasn't concerned that he'd be worried about conflict and obstacles and old ideas. I did wonder a little bit, though, about that green thumb and those shoes.

We all helped River reassemble her Tarot deck, and I put what was left of the lasagna into a plastic container for her to take home to share with her roommates. "Sorry to eat, give a bad reading and run," River said, "but I need to go home and get into some sequins and glitter. Tonight's movie is *The Shining*. Get it?"

"Meh," said O'Ryan.

"I'll watch if Pete'll watch with me," I said. "That movie scares me to death."

Aunt Ibby said she'd pass on the movie, thanked us for dinner, said she'd talk to me tomorrow about "that other thing" and followed River and O'Ryan out my back door.

Pete and I loaded the dishwasher and finished off the pot of coffee. "What's the 'other thing'?" he asked.

"I don't know yet," I admitted, "but she said she's found out something more about James Dowgin."

"You're planning to tell me all about it, right?"

"I told you I would."

"And the visions? You'll tell me if you have any more? Even if you think they don't make sense?"

There was an intensity in his voice that hadn't been there earlier. "Nothing new in the vision department I'm glad to say." I watched his eyes. "But you sound concerned. Is there something about this case *you're* not telling *me*?"

Oops. I'd said "case" right out loud. Maybe he hadn't noticed.

No such luck. The vaguely apprehensive look and tone disappeared and he smiled broadly. "A case, huh, Nancy?"

I felt my face flush. "You know what I mean. The problem. The question. The missing piece of the puzzle."

"I know." He reached for my hand. "I'm just teasing. I know you think there are problems to solve—questions to answer about Emily Alden's death. There's just no puzzle there, babe. The answers are in the M.E.'s report. It was a sad, tragic, avoidable accident."

"But you're interested in what Aunt Ibby and I might come up with anyway, aren't you?" I insisted. "You think there's a chance, even a little one, that Dorothy could be right. I promised to tell you everything we find out. What aren't you telling me?" I squeezed his fingers. "Come on. Fess up."

"Okay. I went back over the paperwork we had on the case."

"Ha! *You* said case!"

He pretended not to hear me. "It's probably nothing. It was about the party—or whatever it was at the Shoreses' place that night. According to Emily's letter to her sister, she thought that the get-together was in her honor, a celebration of something she'd done."

"That's right. I saw the letter myself."

"I checked my notebook. When I asked what the party was for, both Mr. and Mrs. Shores gave the same answer."

"Which was . . . ?"

"There was no particular reason. They said they often

hosted small cocktail parties and occasionally invited one or two of their employees to mingle with their other guests."

"That's odd. Did you check with the other guests?"

"Of course. There were only two. An elderly couple. Very nice folks. Both hard of hearing. They remembered Emily as a 'nice girl.' They left early."

"They didn't say anything about the party being in Emily's honor?"

"I would have noted it if they had."

"Interesting," I said.

"Kind of."

"Very."

"Yeah. Okay. I'll talk to them again. Probably nothing. I told you. They're old. Hard of hearing." He stood, yawned, and stretched his arms over his head and looked at the Kit Kat clock. "Getting late. Are we going to watch River's scary movie? I'll stay here so you won't be scared if you like."

"I like," I said.

I didn't even stay awake until the end of the movie. Just as well. It's such a nightmare-inducing masterpiece. I did get to see River shining in her sequins and glitter though, with a neckline to rival some of Wanda's best. Pete went to work early and brought me coffee in bed before he left. What a guy.

I skipped breakfast. Mr. Pennington had scheduled an eight o'clock teaching staff meeting in the top floor suite of rooms where the Trumbull family had lived back when their department store was the center of Salem's downtown activity. A Pennington staff meeting always meant coffee and doughnuts with my fellow instructors at the long mahogany table in the Trumbulls' handsomely restored dining room, along with a thirty-minute "state of the Tabby" speech from the school's director.

When all of the Tabby teachers are gathered together in one place that way, it's always a bit of a surprise to realize how many of us it takes to operate the Tabitha Trumbull Academy of the Arts. Although my department, TV production, manages with just me at the helm, several of the classes require a full complement of instructors. Dance, for instance, has several including ballet, tap and ballroom disciplines. The Theater Arts group takes up a whole side of the table covering elocution, costume design, makeup, lighting, production and direction. Art has just two—who somehow manage to teach an amazing variety of techniques and media. Add to that the writers, singers, musicians . . . well, you get the idea. There are a bunch of us. And that doesn't count the housekeepers, carpenters and custodians who keep the old place from falling apart, and the office staff who keep track of bill paying, tuition collecting, scholarship awards and government grants.

Mr. Pennington had apparently been considering the sheer numbers of us, including students. After giving us a brief—for him—rundown of Tabby facts and figures, he announced a new schoolwide exercise.

"In consideration of today's climate of possible or perceived dangers—whether man-made disruptions or acts of nature," he said, "I feel it imperative that we implement a plan to aid in the protection of all concerned."

Here he did one of his elongated dramatic pauses—intended to draw particular attention to the utterance to follow. It had the desired effect. The room was hushed and all eyes were focused on him.

"The board of directors had at first considered the installation of an alarm system for each and every classroom." A shake of the head, eyes closed. "Alas, the building is so old, so solidly built and with such a maze of wiring that the expense of such a system is financially unfeasible." He raised one hand. "But do not despair! We have a solution. This very day, each of you will be presented with a personal alarm device." He held up what appeared to be a white jewelry box. Inside was a simple oval pendant on a cord. "It's on the order of those worn by the elderly or infirm to summon assistance. One of these shall be worn on your person or concealed within reach of your desks during school hours. A press of the button summons armed security. Simple. Effective. Hopefully never needed."

There was a ripple of conversation, an undercurrent of nervous laughter, a few comments about falling and being unable to get up. Personally I thought the panic button was a good idea, remembering a time or two there in the Tabby when I could definitely have used the thing. After announcing an upcoming performance in the school theater, a special Saturday lecture on diversity in curriculum and the gift of costumes from a defunct Shakespearean road company in Vermont, he spoke briefly about the upcoming Day of the Dead event and congratulated me on the creation of a new celebration for Salem.

We were dismissed with several minutes to spare before the start of classes. I stopped to chat with some of my fellow teachers, received assurance from the office manager that he'd help with the permitting process facing us, helped myself to an extra half cup of coffee and finished off the crumbs of my second cinnamon doughnut. I took the elevator down to the mezzanine and managed to get to the classroom ahead of my students, but not ahead of a tall man wearing a green coverall with SECURITY embroidered on the breast pocket. He carried a cardboard carton filled with the white jewelry boxes we'd seen at the meeting.

"Here's your alarm button, honey." He looked me up and down, pausing at the bustline and smiled. "Want me to help you put it on?"

"No thanks," I said, backing away a little. "I can handle it."

"You think the old man is expecting trouble?"

"The old man?"

"Pennington. The guy who ordered all these."

"No. I don't think so at all. Just being cautious. Am I supposed to shut it off somehow when I leave for the night?"

"Nope. It's in the on position all the time." His smile was more like a leer. "Does a pretty lady like you worry about ever working late in here? Being all alone?"

I tucked the white box into my purse and took another step back.

The twins appeared, just as the opening bell sounded. They stood, one on either side of the man, towering over him. "Problem, Ms. Barrett?" Roger asked.

"Problem?" Ray echoed.

"Everything's fine," I said. "This gentleman was just leaving."

"You know the way out, fella?" Roger gestured with a motion of his head toward the mezzanine landing.

"Yep, sure do." Hurriedly, the man tucked the carton under his arm. "Have a nice day."

Ray watched the retreating back. "That one bothering you?"

"Just made me a little uncomfortable is all. Thanks."

The two started for their seats. Roger turned and faced me. "We've always got your back, you know, Ms. Barrett."

I'd never thought about the pair of retired policemen "having my back" as Roger had put it, but it was a decidedly comforting thought. "I appreciate that," I said, meaning it. "And please call me Lee."

"Yes, ma'am," they said in unison.

The women arrived all together, bringing with them a happy sound of chatter and laughter into the wide expanse of long-ago retail space. They took their respective seats beneath the sound insulating canopy covering our simulated broadcast studio.

"Missed you at breakfast, Lee," Hilda said.

"Staff meeting," I said. "Free coffee and doughnuts with the boss."

"Good deal," Therese sat behind the news desk. "Was it in the big beautiful dining room in the penthouse?"

"A penthouse? This place has a *penthouse*?" Dorothy sounded incredulous.

"I've heard about it before," Shannon said. "The Trumbulls used to live up there."

"It's haunted, you know." Therese was matter-of-fact about the top-floor ghost. "Tabitha Trumbull is still up there. Isn't she, Lee?"

"So they say."

"Is there really a ghost up there, Lee? Have you seen it?" Hilda persisted.

I dodged the question. "That would be hard to prove." I managed a laugh. "There have been some strange happenings in those old rooms, that's true. But Tabitha didn't show up for doughnuts and coffee this morning and as far as I know, nobody's claimed to see her lately."

A loud guffaw from one of the twins. "Come on ladies. Ghosts in the cemetery. Ghosts in the attic. You've all been reading too much of that ‘haunted Salem’ literature. Let’s get back to reality.”

I was grateful for the change of subject, but Dorothy wasn’t ready to let it go. “I hope there really are ghosts,” she spoke softly. “Ghosts that can come back and tell the living about the things that happened to them when they were alive.”

I knew she wasn’t talking about Giles Corey or Tabitha Trumbull.

# CHAPTER 17

We did "get back to reality," after all. I related my conversation with Marcia from city hall, and with the Tabby's office manager, which helped to allay some of the fears we'd all had about being sure everything was legal.

"All the T's crossed," Ray said. "That's the way to do it."

"All the I's dotted," Roger added. "That's the way."

Mr. Pennington had come up with some grant money from an endowment for the arts fund to pay for the printing of the Day of the Dead brochure. We hadn't selected a date yet for the sugar skull cookie baking project, but I promised to clear that with Aunt Ibby. In short, things were moving along nicely. We spent much of the day working on some of the technical aspects of TV production, using the quite expensive, brand-new textbooks the Tabby had provided for us. I gave the first homework assignment of the semester. Everyone would study the section on interviewing skills, in preparation for the next day's program.

I didn't get any one-on-one time with Dorothy, but since I didn't have the new information on James Dowgin Aunt

Ibby had promised, I had little to offer in the "what happened to Emily" department. Shannon reported that she'd made "sort of a date" with the handsome blue-eyed gravestone rubbing building superintendent for the following Thursday night and we all looked forward to hearing about that . . . all of the women anyway. The twins just gave their usual synchronized exasperated head shake and eye-roll.

The closing bell dismissed us all in apparent good humor, looking forward to the next day. I hurried home, anticipating hearing what Aunt Ibby had learned about James Dowgin. I didn't have to wait long—she and the cat met me at the back door.

"He had a library card," she announced, ushering me into her kitchen. "Come on in. I'll tell you what I found out."

I followed obediently, with O'Ryan tagging along behind me. "A library card, huh? At your library?"

An eye-roll worthy of the twins. "Of course, at my library. Here. Sit down. I've checked out the same books your James selected for reading material while he was in Salem. The library, for heaven's sake! Why didn't I think of it in the first place?"

A stack of books lay in the center of the round table. I sat, as directed, and she picked up the top volume on the pile and handed it to me. *Soil Sampling Preparation and Analysis.* It was a thick, heavy book. (I recognized it as the kind of dreaded college tome that runs the student over a hundred dollars.)

Next came *Inescapable Ecologies.* The subtitle described it as "a history of environment, disease and knowledge."

The only book in the pile I actually recognized was *Silent Spring* by Rachel Carson. It was required reading in my eighth-grade science class.

"So our friend James was studying up on the environment," I said, "and he took Emily with him on a soil sampling expedition. They both worked for the same real estate firm. . . ."

She finished my thought. "And they're both dead."

"Wow," I said. "I'll have to tell Pete about this."

"There's more you'll need to tell him." Her voice was solemn. "Emily Alden had a library card too. She'd also borrowed the one on soil sampling, and after she returned that one, she checked out *Risk of Hazardous Wastes*. Never returned it. You might want to ask Pete if he found the book at the crime scene."

"You agree with Dorothy that it was actually a crime scene, then?"

"It's a possibility. Maralee, I've been thinking about that green-handled trowel in your vision. See the connection?"

I'd already made that connection, and another one. Maybe the dirty boots in that plastic bag in Emily's closet had walked in the soil she'd bagged and labeled. The next question was—exactly where had she and James walked that day?

"I'll call Pete right away," I told my aunt. "He'll want to look at these books."

"Of course. He can keep them as long as he needs to. Oh, and one more thing. The name of the agency in Florida where James worked? It's True Shores."

I hurried upstairs to my apartment, took off my shoes, tossed my jacket onto the bed and speed-dialed Pete.

"Hi babe." There was a smile in his voice. "I was just going to call you. Got a couple of pieces of new information on your friend Dorothy's sister."

"Hi yourself. Aunt Ibby has dug up some new information too."

"Great. Shall we get together and compare notes? Maybe over hot dogs and beer at Greene's Tavern?"

"Perfect. See you in about an hour?"

Greene's Tavern is one of our favorite places. It's a kind of out-of-the-way waterfront version of Cheers—where everybody knows your name—definitely not a tourist destination. Sometimes we join the gang at the bar and get involved in the conversation and other times we sit in a cozy booth where nobody bothers us except to refill a glass or bring more food.

We chose a booth. "You first," I said, after we'd ordered hot dogs and light beer. "And thanks for checking into this. I appreciate it, and I know Dorothy will too."

"Maybe you won't be satisfied with what I've learned. We checked again with her doctor. He's in Boston. She wasn't a regular patient, and she told him she'd used sleeping pills before. She was having a lot of trouble sleeping and it was affecting her work. He'd warned her about taking more than one pill at a time. The M.E. says she had taken three—with quite a lot of alcohol. We don't think she was trying to kill herself. She could have taken the whole bottle if she'd wanted to do that. Doc says she just wanted to sleep and overdid it." He put his elbows on the table and looked into my eyes. "I stopped by at Dorothy's place and photographed those letters. Frankly, I don't think they tell us anything new. Emily's death was an accident. Pure and simple. Just as we said in the first place. I hope we can ease Dorothy's mind about it. I don't know how I'd feel if it was my sister, Marie. I'd probably be looking for a reason too."

I took a deep breath. "I'm not sure how this ties in with the sleeping pills, or if it even does, but the man Emily had a date with that night—James Dowgin—had taken her with him on a soil sample project. He had been getting books from the library about the environment—especially about hazardous waste. She read some of the same books and now they're both dead. At least she is, and most likely he is too. Aunt Ibby is wondering if you found one of those library books in Emily's apartment."

He leaned back against the high-backed booth. Cop voice. "No. But I wasn't looking for one. It was an accident scene, remember?" He frowned. "They both worked for Happy Shores Real Estate. That where you're going with this?"

"My friend at city hall says there's a problem in the wild woods. That's where the mall is supposed to be. Happy and Trudy Shores are ready to start construction there. And Pete? When he disappeared James Dowgin worked for a Florida agency called *True* Shores. Another coincidence?"

He didn't say anything right away, just took a bite of his hot dog and looked thoughtful.

"You said you had a couple of pieces of new information," I persisted. "Want to tell me what the other one is?"

He hesitated. "I will, but what you just told me makes me rethink what I was going to say."

I waited for him to continue. "Is it about James?"

"Yes. I was going to tell you he's in the clear on all this. He didn't keep that date with the girl after all. We checked with DMV and DOT. His car showed up passing through toll booths heading south in the late afternoon that day. Traced him all the way down to North Carolina. No way he could have come back in time to see her that night."

"She must have been disappointed," I said. "Maybe that's why she thought she needed pills to get to sleep."

"Maybe. But all this about both of them studying books about soil contamination makes me wonder . . ."

"About?"

"About a problem with the dirt in the wild woods. I'll be checking on that first thing tomorrow morning."

“My city hall friend said there was some talk about endangered birds.”

“I’ll check on it.” Cop voice was gone. Conversation about Emily Alden, True Shores and soil samples was over. He smiled. “Want another hot dog?”

# CHAPTER 18

It was still fairly early when we got back to Winter Street from Greene's Tavern. "Think your aunt would mind if I come in and grab those library books you told me about?" Pete asked as he pulled into the parking space next to the garage.

I looked toward the house. "Kitchen lights are still on," I said. "I'm sure it'll be okay."

Aunt Ibby was, as I'd guessed, wide awake—and busy. Even before she answered our knock at her kitchen door, I was aware of a wonderful smell. "She's baking," I said.

"I'm available for taste-testing." He sniffed the fragrant air as the door swung open.

"Come in," my aunt said. "You're just in time to try Tabitha's vanilla bread pudding."

"I came to borrow the library books," Pete said, "but I'd never turn down an offer like that one."

The books were still stacked on the table and Pete silently browsed through the thickest one while Aunt Ibby topped two bowls of the hot pudding with hefty dollops of whipped cream—a large bowl for Pete, a smaller one for me.

She waved a large wooden spoon toward me. "I'd like your opinion." She pointed the spoon in Pete's direction. "Tell me what you think."

"I think we may need to take another look at it."

"The pudding?" I asked.

"The Alden thing. The late date. It doesn't add up quite the way we figured." He put the book aside and picked up his spoon. "Tabitha scores again. Pudding is perfect."

I waited for Pete to say something more about "taking another look," but he grew quiet again, eating slowly and at the same time sneaking the occasional peek at the text in the open book.

Aunt Ibby didn't join us at the table, claiming she'd already done quite enough tasting during the preparation process. She began her usual orderly kitchen cleanup, while I nibbled at the delicious, but highly caloric dessert.

I put down my spoon. "It's kind of an unusual thing to try so late at night."

Pete looked up. "The Alden thing? The late date?"

"No. The pudding."

We both laughed at that and Pete closed the book, putting it back onto the pile. "I'll just take these along with me and try concentrating on one thing at a time." He stood and carried his empty bowl to the sink. "Thanks, Miss Russell. That was great. And thanks for digging up the library connection."

"Just a minute, Pete," she said, opening a drawer. "Here's a nice bag to carry them in. Maralee gave it to me." She handed him the canvas bag with the H.S. monogram on it. "I hope the books will be useful."

"Could be," he said. "They just could be. Walk me to the door, Lee?"

Licking a bit of stolen whipped cream from his whiskers, O'Ryan led the way out of the warm kitchen and outside into the early fall chill. Pete put the bag of books down on the steps and pulled me close for a lingering good night kiss which spoke volumes.

"I'll call you tomorrow," he whispered. "Be careful. I love you, you know."

"Love you too," I said. "Be careful."

Turning to go back inside, I looked around for O'Ryan. There was only a pale sliver of moon and a little light from the street lamps on Oliver Street filtered through the trees. I noticed the white cat first, then watched O'Ryan as he crept along the fence top until the two faced one another. They stood there, silently, about a foot apart. I listened attentively, wondering if the usually talkative O'Ryan would break the silence. He didn't. As I watched, the two cats simultaneously nodded to one another. O'Ryan jumped to the ground on his side of the fence, while the white cat disappeared into the next yard.

"Come on, cat," I said, opening the door and waiting for him to enter ahead of me. "What was that all about?"

"Mmm—mmm," he said, looking back at me and starting up the stairs to my apartment. I took that to mean "none of your business," and didn't pursue the matter. O'Ryan headed straight for the bedroom and curled up at the foot of the bed.

Tired, but not quite ready for sleep yet, I donned pajamas and opened my laptop for just one more search for information on the elusive James. I found an H. J. Dowgin listed under Massachusetts Real Estate Agents. It was a bare bones listing, showing a black-and-white photo—as Emily had observed in her letter, he was good looking. He had a valid real estate license and a degree in Environmental Science. I recognized the e-mail address as the one I'd seen on the advertising material in the canvas bag. It belonged to Happy Shores Real Estate and there was no point in trying to contact him there. Or most likely anywhere. I closed up the laptop and joined the sleeping cat in the bedroom.

River's ideas about *feng shui* for my apartment included the fact that I shouldn't be able to see my own reflection from the bed, so I kept the full-length mirror angled accordingly. I climbed into bed, careful not to disturb the sleeping cat and took a quick glance at the mirror. It reflected, as it was supposed to, one corner of the kitchen counter, part of the Lucite table and one of the tall windows. What it was not supposed to reflect was a white cat sitting on the fire escape outside, its nose against the pane.

"Jesus, O'Ryan!" I squeaked, startled. "What's your friend doing out there?"

The big yellow cat opened sleepy eyes, stretched and padded across the covers to where I sat, bolt upright, peering into the mirror. The white cat's reflection, unmoving, stared back at me. O'Ryan looked from the mirror to me and back, then returned to his position at the foot of the bed and lay down.

"What's the matter with you?" I prodded him with my foot. "Tell it to go away."

"Naaa," he complained.

"Oh for heaven's sake. I'll do it, lazy bones." I stepped into the kitchen, flicked on the light switch and approached the window. No white cat. "It's gone," I grumbled, "not that you care." I turned off the light and climbed back into bed "Now maybe I can get some sleep." I looked once again into the mirror. The white cat was still there.

It took several double-takes—mirror to window, window to mirror before I figured it out. The mirror cat was a vision. There was no cat on the fire escape.

The cat in the mirror blinked away just then, and the reflection showed the things that were supposed to be there.

The visions have always been disturbing. They've often been frightening. But I couldn't remember a time when they'd been so confusing. None of them seemed to have any logical relationship to one another. There was the woman in the bathtub. Emily Alden. There was a green-handled garden trowel. Whose was it? There were some shoes. Mine, Dorothy's, the giant display shoe and a pair of dirty work boots. And now a white cat who might live next door.

"Well," I said to the cat at the foot of the bed, who was clearly not listening, "I promised to tell Pete about any visions I might have. It'll be interesting to see if he can make any sense out of this one."

In the morning I didn't wait for Pete's promised call, but phoned him as soon as I reached my assigned space in the Tabby parking lot.

"What's up? Everything okay?" There was concern in his voice.

"Everything's okay," I said. "Nothing to worry about, but there was another—thing—in my mirror and I promised I'd tell you whenever I saw one."

"Sure. Tell me about it. Was it a bad one?"

"I don't know. I don't think so. I just want to see if maybe you can figure it out—if you can connect it somehow to what's going on."

"I'll try. What did you see?"

I told him first about the white cat—that O'Ryan and I had seen it more than once and that O'Ryan seemed to like it—or to at least tolerate it trespassing on his back fence.

"The cat was there—when you were seeing things?" he asked.

"Yes. In the mirror it was sitting on the fire escape. Looking in my kitchen window. But of course, it wasn't really there at all."

"That's funny," he said.

"It is? What's funny about it?"

"Not funny ha-ha. Funny strange. Funny damned strange as a matter of fact."

"What do you mean?"

"There's a cat like that—at least it's a white cat—that lives in the Alden woman's apartment house. I saw it when I investigated her death in the first place and I saw it again when I went over there to see those letters from her sister that Dorothy has. It was outside on that little balcony that runs along the top floor. I asked Dorothy if it was hers and she said it was just a stray that hangs around there. She figured somebody in the house must be feeding it."

I thought about that. "That's interesting," I said. "It doesn't make things any less confusing, but it does kind of tie things together a little bit, doesn't it?"

"Oh babe, I'm sorry. None of that vision stuff makes a lot of sense to me anyway, you know? But I guess the cat must have some connection to the dead girl you saw. Right?"

"Yes. And it's probably connected to the shoes and the trowel too somehow."

*Probably. Somehow. Maybe.*

# CHAPTER 19

I locked the 'vette and, with an eye toward a gray, overcast sky, hurried to the diner entrance. I'd already decided to skip breakfast with the group, but instead ordered coffee and a Danish to go. With a quick smile and a wave to my class, already gathered at their regular table, I hurried through the side entrance onto the main floor of the Tabby.

I knew that I needed some time at my desk to pull together plans for our Day of the Dead event, especially in regard to integrating them with my ongoing TV production lesson plan—which, after all, was what they'd all signed up and paid for. Also, I thought that an hour or so of intense concentration on things academic might make the whole white cat, green trowel, girl in the bathtub mess recede into the background.

I paused at the mezzanine entrance, looking around the silent, high ceilinged, vast expanse of the place, imagining what it must have looked and sounded like back in the days when it was Salem's largest, and undoubtedly most important, shopping destination. An elevator dominated the wall space on my right and I was startled when the bell chime sounded and the over-the-door light flashed indicating an approaching passenger. The door slid open and Rupert Pennington stepped out.

"Ms. Barrett. Glad you're here. Can you spare me a moment of your valuable time?"

*So much for my hour of intense concentration.*

"Of course, sir." I put my coffee cup and the paper bag containing my meager breakfast on the corner of my desk, and indicated one of the handsome vintage shoe department bentwood chairs. "Please sit down." Avoiding looking at the giant shoe over my desk, I pulled up my own modern and very comfortable leather swivel chair and sat facing him.

"Ms. Barrett," he began, "a matter of some concern has come to my attention." He stopped and grew silent for what seemed to me to be a very long moment. The Tabby's executive director at a loss for words was something I'd not seen often.

"Is something wrong, Mr. Pennington?"

He leaned forward and an uncharacteristic frown crossed his face. "I'm not exactly sure, Ms. Barrett," he said, "but it has to do with you—or at least with your class—so I thought it best to bring it to your attention."

"Go on." I reached for my coffee.

"Actually, the matter is of enough concern to have initiated the distribution of the alarm pendants."

It was my turn to frown. "And this has to do with me? What in the world is going on?"

"The school has received a threat. A veiled threat to be sure, but one which causes me to worry, Ms. Barrett."

"Have you called the police? What kind of threat?"

"I have contacted a private security firm," he said. "It doesn't seem to be a police matter."

"If you think it requires an alarm system, it's probably

a police matter. Tell me what this is all about." I glanced pointedly at my watch. "My class will be arriving soon."

I knew I sounded bossy. Even rude. But I didn't like the sound of this "matter of concern" one little bit.

He reached into his inside jacket pocket and withdrew a folded piece of paper. "This was delivered by a messenger the day before yesterday. You may read it." He pushed the thing across the desk.

The message was printed in a standard typeface. It was short.

> Your school is involved in something that's none of your business. Tell that nosy teacher to stop asking questions about the accident. Just stick to the graveyard and stop snooping into other people's personal problems.

He pointed to the paper. "You see why I think it involves you and your class. You're the only ones involved with a graveyard. Have you been asking questions about an accident of some kind? Something that might be regarded as—pardon my asking—snooping into someone else's personal problems?"

I ignored the question. "I'm going to call Pete. May I keep this letter? I'm sure it's nothing serious., but I'd like to have him check it out all the same."

"Of course, if you think it's important. But I must ask you to be discreet, Ms. Barrett." He stood, unsmiling. "I trust you'll be careful not to bring any *further* unpleasant publicity to the academy."

That "further" didn't escape me. A couple of times since he'd hired me, I'd been kind of involved in a little unpleasantness at the Tabby. Okay. I'd been directly involved in some definitely unpleasant happenings. I took his warning seriously. I liked my job and I had no intention of letting Dorothy's questions about Emily's death mess up my future employment. I decided to call Pete at the first opportunity and to turn the letter and the entire matter over to the police. If there was anything more to be learned about Emily Alden, it was none of my business. I figuratively washed my hands of the whole thing.

"Don't worry, Mr. Pennington," I assured him, stuffing the letter into my purse. "I'm sure Pete can straighten this out. There's no reason to involve the school at all." And in my mind, there really wasn't—except for the fact that Dorothy was one of my students. I'd just tell her that I'd teach her all I could about interview skills, investigative reporting and TV production . . . all strictly by the book. But as to actual investigation of Emily's "accident," she'd do well to let the police handle it—and to accept their conclusions about it.

I meant every word, and after I walked with my boss back to the elevator, watched the door close behind him and saw the lighted arrow pointing up to the second floor, I turned back toward my desk—where the swirling colors and pinpoints of light had already begun in the shoe.

I wanted to look away, to close my eyes, but I didn't—couldn't—do either. I moved slowly closer to the desk, watching the picture form.

The white cat, its nose pressed against a windowpane, stared at me. As I watched, the cat's face moved closer—closer—until all I saw was the eyes. Then something changed. Those eyes were no longer green, no longer featured the familiar cat-striped pupils. They were no longer cat's eyes at all. Peering through the window was a pair of blue eyes. Cerulean blue eyes.

Thankfully, the clatter of feet running up the stairs, the chatter of voices interrupted the disturbing vision. It blinked away and the black shoe once again became just an old display piece. But the thought of those haunting blue eyes didn't go away.

I sat down quickly, busied myself with rearranging papers on my desk, lining pens and pencils in a row, willing myself to focus on the day's work ahead, and on my very recent decision to turn everything over to the police to handle. Especially that letter in my purse.

"Lee?"

I looked up and faced a smiling Dorothy. "Yes? Good morning, Dorothy. You look happy today."

"I feel pretty good. I talked with my stepmother last night. She sold Emily's VW and the new owner found Emily's phone between the seats. She's sending it to me. Paula said she'd thought the only thing Emily had left in the car was the dirty old boots that were in the trunk, and she'd bagged those up and left them in the closet."

"Did your stepmother say anything about what was on the phone?"

"She didn't have the charger, so she hadn't tried to look at it. I don't think she wanted to anyway. She wouldn't want to see pictures of Emily, messages." The smile had disappeared. "You know, I'm not sure I want to either."

"We really need to see what's on it," I said, letting that "we" slip out. "I mean," I corrected, "you need to look at it and if there's anything the police should see, you need to call them."

"Okay." She backed away from the desk, looking puzzled. "I'll tell you as soon as I get the phone from Paula."

I nodded, and returned my attention to the pens and pencils.

*Letting go of all this isn't going to be easy.*

I managed to clear my mind of things that didn't belong in the classroom, and before long we were all productively involved in watching an instructive video on digital editing. I followed up with a brisk question and answer session. Things were going well. I was pleased with the class—and with myself as instructor. Making the transition from my years of in-front-of-the-camera background in TV to the role of educator in the craft had not been an entirely smooth one. I reminded myself to be grateful to Mr. Pennington for the opportunity he'd given me, and to stop getting myself involved in things which could damage this almost-new career.

The thought of the letter I'd so recently stuffed into my purse intruded on my introspection. The printed words were more frightening than I'd let on to Mr. Pennington or maybe even to myself. I'd promised to turn the thing over to Pete and I could hardly wait to do it, to get rid of it, to disassociate myself from other people's problems.

But how was I supposed to disassociate myself from the blue-eyed cat thing, the trowel in the dirt, the shoe slide show and the body in the bathtub?

# CHAPTER 20

I was in a hurry to leave the Tabby that afternoon, realizing that the letter had me more spooked than I cared to admit. I practically sprinted across the parking lot to my designated space. I even peeked inside the car windows before unlocking the doors, glad at that moment there was no backseat. At least I wouldn't have to replay that old nightmare of looking up into the rearview mirror and seeing someone looking back at me.

It was Aunt Ibby's late day at the library so I knew I'd be alone in the big house for an hour or two. O'Ryan waited for me inside the back door and I scooped him up in my arms, burying my face in his warm fur. "I'm happy to see you, boy," I whispered, and carried him all the way up the two flights of stairs. If he was surprised by the unusual display of affection, he didn't show it, just snuggled against my shoulder, purring loudly.

Once inside, with the door securely locked, I put O'Ryan down thinking that he'd make his regular supper time dash for the kitchen. But he didn't. He just sat there, looking up at me. "It's okay," I said, stooping to pat his head. "I'm all right. A little bit scared is all. Don't worry.

Come on." I led the way down the hall to the kitchen with my big yellow pal close behind. Even after I'd served his *Chicken Liver Pate in Cream Gravy with Peas and Carrots,* he glanced up and down from his bowl, keeping me in his line of vision.

I hung my jacket on the back of one of the Lucite chairs, pulled my phone from my purse and texted Pete. *Mr. Pennington got an anonymous note saying the nosy teacher should butt out. Call me.*

"It'll be okay," I said aloud, more to myself than to the cat. "The cops will handle it." It didn't take long for Pete to respond. I hadn't thought it would.

"What have you gotten yourself into?" came the cop voice. "Exactly what does the note say? Never mind. I'm coming over right now." Softer voice. "Are you all right?"

"I am," I said, unexpected tears gathering at the sound of his voice. "But I'm scared. A little bit."

"I'm coming over right now," he said again. "Is your aunt with you?"

"No. I'm alone."

O'Ryan looked up. "Meeow?"

"I mean, I'm with O'Ryan."

"Okay. On my way."

It was one of those times when the clock seems to stand still. I must have looked at it a hundred times just to be sure it was running. But the Kit Kat's coordinated tail and eyes continued to move reassuringly back and forth and before twenty minutes had crept by, I heard Pete's key in the lock. The cat and I met him at the door. He didn't say anything, just held me for a long moment. When he spoke, his voice was husky with concern.

"That sounded to me like some kind of threat. Is it?"

"I think it could be. It's in the kitchen. Come on." My

purse was still on the table. I sat down and pulled the note out, handing it to Pete who sat across from me. "Mr. Pennington has hired private security," I said, "and he gave everybody one of those 'I've fallen and I can't get up' buttons. So I'd say he's taking it seriously."

He studied the paper, then laid it flat on the table. "Jesus, Lee, what the hell have you gotten yourself into this time? Do you have any idea what this is about?"

"I really don't," I said, "except that it has to be about Emily Alden and I've already told you everything I know about that."

"Let's go over it again." Cop voice. Notebook on the table. Pencil poised. "Start with when Dorothy asked you for help."

I went over it all carefully, trying to remember every detail, every conversation, every observation since that first ride to the Howard Street Cemetery when Dorothy had told me why she'd taken my class. He took notes and occasionally asked a question, but I talked nearly nonstop for an hour, ending with the information Dorothy had given me about the phone call from her stepmother. "I told her that if there was anything on Emily's phone that she thought was important, she should call the police."

He finally put the notebook and pencil down, leaned back in his chair and looked at me for a long, silent moment. "You know," he said, "there may be more going on here than I thought. You could be right about . . . some of it."

"What about the note? The threat? What should I—we—do about that?"

"First of all, you'll do what it said. Stop meddling and we'll suggest that your aunt do the same. Stick to your cemetery project. Keep the relationship with Dorothy Alden on a student-teacher basis. I'll touch base with her, have a talk with Pennington, check out that alarm system and get an analysis of this note." He picked it up by the edges. "Got a gallon-sized plastic Baggie?"

"Sure," I said, wishing I'd been more careful of the thing when I'd stuffed it into my purse. I got up and opened the plastic wrap, aluminum foil, waxed paper, plastic bag drawer. "Here you go. Want coffee?"

"Yeah. Of course. Got any food?" He carried the carefully bagged note into the bedroom.

I opened the freezer. "A three cheese pizza, a couple of beef pot pies, spinach soufflé, half a chocolate cake and the remains of that bottle of sangria from the other night," I called.

"Sounds good." He rejoined me in the kitchen

"Which one?"

He smiled. "All of it. I'm hungry." He joined me at the kitchen counter and put his arms around my shoulders, pulling me close. "Don't worry, babe. It's going to be all right. We'll get to the bottom of this. Just be careful. Don't take any chances. Promise?"

"I promise." I meant it too. "Oh" I said, remembering the cat-thing in the shoe. "I have one more vision to tell you about."

"Shoot."

I described the white cat looking through the window, almost the way it had in the other vision. "But then, the cat face—at least its eyes—changed. They turned into blue eyes. Human blue eyes. In a cat's face. The same eyes Dorothy's building superintendent has. His name is Dakota something."

"Dakota Berman," Pete said in his cop voice. "Already checked him out. He has a little juvie record. Nothing recent. Nothing real serious."

I knew better than to ask any questions about Dakota

Berman's police record. "You start the coffee," I said, "and I'll start cooking—or thawing as the case may be."

The meal turned out to be surprisingly tasty—or else we were both so hungry it just seemed that way. After dinner I asked Aunt Ibby to come upstairs. Pete's warning to stop meddling applied to her as well as to me. I knew before I heard her knock on the kitchen door that following that advice was going to be easier said than done—for both of us.

My aunt, bearing a bottle of Kahlua "to perk up the coffee," joined us at the table. "What's going on? You two look kind of grim. Something wrong?"

"Not exactly," Pete said, perking up his coffee, "but something to be concerned about."

He explained about Mr. Pennington's note and went into quite a lot of detail about the importance of both of us minding our own business.

"May I see the note?" she asked.

"Of course." He disappeared into the bedroom and I heard one of the secret compartments of my antique bureau creak open. Aunt Ibby raised an eyebrow. "Must be important," she said, "to rate being hidden."

"It kind of is," I agreed, as Pete came back into the room and laid the plastic-covered message in front of her.

She studied the words carefully, then looked up. "Did Rupert save the envelope this came in?"

"I don't know yet," Pete admitted. "I plan to ask him about it tomorrow. I'll need to know a lot more about the circumstances of the delivery. Like a description of the messenger. Was it from a standard messenger service or just some guy off the street wanting to earn a couple of bucks."

My aunt nodded, using her "wise old owl" look. "I'd bet on the latter."

Pete persisted. "So may I count on your—uh—discretion in the matter?"

Aunt Ibby cocked her head to one side and perked up her own coffee. "You mean, like—keep your nose out of it, you meddlesome old biddy?"

"I wouldn't have exactly put it that way." Pete smiled. "But, well, yeah."

"I'll do my best," she said. "But I do have a curious turn of mind, you know. And there are library books involved. I guess my niece told you about the soil sampling research both Emily and James were doing?"

"She did. And I'll take it from here. You don't need to help. Honestly."

She put a finger to her lips. "I'll be the soul of discretion. I promise. I'll keep my nosiness within the confines of the public library. Okay?"

"Guess it'll have to be," he said. "And you, my snoopy girl detective, you'll behave too?"

"I will," I said, dumping a healthy slug of Kahlua into my cup. "To the best of my ability."

Pete picked up the plastic-covered note and returned it to the bureau in the bedroom while Aunt Ibby finished her thoroughly perked-up coffee. She declared between that and the sangria, if she had another she wouldn't be able to find her way home. She gave a fluttering wave of one hand, knocking her wineglass onto the floor. "Oh, I'm so sorry," she said with a muffled giggle. Pete, returning from the bedroom, grabbed the dustpan and brush on his way past the broom closet and with what looked like one fluid motion, swept up the pieces, dumped them into the waste-basket and bowed in my aunt's direction.

"May I walk you home, Miss Russell?" he said. Aunt Ibby, smiling happily, took his arm and they left via the kitchen door with O'Ryan close behind them. Pete returned within minutes.

"Looks like the cat has abandoned us for greener pastures." He picked up our empty cups and carried them to the sink. "We've got the place all to ourselves."

"Thanks for seeing her home," I said. "I like being alone with you." I put the cups into the dishwasher, then turned to face him.

"Me too." He pulled me close. "I wish I could be with you every minute, so I wouldn't worry about you so much."

"I don't mean to make you worry. Sometimes I just get myself into . . . situations."

He smiled. "You sure do. Anyway, I'm with you tonight, so no worries."

"No worries," I agreed. I sighed happily, looking over his shoulder toward the window.

That damned white cat looked right back at me.

# CHAPTER 21

A sharp intake of breath, a little squeak of a scream and I pulled away from Pete's embrace. "Look," I said in a half-whisper. "There."

He whirled, pushing me behind him with one arm, and faced the window. "Oh. It's okay, babe. It's just a cat."

"You see it too?"

"Sure. A big old gray cat." He pulled me close again and smoothed my hair with a gentle hand. "Nothing to be afraid of. Probably just one of O'Ryan's girlfriends checking on him."

"She's a white cat," I murmured, close against his shoulder. "At night all cats are gray," I paraphrased Franklin, "and I'm glad you see her too."

"I get it." He steered me away from the window and down the hall toward the living room. "You thought you were seeing things again, right?"

"Uh-huh. Sure did. Sorry to be so jumpy. Between the note and the blue-eyed cat monster thing . . ."

"I know. Come on. Let's sit on the couch and relax and watch TV for a little while." He reached for the remote. "I think we can catch the late news."

A woodsy scene of trees and bushes filled the screen as the voice of Phil Archer, WICH-TV's senior announcer, commented on the ongoing battle at City Hall. "Although all of the paperwork regarding the proposed shopping mall in the area known locally as the wild woods appears to be in order, some council members object to the continuation of the project due to environmental concerns. However, in an exclusive interview, the owner of the property has told WICH-TV that construction of the parking lot will proceed as planned with an official ground-breaking ceremony on Monday morning, despite the likelihood of protestors."

"Oh boy," Pete said, "guess we'll be busy Monday keeping the tree-huggers and the mall lovers separated and out of the path of the road graders."

A few more local stories preceded the weather report. Wanda predicted a cool but sunny Friday with the possibility of some rain on Saturday. Posing prettily in front of the large weather map, she pointed to a circular pattern close to the bottom of the screen. "We're still keeping an eye on this tropical disturbance which has strengthened a bit since yesterday. Stayed tuned to WICH-TV for continuing updates. *Tarot Time with River North* is next. Bye for now!" With a dimple-flashing smile and the ever popular cleavage-exposing bow, Wanda waved good night to her many fans and River's theme music began.

"Want to watch the scary movie?" he asked.

"I don't think so. Today has been scary enough."

"Okay." He clicked off the TV and pulled me to my feet. "Want to go to bed?"

"Yes, please."

We didn't lose any time walking down the short hall and through the kitchen toward the bedroom. As Pete turned off the kitchen light, I stole a peek in the direction of the window. No cat. I was glad.

Sometimes morning comes too fast, even Friday morning. There was the usual dash to get ready for work, and once again I was thankful for a big house with plenty of bathrooms. (I opted for the pink-and-white one next to my childhood bedroom one flight downstairs.) We took time for a glass of juice apiece, orange for me, apple for him, and shared an English muffin slathered with peanut butter. After a quick good-bye kiss in the back hall, we headed for our respective cars.

It's always seemed to me that Friday is a unique day in the school week, even when the students are adults. Thoughts of the weekend to come make studying secondary to personal pursuits—and concentration on things technical, historical, mathematical or literary pale in comparison to relaxation, restaurants and relationships. Actually, that was probably the genesis for corporate America's "casual Fridays."

I beat my students to the classroom by about one minute. The women arrived first, all abuzz with questions about Shannon's date with the blue-eyed hunk from the cemetery. The twins followed behind and, like indulgent parents, just rolled their eyes and shook their heads without comment. I'd apparently missed some of the preliminary revelations and Shannon was in the process of describing Dakota Berman's apartment.

"You went to a man's apartment on the first date?" Hilda's question fell somewhere between disapproval and admiration.

Shannon gave a pretty, one-shoulder shrug. "Sure. Why not? He's a nice guy. I've dated enough creeps to know the difference. Anyway, he lives in one of those huge old-fashioned houses they've chopped up into a bunch of apartments. He's the janitor or the caretaker or something. Anyway, he gets his place for free. It's in the basement."

"Free is a good deal." Hilda nodded approval. "What was it like? Does he have any furniture? Or is it one of those mattress on the floor bachelor pads?"

"Huh. You must've dated some creeps too. No. The furniture was okay. He said he got most of it at thrift stores and some that people left out by the Dumpster when they moved out." Dorothy seemed to be listening intently, but at that point had made no comment. "You live there, Dot," Shannon said. "You ever find any good stuff out by the Dumpster?"

"Not yet. But my kid sister, Emily . . ." She smiled a sad little smile. "She would have been the first one out there. She was the queen of recycling. Got most of her flower pots that way. Nobody's moved out since I got there though. One family moved in next door to me, but I think that apartment had been empty for a while. If I saw anything out there that I liked, I wouldn't mind taking it though. Living off the grid like I do in Alaska, I'm used to scrounging whatever I can."

"Yeah. Wow." Shannon said. "I can't imagine living like that. Outhouses, bears and stuff. Any cute guys up there?"

"Alaska has more men than women," Dorothy said, "so the odds up there are pretty good."

"You seeing anybody?"

"Not really. The guy who mates on my boat is staying at my place while I'm down here. He takes care of my dogs and we kind of hang out together. Nothing serious."

"Friend with benefits?" Hilda asked.

Dorothy didn't answer that and the twins made a simultaneous throat-clearing noise.

"Well then," I said, realizing that things were getting out of hand, even for casual Friday. "Let's get down to work, shall we? We'll be viewing an instructional DVD on script preparation. It runs for about forty-five minutes. Take notes. Then we'll discuss the possible techniques we'll use for our *Dia de los Muertos* script."

Things quieted down immediately and all eyes were obediently focused on the big screen behind the news desk. I'd seen the film before and anyway I had the teacher's manual, so I was free to let my mind wander.

Unfortunately, but maybe predictably, it wandered down a path where strange cats, gator-ravaged bodies and threatening notes lurked.

*Enough wandering.*

I pulled the Happy Shores notebook and pen from my purse and forced myself to watch the instructions on proper formatting. I took careful notes, writing neatly, even adding a couple of properly numbered footnotes.

*I wonder what's on Emily's cell phone. I'm sure Dorothy will want to show it to me as soon as it arrives.*

Shaking the intrusive thought away, I wrote a whole paragraph on important trends in the short film industry, and another on visual storytelling. By the time forty-five minutes had passed the class had absorbed enough information to keep us all busy up until lunchtime and for a couple of hours after that.

It's not often that we hear the distinctive "ding" which means the elevator has stopped on our floor—largely because so far our classroom is the only one on the mezzanine. Most of the action in the Tabby is on the first floor or the two above us. Neither the top floor "penthouse" nor our between-first-and-second-floor location got many visitors. Everyone looked up from the desks at the sound and the flashing light above the elevator door.

Pete stepped out, Mr. Pennington close behind him. The director wasn't smiling and Pete wore his cop face. The two men approached my desk.

"Sorry to interrupt, Ms. Barrett," Mr. Pennington said, "but there seems to be a matter of some urgency that requires your attention."

I looked up at Pete, and waited for an explanation. He glanced around the room, which had grown completely silent while six pairs of eyes looked expectantly toward us. He spoke in a near-whisper. "Something's come up. I need to talk to you and Dorothy right away." He walked to Dorothy's desk, spoke a few words to her, and she followed him back to where I still sat beneath the giant black shoe. Meanwhile, Mr. Pennington had moved to the front of the news desk.

"Ladies and gentlemen," he began. "Ms. Barrett's presence is required elsewhere. Class is dismissed. We'll see you on Monday. Have a good weekend."

There was a scraping of chairs, a rustling of papers and a low hum of conversation. Dorothy stood silently beside my chair. Therese, Hilda and Shannon put books away and performed the usual end of day straightening up ritual, all the while sneaking worried glances in our direction. The twins left their desks and approached Pete.

"Anything we can do, Detective?" Ray asked, genuine concern showing on his face. "Whatever's going on, Roger and me are available if you need us."

"Thanks," Pete said. "Maybe later. I'll let you know." He herded Dorothy and me toward the elevator where Mr. Pennington stood, impatiently pushing the UP button.

"Pete," I demanded. "Why all the mystery? What's this all about?"

Dorothy still hadn't spoken. The elevator door slid open and the four of us got in. "It's about my sister Emily's murder, isn't it?" Her tone was even—unemotional. "That's what this is all about."

No one answered her question. The elevator stopped on the second floor and we followed Mr. Pennington into his office. Once Pete and Dorothy and I were seated, he closed and locked the door—most unusual for a man who prided himself on his "open door" policy.

Pete reached across the director's desk and picked up a plastic page protector. Inside was a standard letter-sized envelope. He held it up in his left hand, and in his right was the gallon bag containing the wrinkled note. He handed the bagged note to Dorothy. "Dorothy, you should read this before I continue. Mr. Pennington received it from a messenger yesterday afternoon."

Dorothy accepted the bag, her eyes darting back and forth across the page. "See? I told you so. It's about Emily. Her murder. Do you know who sent it? Who killed her?" She slid the bag across the desk toward Pete.

"We checked it carefully for prints, but we weren't able to find anything useful." He looked directly at me. I blushed, realizing that my careless handling of the letter might be responsible for any obliterated evidence. He picked up the page protector with the envelope inside. "Fortunately, Mr. Pennington saved this carefully for us." He gave an approving nod toward the director.

"I thought it could be important," Mr. Pennington beamed. "I held it by the edges with two fingers." He gestured toward Dorothy and me, displaying his two-finger technique. "Played Hercule Poirot in an off-Broadway production of *Murder on the Nile* some years ago. Gained an appreciation of the lawmen. Learned a few tricks of the trade."

Pete held the plastic-protected envelope up and shook it gently. "We were able to lift some good prints from this.

We know who the messenger was. Maybe the same person who wrote the note."

"The killer?" Dorothy rose halfway from her chair. "You know who the killer is? Who is it?"

"We don't know that. We're pretty certain about the messenger though. We're concerned that he's apparently here in Salem. At least he was yesterday."

"Who?" Dorothy and I spoke in unison.

"He's supposed to be dead in a swamp down south," Pete said. "It's the man Emily Alden knew as J.D. His name is H. James Dowgin. We're actively looking for him. You two need to be especially careful. We're taking him seriously." He held up a black-and-white photo. I recognized it as the same one I'd found when I looked Dowgin up on the Massachusetts Real Estate Agents Web site. "We've notified officers statewide to be on the lookout for him."

*I found that picture before you did.*

For me, the thought of being first made up a little bit for the messed-up fingerprints on the threatening note, but of course I didn't say so. After some instructions on being aware of our surroundings, locking doors, keeping cell phones handy, Pete told Dorothy he'd drive her home, and that she should call the station for transportation whenever she needed a ride until Dowgin was found and brought in for questioning. He gave each of us a print of the picture of Dowgin, squeezed my hand, leaned forward and brushed my cheek with a discreet kiss. "I'll call you tonight. Don't worry. We'll catch this guy."

Pete and Dorothy took the elevator and I headed for the stairs. "I'll just run down and make sure everything's put away in the classroom," I told Mr. Pennington. "See you Monday."

"Do you want me to escort you, Ms. Barrett? I'd be glad to if you're the least bit nervous about being alone."

"Thank you, no sir. I'm fine."

"If you say so. I'll print up some photos of that Dowgin fellow and I'll post them on the bulletin boards on each floor."

"Thank you, sir."

I didn't need to worry about being alone. No one had left the classroom yet. Therese, Hilda and Shannon were still at their desks watching TV. Ray stood at the head of the short flight of stairs leading to the mezzanine floor, while Roger had posted himself beside the glass doors leading to the side street.

"You're all still here." I stated the obvious.

Therese clicked the TV off. "We're worried about you and Dot." She looked behind me. "Where is she, anyway?"

"What's going on with you two?" Hilda wanted to know. Ray and Roger are getting all copped out and your boyfriend looked real serious. And where *is* Dot?"

"Pete gave her a ride home," I said. "and thanks for being worried. But I'm okay. Everything's under control."

"You don't sound convinced, Lee. Does she, Ray?"

Ray hadn't moved from his position at the head of the stairs, and didn't answer. I could see that he was visually scanning the floor below. Hilda was right. Definitely all copped out.

"Are you going to tell us what's wrong, Lee? We want to help. Whatever it is. But we need to know what's going on." Therese waved a hand toward my desk. "Come on. Sit down. Spill it."

It only took me a minute to decide. If I was involved in this mess, to some extent, they were too. I gave them an abbreviated account of what we knew about Emily's death and James Dowgin. I read aloud my copy of the note that had been delivered to Mr. Pennington. Naturally I didn't share any information about the visions. I showed them the photo of Dowgin. "If you see this guy in your travels around town, call 911, okay?"

"So are you going to do what the note said? Mind your own business? I know I would!" Shannon's eyes were wide.

"Of course I am," I said. "I mean, as much as I can."

Roger had moved a little closer to the group, while still keeping an eye on the street outside. "Doesn't say *we* have to stay out of it, right?"

From the head of the stairs, his twin answered. "We don't have to stay out of it, right?"

Hilda's expression brightened. "We can get involved as much as we want to. Like real investigative reporters."

"Whoa!" I said, raising both hands. "Slow down, you guys. You aren't investigative reporters yet—and as a matter of fact, neither am I. So we'll all stay out of it. Agreed?"

"As much as we can, like you said." Therese's voice was serious, but she couldn't hide her sly smile.

"Hey, I'm the one being threatened here, if this thing is actually a threat, so it's my call. We stay out of it. Now. Back to Day of the Dead. Okay?"

Collective sigh.

"The twins don't like the design they got for the brochure cover," Hilda broke the silence.

"Oh? What's wrong with it? Ray? Roger?"

Neither man had left his self-appointed post. "We've decided we'd rather have a different photograph. Roger likes the ones Therese took with the morning mist above the gravestones," Ray said.

"But Ray likes the one I took of the tree with the orb thing," Roger offered. "So we think we'd like to go back to the cemetery some morning and take one of both the tree and the mist. Can we do that?"

"I'll call Kelsey Roehl and see if she can get permission for us to go in there before sunrise on Monday morning." She aimed her smile at Ray. "I can't quite see you guys jumping that wrought iron fence!"

Ray straightened his shoulders and pulled in his stomach. "Don't be too sure of that, Missy. We keep in shape."

"We keep in good shape," Roger agreed with his twin.

*I bet they could jump that fence if they had to.*

"Monday morning good for everybody? That is if the weather cooperates. We need that pretty early morning mist. Watch Wanda Sunday night and check. She'll call it 'ground fog.'"

Ray and Roger looked at one another. "We always watch Wanda," Ray said.

"I'll just bet you do." Hilda laughed. "The photo is a good idea though. Want me to call Dorothy? I can pick her up. She won't want to walk to the cemetery in the dark."

"Good idea. Thanks." I'd already thought about Dorothy needing a ride, hoping I wouldn't have to pick her up and face the inevitable conversation about Emily.

It was within minutes of the normal closing time when we all left the classroom. We'd agreed to meet at the east gate of the cemetery on Monday morning, weather permitting. Kelsey had secured the necessary permission and had offered to join us there. Still more concerned about the damned note than I cared to admit—even to myself—I hurried across the parking lot to my car, shielding my eyes with one hand and peering into the windows. I looked around (it could only be called "furtively"), unlocked it and climbed in feeling like a big silly goof.

I wasn't looking forward to sharing all this new information with Aunt Ibby. I knew that despite the state-of-the-art alarm system we had in the house on Winter Street, she'd be worried about my safety. As it turned out, I didn't have to share the information with her. She was already worried when I reached home, thanks to a phone call from Rupert Pennington. She greeted me as soon as I stepped into the back hall, right behind O'Ryan who had already greeted me in the driveway.

"Come in, come in." She held her kitchen door open, looking back and forth between the stairway to my apartment and the laundry room across the hall. "Rupert told me about the threatening note from that man." She looked every bit as furtive as I must have a short time earlier in the Tabby's parking lot, and I couldn't help laughing.

"Come on, it's not as bad as all that. Anyway, it isn't actually a threat. More of an—um—admonition."

"Just the same. It's aimed at you and I don't like it." She took my hand and pulled me into the kitchen, rapidly slamming and locking the door, leaving O'Ryan to push his way through the cat entrance, looking a bit miffed at being left behind. "Sit down," she ordered. "I've been thinking about it all day, even though I woke up with quite a headache. Anyway, I'm fine now and I have a theory."

I sat. So did she. So did the cat.

"That man, H. James Dowgin, faked his own death."

"It looks that way," I agreed, "since if he's the one who delivered the note, he isn't dead."

She looked at me over half-glasses and used her librarian voice. "Obviously. The question then is, what have you been asking about that someone doesn't want answered?"

"Emily Alden's death?"

"That, of course, but something beyond that."

"The idea that she was murdered—that she didn't die of an overdose?"

She tapped her foot impatiently. "Of course she was murdered. But *why* was she murdered? Hmmmm? That's the part H. James Dowgin doesn't want you to know."

"I'll bite. Why was she murdered?"

"The dirt." She sat back in her chair. "It was the dirt all along."

A series of pictures flashed through my mind. Emily's letter about the soil sample. The muddy work boots. The trowel in the dirt. The warring councilors. The borrowed library books. "There was something bad in Emily's soil sample from the wild woods."

"I think so. Doesn't it make sense? If that soil is contaminated somehow, the whole Wildwood Mall project is compromised."

"Cleaning up whatever it is could cost millions," I said. "And somebody doesn't want me to find out what it is."

# CHAPTER 22

Aunt Ibby's theory made a certain amount of sense. Quite a bit of sense, really. But why does James Dowgin want me to stop asking questions? What does the new mall have to do with him? If anyone was going be impacted by the news that there's something wrong with the land, wouldn't that be Happy and Trudy Shores?

"I'm going to find out what kind of businesses were operating there," my aunt announced. "I know there are still several buildings standing on the property but those will be gone by Monday if Happy Shores has his way."

"You think maybe one of them was producing something toxic before they closed?"

"Could very well be. They've been there for years. Long before there were environmental impact studies going on every two minutes. I remember the diaper service was there. Wypee-Dypee. Your mother used them for you. And there was a restaurant supply place. I forget what the others were. Most of the buildings there were torn down years ago when the big malls came, and then the woods took over." She grinned at me. "Remember when I took you for a nature walk in there once?"

"I remember the bee sting and the poison oak, thank you."

"You itched for weeks."

"I remember it well. But aren't we supposed to stop asking questions about this? Stop snooping? We said we would."

"I said I'd keep my snooping within the library walls. I can do that."

"My main problem is going to be keeping Dorothy from getting into trouble over this. And getting me into trouble along with her."

"You have to stay out of it. At least until Pete finds that Dowgin person. I don't like the sound of that note one bit."

"I don't either. But I'll be careful. I'll just be going back and forth to the Tabby during the daytime and I sure won't go out alone after dark." I remembered our class arrangement for Monday morning. "Of course, I'll be hanging around in the cemetery before sunup on Monday for a photo shoot if our plans work out—but the whole class will be there, including the twins—who seem to have appointed themselves my personal bodyguards."

"Have they? That's good. But be sure you tell Pete your plans."

It was the advice I expected to hear and I had every intention of taking it seriously. When Pete arrived at my back door later that evening, he'd hardly taken off his jacket and secured his gun in the bureau before I began to rattle off the details of the happenings since I'd last seen him. Even to my own ears, most of seemed pretty mundane. He frowned when I told him about the proposed early morning trip to the cemetery, and absolutely snapped to attention when I repeated Aunt Ibby's theory about James Dowgin's and Emily's soil samples.

"I gave the chief those library books your aunt loaned us," he said. "He knows a lot about dirt and plants and growing things in different kinds of soil and all that."

I'm sure I looked surprised. I couldn't quite picture hard-as-nails, tough cop Chief Whaley planting seeds or trimming hedges. "Really? The chief?"

"Sure. You didn't know that? His rose garden is always featured when the garden club does its spring tour of homes."

"That's just amazing," I said, sitting down on a stool at the kitchen counter. "What does he think about all this?"

Pete started a pot of coffee then sat beside me. "To tell you the truth, up until today he's being kind of old-school about this one. He's been standing by the M.E. and coroner's reports about Emily's death being a simple OD, and so far he's been content to let Miami-Dade handle the missing guy in the Everglades."

"Didn't you tell him about the note? About me? About the prints on the envelope?"

"Sure did."

"Well? What did he say?"

Pete kind of half-smiled. "He said, 'What's that woman of yours got herself mixed up in now?'"

"So now he believes maybe Emily was murdered? Maybe this Dowgin guy had something to do with it? And that maybe—just maybe *I've* got a little problem?"

"A complete turnaround. You know how the chief is. He has to be convinced, then it's full steam ahead. He's got an APB out on the Dowgin character, who—by the way—has started using his credit cards again. Must have run out of cash. His cell phone hasn't shown up yet though. Too bad.

We could track him with that." Pete poured our coffees. "He must have fed it to the alligators."

"Speaking of phones, did Dorothy tell you that her stepmom found Emily's?"

He nodded. "She did. She'll call me just as soon as she gets it. She says her mom never tried to see what was on it."

"I know. It was too painful for her I guess, to hear Emily's voice or maybe to see pictures of her. It must be awful. Losing a child I mean."

"I'm thinking that phone could turn out to be an important piece of evidence," he said. "And there may be things on it a mother might not want to see or hear."

"That's probably true of most everybody's phones," I said. "Want to go out to eat? I don't feel like cooking."

He didn't feel like cooking either, so we finished our coffee and went to our favorite Italian restaurant—chicken Parmiagiana for me, the classic spaghetti dinner for him. Cheesecake for both of us. I noticed that on the way home, Pete kept a close eye on his rearview mirror. It was both comforting and scary.

He parked on Winter Street, and walked me up to the front door. "Be sure to use the dead bolt," he said, "and set the alarm." As if I didn't always do both! But I knew he was worried about me and I told him I'd be extra careful. We shared a long, lovely good night kiss, I closed the door, put the dead bolt in place, tapped the code into the alarm keyboard, and with O'Ryan scooting ahead of me, climbed the two flights to my apartment. I let myself in and was extra careful about locking and bolting that door too.

Still a little skittish about even looking at the window where the white cat had taken to showing up, I made sure that it was locked, then took a long look outside. No cats in sight, gray, white or otherwise. O'Ryan sprawled across the windowsill and closed his eyes.

"Good boy," I told him, patting his big fuzzy head. "No cats will get past you, either real or imaginary ones." I made the usual preparations for bed—no school on Saturday so didn't have to set the alarm. Surprisingly, considering the day's happenings, I went to sleep almost immediately and slept like the proverbial baby.

I awoke to one of those Saturday mornings when you wish you could just snuggle up on the couch with your favorite blanky, have a bowl of Captain Crunch, watch cartoons and make the grown-up world go away. But of course, that's not the way life works. O'Ryan had left his post on the windowsill and cried piteously for his breakfast. I pulled a pillow over my head. "Go downstairs and bother your aunt," I told him. It didn't work. More crying. Grumbling, I got out of bed, pulled a bag of kitty kibble from the cabinet and dumped some into his red bowl. I reheated the leftover coffee from the night before and clicked on the TV, debating whether I should watch the WICH-TV morning news or Spongebob. The grown-up me won.

Wanda appeared on the screen, bright eyed and as perky as ever.

*Does the woman never sleep?*

The day promised to be overcast with a twenty percent chance of rain. Drivers were warned to be cautious of ground fog which would likely burn off before nine A.M. That tropical depression down south had grown into a tropical storm and was named Penelope.

"Okay. So much for the weather." I said to the cat who'd by then already finished his food. He began his brisk A.M. face-washing, whisker-grooming ritual, while I, barefoot, unwashed, messy-haired and still grumpy, sipped yesterday's coffee and tried to focus on today's news. A new TV morning duo tossed topics back and forth, tag team fashion, mostly local news with a smattering of statewide items. The same shot of the wild woods I'd seen yesterday appeared, followed by a series of still shots of the few buildings remaining on the street-facing edge of the property. Other than being closed up, with plywood over some of the windows and faded paint and a minimum of graffiti, they didn't look all that bad. The Wypee-Dypee sign was still legible on the front of a pale blue–clapboard structure, and a nearby storefront with boarded windows had brass letters spelling out what must have once read HARDWARE but now said simply DWAR. The third place had no visible signage at all. "Kind of sad looking, isn't it?" I addressed the cat who by then had one leg over his head, continuing his morning ablutions. No response. "Do you think Aunt Ibby's right? About the dirt?"

The cat stopped licking the end of his tail for a moment and looked straight at me. "Mmmyyup," he said.

The two on screen discussed the upcoming mall—he with some construction details, she with a wish list of stores being discussed around town. I finished off the old coffee and made new, wondering if the photo of H. James Dowgin would be part of the newscast. It wasn't.

"Guess the chief isn't ready to publicly call James a person of interest yet," I told the cat, who licked one paw and put it behind his ear. "Just a missing person, I suppose. And he's probably right." I opened the refrigerator, poured a glass of orange juice and started back to the stool on the other side of the counter.

"Ouch!" I grabbed my right foot and did a little hopping dance, then sat quickly. With a motion—not nearly as graceful as the cat's—I inspected the bottom of my foot, where a tiny sliver of glass protruded from the flesh. I grabbed a dishtowel and wiped away some blood, then with thumb and forefinger, dislodged the offending shard.

"Guess we didn't sweep up all of that wineglass," I said, limping toward the bathroom in search of disinfectant and an adhesive bandage.

This day was not starting well at all.

I looked into the bathroom mirror. The face looking back at me was not a happy one. "A hot bath would feel good," I told my bedraggled self. I even hummed a little as I filled the tub with hot water and dumped some Peach Bellini bubble bath in too. Within moments, I eased myself into the steaming, hot, bubbly, wonderful relaxing water and closed my eyes.

*Just what the doctor ordered.*

The lovely feeling didn't last long. My eyes flew open.

*The doctor.*

*The broken wineglass.*

*The bubble bath.*

My foot was still bleeding. The bubbles were stained a pretty pink.

# CHAPTER 23

Had Emily stepped on the wineglass I'd seen in my vision? Had the doctor found any cuts on her body? Had her blood made the bubble bath pink the way mine just had? I wanted to ask Pete, but I knew he'd probably already be at work. No bubble baths or Saturday morning cartoons for him. Anyway, even if I called and asked him, he'd know I hadn't stopped meddling.

*But a person can't stop thinking, can she? Thinking isn't meddling. Is it?*

I closed my eyes again, leaned back and tried to find my way back to that happy place where I'd been just a few minutes earlier. Didn't happen. I climbed out of the tub, drained the pink water and started over with nice clean bubbles. Then I soaked for a while, used a nailbrush on toes and fingers, shampooed and cream rinsed, then towel dried and stuck a small adhesive bandage on the by then hardly visible cut on my foot.

I felt better and probably looked better too. I dressed in black capris, white silk shirt and black Capezio flats.

*Now what? All dressed up and no place to go.*

It was too early to call River. She had weekends off,

slept in on Saturday morning and usually had witch stuff going on in the afternoon, and it was Aunt Ibby's day to volunteer on the Bookmobile.

"Guess that leaves you and me, O'Ryan," I said to the cat, who was once again on the windowsill, but this time, facing the room. "Want to go for a walk?"

His ears perked up and he hopped down onto the floor. I took that as a "yes," and went to get a leash from my closet. Yes, O'Ryan is one of those rare cats who'll tolerate a leash. We knew he didn't mind wearing a collar. The witch Ariel Constellation, his previous owner—if anyone can *own* a cat—had dressed him up in all sorts of fancy ones. It was Aunt Ibby's idea to try the leash after an unpleasant experience made him wary of the cat carrier. To our surprise he took to it immediately. Perhaps one of his previous owners taught him to do it—or, less likely—maybe he was a show cat once. Nobody knows much about O'Ryan's background. At any rate, I occasionally took him for a walk on the Salem Common and he seemed to enjoy the attention he attracted and the friends he'd made there. Aunt Ibby had gifted him with an assortment of fashionable leashes. I picked out a bright red leather number with silver conchos for him, chose a red jacket for myself so we'd coordinate and we headed down the front stairs to Winter Street. Per Pete's instructions I remembered to lock my door, lock the downstairs door, reset the alarm and put my cell in my pocket.

We walked toward Bridge Street for a change, instead of to the Common, with O'Ryan attracting stares all the way. Cars slowed down to get a better look or even to shoot the occasional drive-by photo of the unusual sight. I hadn't planned to go to the Howard Street Cemetery, at least not consciously—but in a short time, there we were, standing in front of the graveyard as cars whizzed by on Bridge

Street. O'Ryan put his paws up on the low stone wall and sniffed.

"What do you think, big boy?" I asked, but he strained at the leash, pulling me toward the east gate. I followed his lead and we joined the few tourists who were already inside the cemetery, strolling among the headstones. The cat, ignoring the pointing people and the flattering remarks about such a smart, obedient animal, headed straight for the man with the easel making a copy of a headstone. It seemed that we were about to meet the elusive Dakota Berman.

He didn't look up from his work when we approached. But when O'Ryan peered around the edge of the tall tombstone, the artist, startled, sat up straight and those amazing blue eyes met mine.

"Hello," I said. "You must be Dorothy Alden's friend." I stuck out my hand. "I'm Lee Barrett, Dorothy's teacher at the Tabby."

The smile was just as arresting as the astonishing eyes. His handshake was firm. "How do you do. Dorothy's told me about you. I don't think I've ever seen a cat on a leash before. I mean one that seems to like it."

"His name is O'Ryan. He's quite . . . unusual." I turned to look at the drawing on the easel. The artist's rendering was almost identical to the original, except that Dakota had "repaired" a broken corner and a chipped edge on the monument, and had "erased" a muddy smear across some of the letters. "You've fixed the broken parts," I said. "That's nice."

"I wish I could really fix them. All of them." The smile faded and he gazed across the rows of stones.

"Has Dorothy told you about our plans for *Dia de los Muertos*?" I asked. "Maybe we could raise some interest somehow in getting some restoration done around here."

"I'd like to help with that if I could," he said. "I love this place."

*He loves a cemetery?*

"Uh-huh. It's . . . um . . . interesting," I said. "Well, you're busy, so O'Ryan and I will get on with our walk now. It was nice meeting you. I'll ask Dorothy to keep you up to speed on our celebration." I gave the leash a tug and without a backward glance the cat trotted obediently up the hill toward the resting place of the Hawthorne siblings and the maybe sort of haunted tree.

*Strange guy. I wonder how well he knew Emily.*

I gave myself a mental slap on the wrist. I was thinking like a girl detective. Or at least like an investigative reporter. Also, I was just dying to do a little meddling. Keeping my word to Pete was not going to be easy.

O'Ryan displayed quite a lot of interest in the Giles Corey tree, sniffing all around the base, digging a little beneath it and looking up through the tangled branches as though he'd like to climb it. Was this plain old cat curiosity, the scent of other animals, or did he sense something else about it? He suddenly stopped digging, sniffing, gazing and sat down on his haunches, his eyes fixed on something just to the left of the tree. I followed the green eyes. There was nothing there. O'Ryan growled, deep in his throat and kept right on gazing at the nothing.

I let him sit there, staring, until I began to feel strangely uncomfortable. I gave the leash a tug. "Come on. Let's look around the rest of the place, then I'll take you to the Common." He backed away a little, then obediently trotted ahead of me toward the Howard Street gate.

Dakota Berman was right about the state of repair of the ancient stones. Some of them lay on the grass in pieces, others so eroded by time and climate, the names were no longer legible. Maybe our video, in addition to showing a happy, colorful celebration, could call the community's attention to the sad and downright disrespectful condition of some of the old monuments. Maybe we could start an "adopt-a-gravesite" movement! In a place like Salem it just might work.

We exited onto Howard Street. From there it was a straight shot uphill to the Common. I congratulated myself on steering my thoughts away from forbidden subjects and back to the classroom where my head belonged.

The big yellow cat on the leash had become a familiar sight on the Common, and no longer attracted quite as much attention as he used to. We visited the hot dog man and the pigeon lady, and O'Ryan watched, but did not attempt to chase, the squirrels. We stopped for a moment and saw some gardeners planting marigolds around the bandstand. Of course, they all used trowels which sent my thoughts whizzing back to Emily and broken glass and dirt samples and the threatening note and murder.

I stopped at the popcorn cart and bought a bucket of the warm, white, buttery stuff for a delicious and reasonably nutritious—if somewhat decadent—breakfast. Crossing Washington Square we headed home to Winter Street, forbidden thoughts still churning in my brain. What if Aunt Ibby was right? If H. James Dowgin was in fact not just a missing person but a killer, or at least a threatening note writer, I could be in danger.

*He might be watching me right now. Was he one of the drive-by cat photographers?*

I'd managed to creep myself out. Looking over my shoulder, just like they do in the movies, I walked faster. I wished I'd worn sunglasses so I could really study faces of people on the Common, or the drivers of passing cars. O'Ryan grew annoyed when I yanked on his leash just as he was greeting a poodle friend of long acquaintance.

"Mrruf," he said. "Mrouw."

"You're right," I told him, slowing my pace. "I'm being silly. Paranoid, even. It's a beautiful day. I'm in a public place a block from home. No one is chasing me or even watching me. Watching you, maybe, since you were just nose-to-nose with a dog and that's a little odd, but I'm fine."

We rounded the corner to Winter Street. Did I catch a motion behind the giant Civil War monument on the corner? Was someone standing behind that chestnut tree? Had that silver van driven past me twice?

*Maybe I'm not so fine after all.*

"Come on, cat," I said, getting a firm grip on my popcorn bucket and breaking into a jog. "Let's run to the front door."

Once safely upstairs, locked and bolted inside my apartment with the cat de-leashed, I sat by the window, checking first to be sure it was still locked and that there was no white cat on the fire escape and took a deep breath. Meddling or not, I was scared. Pulling my phone from my pocket I texted Pete.

# CHAPTER 24

I didn't exactly tell Pete that I was frightened, but must have managed to sound urgent enough to prompt him to call me within five minutes of my text.

"What's going on, babe? You're upset."

"I am," I admitted. "I keep thinking about Aunt Ibby's theory that Dowgin killed Emily. That he's threatening me because . . . because why? I don't know anything about the man. I'm literally walking around looking over my shoulder and you know that's not like me."

"I know." His voice was calm. Comforting. "We'll have him in custody soon. I promise. He's used a credit card to buy gas, so we've sent his photo around, alerted gas stations to be on the lookout for him." He paused and I could almost see the frown. "Walking around where?"

"Oh, I took O'Ryan for a walk. Down to the cemetery and over to the Common."

"The cemetery again?"

"Uh huh. We visited the grave rubbing guy. Dakota Berman. Seems nice."

"Yeah, well, let's cut down on the random walks for a

bit, okay? Dowgin is just a missing person at this point you know, but no sense tempting fate."

"Tempting fate. You sound like River," I said. "I'll be careful. How's your card reading working out anyway? Any deceptions, obstacles or unpleasant news yet?"

"Lee, I'm a cop. I deal with deception, obstacles and unpleasant news every day. But no, nothing unusual. I'll come over after work today, okay? And I have tomorrow off so maybe we can do something."

"That'd be great," I said, meaning it with all my heart. I didn't want to be alone and I knew that he knew it. What a guy. We made plans to catch an early movie, have fried clams at Dube's and spend the rest of the evening at home. Then we'd think up something fun to do on Sunday.

Things were looking up. My afternoon was blessedly uneventful, with barely a thought of murder to interrupt the mundane Saturday chores like dusting and catching up with laundry. Aunt Ibby finished her Bookmobile shift and we played a game of gin rummy for pennies at her kitchen table. She won. (Two dollars and three cents.)

By the time Pete arrived my frame of mind was so much improved that I felt a little embarrassed about having sent that semipanicked text. I'd changed into skinny black jeans, a super-soft baby blue cashmere sweater and black leather booties with three-inch heels. A black leather vest would keep the evening chill away and for once my hair behaved so I didn't feel as though I should hide it under a hat. I could tell by the look in Pete's eyes and the long, lingering kiss he greeted me with that he approved. I wanted to ask him about the broken wine-glass and the pink bubbles I'd seen in my vision, but why break the mood? Visions could wait.

I won our ritual coin toss at Cinema Salem and got to

pick the movie—the newest *Jason Bourne*. I'd already had enough popcorn for one day, so I settled for a Mounds bar. After the movie the fried clams at Dube's were fabulous as always. It was still pretty early so we took a ride along the shore road, which took us past the wild woods.

"Pretty quiet here tonight," Pete said. "But Monday morning when the heavy equipment trucks and the protesters face off—oh boy—that'll be some fireworks."

"I'll bet. Hey, look. There are lights on in one of the buildings. Is that okay?"

"Yeah. We've had a few calls about those lights being on in there lately. The water has been turned on again too. Checked it out. The owners have permission to see if there's anything in there they want to salvage before they start to demo the places next week."

"Looks like it's the Wypee-Dypee building. Did I tell you my Mom used those diapers on me?"

"I'll bet you were the cutest little red haired baby in Salem! Ready to go home now? Or do you want to take one last stroll in the wild woods?"

"No thanks. I'm still allergic to poison oak. Ready to go home." I looked at the clock on the dash. "We can catch the late news if you want to."

We pulled into the driveway next to the garage. Pete locked his car and took my hand as we walked along the path past the garden and up to the back steps. I sneaked a quick glance toward the tall fence at the edge of our property, half expecting to see the white cat. She wasn't there. When we got upstairs she wasn't at the kitchen window either.

*Am I glad she isn't there? Or do I miss her?*

I didn't mention the white cat, or the lack of her, to Pete.

I didn't even stay awake for the late news and I don't think Pete did either.

I awoke to the smell of fresh coffee and the sound of Tammy Wynette singing a "somebody done somebody wrong" song on the radio. Two sure signs that Pete was in the kitchen. I joined him at the counter and poured myself a cup of the lovely stuff.

"Is there something special you want to do today?" He passed me the half-and-half. "Or shall I be tour director?"

"Not sure," I said. "What do you have in mind?"

"Ever been to the Topsfield Fair?"

I smiled at the thought of it. The memories. "Not since I was a kid! What a great idea!"

It was a great idea. Topsfield is only about ten miles north of us, and though Salem is every bit a city, Topsfield looks and feels like a small country town—complete with cornfields and cows. The fair, one of America's oldest, was every bit as wonderful and magical as I'd remembered it. We got there early, saw draft horses and baby goats, watched the tractor pulls, marveled at the giant pumpkin contest. (Saw one that weighed 1,992 pounds!)

We were at the funnel cake stand for the second time when Pete said, "Don't turn around now, but after a minute or so, take a look over toward the fried Oreos. There's a guy over there wearing a Pittsburgh Steelers shirt. Anyone you know?" It wasn't in a cop voice, but sounded like cop words. I tried very hard to be totally casual about it, and looked in the direction he'd indicated. Got a good look at the man. About six feet tall. Tanned. Balding. Thin.

"Never saw him before in my life," I said. "Why?"

"He's been with us since the parking lot. Driving a

maroon Ford pickup." He frowned. "I didn't notice him following us from Salem, but he could have. Ran the license plate. It's a rental."

"Following me?" My voice sounded squeaky. "Couldn't he just be coming to the fair? Maybe he likes to see the same things we do."

"Maybe. Got your phone?"

"Sure."

"Make believe you're taking my picture but zoom in on him."

"Okay."

Pete faced me, smiling a big fake smile. I made sure Pittsburgh guy—who wasn't smiling—was in the frame and clicked off a couple of shots, then sent them to Pete's phone.

"Good. Come on, let's go to the bee and honey exhibit." He took my hand. I dragged along behind him like a little kid. I like honey all right but bees are not my favorite creatures. The bee and honey thing didn't take up much space and there weren't a lot of people gathered around it. The man was there though, leaning against a fence just across the way from the honeycomb table and pretending not to see us.

I almost giggled. "Pete," I said, "if he's tailing us he's not very good at it, is he?"

"He isn't," Pete agreed. "Come on. Let's ditch him. Want to see the ax women loggers from Maine?"

"Sure."

We cut around the edge of a field where the ox pulling contest was about to begin, ducked behind a parade of thirty-two Royal Canadian Mounted Police and wound up in some good seats for the ax women loggers. The girls were awesome and Pittsburgh guy apparently missed the show. It was nearly sunset when we went back to the parking lot. The maroon Ford was gone.

*Maybe he wasn't following me—or us. Maybe he just likes funnel cakes and giant pumpkins and baby goats and bees.*

When Pete dropped me off at home, it was still fairly early so I knocked on Aunt Ibby's kitchen door, knowing she'd like to hear about the fair.

"It was just as I'd remembered it," I told her. "But maybe bigger and with more weird food. Did you ever have fried Oreos?"

"Never. But I'd try one. Did you?"

I admitted that I had, and told her about the Royal Mounties and the baby goats and the giant pumpkin and the girl loggers from Maine. "Something odd happened while we were there," I said, knowing that the possibility of our being followed around the fairground would worry her—but wanting her thoughts about it.

"What did he look like?" she wanted to know.

I pulled out my cell. "Look. I have a picture." I pointed. "See. He's behind Pete. Right there."

She reached for her glasses and peered at the screen. "The fellow in the Steelers shirt?"

"Yes. That's him. You don't recognize him do you?"

"No. But the Steelers shirt interests me."

"Huh?"

"I did a little more digging into that Dowgin person's background. He's originally from Pennsylvania. Edgewood. A very nice suburb of Pittsburgh." She scowled. "A coincidence?"

"Maybe. There are lots of Steelers fans around." I said, hoping for coincidence but anticipating something more ominous. "Do you think Pete knows about the Pennsylvania connection to Dowgin?"

"I'm pretty sure he must. It wasn't very hard for me to find."

I thought about that for a minute. "Do you want to see what else we can find out?"

"Right now?"

I nodded. "Right now."

# CHAPTER 25

I followed my aunt into her office. She sat at her computer and I pulled up a chair close beside her. "I'm going to log into my library account," she said with a sly smile. "That way I won't be exactly breaking my word that I'd keep my research limited to the confines of the library."

"We promised to tell him everything we learn though, so we'll have to do that."

"Of course." Her fingers flew across the keyboard and within what seemed like seconds we were looking at the page of a yearbook. She zoomed in on a photo of a young man. A young H. James Dowgin. No doubt about it. "Jimmy Dowgin. Class of 2003 University of Pittsburgh."

"That must be where the degree in Environmental Science came from. I wonder how he wound up in real estate."

"There could be many reasons for that. I'm guessing it was financial. Probably more money in sales than in consulting right now."

"Makes sense. But if the alligators didn't eat him, and

they obviously didn't, how did he become a missing person?"

She spread her hands apart. "Don't know. What do you think?"

"The falling into the water scenario was staged. But did he stage it? Or did somebody else?"

She gave me a long look. "You're thinking if he staged it himself, he's hiding from something."

"Or somebody."

"And if somebody else did it, *they're* hiding something."

"Right." I tapped my fingers on the edge of her desk. "But now he's come out of hiding and it has something to do with me. Something I don't like."

"I don't like it either, but as you say, he's come out of hiding so it won't take long for the police to find him. You'll see."

"I think you're right. And Pete seems confident too, although he warned me about taking random walks around Salem," I said. "Tempting fate, he calls it."

"Sounds like River."

"I know. I'm going to talk to her about the Steeler guy. That really puzzles me."

"Oops. Look at this." She tapped the screen. "I searched the team name and see what popped up. Monday night football. The Pats and Steelers are playing an early season game in Foxboro tomorrow. That probably explains the presence of your mystery man in the area."

"Whew." My whole body relaxed. "Of course. You're right. He's here for the game along with lots of other Pittsburgh fans. And that's why he's driving a rental. What a relief."

"Sometimes the simple answer is the best one."

"Makes me feel a lot better. Guess I'll just run along upstairs and go to bed. Thanks for helping."

"Thanks for meddling, you mean?" She smiled and shut down the computer. "Good night, dear. Sleep well."

"Good night. Where's O'Ryan?"

"He went upstairs right after you came in. He must be waiting for you in your place."

I climbed the curving front staircase up the two flights and unlocked my kitchen door. Aunt Ibby was right about O'Ryan. He sat on the windowsill, facing through the glass, nose to nose with the white cat on the fire escape.

He turned and jumped down onto the floor, skittering across the tiles to greet me with the usual purring and ankle rubbing ritual. I picked him up, holding him close while looking past him toward the white cat. She opened her mouth in a silent meow and cocked her head to one side, not moving away from her position at the window. O'Ryan looked up at me, giving my chin a lick, then squirmed to get down. He returned to his spot on the windowsill.

"Do you think she's hungry?" I asked him.

"Mow." He said, which had a positive sound to it.

"Okay. I'll give her some of your kitty kibble. Is that what you want?"

"Mmlik," he said.

"All right. Milk too."

I took two bowls from the cabinet and filled one with kibble, the other with milk. I unlocked the window, lifted the sash and placed them on the iron rails outside. She certainly appeared to be hungry, hunched down over the food. I smiled, gave her head a tentative pat and began to lower the window.

That's when I noticed a Ford pickup driving down

Oliver Street, passing right beneath a streetlight. Was it maroon? I couldn't tell. I wanted to call Pete but what would I say? A pickup truck just drove past my backyard? Big deal.

I wasn't going to sleep very well after all. To make things worse, Wanda's late weather forecast promised a rainy morning, so there went our hoped for photogenic ground fog. I blasted an e-mail to all of the class, telling them we'd meet at the usual time at the Tabby and to hope for misty weather on Tuesday.

Monday dawned just as Wanda had promised. There's usually nothing romantic or attractive about a rainy day in Salem, Massachusetts. The sky turns a uniform mouse-gray, there's a chilly dampness permeating everything and people get grouchy. The rain fell straight down giving the city a relentless pummeling. With an inward resolution to punch the first person who chirped, "We really needed the rain," I donned a hooded yellow slicker, jeans and Patriots sweatshirt, pulled on rubber boots and headed out. I paused on the way and tapped on Aunt Ibby's door. "If you see a white cat in the yard, and she's getting wet, I think it would be okay to let her in," I said. "See you tonight."

I slogged my way to the garage, stamped muddy feet vigorously before stepping into the 'vette, backed out onto Oliver Street and drove extra carefully to the Tabby—assuming that all the other drivers on the road felt as crabby as I did.

Things seemed better within the warmth of the diner, as I joined the twins at the counter. The rest of the class hadn't shown up yet and I hoped none of them had missed my late night e-mail and gone to the cemetery after all.

"Good morning, Ms. Barrett," Ray greeted me. "Nice weather."

"For ducks." Roger completed the cliché. "Good morning."

"Hi guys," I said, taking a vacant seat next to Ray. "What's new?"

"Not much," Roger said. "Did you have a good weekend?"

"I did. Pete and I went to the Topsfield Fair. Ever been to it?"

They beamed identical smiles. "We go every year," Ray said.

"Every year," Roger echoed, his smile fading. "Is everything going okay for you? I mean, any worries?"

I made the quick decision to tell them about the Steelers man, gave a quick rundown of what had happened and showed them the photo on my phone. "He drives a maroon Ford pickup with rental plates." I didn't mention the truck I'd seen from the kitchen window.

"Can you zoom in on that guy and make us a couple of prints? I've got an idea." Ray poked his brother with an elbow. "You thinking what I'm thinking, Rog?"

"The game?"

"Right. The game."

I looked from one to the other, bewildered. "Game? What game?"

"Pats and Steelers. They're playing tonight. You follow football?"

I pulled the Velcro closing of the slicker open, revealing my Patriots sweatshirt. "Sure. Why?"

"They usually put on extra security in Foxboro for Steelers games," Ray said.

"Steelers fans. Rowdy bunch," Roger offered. "The Pats like to hire ex-cops. Like us."

"So if you two are working the game, you can look for this man." I thought about that. "There'll be thousands of people there."

"Yeah. But we can watch the gates, the concession stands, we can walk the whole stadium."

"Ray knows the photographer who puts shots on the JumboTron," Roger said. "He'll scan different sections for us. We've done it before." He gave his twin another poke in the ribs. "Ray thought his girlfriend was there with another guy."

I couldn't help myself. "Was she?"

An embarrassed laugh from Ray. "Yeah. It was her father."

By this time the rest of the class had appeared, motioning us to the back booth. The twins assured me that they'd call in right away and volunteer for security duty in Foxboro. "When we locate him, we'll find an excuse to talk to him, check his seat number, you know, hassle him a little. At least we'll get his name."

"Thanks so much," I said. "I really appreciate your help. Pete will too."

"Our pleasure." Roger waved away my thanks. "We get paid and get to see the game too."

I joined the group who were already seated at the back of the diner, leaving the twins at the counter. "Good morning all." The booth had a coatrack attached, and I added my slicker to the damp mass of outerwear already there. "Sorry the weather didn't cooperate for our early photo shoot. Tomorrow will be better."

"A lot of stuff got canceled because of the rain," Hilda said. "We were listening to the radio on the way over here.

They said that the groundbreaking ceremony for the new mall was being postponed."

"Don't blame them. The ground will be pure mud." Therese motioned for the waitress.

Shannon gave a pretend moan. "They'll never get it built at this rate. I can hardly wait for the grand opening."

"I was hoping it would be open before I have to go back to Alaska," Dorothy said. "I don't get to go mall shopping very often up there."

"Sorry to burst your bubble, hon, but it'll take a year or two at least to build the thing. When do you have to go home?" There was real concern in Hilda's voice. "Are you going to be able to finish the semester?"

"I think so." Dorothy smiled. "At least I hope so. I like this class—and all of you. It just depends on . . . circumstances."

"Do you have to get back to your fishing business?" Shannon asked.

"Or the cute guy you fish with?" Hilda added.

"I didn't say he was cute."

"Is he?"

Dorothy blushed. "Well, yeah, he is. I've missed most of the halibut and salmon season already, but he's doing okay without me. And we can fish other groundfish most of the year. The way things are going, it looks like I'll be sticking around here for a while." She aimed a meaningful glance in my direction.

I could understand her frustration. We weren't getting any closer to finding Emily's killer—if, indeed she'd been murdered—and it looked more and more as though she had. Besides that, we needed to worry about our own safety. Or, according to the note with James Dowgin's fingerprints on it, at least I did.

I was making a real effort to stick to my lesson plan.

After all, my students had paid a not insignificant sum to take the TV Production course, and had every right to expect to learn skills which might lead to a career in the TV industry. Since they'd become somewhat involved in Dorothy's problem—and, by extension, mine—I needed a way to keep the *Dia de los Muertos* project front and center and at the same time to use the techniques we studied along with our individual talents to help figure out what had happened to Emily. Without actually meddling, of course.

As soon as we all got to the classroom I proposed a problem for the class to solve. "Let's assume that we're investigative reporters and we've be asked to check out a 'person of interest.'" I propped a small white board against the bottom of the screen and picked up a black marker. "We don't know his name or anything about him. But we do have a recent photo. Very recent. It was taken yesterday."

I asked Therese to put the photo of the man in the Steelers shirt on the big screen. "Okay. There he is. What can we learn about him from this picture? Anybody?"

"He's a Steelers fan," Roger said.

"That's right," Ray agreed. I wrote "Steelers fan" on the board.

"Not necessarily," Dorothy said. "He could have bought that shirt at a yard sale."

"Good one, Dorothy." I hadn't thought of that possibility. I wrote. "Secondhand shirt?"

"It looks like he's at an exhibit of some kind," Shannon moved closer to the screen. "What's that thing behind him? Is it a cage?"

"Looks like there's bugs in it," Hilda pointed. "See? Bees. Definitely bees. You can see the wings. But there's something else behind the cage. It looks like a big ice cream cone."

She was right. I remembered the ice cream stand. The sign was just outside the bee exhibit.

"I think he's at a carnival or a farmer's market. Something like that," Shannon said. "It's not just about the bees."

"You've almost got it, girl!" Ray punched a fist in the air and his twin said, "Almost!"

"You guys know where it is?"

"We can't tell you."

"A fair," Hilda interrupted before I could explain that the twins had a little lead on the topic. "The county fair. It's over in Boxford or Ipswich or someplace like that."

"Topsfield," I said and wrote Topsfield Fair on my board. "But what does that tell us about the man?"

"He's nearby. Topsfield isn't far from here." Therese had been quiet until then. "He's not interested in the bees. He's not looking at them. He's looking right at the camera. Or whoever is holding the camera."

*That would be me.*

# CHAPTER 26

I had no ready response to Therese's observation. I stared at the picture of the man on the giant screen, my marker poised. He wasn't a particularly sinister looking person—quite ordinary really. The state-of-the-art TV screen a generous government grant had provided for the Tabby showed him in much finer detail than the smart phone had revealed. I scribbled "Subject looking at photographer" on the board and tried not to think about what that might mean.

"Any more information we can gather from the photo?" I asked, looking around the room at six faces, all intent on the screen.

"He's wearing a nice watch," Hilda said. "Not a Rolex, but nice. An Omega, maybe. Like James Bond wears."

"Good observation, Hilda," I said, writing "expensive watch." Anything else?"

"Is that a tattoo on his other arm?" Dorothy pointed. "Or part of one?"

"Can you zoom in on it, Therese?" Dorothy was right. The lower half of a skull was visible beneath the left sleeve of the yellow T-shirt. There were some letters under it.

The left arm grew bigger on the screen, and the skull more distinct. It wore a helmet.

"The man's a vet," Roger said. "Army. Can you make out the words, Ray?"

"Forty-fourth something. Begins with an E."

"Engineer, probably. Afghanistan I'm thinking. I don't know how we'd check it out though."

"Pete probably can," I said, writing faster. "Army vet. Afghanistan?"

"Hey, we're pretty good, aren't we?" Shannon sounded both surprised and pleased. "And all this is just from looking at a picture."

"I know," Hilda said. "This is fun. Let's put that note up on the big screen. Maybe we can find something in that too."

"We can do that," I agreed. "First, any more on this photo?"

Roger and Ray looked at one another. "Shall we tell them now, Ms. Barrett?" Ray asked. "Why we're looking for this subject and how we're going to find him tonight?"

"Lee," I said.

"Right. Shall we?"

"Go ahead."

In their usual tag team fashion, the men explained why we were interested in this particular fairgoer and detailed their scheme for finding him at the Patriots-Steelers game.

"Oh this isn't good," Dorothy faced me. "He was following you? What if he's after you all because of me!"

I tried to calm her. "We don't know that he was following me at all. Chances are it's nothing. I thought it would be a good exercise in observation for the class—and it was. Now let's take a look at that letter."

I retrieved my copy from the desk and asked Therese to scan it onto the screen. The wrinkles and folds were obvious and once again I regretted my carelessness with the evidence. Unlike the Steelers shirt man, we *knew* that this letter involved me.

Like the photo of the man, the big high-definition screen gave a new perspective to the paper and the words on it. "Remember," I said, "there are fingerprints on the envelope and the police have already identified that person and are searching for him. He was a coworker of Dorothy's sister named James Dowgin. We don't know whether or not he was actually the author of the letter. What can we learn from this?" I drew a line with marker under what I'd written on the white board so far, then pointed to the screen. "Who wants to start?"

Hilda began. "Well, in the first place they knew this school was involved. That's why it was delivered to Mr. Pennington."

Shannon waved her hand. "Whoever it is knows about the cemetery even though we haven't done any publicity yet."

"That's right," Therese said, "and they know we're snooping around in somebody else's business."

I wrote "Pennington" and "Cemetery" and paused while I searched for a more polite word for snooping.

Hilda came up with it. "We're *investigating* somebody else's business sounds better," she said. "But hey! What if it's one of *us?* We all know those things. What about that?"

"That's just crazy," Dorothy said. "Plenty of people know what we're doing in the cemetery. Kelsey knows, and Dakota and whoever Lee talked to at city hall and the people who've seen the layout of the brochure . . . plenty of people. It can't be one of us."

"Of course it can't." I pointed to the screen, "Now, back to the letter. Anybody see anything out of the ordinary?"

"What's that brown smudge there in the corner," Ray asked. "See it?"

"I'm afraid that was my fault," I said. "There was half an Almond Joy in my purse when I put the note in. Sorry."

Roger frowned in my direction. "It's real important to preserve evidence carefully. Keep it from getting contaminated."

"Like with chocolate," Ray said. "Contaminated."

I sighed. "Right. What about the typeface? Anything there?"

"Times New Roman," Shannon said. "Nothing unusual about it."

"He knows about the teacher. That's you, Lee." Dorothy said. "And he knows it's about other people's business. That's me. And if the one who wrote it is the Dowgin guy, I'm scared."

She was right of course. Maybe I shouldn't have involved the rest of the class after all.

*Too late to worry about that. They're all involved already.*

"You know, this is so interesting," Hilda said. "I feel like we're really learning a lot about investigative reporting."

"I know," Shannon said. "Best class I ever took. I mean, it's real life investigating. Maybe we'll catch a real bad guy!"

I put down my marker and raised both hands. "We're just investigating, Shannon. Fact finding. Searching for the truth. It's not our intent to actually catch anybody. That's a job for the professionals."

"Like us. Me and Ray," Roger declared. "We're still pros." He gestured toward the screen. "You're not going to get anything more from that letter though. Contaminated."

It seemed like a good time to change the subject.

"Good job, everyone. That was an excellent exercise in

basic investigation." I popped one of my favorite teaching tools into the system. "We'll watch a good DVD on interviewing. Barbara Walters is the narrator. It's from her book *How to Talk to Practically Anybody about Practically Anything.*"

Barbara deftly took over my job for the better part of an hour. I texted Pete and told him what the big screen had revealed about the mystery man's tattoo and the James Bond watch. I hesitated about mentioning the twin's self-appointed search at Foxboro and decided against it. After all, I reasoned, it was their idea, sort of a voluntary homework assignment. Anyway, probably nothing would come of it. I pulled the Happy Shores notebook from my purse and copied the words from the whiteboard into it. Then spent a few minutes staring at the words.

*What does it all mean?*

By the time the credits rolled at the end of the video, it was lunch time. The rain had lessened, and most of the group headed off in different directions for lunch or shopping or both. Dorothy stayed behind, quietly watching me as I returned the letter and photo to my desk and the notebook to my purse.

"Yes, Dorothy?" I wished she wouldn't look at me that way, with her frightened eyes.

"Will you come down to the diner with me?"

"Of course I will. But don't worry so. The police will have that Dowgin fellow in custody by the end of the day. You'll see. And if he knows anything about what happened to your sister, Pete will find out."

"But why would he . . . or anybody want to hurt Emily?"

Again, I hesitated. Pete didn't want me to get too involved with Dorothy. But would it do any harm to share Aunt Ibby's theory about the dirt in the wild woods with her? Maybe it would even help her to recall something helpful to the police. So I told her, briefly, what my aunt had suggested about the soil being contaminated somehow.

A little smile flickered across her face. "Contaminated. Like the letter in your purse. Only not with chocolate I'll bet."

"I have an idea," I said. "Let's go over to my place for lunch. I can throw something together. It's not far and you can meet my aunt. And our cat, O'Ryan."

She agreed and before long we were driving through a light rain toward Winter Street. I tried to keep the conversation light too. "We still have to make plans for that sugar skull cookie baking project," I said. "The picture in the magazine looked so cute."

"The *calavera,"* she said.

"Exactly." I pulled up and parked in front of the house. "Here we are."

Dorothy climbed out and, shading her eyes with one hand, looked up. "Wow. You have a big house."

"Not all mine," I reminded her. "But I have a few rooms on the third floor to call my own."

"Big house," she said again. "Pretty too. Hey, didn't you say you had a yellow cat?"

"We do. Big yellow cat. Name's O'Ryan."

"Is the white cat yours too?" She pointed toward the bay window in Aunt Ibby's front living room. There she was. The white cat. On the inside this time, looking out.

# CHAPTER 27

Aunt Ibby rushed out into the front hall as soon as she heard the door open. Naturally, O'Ryan was already there, waiting to greet us.

"Maralee! Is everything all right at school? You're home so early!"

"Everything's fine. I should have called and warned you that we were coming, but it was kind of a last minute decision. This is Dorothy Alden. We're just going to grab a bite of lunch, and I wanted her to meet you and O'Ryan."

"So very happy to finally meet you." My aunt took Dorothy's hand in both of hers. "I'm sure you know that I've heard a great deal about you, and I'm so terribly sorry for your loss. I understand what it's like to lose a sister."

"Thank you. You've lost a sister too?"

Aunt Ibby nodded. "Maralee's mother. Her daddy too. A dreadful plane crash. The pain of that kind of loss never goes away." She hadn't let go of Dorothy's hand, and drew her into the living room. I followed. "You girls come on out to the kitchen and have lunch with O'Ryan and me." The white cat on the window seat cushion stood up and stretched, hopped down to the floor and trotted along behind us. "Oh, that one is a friend of O'Ryan's. She's just visiting."

"There's a white cat like that one that visits where I live too," Dorothy said. "It peeks in the window sometimes but I haven't been able to coax it inside. I don't think it could be the same one."

Ben Franklin's line about all cats being gray popped into my head again and I realized that I'd begun to call the white cat "Frankie" in my mind, although I'd never said it aloud.

Dorothy's statement puzzled me. "But you're on the top floor. How would a cat get up that high unless it came from one of the other apartments?"

"I wondered about that too," she said. "There's a tree near the far end of the house. I saw the cat climb the tree, run along a limb and jump onto that long balcony that wraps around the fourth floor. It just hopped from one section of balcony to the next," She squinted at Frankie. "And apparently peeked into everybody's windows."

Frankie licked a paw, passed it daintily across her face, and looked the other way.

As usual, Aunt Ibby provided a delicious lunch on incredibly short notice, and as the three of us sat at the round table enjoying chicken salad sandwiches, fresh peaches, avocado slices and hot tea, my aunt explained once again her idea that Emily might have discovered something amiss at the Wildwood mall site, something that someone didn't want revealed.

"Trudy and Happy Shores?" Dorothy sounded incredulous. "I don't think so. Emily really liked them and I know they liked her. Trudy Shores told me so."

"It wouldn't have to be the Shoreses, dear. No indeed. A project of that magnitude involves many people. For instance, we don't know yet what that Dowgin man's involvement is. Is it possible that Emily might have learned something that *he* didn't want anyone to know about? Hmmm?"

"But Emily liked him too, and he seemed to like her. Maybe she was just too trusting of everybody."

"Some people are, and that's not always a bad thing. Usually they're trusted by others too."

Dorothy's expression brightened. "That's true. I think everybody trusted Emily."

"I wonder if James Dowgin trusted her with something that *someone else* didn't want her to know about," I said—almost to myself. "What about that?"

"And now that she's dead, he's back in Salem. What for?" Aunt Ibby refilled our tea cups. "And why would he send that warning note to Rupert? A warning note intended for you."

"According to Pete, Chief Whaley has finally come around to the idea that Emily's death might not have been an accident, so the police are seriously looking into the note and the fact that Dowgin delivered it. I don't think it'll take long for them to figure it all out."

"Meanwhile," Dorothy said. "The whole class is investigating."

"Really?" One of Aunt Ibby's eyebrows shot up. "The whole class? How so?"

I told her about the picture of the Steelers man on the big screen and how the class had made observations about him. "It seemed to fit into my lesson plan. A good exercise in investigational skills."

"I guess that's not actually meddling in police business," she said, "but you must tell Pete what you've observed."

"Already done," I assured her. "We'd better get back to school. Thanks for lunch."

"My pleasure," she said, "and I'm so happy to have met

you, Dorothy. Please come again soon. I'd love to hear about your home in Alaska."

"It's nothing like this one, believe me," Dorothy said. "And thank you. I'd love to come back."

We said good-bye to the cats, who, along with Aunt Ibby, followed us to the front door. O'Ryan watched from the window while my aunt engaged the alarm system but Frankie scooted out the door ahead of us.

"Looks like she's more of an outdoor cat," I watched her run around the corner of the house heading for the backyard. "I'm surprised that she came inside at all."

"It was pretty rainy this morning." Dorothy climbed into the passenger seat. "Cats don't like getting wet."

I made a U-turn around the Civil War monument and started back to the Tabby. "True. It's clearing up nicely. Hopefully, our early morning shoot will be successful tomorrow. Are you coming?"

"I'm planning to. Hilda's going to pick me up. By the way, would you mind if Dakota Berman joins us? I told him about it and I know he must have been disappointed when it got washed out today."

"We'd welcome him. I'll bet he has some information to share about some of those old graves."

"Probably. *If* you can get him talking. He's awfully quiet. I've tried several times to get him to share what he remembers about Emily, but haven't had much luck so far."

"That's too bad."

"Oh, he doles out little bits of information sometimes. Enough to convince me he knew her better than he's letting on."

"Oh?" That was a surprise. "What do you mean? What did he say about her?"

"Most of it was pretty general but once he said that she sometimes let him set up his easel on her balcony because the light is so much better than in his dark little place in the basement."

"That was kind of her."

"Uh-huh. She was kind. He used to use the balcony of the apartment next door while it was vacant, but when the new people moved in he asked if he could use hers."

"And she was okay with that?"

"Yeah." Dorothy sounded doubtful. "But she let him use his pass key and paint up there when she wasn't home. I think he might have been hinting that I should do the same."

"What did you say?"

"He didn't actually ask, you know. Just hinted around about how much he appreciated it. So I just flat out told him I wouldn't be comfortable with an arrangement like that."

"Good. I wouldn't like it either." We pulled into the Tabby parking lot with five minutes to spare before class time. "Are you thinking the arrangement with Dakota might have been more than friendly?" I asked. "Because if you are, that could be important information to share with the police."

She shrugged. "I don't know. The thought had crossed my mind of course. He is such a handsome guy, and Emily wasn't in a relationship with anyone else as far as I know. I really don't have any kind of proof."

I locked the 'vette and we crossed the lot, stepping over remaining puddles. "You could talk to Pete about it. You don't need to prove anything."

"Okay. If you think I should."

"I do." We entered the Tabby's front door just in time to see Therese, Hilda and Shannon approaching with varicolored boxes and bags indicating visits to several of Salem's specialty shops and fashion boutiques. Together we climbed the stairs to the mezzanine where the twins were already seated facing the TV watching an old rerun of *Family Feud.*

Roger stood when we approached. "Ms. Barrett, we were thinking . . ."

"Lee," I interrupted.

"Right. Lee. Anyway, we were thinking maybe Ray and I could leave early today. We need to go home and change into our security guard uniforms and we still have to drive to Foxboro."

"You guys got the security gig? Cool." Shannon tossed her pink-and-purple bag onto an empty chair and took her usual seat.

"That's great." Helga added her bag to the pile. "But you really think you can find that man among a sea of yellow-and-black Steelers shirts?" She consulted her phone. "There are sixty-six thousand, eight hundred and twenty-nine seats in Gillette Stadium and this game is probably a sellout."

"It'll be a challenge," Ray admitted. "But it's worth a shot."

"The worst that can happen is you two get to see a game free." Therese said.

Roger smiled broadly. "And we get paid for it. What do you say, Ms. Barrett? Lee? Can we leave early?"

"Yes, of course. Leave whenever you like. I'm sure we'll all be watching the game tonight."

"Looking for you two," Shannon promised. "Bet you guys look cute in uniforms."

Neither twin replied, but couldn't hide identical smiles.

"Why don't you go along now," I told them. "We're going to read a chapter on creative strategy. You can catch up later." I passed out the Advertising and Promotion textbooks and reminded the twins of our early morning cemetery photo shoot. "If the game keeps you up too late, don't worry about it. We'll take plenty of pictures for you."

We'd really need some creative strategy if we were going to pull off our after-Halloween extravaganza. There wasn't a big budget to work with so every bit of talent and ingenuity we could muster would be needed. I was pleased with the dedication and interest the group displayed—whether tramping uphill in a maybe-haunted cemetery or diving into a thick textbook. The afternoon seemed to fly by as we took notes, brainstormed and generally immersed ourselves in promotional possibilities.

When the bell announced five o'clock, I made sure that Dorothy had a ride home, reminded everyone once again to check the weather report in the morning and, if ground fog was indicated, we'd meet on Howard Street at six A.M.

# CHAPTER 28

Pete and I try to watch the Pats games together whenever we can. His shift wouldn't be over until a little after the kickoff, so we agreed to meet at Greene's Tavern. It isn't too far from the police station and I feel perfectly at ease there, even without Pete. I know the owner, Joe Greene, and his daughter Kelly had been one of my students the previous year. I took a seat at the end of the bar, facing the door, and put my purse down on the stool beside me, saving it for Pete. I was happy to see Kelly there. She'd landed a position as an intern at a Boston TV station, but often helped out at the tavern.

"Lee! Glad to see you." She gave me a hug across the bar. "Pete coming later?"

"As soon as he gets off. How are you doing? Loving the TV job?"

"I do." She grinned. "I learned so much from your course. Is this year's class as much fun as we were? Therese still drops by sometimes and she says you've got a couple of ex-cops, a woman from Alaska, and you take field trips to the cemetery."

"All true and it's a good group so far," I told her. "Your class wasn't all fun and games, you know!"

Her expression turned serious. "You've got that right; but we still learned a lot. You want a light beer while you're waiting for Pete?"

"Yes, please." I looked at the Budweiser clock behind her. "Kickoff in about twenty minutes. We'll probably have pizza or something later."

She looked toward the door. "Place'll start filling up soon. Big game. Wish I could be there."

"The two ex-cops you mentioned? They're twins. Roger and Ray Temple. They're working security tonight at the stadium."

"Cool. They get to watch the game and get paid for it too."

"That's exactly what they said." I dropped my voice. "They're also looking in the crowd for a particular Steelers fan Pete's interested in talking to. We're working it into our course on investigative reporting."

"That's even cooler, though I'm surprised that Pete let you do it."

I didn't know exactly how to respond to that, so I didn't say anything.

"Uh-oh. He doesn't know about it?"

"Not yet. They just thought it up today. I'm going to tell him about it tonight." I knew I sounded defensive. "It's definitely a long shot. What are the chances of finding one guy in all those thousands of people? Anyway they volunteered. Self-imposed homework."

Kelly smiled and went to wait on another customer, but came right back. "Why does Pete want to talk to the Steelers fan? What did he do?"

*I've said too much. That's what happens when I meddle.*

"Probably nothing at all. Forget I mentioned it."

"Okay." She made a zipper motion across her lips. "But if it *is* anything, you have to promise to tell me."

"Promise," I said. "But I think the guy is just a regular Steelers fan who isn't involved in anything suspicious at all. Just a random picture I took of a man at a fair."

I hoped very much that I was right about that.

Kelly was correct about the place filling up fast. Patrons poured into the long room, many opting for booths and tables and quite a few at the bar. I had to explain more than once that I was saving the seat next to me, and some people didn't seem too pleased about it. The game was well into the first quarter when I looked up and saw Pete approaching. I snatched up my purse and waved.

"Over here, Pete."

"Sorry I'm late, babe. No score yet?" He sat on the stool and motioned to Kelly.

"Not yet. Tom Brady's been waiting for you to get here I guess."

"Good old Tom." He put his arm around my shoulders and pulled me close for a brief kiss on the cheek. "How was your day?"

"It went well. This class is really into learning everything they can. They did an excellent job of analyzing that picture, don't you think?"

"That fancy screen makes a difference. The chief said he'd like to come by the school some time and take a look at it. Okay with you?"

"Are you kidding? We'd be thrilled with the attention. Chief Whaley. Wow."

"Yeah. We blew that picture up as much as we could but it's not the same quality as yours I'm sure. Of course, the whole thing is probably nothing." Pete thanked Kelly and sipped his beer. "The man is likely just a football fan who happened to tag along behind us."

"I think so too." I took a deep breath. "The Temple twins have volunteered to do a little extra homework." I watched his face.

"Homework? About the guy in the Steelers shirt?" There was a little cop-voice edge to the words and he didn't take his eyes from the TV.

"Yeah. They had a chance to work security at the game tonight. So they're going to try to find him. Ask to see his ticket. Get his name for you."

"And you said it was okay?"

"Sure." I sounded defensive again. "It was their idea. They wanted to do it. Anyway, what chance do they have of spotting one person in a crowd that size?" I pointed at the screen just as the Patriots scored a TD and the whole place erupted in cheers.

We both stood up and joined in the yelling. After the extra point, the room quieted and a commercial came on. Pete gave a long sigh. "I know Ray and Roger are ex-cops. They know, more or less, what they're doing. But the rest of your people are rank amateurs. They could get hurt. They could get *you* hurt. Don't encourage any more playing detective." His tone softened. "Dorothy's sister is dead. You have been threatened. We may have been followed at the fair. This is not an eighth-grade science experiment. For God's sake, Lee. I love you. I don't want anything to happen to you and I can't be with you every minute."

His look was so sincere, so forlorn, it made me feel guilty. "I'm sorry," I whispered. "I'm sorry."

"Just try to be more careful." He took my hand, looking into my eyes. "Please try not to do things that can put you in harm's way."

I didn't answer right away. Was a predawn trip to a cemetery in the harm's way category?

Another touchdown gave me a little time to think. The

Steelers scored it, so loud boos replaced cheers and all eyes were on the screen while they made the conversion. More boos.

When things calmed down, I said, "We're going to do some cemetery photography tomorrow for the Day of the Dead brochure."

"Pictures of grungy old tombstones?" He smiled. "Sounds like fun."

"Tombstones in the morning mist. Kind of spooky."

"Morning mist?"

"Ground fog. Six-thirtyish."

"Photo shoot in the dark?" Cop voice back.

"Sunrise. We'll all be together. The whole class, along with a ghost tour guide. What could go wrong?"

His expression softened. "Well, I guess there's safety in numbers like that. Sounds like a damp, soggy, creepy field trip to me though. Have fun."

The game was at halftime by then, with the score tied seven-seven. We ordered a large onion and pepperoni pizza and turned the conversation to more pleasant and less controversial things—like football and plans to spend a weekend in Maine sometime soon.

We both paid special attention between plays to the crowd shots and the close-ups of Foxboro fans. I guess we were halfway hoping—and at the same time doubting—that we'd see the man who'd followed us around at the Topsfield fair.

Hilda had been right about the sea of people wearing yellow-and-black Steelers shirts. And with the fast panning action of the camera, they all looked pretty much alike to me. We did spot one familiar face though. A clear shot showed Happy Shores seated in the first row, midfield with some Patriots front office executive types.

Pete leaned forward, concentrating on the image. "Happy looks happy all right."

"Who wouldn't be with those seats," I said. "Must be nice."

"They haven't announced a new date for the groundbreaking thing yet. I heard they're planning now to demo the old buildings first. I might take my nephews over to watch. Kids like that kind of stuff. Boom! Flattened."

"I watched when they were taking down St. Joseph's Church," I said. "It was exciting and sad at the same time. Aunt Ibby is still upset about the old Salem depot and the Paramount Theater being destroyed."

"There's nothing historic or beautiful about the diaper laundry and the others. Good riddance."

We jumped out of our seats again as the Patriots scored again. Fourteen to seven. The mood in the tavern was upbeat. They scored again. Joe Greene bought a round for the house. There was no more talk about the graveyard or poor dead Emily or threatening notes. There was pizza and beer and the Patriots defeated the Steelers. All was right with our world.

Pete followed me home in his car, then walked with me to the door. We both had to get up early—me especially—so he didn't come inside. We shared a good night kiss on the back steps, and he waited until I unlocked the door and was safely inside before he left.

O'Ryan was waiting for me, and Aunt Ibby's lights were out so I tiptoed up the creaky back stairway with O'Ryan hurrying ahead on big, silent cat feet. He was already inside, via the cat door, when I got all the locks undone and joined him in the living room.

I'd just reached the kitchen and clicked on the light switch when my phone buzzed. I fished it out of my purse. "Hello?"

"Ms. Barrett? Lee? This is Roger. Roger Temple."

"Yes, Roger. That was quite a game."

"Sure was. Look, I wanted to let you know we really looked for that guy every minute during the game. Ray even missed the second TD."

"Oh, that's a shame. Thanks though, for giving it a good try. It was, as you said, a longshot."

"Yup. Sure was." Short pause. "We didn't find him till *after* the game was over."

I wasn't sure I'd heard that right. "You *did* find him?"

"Sure did. We're on our way home now. Couldn't wait to call you." There was a shuffling noise. "Wait a minute. Ray wants to talk."

"Hi Lee. This is Ray." I could almost hear the grin in his voice. "Son of a gun walked right up to me and asked directions to the P10 parking lot. I didn't recognize him right away. Wasn't wearing that Steelers shirt, y'know? Had a Steelers cap, but a plain shirt."

Roger interrupted. "We were parked over there too, so we just talked to him, friendly like, about the game, and told him we'll walk him over there and help him find his truck."

Ray spoke again. "You were right. It's maroon."

Roger laughed. "We were just chatting him up, telling him about being twins, and he says he's got a brother too, but not a twin."

I couldn't bear the suspense any longer. "Ray! Roger! Get to the point! Who the hell is he?"

"His name is Billy. Actually it's William but he goes by Billy. Billy Dowgin. How about that?"

I sat down on the Lucite chair next to the kitchen window. "You mean, out of six thousand, eight hundred and twenty-nine people at that game, this man walked right up to you?"

"Honest to God, Lee. That's what happened. We're still laughing about it. Son of a gun just walked right up to us."

"And his name is Dowgin. Billy Dowgin." This conversation had started to take on an eerie, almost nightmarish quality.

"The same name as the note messenger. Right?"

"So it seems. Tell me, did he give you guys any more information?"

"We have no authority to ask him any questions. We're just security. But it's a bit of a hike to that parking lot you know, so we talked back and forth about different things. We told him we were retired police officers. He said he was a department store manager in Philly. Here on vacation."

Roger spoke again. "We told him about the Tabby being an old time department store. He said he'd like to see it. So who knows? He might walk right in some day."

"I guess he might. Good job, you two. I'll tell Pete what you found out." The thought of Billy Dowgin wandering into my classroom was too crazy to believe. I hoped Pete could make some sense of it. "Will you be joining us at Howard Street in the morning? Six o'clock?"

"We'll be there." That was Ray. "I can hardly wait to tell the girls. They'll never believe it. Good night. See you in the morning."

It *was* too crazy to believe. I began to wonder who was stalking who. I punched in Pete's number.

# CHAPTER 29

I was glad I'd already told Pete what the twins had planned for their football game surveillance. Otherwise this latest bombshell would have been pretty difficult to explain. I began as soon as he answered.

"I don't know whether this is a good thing or a bad thing, but here goes. The twins actually did find the Steeler guy at the game. Or maybe he found them. I'm not sure at all what's going on."

I repeated the whole story, just as Ray and Roger had relayed it to me. Pete didn't interrupt even once. His silence bothered me, but I kept going right up to the part where it was possible that Billy Dowgin might walk into my classroom. "What if he does?" I asked. "What do I do then?"

He sounded calm, composed, not coplike. "Take it easy, babe. The parking lot meeting may have been a coincidence, that's true. But you know how I feel about coincidences."

I knew.

"If it isn't a coincidence, this Dowgin *was* following us in Topsfield and *is* interested in you. We know his brother delivered the note to Pennington. The chief's been analyzing it. Was it actually a threat, or is somebody trying to warn you about something?" Concern had crept into his voice by then. "I'm going to wake up a sheriff and deputize the twins. They'll be with you during the day and I'll be with you as much of the rest of the time as I can. It won't take long for us to pick up one or both of the Dowgins."

"What should I do? Do I just go about business as usual?"

"Yes. But be aware of who's around you. Don't go anywhere alone. If you feel nervous about anything at all, call the station. I'll leave word to send a cruiser, wherever you are, no matter where, no matter what time. You understand?"

"I do. I feel better, talking to you. I don't like this—whatever it is. And I'm worried about Dorothy. She's at the center of it all. To tell you the truth, I'm worried about all of them—all my students. They seem to think it's an adventure, a class project, a mystery for them to solve."

"Keep the classwork academic. Concentrate on the cemetery stuff. Get away from the note and the Dowgin brothers as much as you can. We're keeping an eye on Dorothy, and we're taking another look at the circumstances of her sister's death. That seems to have been the beginning of all this. As a matter of fact, I'm planning a trip into Boston to talk to her doctor again about those sleeping pills."

"I hope this will all be over with soon," I said.

"Want me to come over?"

"No. It's late and I'm all safely locked in with my guard cat. I just needed to talk to you. To tell you what the twins had done."

"It was probably a good thing, even if it would have given the chief fits if he'd known about it. At least we have a name now."

"Right. I hope there are no more Dowgin brothers though."

"Hope not. Good night. I love you. Talk to you tomorrow. You still planning the soggy creepy cemetery visit in the morning?"

"Yes. You said it would be okay."

"That's right. It is. But I may have a cruiser do an extra drive-by."

"Thanks. Good night. I love you."

I put the phone down on the table and leaned back in my chair and reached out to pat O'Ryan who'd jumped up onto the windowsill while I was talking to Pete. He leaned his head into my stroking hand and gave my palm a lick. "I love you too, O'Ryan," I told him, meaning it sincerely. "I'm so glad you're here with me."

"Mmmrow," he said, and turned his big head toward the window. I twisted in my chair and followed his gaze. The white cat, looking gray in the dimness, was on the side yard fence.

"There's Frankie," I told him. "That's what I've named her. Okay with you?"

"Meh," he said, which I took to mean he had no objection. I set the alarm for five o'clock, laid out my clothes for the next day, prepared the coffeemaker for fast morning duty, checked the weather channel for the latest forecast and fell into bed.

O'Ryan was already up when the alarm sounded, and waiting for his breakfast when I stumbled out of the bedroom and headed down the hall to the bathroom. A look out the window told me we'd picked the right day: Winter Street was already socked in with fog, so Howard Street was sure to be perfect for our photos.

By five-thirty, dressed in jeans, sweater, jacket, boots and with an old knit cap pulled over my hair, I filled a to-go cup with coffee and said good-bye to the cat who was hunched over his red bowl of kitty kibble.

I tiptoed down the stairs—this hour was early even for Aunt Ibby to be awake—and hurried to the garage. I sneaked a look toward the neighbor's fence, but if Frankie was there, she blended in with fog so well she was invisible.

I thought I'd be the first one to arrive, but Hilda and Dorothy were waiting in Hilda's car with the heater running. Kelsey Roehl stood inside the gate, back to us with arms outstretched, which I presumed might be some sort of ghost-repellant ritual. By the time I'd climbed out of the 'vette the twins had arrived followed by Therese, Shannon and Dakota Berman—who'd apparently shared an Uber ride. I was both surprised and gratified by the interest they'd all shown, especially on a dreary, foggy, early morning at such an unlovely destination.

By the time everyone had gathered at the entrance, Kelsey had finished her whatever it was, and greeted us with a welcoming smile. "Welcome to my world," she said, "of ghoulies and ghosties and long leggety beasties and things that go bump in the night."

Hilda looked up from her smart phone. "Old Scottish prayer, right?"

"Right!" Kelsey sounded surprised. "Are you Scottish?"

"No," Hilda said. "Googleish."

Our laughter broke the tension of the moment. Shannon introduced Dakota to those who hadn't yet met him. Polite remarks were exchanged and, single file, we followed Kelsey up the hill on the right side of the cemetery. Fog is known to muffle sound and the sounds of passing cars sounded very far away. Workmen had not yet arrived at the construction site next door, so all was silent.

"Want to separate and head in different directions for

a variety of angles before this fog lifts and we lose the magic?" Therese called from just behind Kelsey. "Cameras ready everybody?"

I could see the top of the tall Richard Manning monument just ahead, poking up through the cloudy mist. Roger (or Ray) answered from behind me. "We'll go up near the ghost tree, okay?"

Ray (or Roger) responded, "No such thing as ghosts."

"Dorothy and I are following Therese and Kelsey," Hilda announced. "We don't want to get lost in this place. Shannon and Dakota already went down front where Dakota likes to make those fake rubbing things."

That left me standing alone beside—or above—the Manning/Hawthorne remains, vaguely wondering what the connection between those families might be. "Okay," I called in a general answer to all of their fog-shrouded pronouncements. "Everybody meet me back at the same gate we came in through when you finish shooting."

There was no response, but I assumed everyone knew enough to do that anyway. The sun had started to come up which made the fog shimmer. It was quite beautiful, in a weird sort of way, and I stepped ahead into that glistening grayness.

Not a good move.

One booted foot hit a muddy patch of loose earth and I felt myself sliding sideways down a little incline. It was a short drop and I felt the low wrought-iron fence that borders the place with my right hand, so I knew approximately where I was. I wasn't hurt, but the feeling of falling, of being out of control, is unpleasant under the best of circumstances. In near darkness, with limited vision, in a graveyard, it's truly distasteful—and in this case, quite damp.

I scrambled to my feet, still holding onto the fence, and moved ahead slowly and carefully, wishing every second that the damned fog we'd spent two days hoping for would go away.

My left foot hit something soft. I shuffled my right foot ahead and it touched the same thing. Leaning forward, I gingerly reached down with my left hand. There was something in my path, something large and wet and made of cloth. Moving my hand gently upward on the thing, the texture beneath my fingers changed. Still wet, and cold, but not cloth. It wasn't until I touched its mouth that I knew what I'd found.

If it wasn't so terribly cliché under the circumstances, I'd say my scream that foggy morning would have wakened the dead.

# CHAPTER 30

I clawed and climbed my way up that little embankment, yelling at the top of my lungs. The twins were the first to reach me. The ghost tree they'd chosen to photograph was just past the Manning tomb and the two of them came hurtling out of the fog to where I'd landed, half standing, half crawling on the straggly grass.

"Jesus, Lee. What happened? Are you hurt?" That was Ray.

"There's somebody . . . something . . . a face. . . ." I struggled for words as Roger, with an arm around my shoulders, gently lifted me to my feet.

"Can you walk? Are you okay?"

By that time the others had begun to appear and the fog had begun to lift. Dorothy stood silent and Kelsey peered at me, eyes wide. "You saw a face? Was it an old man?"

"I didn't see anything. I touched it. It's down there." I pointed in the direction of the gulley next to the fence, but turned my head away, not daring to look.

"Come on, Lee. It's okay. There's nothing there." Hilda was on one side of me and Therese on the other, with the twins following behind. "There's a bench over here. Come and sit down." I allowed myself to be led away from the Manning tomb—from the fence—from that thing below, to the comparative comfort of a cement bench, positioned on one of the highest points in the cemetery. I sat obediently, trying to force my brain into gear, to make sense of what was happening there in the fast-dissipating fog.

Shannon and Dakota were the last of the group to respond to the commotion and I overheard their worried, whispered questions to Kelsey. "Did she really see a ghost? Do you think it was old Giles Corey?"

The guide's answer was guarded. "I hope not. I mean if she did I hope it wasn't *him*. If it was, something really bad will happen in Salem. It always does."

"I didn't see a ghost," I insisted, surprising myself with the strength of my voice. "Not a ghost. Something—somebody real. Somebody's down there." I stood, legs wobbly, and pointed again to the gully beside the fence. Then, irrelevantly, "And I dropped my camera down there too."

"I'll get it for you, Ms. Barrett. Don't worry." Dakota Berman spoke softly. "I know my way around this place, fog or no fog."

"Wait a minute, kid," Roger put a restraining hand on Dakota's arm. "We'll do it. Ms. Barrett—Lee—she saw something there that scared the bejesus out of her. We'll check it out." He pulled the collar of his jacket aside and I caught a flash of something shiny. "It's okay. I'm a deputy. So's Ray."

*How did Pete do that so fast? He must have deputized them last night.*

The twins lowered themselves into the space next to the fence, feet first from a sitting position.

*They're going to have wet bottoms.*

I could see both their heads and shoulders above the

grass. They were each looking down. Ray was the first to speak. "Holy shit."

Roger held up both hands. "Stand back, everybody. We have a situation here. I'm calling 911. Try not to disturb anything."

The two men pulled themselves up over the bank, Roger with his phone to his ear. "Howard Street Cemetery, west gate," he said. "That's right. A male. Deceased."

Barely a minute had passed when we heard the scream of a siren and saw the flashing lights of a police car.

"Must have been right in the neighborhood," Roger said.

*Pete's extra drive-by.*

The cruiser pulled up, quickly followed by two more. The twins, along with Kelsey, went out onto the sidewalk to meet the approaching police. Therese and Hilda leaned over the nearby fence watching the action below. The officer in the lead had his gun drawn. I retreated to the bench with Shannon and Dorothy following. None of us sat on it though, heeding the command not to disturb anything, and for a long moment, none of us spoke, just listened. There was the crackle of police radios and cross talk and another siren screaming as an ambulance approached.

*No need for an ambulance. Whoever I touched down there is dead. Very dead.*

By this time a crowd had started to gather. Word of trouble gets around fast in Salem. Police bands on home radios are pretty common here. The sun was well over the horizon by then and the fog was completely gone. The ambulance attendants approached the west gate just as I spotted the black car belonging to the medical examiner pulling in next to the construction site. I was acquainted with the M.E. We'd met before on a couple of unfortunate occasions.

"So it wasn't a ghost you saw, Lee." Shannon was

wide-eyed. "A body. Wow. No wonder you screamed. What'd it look like?"

"I didn't really see it," I admitted, surprised that my voice sounded so normal. "I kind of tripped over it. I felt it."

"Eeew." Hilda wrinkled her nose. "You actually *felt* it? I've never even *seen* a dead person, let alone *touched* one."

"You've never seen one?" Therese was incredulous. "Don't you go to funerals?"

"I've been to funerals," Hilda said. "I just don't look at the dead person."

"I saw my grandmother when she was dead," Shannon said. "But that's a lot different than what happened to Lee. What about you, Dakota? Ever see a dead person?"

"I don't want to talk about it. I'm going over to see what the cops are doing." Dakota hurried away from us, joining the twins next to the Manning tomb.

"What's wrong with him?" Therese asked.

"He doesn't want to talk about it because he's the one who found my sister," Dorothy said. "He told me."

That surprised me. Pete hadn't told me that and it wasn't in the newspaper report either. But of course, Dakota was the building super, with keys to all the apartments, so it made sense that he'd be the one who'd opened Emily's door when her mother hadn't been able to reach her by phone that day.

"Oh, I'm sorry I asked him that, and I've made you sad too, Dorothy." Shannon apologized. "I'm so sorry."

"Not your fault," Dorothy said. "But who's the poor guy they just found? That's what I'd like to know. Look. They're bringing him up on a stretcher."

We all turned to look. The body was wrapped with a dark blue blanket or maybe it was a body bag. Whatever it was, we could tell that it was wet. The clothing on whoever was under it must have soaked through. Another siren announced Pete's arrival on the scene. He hardly ever uses it when he's driving his Crown Vic, but he was clearly in a hurry.

Pete stopped and spoke to the uniformed officers first, then to the M.E., who'd followed the stretcher to a waiting van. I watched as he moved the dark blue covering away from the top of the form on the stretcher. He nodded, replaced the fabric, then pulled out his notebook. The stretcher bearers continued to the van with their sad burden and the M.E. returned to his own car. With one of the cruisers leading the grim parade, all three vehicles moved away from the cemetery and proceeded down Bridge Street. Pete watched them depart, then turned and headed up the sidewalk to the west gate. I waved, a little fluttery wave, knowing he'd already seen me—and so very glad and grateful to see him.

Pete hurried up the steep rise to where we'd all gathered behind the empty bench, the twins flanking us, Ray on the left of the group, Roger on the right. "You've all had quite a morning," he said, "and you've handled a bad situation really well. Chief Whaley says you can all go back to the school now. I'll follow you over there. Lee, you and the Temples actually saw the . . . um—body, so we'll have some questions for you today. If we have questions for the rest of you, we'll conduct those interviews at the school too. We're yellow-taping the west side of the cemetery while we check out a few things, so we'll ask you to exit on the other side."

The questions from the class came quickly.

"Do you know who the man is?"

"What happened to him?"

"How did he get so wet?" Ray wanted to know. "It didn't rain last night."

"That's true," Roger said. "Looked like his clothes were soaked through."

Pete held up both hands. "I can't discuss it right now. You all know that. Does everybody have a ride back to the Tabby?"

"We have three cars between us," Hilda said. "We can fit everybody in okay."

"Good. Lee, I'd like to speak with you a minute before you leave."

"Of course." I moved closer to him, then looked back at the group. "Who's riding with me?"

Shannon raised her hand. "Me, if that's all right with you. Kelsey's already left and Dakota's going to walk home. Pete said it was okay."

Pete nodded his agreement and I pulled the keys from my pocket and handed them to her. "Here. Let yourself in. I won't be long."

I watched as the group trudged across the grass, passing orderly rows of tombstones, once again single file behind Kelsey, who—I could tell by her gestures—continued to deliver her ghost tour information.

Pete put both hands on my shoulders. "God, Lee. Are you all right? The twins are worried about you. So am I." He pulled me close for a moment and whispered, "I wish I could be with you every minute," then stepped back and looked into my eyes. "There's something I need to tell you before you leave. Roger and Ray already know about it, so they may have told the others by now."

I frowned. "What is it?"

"The body. It's James Dowgin. No doubt about it."

"Oh dear. Pete, was he . . . was he murdered?"

"I don't know. The doc says no visible sign of trauma from his cursory exam. We'll know better when we get him to the morgue. Are you sure you're all right to drive?"

"Yes. I'm fine. I promise. I'd tell you if I wasn't."

"Okay. I'll be along just as soon as I finish up here."

"They're not going to close the whole cemetery are they?"

"No. We're only taping the area where he was found and the west gate. Probably the parking lot outside the gate too. We've informed the city to keep the riding mowers out for a while."

I headed for the parking lot where Shannon waited. Pulling my phone from my pocket, I speed dialed Aunt Ibby. Between the various media outlets and Salem's efficient gossip grapevine, I knew that news of a fresh body in an old cemetery would travel fast. I wanted her to hear it from me first.

I wasn't first.

"Maralee, dear! I was just about to call you. Is it true? Someone found a dead man in the same cemetery where you went to take pictures?"

"It's true." I kept my voice calm and steady. "I'm just leaving to go back to the school right now. The police have everything under control and Pete's going to meet us all at the Tabby. It was pretty frightening, but everyone is okay. I'll call you as soon as I can and tell you all about it."

"Well then dear, if you're sure you're all right." She paused. "You didn't actually have to *see* the poor dead man, did you?"

I hesitated for about a second, then answered truthfully. "No. I didn't see him."

*But I did actually put my hand directly onto poor James Dowgin's dead mouth.*

# CHAPTER 31

Shannon was in the passenger seat of the 'vette waiting for me. She'd locked the car. Smart girl. I tapped on the window and after a moment of studying the instrument panel, she opened the doors and I slid into the driver's seat.

"Well, this morning didn't go exactly as planned, did it?" I said, stating the obvious as I pulled out onto Bridge Street.

"Sure didn't. That was awful—about you tripping over that body—the Dowgin guy everybody's been looking for. The twins told us. Makes me shiver just thinking about it."

"I'm guessing there'll be a few nightmares about it in my future."

"In Dakota's future too I guess. Did you hear what Dot said about him finding her sister's body?"

"I did," I said. "She hadn't told me about that before. I guess Dakota hadn't mentioned it to you either?"

"No. But then, I haven't known him very long and he's so darn quiet. He's told me hardly anything about himself."

"Strong silent type, huh?"

She smiled at that. "Yeah, but he sure is cute. And those eyes really get me!"

The thought of the cat face with Dakota's eyes gave me a chill. I was glad to pull up to the Tabby where there might be some sort of normalcy. "Here we are," I said, a little too heartily. "I hope we got some good shots for the brochure."

"Did you get your camera back?" Shannon asked. "I heard you say you dropped it when—you know."

I'd forgotten to ask Pete about my camera. "I didn't," I told her as I eased the 'vette into my accustomed parking space. "But I hadn't taken any shots yet anyway. I hope they found it. It's a good one. Takes better pictures than my phone does."

"I hope you get it back. Dot says that her mother is sending her sister's phone to her." Shannon stepped out of the car and faced me across the convertible top. "That's a little creepy, if you ask me. I mean hearing a dead person's last messages or seeing their last pictures."

"I hadn't given that much thought," I told her as I scanned the lot, noting that the other two cars were already there. "But yeah, it would be kind of creepy." I thought about my dead parents. If smart phones had been invented back then, would I have wanted to see and hear those things? I still don't know the answer to that.

I locked the car and we entered through the diner, thinking that some of the class might have stopped to warm up with some coffee, which sounded like a good idea to me. I was right. All of them were seated at the usual table even though it was a little early for lunch.

Shannon and I joined them. It was, as one might expect under the circumstances, a more subdued group than usual. Even our regular waitress who liked to kid around with us spoke in a hushed tone, asking quietly, "Coffee, Ms. Barrett?"

"Yes, thanks,"

I knew it was my job to get the students out of this pervasive gloom and back into learning mode, but from the looks of the faces around the table, it wasn't going to be easy. I decided to plunge right in.

"This morning was bad," I said, "and until the police get things straightened out I'm afraid we could be in for more unpleasant surprises. I want all of you to remember that you are pursuing careers in television, which may often involve the seamy side of life. You're all familiar I'm sure with the old media adage—'if it bleeds, it leads.' Well, you had a firsthand experience this morning. Did any of you come away with useful video of the happenings at the cemetery? Video that might interest WICH-TV?" I looked around. Some of the faces had brightened already. "What are you doing sitting around drinking coffee? Call the station." I rattled off the station's number from memory. Bruce Doan would want those images right away. "This could mean your first TV credit. Go for it."

Both twins, Therese and Hilda grabbed their phones. Ray stood and headed for the door, phone to his ear, with Roger close behind. I hadn't had a chance to film anything at all and Dorothy and Shannon apparently felt that they'd not captured any images of importance either.

With the beginning of the school day still a good hour away, I suggested that those of us who didn't have videos to share might begin to write down our impressions of exactly what had happened at Howard Street. "Pete will be along soon to interview each of us, and having written notes to consult will be helpful, I'm sure. Shall we go up to the classroom?"

That's what we did. The room was quiet with only the sounds of pens scribbling on paper and the muted tap of laptops. The twins were first to rejoin us, both smiling.

They were followed by Therese and Hilda who looked pleased with themselves too.

"How'd it go?" I asked. "Was the station interested?"

"You bet," Ray said. "They told us all to send what we had. They're going to do a fast edit on it. Can we turn on the TV?"

"Sure."

Therese had already turned on WICH-TV's morning programming. Scott Palmer, speaking with what I perceived to be his "respect for the dead" voice, stood on the Howard Street side of the cemetery, with a good shot of some of the oldest gravestones in the background. I guessed that the police must still be working on the opposite side of the place or else Scott would have been smack in front of that west gate.

"An early morning 911 call brought Salem police to this historic cemetery—the second oldest in Salem. A group of students from the Tabitha Trumbull Academy of the Arts, Salem's newest school, were here for a predawn photo shoot, when one of them made a frightening discovery. A dead body was found at the edge of this graveyard, adjacent to the old Salem Jail and, legend tells us, near the site of the Salem Witch jail, where, in 1620, those accused of witchcraft were imprisoned. The identity of the deceased man found here at approximately six A.M. is being withheld pending notification of his family. WICH-TV has exclusive video of police activity at the site this morning, courtesy of the TV Production class at the Trumbull Academy." (This last pronouncement was met with smiles, thumbs-up signs and fist bumps from the assembled classmates.)

The video began in relative darkness with the camera panning across a long row of tombstones. Then, with the sky brightening, we saw red, white and blue lights of the approaching police cars and ambulance. The actual removal of the blanket-covered body had been captured with startling clarity. Then a zoom lens played across the faces of a crowd of onlookers as the body was placed on a gurney and trundled to a waiting police van.

I didn't really hear Scott Palmer's narration after that. I was busy trying to process one particular image which had flashed too quickly across the huge screen.

I'd seen the man's face for what seemed like only a nano-second, yet it was engraved on my consciousness. Recognition was immediate and terrifying. The idea that he'd been there on this day, at that moment, perhaps just a few feet away from where I'd fallen, froze me with fear. A plain black ball cap partially covered his face, but I knew immediately who he was, even though he wasn't wearing the Steelers shirt.

# CHAPTER 32

Had any of the others seen him? Within seconds that question was answered. Hilda waved in the direction of the screen. "Therese, can you back that thing up? Take it back to the crowd scene. I think I saw . . ."

Ray interrupted. "I saw him too. It was that guy we talked to at the game last night, right Roger?"

Roger agreed with his brother. Therese tapped a few buttons on the console and focused on the frame showing Billy Dowgin. He was in the row of people closest to the west gate.

"Hey, I think that was from one of yours, Roger," Ray said. "You were standing near the gate."

"Could be mine. I didn't notice him while I was shooting though. They did a good job splicing our stuff together. Looks like one of those big network multicamera jobs, doesn't it Lee?"

I found my voice. "Darn near. They did a good job all right, especially on such short notice, but you all did a great job. You kept filming in spite of all that was going on." My heart was pounding and I tried to keep the fear from sounding in my words. "That man, Billy Dowgin, was pretty close to us. Makes me wonder if the police noticed him there too."

"He must have known his own brother was laying there in the dirt." Therese sounded matter-of-fact. "Why else would he be hanging around?"

Ray's answer was ominous. "Maybe he didn't know. He could have been there just to watch us."

*To watch me. At the cemetery and at the fair and who knows where else?*

The paused frame showing Billy Dowgin still loomed on the TV when Pete, with two uniformed officers, strode into the room. "See you spotted him too," Pete said with a tilt of his head toward the screen. "Good work. We've already picked him up."

Relief replaced fear in an instant. I resisted a strong temptation to run across the room and into his arms, like the woman in those slow motion shampoo commercials. Instead I composed myself and said quite calmly, "That's welcome news, Pete. We've all made some notes on what went on this morning. Hope that'll be helpful."

A quick half-smile from Pete before he shifted into full cop mode and addressed the class. "Thank you. Officer Marr, Officer Costa and I will take your statements. I hope we won't take up too much class time and we appreciate your cooperation. Mr. Pennington has arranged for us to use three of the small study areas on the main floor." He pulled a sheet of paper from his pocket and read from it. "Ms. Mendez, if you'll follow Officer Marr downstairs, Ms. Alden please follow Officer Costa, and Ray Temple, you'll come along with me. This shouldn't take too long." A brief nod from Pete in my direction, and the three designated students, notes and laptops in hand, fell into step behind the three men and started down the stairs.

With half my class missing I went back to my standard

"Plan B"—the textbooks. "Let's look at chapter fifteen in the advertising and promotion books. It's on using the Internet as a powerful advertising tool. We'll be working on promoting *Dia de los Muertos* as economically as we can. Let's see what ideas we can come up with."

"What do you think they're talking about down there?" Shannon asked, opening her book and flipping through the pages.

"It's likely the standard stuff that they always ask witnesses," Roger said, opening his own book to the proper page. "Where were you standing? Did you have a clear view of whatever? Did you see whoever? That kind of stuff."

"I think it might be better if we don't discuss this among ourselves until after the interviews," I suggested. "Is that right, Roger?"

"Yes, Ms. Barrett, um—Lee. You're right."

"Well," Dorothy said, ignoring both of us. "We didn't have a clear view of anything. We were in a pea-soup fog."

"True," Roger agreed. "That was the point of our being there. But Ray and I saw something."

This was getting out of hand. "Okay," I said, using my Aunt Ibby librarian voice. "Hit the books."

That worked. The room grew quiet except for the usual Tabby sounds of student traffic and random loudspeaker announcements from Mr. Pennington. I'd already studied the chapter in question, both for class prep and—in a prior edition—at Emerson College in my student days, so I pulled out my own notes on the morning's happenings.

I'd noted all of us who were present. I gave the approximate time I'd arrived there. Weather conditions. Cars in the parking lot. Directions in the cemetery (as far as I could recall) that each of us had taken. My position when I'd slipped into the gully. How I'd tripped and touched the body. The wet body. I added that to my notes. I remembered that the clothing on the person was so saturated it had "squished" under my hands when I'd fallen forward against it. Was that important? I didn't know.

The interviews took longer than I'd expected. More than half an hour had passed and all three had finished reading the chapter before Pete and the two officers returned with the rest of my class.

Everybody looked normal. No signs of anxiety among them as they resumed their seats. Hilda even looked somewhat pleased, but that may have been because her interviewer, Officer Marr, was quite handsome. The second shift, Roger, Therese and Shannon, trooped out of the room and down the stairs, leaving me as the lone witness yet to be questioned. I guessed that was because Pete would do it later.

I repeated the textbook chapter number, but the three clearly wanted to talk about their respective interviews. I wanted to hear what they had to say too, so I didn't pull the librarian thing on them.

"I didn't have much to tell him," Dorothy said, "I mean about what went on in the fog. I was in the wrong place to see anything anyway. I told him what I knew about James Dowgin—him being a friend of Emily's and all. They asked me about Dakota Berman too, like where did he live before he came to Salem. I don't know. I told the cop he should go ask Dakota that stuff."

"What did he say?"

She shrugged. "Said somebody else was interviewing Dakota."

"Maybe Shannon can answer some of that," I said. "She seems to know him better than the rest of us do. How was your interview, Ray?"

"I can't tell you too much. I'm a deputy now, you know."

Did he puff out his chest a little when he said that? "But Pete was mostly interested in the part about us, me and Roger, finding the body."

"That was the awful part, wasn't it? Did you know right off who it was?"

"Yep. Right away. Looked just like his picture. Even had a peaceful look on his face." He held up one hand. "But hey, I shouldn't be talking so much. I know better. Deputy, you know."

"Has anyone talked to you yet, Lee?" Dorothy asked. "After all, you were the first one to know that the poor guy was dead."

"No. I haven't been called yet," I said. "I didn't know who it was but I was pretty sure that he—or she—was really dead."

"'Was really, most sincerely dead,'" Hilda sang the old tune from *The Wizard of Oz* softly, then looked around. "Ooops. Sorry. That was inappropriate. Couldn't help it. Everyone is so gloomy around here."

"You're right" I said. "Enough gloom. Back to work. While you were being interviewed we read about using the Internet as an advertising tool. We're going to need all the promotion we can get—as inexpensively as we can get it—for our video project."

"I was thinking some of the fog footage we got this morning. . . ." Hilda paused mid-thought. "Can it only have been this morning . . . what a long day."

"What about the footage?" I prompted.

"Oh, yeah. A picture of a tombstone might make a really good opening shot, with information, time, date and all that played across the part of the thing sticking up above the fog."

"Sounds good," Ray agreed.

"I like it," I said. "Let's read the chapter, then maybe

we'll run through the footage we shot again. See what might fit where."

With a minimum of grumbling, the three resumed their usual seats. I pulled out my Happy Shores notebook, turning to a fresh page and, once again, noted the happenings of that bizarre morning. This time I included several personal notations which, while not appropriate for a police report, might help me to make some sense of the situation.

Billy Dowgin—brother of James Dowgin—must have followed me to the fair. He may have been driving the truck I saw on Oliver Street. He was outside the cemetery this morning. Why is he watching me? Following me? Should I be afraid of him?

He may be trying to find me alone so he can harm me somehow. Why? Does he think I know something about Emily's murder? If it was a murder? What do I know about it? I think it has something to do with the soil sample she took with Billy's brother.

What if he isn't trying to harm me? Why else would he follow me? Idea: Is he trying to protect me? From who? What? Was James Dowgin trying to harm me? Is that why he's dead? Would his own brother kill him to protect me? Probably not. Then who wanted James dead? Why? Does Billy know who might have killed his brother? Does that mean he's in danger too? Were both of the Dowgins trying to protect me, not harm me?

*Wow! New concept! I need to tell Pete about this.*

I closed the book, returned it to my purse and looked around the room. My students were still reading. The TV screen was blank. I swung around in my swivel chair the way I used to when I was a kid—forgetting for the moment that a half-circle turn would bring me face to face with the giant black shoe.

Swirling colors. Twinkling lights. Darkness. Then a form drew closer. A woman. I didn't recognize her. She was pretty in a girl-next-door sort of way, with short brown shoulder-length hair, wide-set eyes and a sweet smile. She seemed to look directly at me, then put her finger to her lips. She winked, cupped her hand and put her ear to a wall.

Listening.

# CHAPTER 33

The vision faded away. The shoe was just a big, out-of-style shoe once again. I swung my chair around to its front-facing position just in time to greet the three returning from their interviews. I raised one hand in welcome, attempted a smile and tried to erase the lingering image of the listening woman.

Not too long ago seeing a scene like that in an inanimate object would have made me run screaming from the room. But somehow it had become a matter of course, something I'd learned to accept—but still something I dreaded. Now, within just a few seconds of a vision, I could face a room full of students with a smile and pretend there was nothing strange going on at all.

*I'm afraid I'm getting pretty good at it.*

There was no point in trying to dissuade the students from discussing their interviews with one another. And to be honest, I was as curious as the others.

Therese resumed her seat behind the news desk. "I thought the cop would only want to talk about the body in the cemetery. I wonder why he asked me about those

Shores people. Happy and Trudy. I barely know them. Did they ask any of the rest of you guys about them?"

Dorothy closed her textbook. "Officer Costa asked me about them too. In fact, he asked me the same questions over and over as if he thought I'd give a different answer."

"What did he want to know?" Hilda asked. "I only knew them because my parents bought a house from them once."

Dorothy frowned, then answered. "He kept asking me if Emily seemed to be afraid of either one of them. If she'd had any arguments or anything. I told him she seemed to be fond of them both. They liked her. She liked them."

That was the impression I'd had too. I could understand the question though. Emily had been at a party at the Shoreses' the night she died.

"He mentioned them to me too," Shannon said, "but mostly he wanted to talk about Dakota and if Dakota had ever talked to me about Emily or about that James Dowgin guy."

"Had he?" Ray asked.

"Yeah. A little. I told him what I could remember."

"Like what?" Roger had closed his textbook too.

Shannon looked from one twin to the other. "Dakota really felt bad about Dorothy's sister dying like that. She was nice to him. Used to let him paint on her balcony sometimes. But he didn't really know the Dowgin guy. Only saw him a couple of times with Emily. Never got introduced to him or anything."

"What did they want to know from you two? Ray? Roger?" Therese fixed Roger with a blue-eyed stare. "Come on. You can tell us. We're all in this together."

Roger looked at his brother and shrugged. "I guess it'd be okay. See, we not only found the body." He nodded in my direction. "I mean Lee actually found it but she didn't know what—or who—she'd found. Then we were the ones who caught up with Billy Dowgin at the game."

"Or he caught up with us," Ray pointed out. "Still don't know which."

"Did they ask you about the Shoreses?" I asked.

"Not me," Roger said. "You, Ray?"

"Nope."

"Hey," Dorothy's usual soft tones were replaced by louder, more urgent words. "Did any of you get the idea that they're actually looking into my sister's murder?"

"They didn't exactly call it murder," Hilda said, "but yeah, her name was mentioned and that's where all the questions about the Shores couple were coming from I think."

"Uh-oh." Therese pointed toward the mezzanine entrance and stage whispered, "Here comes Detective Mondello. Better change the subject."

I looked to where she pointed. So did all the others, as Pete strode toward us. He acknowledged the class, using his cop voice. Cop face too. "Thank you all for your cooperation. I'm going to borrow your teacher for a short time." He approached my desk. "Mr. Pennington says he'll sub for you if you like. Shouldn't take too long. Just a few questions."

I stood. "No need for a sub." I picked up the textbook we'd used and faced the students. "Okay, everybody, make a list of the useful strategies you learned from the chapter and apply them to the project. Remember our low budget."

Following Pete, I left the classroom and climbed the stairway to the second floor. "Mr. P. said we could use his office," he said, sounding like himself again. "More private."

"Okay," I said as we approached Mr. Pennington's open

door. "I've been thinking about the Dowgin brothers. Quite a lot."

"Not surprising," he said. "Want to talk about it?" We entered the office and Pete closed the door behind us. He sat in Mr. Pennington's chair behind the huge oak desk that had once belonged to Oliver Wendell Trumbull. I sat facing him.

"It's kind of a theory I thought up." I spoke hesitantly, searching for the right words. "I've been thinking that maybe we have the brothers all wrong. Maybe James Dowgin's note was meant to warn me, not threaten me. Maybe Billy Dowgin is watching, following me to protect me, not to harm me. What do you think?"

His expression was doubtful, but he nodded and said, "Worth thinking about. I'll run it by the chief. But for now, I'd like to ask you about the connections between Emily Alden and the Shores couple. Happy and Trudy."

I would have liked to talk about my theory instead, but hey. He's the cop. Not me.

"I'll tell you what I can but I don't know what I can add to what you've already learned."

"Sometimes we know things we don't know we know." He's told me that before . . . and he's always been right about it. Pete pulled the ever-present notebook from his inside jacket pocket.

"You told me that you'd called the Shoreses' office about James Dowgin once."

"Right. I was looking for information about him for Dorothy."

"What did you learn?"

"Nothing, really," I said. "They had a rehearsed line about him. I guess anyone who asked got the same story."

"What did they say? Can you remember?"

"I think so. It was something like 'there is no agent here

by that name. May I connect you with another of our happy agents?'"

Pete wrote in his notebook, then looked up. "That's it?"

"Afraid so. That's it."

"Did you ever see James Dowgin yourself? I mean before you found his body? Think carefully."

"Of course not. I would have told you if I had." I couldn't keep the little edge of annoyance from my voice.

"Maybe not in the Shoreses' office or here at the Tabby. Think outside the box."

"No. I'd never seen him before . . . wait a minute. Outside the box. Boxes. Shoe boxes!" I halfway stood up, then sat again. "I didn't really see him. I mean it wasn't really him. I didn't recognize him then but I'm sure it was him!"

Pete put down his pencil and spread his hands apart in a helpless gesture. "Could you make that a little clearer?"

"It was the pitchman. The shoe salesman. In the mirror. I mean in the vision. The shoes were in boxes."

"You told me about the shoe vision. I didn't know there was a man in the vision."

"It didn't mean anything at the time. But it *was* James Dowgin." The thought made me happy. "See? You were right again. I knew something I didn't know I knew."

"Good." He'd picked up his pencil again. "Any more visions I should know about? Even ones that didn't mean anything at the time?"

"There was one in the giant shoe today," I told him. "It was a young woman. I didn't recognize her. She was listening to something through a wall. She did this." I cupped my ear with one hand and put a finger to my lips with the other.

"I see. Want to try some more word association? Since the word boxes reminded you of something, how about the word wall? Ring any bells?"

I squeezed my eyes shut, thinking about walls.

*Walls. A wall. The Berlin wall. The wall on the southern border. The Great Wall of China. The walls in my house.*

Ding! Something rang a bell. I opened my eyes.

"It's the wall in Dorothy's apartment. Emily's bedroom wall. Dorothy said the walls in that place are so thin you could hear a mouse—um—break wind in the apartment next door." I thought about the woman in the vision. "Maybe the vision girl is Emily," I said, excited. "I saw her in the mirror when she was dead in the bathtub, but her hair covered part of her face. I've never seen a picture of her. Have you?"

"Only the autopsy pictures," he said. "I'm sure you don't want to see those. Her face was blotchy and swollen. Not at all as she must have looked when she was alive."

"Dorothy must have some. I never thought to ask and I didn't notice any photos at all when I was in the apartment. Has Emily's phone arrived in the mail yet? There'll be pictures on that I suppose."

"We've asked the building super, Berman, to watch for it in case somebody has to sign for the package and Dorothy isn't there." He wrote something in his notebook, then looked up. "I noticed that about the apartment too. Neat and clean but no personal stuff around at all." He smiled. "Not like your place."

"I know," I admitted. "I like all my stuff. But some people don't like clutter. Minimalists, they call them. Emily must have been like that, and I guess Dorothy's place in Alaska has only the basics for survival. But she must have pictures of her sister. I'll ask when I get back to class. I'll bet the listening girl *is* Emily."

"Maybe." Pete concentrated on his notes, not looking at me. I know he's uncomfortable with my visions. I am too, but they've provided answers, solutions sometimes, to cases he's worked on. "Thin walls between the apartments, you say?"

"That's what Dorothy told me. She says the neighbors are reasonably quiet though, except for some country music once in a while."

He smiled at that, because it's his favorite music too. "Nice neighbors. We questioned them, but they didn't live there when Emily died. Berman says the place had been vacant for quite a while."

"Did he tell you he used to set up his painting easel on that balcony? For the light, you know."

"No, he didn't. The balcony of the apartment next door?"

"Yep. And after it was rented, he used Emily's balcony."

Pete put down his pencil and looked at me. Cop face. Cop voice too. "Why didn't anybody tell me that?"

"I don't know. I guess you didn't ask. Is it important?"

"Maybe." He picked up the pencil. "Anything else?"

"Dorothy says he kind of hinted around that he'd like to use her balcony too." I thought about the narrow windows in the basement. "It must be really dark in his place. Artists need light."

"Don't tell me she lets him." There was annoyance in Pete's voice.

"No. But Emily did, Pete." My voice rose. "And she let him use his pass key to come into the apartment when she wasn't there!"

He wrote quickly, closed his notebook, leaned back in the chair and tapped his fingers on the book cover for a long, quiet moment. "All right. I'll walk you back to your classroom now. And thanks." His voice softened. "This has been helpful." He stood, came around the desk as I got out of my chair, bent and kissed my cheek. "See you tonight? I'll bring Chinese."

"Deal," I said, opening the office door. "Would you bring a little extra in case Aunt Ibby joins us? She loves that crab Rangoon."

"I will," he promised. "I may be a little late. Going to stop by and have another visit with your artist friend. By the way, Chief Whaley has released your camera. I can stop by the evidence room and pick it up for you."

I thought about that for a minute. Thought about where it had been. "Don't bother ," I said. "I don't think I want it back after all."

# CHAPTER 34

I hadn't had a chance to call Aunt Ibby to catch her up on all that had happened on this very strange day, and I knew she'd be waiting anxiously for me to come home. I pulled my car into the garage next to the Buick and hurried across the yard to the back door. O'Ryan purred a happy welcome as I fumbled for my keys. I took a quick glance toward the neighbor's fence. No Frankie.

Aunt Ibby's kitchen door was already open when I stepped into the back hall, and she stood waiting for me in the doorway. "Maralee, you come right in here. Tell me every little thing! I saw the video on television. They even gave credit to your class. You must be so proud of them!" She took my hand and pulled me into the warm, welcoming room. "Coffee's on. Sit down."

I sat, and attempted to tell her every little thing, beginning with the surprising identity of the corpse. When I was done, I decided to run my new theory about the Dowgin brothers trying to warn me of danger by her. I wound up with my vision of the listening girl.

"That's a lot to absorb," she said. "A lot to think about."

"I know. We can talk about it some more later." I stood,

picked up my purse and prepared to go upstairs. "Pete's coming over with Chinese for dinner and you're invited," I told her.

"Thank you dear. I'm in the middle of working on a pie, so you can start without me. Save me some left-overs though, and I'll bring dessert. I have another book about soil I want to show to Pete. I'll bring that along too."

As promised, Pete arrived—just a little bit later than usual—bearing the familiar brown paper shopping bag emblazoned with a fierce red dragon. O'Ryan, as usual, had accompanied him up the back stairs and stood next to me, watching as I placed each enticing, slant-sided, wire-handled box on the counter.

"Smells great," I said.

"So do you." Pete pulled me close for the kind of kiss that could delay dinner. O'Ryan intruded on that idea by pushing his big fuzzy head between us and uttering a plaintive "Meeaow!"

I had to laugh. "I think he smells the crab Rangoon."

"All right O'Ryan. There's some shrimp Kung pao in there too," Pete said. "Be a good boy and maybe you can have a little bite."

I set the Lucite kitchen table with plates, wineglasses and chop sticks, but left the food in their neat little boxes with the red pagodas on the sides, and the sauces in those tiny clear plastic envelopes just because I love the way they look. The fortune cookies, however, always go into an antique, blue-and-white, lotus-patterned bowl. Call me crazy.

I turned the radio on to the soft rock station, Pete poured the wine—a pleasant chardonnay—the cat positioned himself under the table and we clicked our glasses together in a silent toast.

"Well," I said, "aren't you going to tell me?"

"Tell you what?" he said with that innocent look he does so well.

"You talked with the artist? Dakota Berman?"

"I did."

"And?"

He hesitated. "I'll tell you what I can, Lee." He unwrapped the chopsticks and handed me a pair. "Egg roll?"

"Yes, please. I understand. Police business."

"It is, but it's your business too. Berman readily admitted that he sometimes used his pass key to enter Emily Alden's apartment. That she'd given him permission to use her balcony to take advantage of the light there for his painting."

"And that he'd used the balcony next door when that apartment was vacant?" I opened the chicken fried rice box, helped myself, then passed it to him.

"Yes. He was perfectly open about it. Didn't seem to see anything wrong with it."

"I suppose there *isn't* anything wrong with it," I said, "as long as he had permission."

"Right. I asked him about his—um—relationship with Emily. He called her Miss Alden. Claims it was a tenant-super relationship. Her rent was always paid ahead of time. She never complained about anything. He was careful to lock up after he left her place and to be sure to leave the balcony just the way he found it. Sometimes, if the plants looked as though they needed watering, he'd take care of that."

Pete stopped speaking, speared a plump shrimp from the Kung pao and slipped it to O'Ryan.

"That's it?" I said.

"Pretty much. Oh, I spoke to the chief about your theory that the Dowgin brothers might have been trying to warn you, not threaten you."

"I've been wondering about that. What did he say?" I sampled the Moo Shoo chicken, then wrapped it in a soft pancake. "This is good. Try one."

"After the chief talked to Billy Dowgin, he came to the same conclusion you did. The poor guy had no idea that it was his brother we'd found dead in the cemetery. Chief said he cried like a baby when they told him." Pete helped himself to the Moo Shoo. "I don't know everything that was said between the chief and Billy Dowgin, but apparently James was worried that someone might come after you the way he figured they'd done to Emily. He believed somebody had made an attempt on his life in Florida—that's why he'd faked his own death down there. Billy claims that's why his brother sent that note—to try to scare you away from learning what actually happened to Emily."

"What made James think someone in Florida was trying to kill him? And who is 'someone'?"

"Chief didn't tell me the details, but Billy thinks it has something to do with Happy Shores. Chief's not so sure. Me either. The M.E. hasn't come up with cause of death for James Dowgin yet, but it seems kind of unlikely that he'd die of natural causes in a public cemetery, doesn't it?"

"Emily and James both worked for Happy Shores," I said, helping myself to a second egg roll. "And they both took soil samples from the wild woods area. And now they're both dead. What if they found something wrong with the dirt? Something really bad?"

"Checked with city hall. All of the soil and water tests came back okay. Main problem with the mall site seems to be that it might be displacing some pileated woodpeckers or snail darters or something."

"I know, but I keep thinking about that trowel full of dirt. Aunt Ibby has been doing some more research on soil contamination. She has another book for you. Shall I call her and see if she's ready to come up? At least hear what she's got to say about it?"

"Okay with me." He gave a noncommittal shrug, then grinned. "Tell her we have plenty of crab Rangoon."

I phoned my aunt and by the time I'd set another place at the table there was a gentle knock on the kitchen door. "I'll get it," Pete said.

Aunt Ibby carried a slim dark red book under her left arm and balanced a pie pan in her right hand. "Key lime pie," she said, putting the pie with its mile-high meringue on the counter and handing the book to Pete. "Here. It's a nineteen-twenty self-published memoir. I found it just this morning in the genealogy department. A retired World War I soldier named Charlie Putnam wrote it. I think it will answer some questions. I put a bookmark in the chapter I think will interest you both. My goodness, it smells good in here. Is that the crab Rangoon?"

My aunt investigated the assorted open cartons of Asian delights, concentrating mainly on the golden brown, crab and cream cheese filled wontons. I cut myself a slice of pie and concentrated on that. Pete put down his chop sticks and opened the red book, focusing *his* concentration on the bookmarked chapter.

Within about half a minute, he pushed his chair back, put the book down and stared across the table at my aunt. "Holy crap, Ms. Russell," he said. "Have you told anybody else about this?"

# CHAPTER 35

"Not a soul," my aunt said, placing a plump wonton on her plate. "Not even Maralee. Saved it for you."

"This is dynamite—if it's true," he said.

"Of course Sergeant Charlie Putnam is long gone," she said, "and I doubt that there are any surviving witnesses to his story, but it surely has a ring of truth to it, doesn't it?"

"What is it?" I wanted to know. "What's dynamite?"

Pete picked up the book, opened it to the marked section and, wordlessly, handed it across the table to me.

"Don't get any of that meringue on it, dear," my librarian aunt warned, moving my plate out of the way. "I borrowed it from genealogy. They're very picky."

The section of interest was approximately in the middle of the book. A quick peek at a couple of the preceding pages showed me that this particular volume of Sergeant Putnam's memoir covered his army days between 1918 and 1920.

In 1918, when the United States was still fighting in the trenches of Europe, Salem was apparently not a bad place for a young soldier to be. There was a serious influenza epidemic going on, but Sergeant Putnam had escaped its ravages, and wrote about how much he enjoyed the city's motion picture theaters, the vaudeville shows and the roller skating rinks. He mentioned that the military, facing chemical weapons for the first time, had leased property in various Massachusetts counties, to establish laboratories and testing sites where researchers could mix poisons and test the substances' killing potential. It was at one of these sites—in Salem—that young Charlie Putnam served his country.

In 1920, after the armistice was signed Charlie wrote that the government closed down the project. There was no more need for chemical weapons. He reported in his memoir that he and his buddies dug deep pits behind their barracks and buried artillery shells and glass jugs full of lethal compounds and that was that.

There was a grainy black-and-white photo of the young soldier in his uniform standing in front of rows of what looked like hundreds of glass bottles. A long barracks building was in the background.

I looked up from the book. "You think that Charlie was stationed in the wild woods?"

My aunt nodded. "Sure do, though it probably wasn't all woods back then. There aren't any records I could find of the testing labs or the disposals. But there was a record of a small, fifty-acre farm being leased to the army for housing troops. It appears to have been located just about in the center of what we call the wild woods today. I believe the mall site is a little bigger than fifty acres but not by much."

Pete caught my eye. "See what I mean? This is dynamite. If that mall site is contaminated with poison gas or God knows what, there's no way they can start building anything there."

I finished the thought. "If Emily Alden and James

Dowgin discovered something toxic in the soil samples they took, they probably reported it to the Shoreses."

"Bingo," Aunt Ibby said. "Do you have any idea what it would cost to clean up a mess like that?"

"Millions, I'd guess," Pete said.

"*Many* millions," Aunt Ibby agreed. "Did you get fortune cookies, dear?"

I passed the blue-and-white bowl to her. "That could be why Happy and Trudy are so anxious to get the grader and cement truck to work. Maybe they know exactly where the bottles were buried and they plan to bury them for good. Under a parking lot."

"All this is going to be hard to prove," Pete sounded worried. "We'll have to get permission to do some more soil tests."

"You said the tests had all come back okay," I said. "My friend at city hall told me the same thing. Maybe we're wrong about all this."

Aunt Ibby selected a fortune cookie and passed the bowl to me. "The initial testing doesn't cover every inch of huge acreage, you know. It's possible that Emily and James just happened to dig on Charlie's waste pit. If the army didn't record what went on there, there'd have been no reason to do an active search for bombs and poisonous chemicals. Nobody alive knew anything about it."

"The dust-up at city hall about the birds could keep the construction tied up for a while," I said. "Might give us enough time to get more tests done. That's *if* we knew exactly where to dig."

"There's no *we* here, Lee. You promised to keep out of it, remember? That's even more important now that there could be poison gas implicated." Pete frowned. "But I'll bet you're right about the location."

"If Happy and Trudy *do* know where the toxic dump

is, it must be somewhere within the space where they plan to pour the paving for the parking lot."

"Big area," he said.

"I wonder," Aunt Ibby said, "if the city hall has records of the land they leased to the army during World War One."

Pete snapped his fingers. "Wouldn't be a bit surprised. I'll put somebody on it first thing tomorrow. Say, did either of you watch the weather tonight? Any more rain coming our way?"

Aunt Ibby nodded. "Sure is. That tropical storm, Penelope, is working its way up the coast. It's already at the outer banks of the Carolinas. We'll be getting bands of rain from it by tomorrow or the next day. Wanda says we may even be under a hurricane watch before long."

"The rain may postpone the groundbreaking ceremony they're planning, and the birds' rights protesters will delay things even more." Pete helped himself to a fortune cookie and passed the bowl to me. "I'll see what the chief wants to do about getting more samples taken. It's still private property you know, so without proof of anything illegal going on, we may have a hard time with this."

"Everything happens for a reason," Aunt Ibby said.

"What?"

She waved a tiny slip of paper. "My fortune. 'Everything happens for a reason.' What does yours say?"

I opened mine. "'Finish the work on hand,'" I read. "Good advice I guess. Yours, Pete?"

"'If you are happy you are successful.' Can't argue with that one," he said. "I'll be even happier with a big slice of that pie."

"No problem." I cut a generous slice of pie for Pete and set out coffee mugs for all of us. The conversation turned from toxic waste dumps and the Dowgin brothers to plans for my class's Day of the Dead celebration. I remembered to tell Aunt Ibby about the sugar skull cookie idea and she agreed to help as I'd known she would.

It was still early when I'd packed the last of the Chinese food into a covered bowl, and wrapped the remaining couple of slices of pie in foil for Pete to take with him to work in the morning. The dishes were done, the kitchen cleaned up and Aunt Ibby and O'Ryan had left us to go downstairs to watch *Jeopardy.*

Pete looked at the clock. "Too late for a movie, and we sure don't need any more food. Want to go for a ride before it starts to rain?"

"Good idea," I said. "Where to?"

"I don't know. Maybe we'll just ride around until we get lost."

"That might be fun," I said. "I'll get my coat. Let's go."

Carefully locking the doors behind us, we left via the back stairs and hurried through the yard to Pete's car parked in the driveway. He held the passenger side door open for me, and I paused a moment to look at the fence where I'd sometimes seen the white cat, Frankie. She wasn't there.

Pete noticed. "Looking for that cat?"

"Kind of," I admitted. "She creeps me out when I *do* see her, and I worry about her when I don't."

"Not much point in worrying about cats," he said. "All the ones I've ever met are pretty independent. They do as they please, go where they want. Anyway, they have nine lives." He climbed into the driver's seat and we backed out onto Oliver Street. "How many of his lives do you think O'Ryan has used up?"

"I don't even want to think about that," I told him. "We have no idea how old he is or—as Aunt Ibby would say—who his people are."

We turned onto Bridge Street, heading toward Beverly.

"Let's swing by the wild woods," Pete said, taking a right onto a narrow road. There was no street lamp on the corner, and no identifying sign giving the name of the street. I didn't recall that there ever had been.

There were a few cars with their lights off parked along the edge of the street. "Just kids making out," Pete said with a grin. "A cruiser comes by every hour or so just to be sure everything's okay. Look, babe. There are lights on again in the diaper laundry. Let's check it out."

There were still a few sections of cracked paving in front of and next to the blue building. Pete pulled into what I guessed must be the remnants of a parking lot for the old diaper delivery trucks. There was a large dump truck parked there, just below a long wooden loading platform. Bright light shone from a large roll-up door and we heard the clank of metal-on-metal as two men tossed sections of pipes and pieces of ductwork from the platform into the waiting truck bed.

"They're salvaging what they can before the demolition begins," Pete said. "Looks like copper pipe there. That'll bring a few dollars. Mind if I stop and speak to those guys for a minute?"

"Sure. Go ahead."

He climbed out and I rolled the window down so I could hear what was being said. Nosy me. One of the men reached down from the platform and handed Pete a piece of paper which he glanced at, nodded, smiled and handed back. The other man kept tossing things into the truck. Noisy things that kept me from overhearing anything. Then Pete turned back toward where I waited, waved to the men and called. "Good luck with the tubs," and climbed back into the car.

"What was all that about?" I asked. "I tried to listen."

"Of course you did. I saw you sticking your head out

the window." He chuckled. "Don't worry. You didn't miss anything. I checked their paperwork. They have permission from the owners to strip the place."

"What was that you said about tubs?"

"Seems the laundry washed the diapers in a series of gigantic tubs in very hot water with special detergent. They've managed to remove the water pipes okay but they're going to have to come back with special saws and more man power to get the huge tubs out of there. Quite a job."

"I guess they're earning their money," I said.

"Yep. There are a whole bunch of five-gallon drums of detergent in there too. They haven't figured out where they can sell that but it must be worth something."

"Good recycling," I said. "Dakota Berman and Emily Alden would approve."

"What made you think of those two?"

"Just popped into my head. Dorothy and I were talking about it. Emily and Dakota didn't like to see things go to waste that could be useful to somebody else."

We drove away from the lighted clearing and headed along the shadowy, woodsy part of the street. Pete had dimmed his headlights (as a courtesy to the young lovers I presumed), and as my eyes became accustomed to the darkness I saw tiny flickers of light among the trees. "Look Pete. Fireflies! That's something you don't see often in a city this size."

"I know," he said. "Fireflies and bumble bees. They're both getting scarce. The new mall will displace a bunch more of them I suppose."

"That's kind of too bad, isn't it?"

He shrugged. "Progress. Babies don't need cloth diapers anymore and maybe the city doesn't need fireflies and bees."

We drove into Beverly and rode along the waterfront past Lynch Park with its popular beach and beautiful rose garden. "Sometimes you can smell roses and salt water when you drive past here," I said.

"And in the summer, coconut suntan lotion," Pete added.

I love it when our minds seem to work alike.

# CHAPTER 36

"Finish the work on hand," the fortune cookie had instructed, and that advice was foremost on my mind as I drove to work the next morning. With the radio tuned to my favorite 70s station, the windshield wipers matched the rhythmic backbeat of Blondie's "Sunday Girl" as Aunt Ibby's (and Wanda's) prediction of rain proved to be correct.

There was certainly plenty of work on hand needing to be finished, and most of it had to do with my job as Television Production instructor at the Tabby. All the other things gnawing at the edges of my mind—like poisoned dirt, white cats, and dead bodies in the cemetery that didn't belong there—would have to be put aside in favor of *Dia de los Muertos.*

The city business, permits and the like, needed to be confirmed before we could do anything else. As soon as that was taken care of, the twins could begin the distribution of their brochures to merchants. I'd volunteered to take care of publicity which meant using all the media contacts I could muster, all the favors I could call in and all the tricks of the trade I could implement to pull this off on budget and on time.

I joined the group in the diner. The twins were in their preferred spots at the counter, but everyone else was seated in the booth. Rain gear in various fabrics and colors hung from the coat hooks and was draped over the ends of the booth. Umbrellas poked out from beneath the seats. I added my hooded yellow slicker to the pile. "Morning," I said. "How's everybody?"

The medley of replies was typical of Salem rainy weather complaints. Dorothy looked around at her classmates and mumbled, "Sissies." It was a deserved remark, considering Dorothy's recent far, far north environment, and it brought smiles from the others.

"She's right," Therese said. "We are sissies. Save the crabbing until we get some *real* bad weather."

"Like that hurricane," Hilda said, consulting her phone. "It's off the mid-Atlantic coast now, off Maryland. headed east northeast at ten miles an hour. Sustained winds at sixty miles an hour. Northeast preparing for impact." Her tone was matter-of-fact. "That's us."

"It'll probably go out to sea," Shannon said. "That's what they said on the radio."

"Hope so," I said. "I heard the same report."

"There'll be great surf on all the beaches then." Shannon beamed. "Maybe some of those hot surfers will be around. I love watching them."

"Me too," Hilda said, putting her phone on the table. "Maybe we can get some good pictures of surfers for Mr. Doan's station."

"Right, Hilda," I said with a laugh. "You're thinking like a professional. But today, hurricane or no hurricane, we need to step up the pace and get things moving on our project. Halloween comes early in Salem. We have only a few weeks before the craziness starts."

"That's true. We have a lot to do. But, you know, that's a smart idea, about the surf pictures," Therese said. "And if we get hammered by the storm we can get some great disaster pictures. Maybe we can get the big Boston stations interested." She paused, both hands in the air. "Not that I'm wishing for a disaster. I'm just saying."

Roger walked over to the booth and leaned toward me. "Let us know when you're ready to go upstairs, Lee," he said. "We'll accompany you." It was the first time I'd heard genuine cop-voice from either twin and it made me smile.

"Thank you, Roger. I appreciate that."

He returned to his stool at the counter and spoke briefly to Ray, who turned in my direction giving a mock salute. Hilda had apparently overheard the exchange between Roger and me. "Is the situation bad enough that you need bodyguards?" she whispered. "Should we all be worried?"

I hesitated a moment before answering. "We should all be careful," I said, loud enough for all four of the women to hear. "Just as Pete told us. Be aware of your surroundings. Stick together. Billy Dowgin is in custody and James Dowgin is dead. Were they involved in some kind of crime? We don't know. We'll proceed with our lives as usual . . . just a little more carefully. Okay? And as soon as everybody is ready we'll go to the classroom."

We all dutifully trooped up the stairs to the mezzanine with Roger in the lead and Ray bringing up the rear just as the bell rang. *With Ray and Roger being deputized, I wouldn't be surprised if they were both packin'*. I was glad the two Boston cops had joined my class. I thought probably the others were too, though none of us expressed it at that moment.

It was a subdued group that faced me as I took my usual seat beneath the shoe. "Therese, want to turn on WICH-TV? The morning news program should still be on. Let's see what kind of weather we can expect and plan our indoor and outdoor classes accordingly. We may want Kelsey Roehl to give us tours of some of the other Salem cemeteries since it's going to be a citywide event."

"More cemeteries?" Shannon pouted. "I thought we were going to make cookies and do some fun stuff."

"We will," I assured her. "As a matter of fact my aunt has agreed to help us with the cookies. Shannon, would you check on prices for the skull-shaped cookie cutters? I'll order them right away and get the ingredients together. I'll talk with the station manager and offer him an instructional program on *calavera* that he can run next month."

Hilda gave a brief explanation of the meaning of *calavera*, which covers not only sugar skull cookies, but all kinds of tchotchkes and memorabilia in keeping with a more or less lighthearted view of death. We all focused on the weather map looming large on the screen. Scott Palmer's voice-over gave the position of the center of the slow-moving storm and suggested that New Englanders would do well to be prepared. (I knew he was envisioning himself standing on the beach mid-hurricane, with waves crashing behind him, limbs of trees flying by, just like the big network boys do.)

"Doesn't look too bad," Roger said.

"Little storm," Ray offered. "No big deal."

"Let's hope not," I said. "This is good weather for another brain storming session. I know you've all been thinking about more than cookies. Any new ideas?"

Dorothy spoke hesitantly. "This isn't exactly about the

project, but since the cemetery and the dead man and Lee and all of us and my sister's murder are all mixed up together maybe I should talk about it."

She had everyone's attention.

"Go on, Dorothy," I said.

"I just got a text from Dakota. He says there's a package in my mailbox from Paula Alden. He wants to know if he should bring it over here."

"Your sister's cell phone," I said. "You don't happen to have a charger for it with you, do you?"

"No. It's in the apartment." She looked down. "Dakota has a key. Should I tell him where it is and have him bring that too?"

"I have a charger in my car. Maybe it'll work on her phone." I didn't like the idea of the artist going into Dorothy's place, and began to say so. "It might not be wise . . ."

Dorothy interrupted. "Why not? There's nothing in the place worth stealing. Not that I think Dakota is dishonest anyway."

"He's not." Shannon jumped to her new friend's defense. "Anyway there could be something important on it. Something us investigative reporters need to know."

"We're not . . ." I began, but Dorothy was already texting.

There was an excited buzz of conversation. Scott Palmer got clicked off mid-forecast and Roger and Ray moved their chairs closer to Dorothy's desk.

"I'm going to call Pete, Dorothy," I said pulling my own phone from my pocket. "There may be evidence on her cell that they need to know about if, in fact, your sister's death wasn't accidental."

Her eyes narrowed. "You know it wasn't accidental."

Pete answered my call on the first ring. I lowered my voice and told him what was going on.

"She told him he could go into her apartment?" he sputtered. "What the hell is she thinking? I'm coming over there. If Berman gets there first, get that phone from him and hang onto it."

# CHAPTER 37

"Pete's coming over," I said in an ever-so-casual tone, putting the phone back into my pocket. I managed to stay with my fortune cookie inspired resolve and we resumed the brainstorming session. There were a few rather half-hearted suggestions for publicity, but everyone was pretty much focused on the mezzanine entrance. Who'd arrive first, Dakota or Pete?

Actually, they arrived together. Dakota carried one of those if-it-fits-it-ships boxes from the post office along with a handful of wires I recognized as a phone charger. Pete was right beside him. When the two approached the classroom area, Dakota handed the box and charger to Pete, then moved to the back of the room where he stood quietly. Alone.

I knew that Dorothy had watched the exchange. She walked toward Pete, and at the same time looked back to where Dakota Berman stood by himself. Pete handed her the package. "It's addressed to you. It's your property. But I'd appreciate it if you'd let us examine it. It may help us figure out what happened to your sister that night."

I watched Dorothy's face. She handed the package back

to Pete. "You can have it first," she said. "I'm not sure I'm ready for it yet." She looked again at Dakota, then returned to her seat.

Pete put the box on my desk. "Want to put this away for me for a while? I'd like to borrow your class and your big screen for a few minutes. I was impressed with the job you all did with the picture of Billy Dowgin. I have another picture I'd like to see in that kind of detail."

I slipped the box and charger into my bottom desk drawer, the one with a lock on it. "Of course you can. It'll work nicely with next week's lesson plan. Our next chapter is on 'tools of the investigative reporter's trade.' This fits right in. Therese knows more about the mechanics of the screen than I do," I admitted, "so I'll turn you over to her."

Pete moved over to the news desk, while I spoke to the class. "You all did such a good job of observation when we enlarged the photo of 'the anonymous fairgoer'—who turned out to be Billy Dowgin—Pete has another to test your powers of observation." I gestured to the screen. "Is it another anonymous person, Pete?"

Pete reached into his inside jacket pocket. "Nope. This time it's a picture of a place, not a person, and there's some detail I haven't been able to magnify enough with the equipment we have at the station." He handed a photo to Therese. "That one. Can you blow it up?"

Therese flashed a dimpled smile. "That sounds subversive, doesn't it? Sure I can. Just watch the magic machine."

"Wish the department had one like it." Pete watched as she manipulated the picture into place and huddled over the controls. "Ninety-inch screen, right? Six feet by eight feet? How much did a thing like this cost? Any idea?"

"Mr. Pennington says around twenty thousand," I told him. "Government grant."

Pete let out a long low whistle and at the same time there was a collective gasp as a six by eight foot picture of an apartment building appeared.

"Hey, that's my place," Dorothy exclaimed. "Look. It's an old picture. That could be Emily's Volkswagen in the parking lot, isn't it, Dakota?" The young man moved closer to the screen. Not speaking, but nodding agreement.

"What are we supposed to be looking for?" Shannon wanted to know.

"Maybe something," he said. "Maybe nothing. Can you zoom in on the top floor please, Therese?" Pete asked.

She zoomed in for a tight shot of a section of the top floor balconies.

"That's my place for sure," Dorothy said, "and look, there's my balcony. I can tell by the plants. It's the only one with plants. See there's nothing on the one next door except—what's that thing?"

"That's an artist's easel," Hilda said. "Yours, Dakota?"

Dakota Berman, those amazing cerulean blue eyes suddenly wide, turned and hurried through the doorway toward the stairs leading to the first floor—and the exits.

Ray was closest to me and I looked up at him. "What was that all about? He bolted like a scalded cat," I said, immediately regretting the unfortunate metaphor.

"Don't know." Ray frowned, watching the young man's departing back. "Looked like as soon as he saw that close-up he beat it out of here."

I caught Pete's eye and tilted my head toward the stairway. He nodded, acknowledging that he'd seen Dakota's hasty exit. A look was exchanged between Pete and the recently deputized twin. Pete gave an almost imperceptible lift of his chin. Returning the motion, Ray followed Dakota down the stairs.

Pete spoke a few words to Therese and she zoomed in

more tightly on the balcony with its many plants. "I thought this screen might give us a clearer picture," he said, "and it does. There. See him? There's a man standing there. Can you get any closer?"

"Maybe a little. There. Uh-oh. His back is to the camera. Can't see his face at all. Sorry."

Dorothy jumped up and practically ran to the news desk. "Whoever it is is looking in my glass doors. I mean *Emily's* glass doors. Where did you get this, Pete?"

"It was mailed to the chief," Pete said. "He spotted the figure on the balcony right away and we magnified it as much as we could without being able to ID the man. Still can't, but chances are we have a good idea of who it is."

"It's Dakota, isn't it?" Shannon spoke up. "But so what? He's the building super. He can look at anything he wants to in that building."

"You're right," Pete said. "He can. So why did someone want the chief to see this particular picture?"

"I've seen it before," Dorothy said. "Or at least one almost exactly like it. It's in a flyer about apartments for rent in Salem. It's an ad for the apartment next door to me. It was in a bag the Shoreses gave me. I gave it to Lee." She looked at me. "Do you still have it?"

"I gave it to Pete."

Pete reached into his pocket again and pulled out a colorful folded brochure. "I have it. I recognized it too. You're right. It's almost the same, from a slightly different angle. There's no Volkswagen in the parking lot and no one on the balconies."

Ray and Dakota arrived at the head of the stairs. The young man, his head down, walked a few steps in front of Ray and approached Pete. The room was quiet. The blown-up photo still loomed on the screen.

"It's me up there." Dakota spoke softly. "I knew about

the pictures because Mrs. Shores called and asked me to take my easel in and stay off the balcony because I'd ruined the shot for their advertisement. See, they don't ever want people in the pictures without what they call a model release. Some legal thing. So I did what they said and they came over the next day and took another picture for the ad." He raised his voice and lifted his head. "But I don't understand why somebody would send that picture to you. I didn't do anything wrong, did I?"

"Not that I know of," Pete said. "So why did you take off when you saw it?"

The reply was barely audible.

"What did you say?" Pete asked.

The artist looked down at his feet again. "Because it looks like I was peeking in Emily's window."

All heads turned toward the two men. Pete spoke quietly, not in cop voice. "Were you?"

Dakota Berman nodded. "Maybe."

Therese silently handed the photo back to Pete, who moved from his position at the news desk and stood in front of the man. "Would you come down to the station with me and talk about this there?"

"Okay. I'm not under arrest, am I?"

"No. We're going to talk. That's all."

"Okay."

The two moved toward the stairway. "Thanks everybody. I'll be in touch about that phone, Lee."

Nobody spoke for several seconds. Long seconds.

Hilda broke the silence. "What just happened?"

Dorothy, who'd been standing since the photo of the building had appeared on screen, returned to her own desk. "Maybe Shannon's boyfriend is a Peeping Tom. I hope not."

"What if he's peeking at you too, Dorothy?" Therese asked. "It's too creepy to even think about."

Shannon sounded close to tears. "That's a terrible thing to say about him. I'm telling you he's a good guy. Stop it!"

The twins looked from one woman to another, undoubtedly confused by the cross talk.

*Time for teacher Lee to intervene.*

First I took the small key from my top drawer, inserted it in the lock on the bottom drawer, turned it and put the key in my jeans pocket. I raised my hand for silence, thinking as I did so that it was how we restored order back in my Brownie Scout days. It still worked. Eyes turned to me, mouths shut.

"All right everybody. Let's be professional. To repeat Hilda's reasonable question, 'what just happened here?' The facts. Not conjecture. Let's think like professional investigative reporters would." I pointed to Roger. "You first, Roger. From the perspective of a peace officer, what just happened here?"

He squinted his eyes together, then rolled them upward. "Well, a photograph of an unidentified individual was shown on a big screen TV. A known individual in the room suddenly left the room. Ray went after him and accompanied him back." He paused, looking at his brother, then resumed. "The individual admitted that he was the person in the photo. That's what happened."

"Thank you," I said. "Dorothy, what did you observe?"

Dorothy didn't hesitate. "We saw a picture of the building where I live. Dakota Berman lives there too. Therese zoomed in on the balcony of the building and it showed a man on the part of the balcony outside the apartment where I live. Where my sister Emily lived before she was . . . before she died. Dakota told Pete it was him in the picture and that maybe he was looking in the French door to my apartment. That's all that happened."

"Ray?"

"What Roger said."

"Okay. Therese?"

"I was busy working the console so I didn't pay attention to everything else. Afraid I wouldn't be a good witness. I didn't even notice when Dakota left the room. Sorry."

"That's all right. Hilda, how about you? What did you observe?"

"What everyone else said, plus the fact that *somebody* wanted the chief of police to see that picture. The first picture, the one that we saw was, according to Dakota, taken the day before the one in the Shoreses' advertisement." She paused, probably, I thought, for dramatic effect, then continued. "So it had to be somebody from the Shoreses' agency that sent the picture. The question is . . ." Another dramatic pause. "Why?"

"Good work, everybody. You dealt mostly with facts. Very little conjecture. This isn't easy when you know some of the people involved. I'd like you all to record your impressions on paper. I'll do the same. Use your own observations as well as what you've heard from others. Let's see what we can come up with. Remember, we're being investigative reporters now. We're being objective."

I pulled the H.S. notebook from my purse along with a pen. I thought about Pete and his ever-present notebook, put the pen back in my purse and took a nice sharp yellow number two pencil from the top desk drawer.

# CHAPTER 38

It had been another strange day—even for Salem—and it was a relief to be driving home, despite the dreary damp weather. I'd filled dozens of the lined pages in my notebook with a rambling jumble of observations, not just about that day's happenings, but about the dead man in the cemetery, the artist who might be a Peeping Tom, the girl in the bathtub, the soldier who'd buried bottles of poison, even about the white stray cat.

Aunt Ibby had called to tell me that Pete was coming over later in the evening to return Charlie Putnam's memoir. Having heeded her observation about the library's picky genealogy department, he'd made copies of the chapters in question and was anxious to surrender possession of the actual book. She'd invited us both to "have a bite of supper" with her. Good thing. My cupboard, as usual, was pretty nearly bare.

I parked the 'vette in the garage and hurried through the yard. O'Ryan hadn't exactly come outside to meet me—he's not crazy about getting wet—but stuck his head out of the cat door in greeting. I picked up the plastic-sleeved copy of the *Salem News* from the back step and being sure the fuzzy yellow cat head had been withdrawn, unlocked the door and stepped into the hall.

I almost bumped into my aunt, who'd opened her kitchen door at the same time I'd come in. "Oh, Maralee. You have the paper. I was just coming out to get it. Come in. They just said on the radio that they think James Dowgin's death is suspicious." She raised an expressive eyebrow. "Well, duh! As if being found dead aboveground in a cemetery was normal. Let's see what the *News* has to say about it."

I handed her the paper, hung my slicker on a handy peg in the hall and followed her inside. "Pour yourself a cup of coffee," she said, waving toward the coffeemaker and sitting in one of the captain's chairs. She spread the front page of the paper on the tabletop, smoothing it with both hands. "It says here that the body found in the cemetery by a group of students—that's you—has been identified as that of H. James Dowgin. Blah blah blah—they give his birthplace, parents' names—they're deceased—his college, his employment, blah blah blah. Oh, here we go. 'The exact cause of death has not yet been determined. Foul play, however is indicated.' Huh, I hope Pete will give us more details than this. They barely even mentioned the Florida swamp thing." She folded the paper neatly and put it aside. "Pour a coffee for me too, please, and tell me about your day."

I filled two mugs and joined her at the table. I pulled the notebook from my purse. "It was a complicated day," I said. "I wrote it all down. Shall I read it to you? It's kind of disjointed but I wanted to get it on paper before I forgot some of it."

"That complicated? Of course. I want to hear every detail. Isn't that the notebook that was in the swag bag from Happy Shores?"

"It is. I like it." I opened the book. "Another item from that same bag is involved in today's happenings."

"Tell me. I can hardly wait."

I began to read my scribbled, penciled notes. They were quite random, and to anyone except my aunt, would have sounded like a mishmash of fact and fancy. I made a mental note to type this up neatly for the class, omitting all conjecture and following the instructions I'd given the others. Be objective. Deal with facts. But for now—this stream of consciousness muddle of words would have to do.

It took almost fifteen minutes to read it. I finally looked up from the pages. "Well? What do think it all means? It's like a game of connect-the-dots where the dots don't connect or pieces of a puzzle that should fit together but don't."

"I see what you mean. You didn't tell me before about the vision of the white cat with the Berman boy's eyes."

"I didn't?"

"No. That's all right. I think maybe the cat peering into *your* window with those distinctive eyes lends some credence to the Peeping Tom theory, don't you? Even though she's not a tomcat."

"You're right." I was excited. "Pete asked Dakota to come down to the police station to answer some questions. But, of course, the blue-eyed cat is nothing the police department can use."

"I know. But it may lead to something more concrete."

"Speaking of concrete, I forgot to mention that it looks as though the weather may postpone the pouring of the parking lot at the wild woods. Pete's going to need more time to check up on the possible location of the poison bottles. Maybe he found out something today. Did he say what time he'd be over to return the book?" I looked at the clock. So did she.

"Should be any minute now. Want to go upstairs and change? I'll entertain Pete until you get back."

"Okay. Thanks. Be right back. I'll leave the notebook here. Maybe between you and Pete, you might make some more sense out of it. Put together some more puzzle pieces. Connect a couple of dots."

"I'll try. Now shoo. Go on upstairs. Hurry back. I have a lovely chicken and broccoli casserole in the oven. Coffee ice cream with hot fudge sauce for dessert."

When I left via the kitchen door, O'Ryan was already on the second floor landing peering down at me. I caught up with him and together we climbed the final flight and entered my apartment. The cat hopped up onto the old velvet-covered wing chair I'd had reupholstered in a wild zebra print, turned around in a circle or two, then curled up and closed his eyes. Tossing my purse onto the couch, I proceeded down the short hall to the bathroom, shed clothes and turned on the hot shower full blast. It felt wonderful and when I stepped out of the tub, reaching for a towel, the little room was like a sauna.

Wrapping myself in a fluffy white towel, I reached out to clear the mirror's steamy surface. One swipe with a paper towel, and the twinkling lights and flashing colors appeared—superimposed on my wavy reflection. The vision came into sharp focus. It took only seconds for me to understand what it meant.

I picked up the clothes I'd dropped on the floor and shoved them hurriedly into the laundry chute. Towel clad, I raced through the kitchen and into the bedroom. Usually I give some thought to looking my best when I'm going to see Pete. Not this time. Grabbing the first things I saw—faded jeans and a wrinkled Boston Celtics T-shirt—hair a wet mess and barefoot, I dashed out my kitchen door and—sorely tempted to use the banister—I raced down the front stairs and into Aunt Ibby's living room.

"Is he here yet?" I called as I headed through the dining room and into the kitchen. "Is Pete here? I know what happened to James Dowgin!"

"I'm here babe, I'm here!" Pete reached for me, pulling me into his arms. "What is it? Are you okay?"

"Yes. I saw it. In the mirror. I know what happened to him. Maybe it's even how somebody killed him."

"Here. Sit down dear." My aunt, her brow furrowed, pulled out a chair. Pete guided me to it. Obediently, I sat.

"I'm fine" I said. "It was a vision, Pete."

Understanding showed in Pete's face. He doesn't like my visions, but he's learned to accept the fact that they often provide answers to some very difficult questions. He took the chair next to mine, still holding my hand. "Tell me about it."

I got control of my breathing, pushed some dripping curls away from my forehead, and began. "Remember that when they found James Dowgin in the cemetery, his clothes were soaking wet, even though it hadn't rained much during the night. Remember that?"

"Sure," Pete said. "The ambulance guys had a hard time moving him out of the narrow space he was in because of the weight of the wet clothes."

"Pete." I gripped his hand hard. "He was in one of those tubs. At the diaper laundry. I saw it. There was a huge shiny metal drum with a curved cover that was open. There was hot water in it. Very hot water. I could see the steam. There was a blue bucket of white powder being poured into the water. I saw it."

"You saw James Dowgin in the water?"

"No. Just the tub and the soap or whatever it was. But

I'm sure that's what the vision meant. That's how James Dowgin got so wet. And maybe it killed him somehow."

Pete nodded, dropped my hand and stood up. "Miss Russell? Will that casserole keep for a while?" He didn't wait for an answer. "Lee, put on some shoes and we'll go for a little ride. I hope we can get there before those tubs go through a metal crusher." He looked at me. "Better put on a hat too."

I did. Sneakers, jacket and knit hat were hurriedly thrown on and we were out the door, on our way to the no-name street at the wild woods. It's not a long ride from my house, and Pete was definitely exceeding the speed limit. There was time for one question though. I wanted to know what Dakota had told him, so I asked. I got the raised-eyebrow, that's-police-business look and a curt reply. "Not much. Let him go."

The brakes squealed when we pulled onto the broken pavement beneath the loading dock at the Wypee-Dypee Laundry. There was no dump truck in sight, but the lights were on in the blue building. A car marked with the name of a security service was parked at the edge of the pavement.

"Wait here," Pete said. "I'll be right back. I just want to check and be sure the tubs are still here. Then I'll try to get a stop order on the demolition until we can check everything out."

"No way," I told him, looking out the window at the trees which seemed like live things, waving their branches and crowding around us in an unfriendly way. "It's starting to get dark. I'm coming with you."

He sighed. "I should have left you with your aunt, but all right. Looks like there's nobody here except maybe a security guard anyway. Stay behind me."

I stayed behind him. Close behind him. We climbed a

ramp to the top of the loading dock and Pete pounded on a door beside the big roll-up door we'd seen earlier. I heard a radio playing inside. Someone yelled "Who is it?"

Pete pulled his wallet from his back pocket and held it up so that his badge showed. "Police" he said.

"Nate," according to the embroidery on his pocket, peered out. "What's up, officer?" he said, looking past Pete and straight at me. "Anything wrong?"

"No," Pete said. "We noticed your lights. Just checking. Mind if we step inside for a minute?"

"No. Come in. Glad of the company." He moved aside. "Wait a sec. I'll turn down the radio. Gets lonely in here."

I'd never seen the inside of a big commercial laundry before. I was glad the place was brightly lit. The looming shapes would have been frightening in darkness. There were some machines that looked like our washing machine at home, but about ten times bigger. There were gaping holes in the walls with tiny bits of pipe protruding through. I guessed these were places where the workmen we'd seen tossing chunks of metal into the dump truck had harvested their bounty of copper and steel.

"See anything like the . . . you know . . . thing you saw?" Pete whispered.

I turned around slowly. A series of three oblong chambers ran along one wall, with one giant corkscrew-like mechanism running through all of them. The guard pointed to it. "Mean looking, ain't it? It's a tunnel washer. The auger pulls the diapers through the different rinses, fabric softeners and bleach and stuff and dumps them out in a big block at the end."

"Interesting," I said, still not seeing anything resembling the bright metal tub I'd seen in my mirror. I moved away from Pete toward an alcove near the back of the place. There it was. Even bigger than I'd envisioned it. I guessed it must be made of steel. The cover was closed now. It had been open when I'd seen it, but I knew this was it.

"Big sucker, ain't she?" The guard spoke from behind me. I whirled around to make sure Pete was there too. He was.

"What is this?" I asked.

"It's a washer-extractor," the man said. "It's so big a guy can stand inside it for service or maintenance. And when she's runnin', this beauty can extract one heck of a lot of baby poop."

"I'll bet," Pete said. "You know a lot about this place. Do you work here every night?"

"No. Used to. Only two, three nights a week lately. They got another guy, young fella, for the other nights. I think he works cheaper than me. I worked here in the laundry when I was young though." He shook his head and looked genuinely sad. "People don't put nice soft diapers on their kids no more. Damned plastic things with sticky tapes and cartoon pictures on them. No wonder the kids grow up so mean."

I tugged on Pete's sleeve. "This is it," I said. "No doubt."

"Mind if I take a closer look at the washer extractor?" Pete moved toward the huge tub as he spoke. "Can I look inside?"

"Sure." Broad smile. "Don't fall in though. Me with my arthritis and this little lady would have a hard time pulling you out."

Pete returned the smile. "I'll be careful." He reached for the curved cover at the top of the drum-shaped machine and, with some effort, pushed it up exposing the interior. He leaned forward. "This is really deep." His voice echoed strangely from within the contraption. He turned his head.

"Do you have a flashlight I could borrow for a minute, Nate?"

"Got it right here." The guard detached a flashlight from his belt and handed it to Pete. "Whatcha lookin' for?"

"Not sure," Pete said, his voice echoing again as he played the light around the inside of the drum. "Has this thing been used lately?"

"Nah." Nate scoffed. "Not for years. Why? Is it rusted out in there?"

"Not at all. Actually, there's still some water in the bottom of it."

# CHAPTER 39

When Pete reclosed the cover of the washer-extractor and handed the flashlight back to the guard, I noticed that his cop face was in place. "Nate," he said. "Did you work here Monday night?"

The man reattached the flashlight to his belt and paused a few seconds before answering. "Funny you should ask about that," he said. "I was supposed to. I was scheduled for Monday, Tuesday and Wednesday. But late Monday afternoon they call up and tell me not to come in. No reason. They say they just don't need me."

"They used the other guy? The young guy you mentioned instead of you?"

"Uh-uh. Don't think so. See, I can tell when he's been here from the radio station."

"The radio station?"

"Yeah. I listen to the all night talk shows. The ones about aliens and bigfoot and stuff like that. When the other guy has been here, the station's been changed to music. Like rap and rock and that modern crap."

Pete nodded. "So when you came in on Tuesday the other guy's station was on?"

"No sir. It was one I never even heard here before. Long hair tunes. Beethoven and Bach and like that."

"Okay. Thanks, Nate. You've been a big help." Pete pulled out his phone and moved away from me and the guard. When he spoke into it, his tone was urgent, but his voice just low enough so that I couldn't make out the words. I tried to though, leaning in his direction as far as I could without tipping over. Nate was doing the same thing. We must have looked like a couple of cartoon eavesdroppers when we tried to straighten up and look casual when Pete put his phone away and faced in our direction.

"I've called for some backup. CSI, forensics."

"CSI? Does that mean crime scene? You think there's been a crime in here?" The guard looked around the room. "Musta been a long time ago. This place has been closed up since the eighties."

Pete spoke softly, right next to my ear. "There's a couple of inches of water in the bottom of that washer. You're right about James Dowgin being in there and now I have something I can tell the chief."

I didn't say anything but I'm sure the question was in my eyes.

"His shoe," Pete said. "One of the shoes was missing from the body." He tilted his head in the direction of the washer-extractor. "It's in there."

*Another shoe.*

Pete instructed Nate to stand on the platform outside and to be sure nobody entered by either of the two doors there until the police arrived. Pete and I stood beside a smaller door at the end of the building. Pete, with a handkerchief over his hand, checked to be sure the door was locked while I studied my surroundings. A time clock still hung on the wall next to a rack of yellowed cards with names on them. Wheeled canvas carts, like the ones I've seen in coin laundries only larger and deeper, stood in an orderly row, each cart numbered.

"Look at that," I said. Each cart had a big painted black number on its end. There were seven carts but the numbers went up to eight. "There's a cart missing. There's no number six."

"You're right. Did I ever tell you you'd make a good cop?"

"Many times," I said. "And I still don't want the job. But what was James Dowgin doing here? And how did he wind up in that washer? And who dumped him in the cemetery?"

"That's what we're going to figure out." The sound of sirens announced the arrival of the investigating team, and things moved very fast after that. "You don't have to stay if you don't want to," Pete told me. "Want me to call a cab for you?"

"Are you kidding? I wouldn't miss this for anything. I'll stay out of the way, I promise."

I tried to keep my word and even looked around for a chair but whatever office furniture might have been there was gone. I wondered where Nate sat during his long night shifts of guarding the Wypee-Dypee building so I asked him.

"There used to be a folding ladder the workers used to reach the big machines," he said, "like that one the cop was looking at. I always sat on it to listen to the radio, or eat my lunch. But it's gone now. I guess the guys that stripped the pipes musta took it. Now I just find a clean spot on the floor to sit and lean against the wall. Lunch time now. You can join me if you want. PBJ and chips, okay?"

"Thanks," I said. "My aunt's holding dinner for us, but I'll keep you company. Let's sit where we can watch the cops, okay?"

"Heck yes. Not something you see every day in this old dump."

There were about a dozen people moving around the long room—quietly, efficiently, quickly. I recognized a couple of them from other crime scenes where I'd unfortunately been present, but most of the men and women on the team were unfamiliar to me. I knew some of the procedures. The fingerprinting unit concentrated on the alcove where the washer-extractor stood, and on the monster machine itself. The most interesting part though was the retrieval of the shoe from the bottom of the machine. It was, as Nate had told us earlier, big enough so that a worker could get inside. A stainless steel ladder appeared from somewhere, and when the fingerprinting was complete, they slid the cover up and one of the team, in white coveralls and holding a pair of tongs, climbed into the washer.

I fought a strong urge to run across the room and look into the thing, envious because Pete was doing just that. He stood right next to it when the tech reappeared, a brown shoe, dripping water, grasped in tongs. Pete held a plastic bag open, and the tech released the wet shoe into it.

Team members assembled in small groups, making notes, marking evidence bags, speaking a few quiet words among themselves. A woman investigator approached the wall where Nate and I sat. Nate immediately returned his sandwich to a blue plastic cooler and scrambled to his feet. I stood too.

The woman introduced herself as Dr. Fredonia Foster and asked both of our names. She seemed to recognize mine, smiled, and glanced from me to Pete and back, then asked Nate to step outside for a moment so that she could ask a few questions. I wished I could follow them, curious about what he'd have to say, but had to content myself with—to use one of Aunt Ibby's expressions—"standing around like a tree full of owls"—simply observing.

"Observing is exactly what a good investigative reporter does," I reminded myself, and trying to look as unobtrusive as a badly dressed redhead with wet curls sticking out of an old knit cap can, I took a slow turn around the edges of the long room. I drew a few curious stares, but no one seemed to object to my presence. I figured that Pete had vouched for me. Even so, I was careful to avoid touching anything. When I saw Nate and Dr. Foster return from the loading platform, I quickened my step a little and joined them next to the big roll-up door. Dr. Foster thanked Nate, wished me a good evening and returned to her colleagues.

"Everything okay?" I asked the guard, who certainly seemed as though everything was okay. Actually, he looked quite pleased with himself.

"Sure," he said. "She was happy that I pay so much attention to detail." He stood a little straighter. "Guess I was able to help her out quite a bit."

"No kidding," I said, fully aware that I was about to meddle. "That's great. What did you tell her?"

"Mostly I told her how things work around here. I really know the old place inside out. Better than anyone in Salem, probably. Used to work here, you know. Back in the day."

"Yes, I remember," I said. "You must know every inch of the place."

"I do. I told her about how the diapers used to come in dirty and leave spic and spandy clean. Want to know how?"

"Yes. I do," I told him with all the sincerity I could muster. "Sounds fascinating. How did that work?"

"Well, first the truck driver pulls up to the dock and opens the back door of his truck. Another guy comes down the ramp with a rolling hamper. You saw those? They have numbers on them that match the truck numbers. The poopy diapers are in bags you know. The driver tosses the bags into the rolling hamper. The other guy pushes the cart up the ramp and into the laundry. I told her about the different machines, but you've already seen them, right?"

"Right," I agreed.

"Okay. When the driver comes back to start his route the next day, his cart has been hosed out and sterilized and down the ramp it comes, all full of nice clean dry diapers for babies' bottoms. Neat, huh?"

It was neat. I could visualize it. Down the ramp the cart would come. But it wouldn't be full of clean, dry diapers. It would hold the soaking wet remains of James Dowgin. Minus one of his shoes.

# CHAPTER 40

It became clear that we were going to spend more time at the Wypee-Dypee building than we'd planned. I called Aunt Ibby, suggested that she go ahead and eat without us, and regretted turning down Nate's offer of that PBJ.

Since I was involved in all that was going on—after all it had been my vision in the bathroom mirror that had started it—I was pretty sure that I was no longer in the "meddler" category. I decided to push my luck. Thanking Nate for his helpful information about the transportation of diapers, both clean and dirty, I walked over to where Pete still stood beside the washer-extractor. I didn't say anything, not wanting to intrude on whatever was going on, but hoping to give the appearance of being a part of it all.

Pete gave an almost imperceptible nod in my direction and continued his conversation with the tech who'd fished out the wet shoe.

*So far, so good. Nobody has told me to go away.*

"Have it checked for everything," Pete said. "Prints, blood, DNA, forensic chemistry, the works." The tech, carrying the bagged shoe at arm's length, headed for the door.

"Forensic chemistry?" I hadn't heard Pete use the term before. "What's that?"

"Pretty much bugs and leaves and slime," he said. "It's like what Doctor Hodgins does on *Bones*. Entomology, minerology, palynology. All that stuff. Gives us an idea of where the shoe has been. Trace elements. Particulates. They probably won't find much since it's been underwater for a while, but it's worth a try."

Memory of the shoe vision crossed my mind and the proverbial lightbulb went off. "What if you were trying to figure out where a shoe had been and that shoe's been in a plastic bag ever since it was in the place you're trying to find?" The sentence was convoluted, but Pete got it right away.

"The work boots Emily wore on the soil testing trip. They still have dirt on them." He took my hand. "Let's take another ride. These guys can finish up here. Better call Dorothy and tell her we're on our way."

On the way from the wild woods to Dorothy's, I felt more like a detective than a meddler for the second time that night. (It'd have to be a plainclothes detective, I thought with a rueful downward glance. Clothes didn't get much plainer than these.) Dorothy must have been standing beside her admission/intercom panel waiting for us. She buzzed us in the second Pete pushed the button beside the name which still—sadly—read "Emily Alden."

"What's going on?" When she opened the door, Dorothy's voice was excited, her eyes bright. "Have you figured out what happened to her? Was there something on her phone?"

Pete and I looked at each other. Between the vision and the discovery of James Dowgin's shoe, neither one of us had mentioned the phone. "Jesus. The phone. Lee. Where is it? Back at your place?"

I put one hand over my mouth, embarrassed. "Pete. I forgot all about it. It's in the bottom drawer of my desk at the school."

"You don't have it?" Dorothy looked from Pete to me and back again. "Is it still in your desk?"

"I locked it," I said. "Put the key in my jeans pocket."

They both looked at my jeans. "Not these," I said. "It's in the ones I wore to school."

The question was spoken in unison. "Where are *those*?"

Pause. Remembering. "I put them down the laundry chute."

"Safe enough," Pete reassured me. "Don't worry about it. But for now, let's get a look at those boots."

By this time Dorothy appeared thoroughly confused. She deserved to be. I gave a fast explanation about why we wanted to pick up Emily's dirty boots, and soon, bagged boots in hand, we left the apartment with a promise to pick up Emily's phone and be back within the hour.

*How are we going to do that?*

Too vain to accompany Pete into the police station dressed as I was, I waited in the locked car while he carried the boots inside. I closed my eyes, reclining the seat a bit, and realized how hungry I was. I wondered if any of that casserole remained edible. I'd nearly dozed off when Pete returned. "Nice going, babe," he said, sliding into the driver's seat. "There are cleats on those boots and there's plenty of dirt still on them. This may be just what we need to narrow down the location of Charlie Putnam's stash of poison."

"I hope so," I said. "I'd hate to think of a mall going up on top of whatever evil stuff is buried there. I think about little kids, babies in strollers, people eating in restaurants. Pete, people could die if we can't stop it."

"We'll do all we can, Lee. I have a good feeling about

it." I wasn't at all sure about my feelings, as mixed up as they were between reality and things I saw in mirrors and a giant black shoe. He reached across the police radio and patted my hand. "All we can do is do our best," he said. "We don't win them all. But let's go to your place and get that key, and see what we can find out about what happened to Emily. Maybe we can win that one."

We parked in the driveway next to the garage and went into the house through the back entrance. I tapped on Aunt Ibby's door, explained that I needed something from the pocket of my jeans, and followed Pete into the laundry room.

"I haven't washed today," my aunt called, "so whatever it is should still be there."

The laundry, which tumbles down the chute from my bathroom, falls into a deep wicker basket between the washer and dryer. The jeans were right on top. I had a few seconds of panic when I fished into a front pocket and came up empty. The second attempt yielded the key and I held it up triumphantly. "Got it."

So began another wild ride, this time to the Tabby. I tapped my access code into the pad beside the big double glass doors which still bear the gold leaf letters spelling out *Trumbull's*. One door swung open and we entered the lobby. A closed-up school at night must be very similar to a closed-up department store. There were no school noises, no store noises. Lighting was dimmed and the place even smelled different. We climbed the stairs to the mezzanine landing where I pressed the light switch, illuminating the classroom.

As usual, I averted my eyes from the black shoe as I approached the desk. Sitting in my chair, I inserted the key into the locked drawer and reached inside. It was empty.

The voice came from the shadows at the back of the old

shoe department. "I guess you're looking for this?" Dakota Berman approached, both arms upraised, Emily's phone in one hand. I saw Pete reach for his gun. "Don't shoot me." Dakota said. "I'm sorry."

"Put the phone down, move away from it and put both hands on your head," Pete barked.

Dakota followed orders, watching from a distance as Pete picked up the phone, keeping the gun trained on him.

"Okay, Berman. Spill it. What's the story? How did you get in here and how did you get the phone?"

"I took it out of the drawer and stuck it in my pocket when you were all looking at the big screen. I just wanted to see if there was anything about me on it." His voice quavered. "She knew about me. Emily knew about me and the pills."

"The pills?" I asked. "The pills Emily took that night?"

Pete lowered his gun. "Mr. Berman has a record. Selling oxy pills back when he was in high school. Stole them from his grandma's medicine cabinet, right Mr. Berman?"

Dakota nodded, hands still on his head, the blue eyes frightened. "Emily knew about my record. I . . . I thought she might have texted Dorothy or somebody about me. I . . . I thought if you found out you'd think I had something to do with the pills she took that night."

"Did you think we didn't know about your record?" Pete asked. "What were you going to do with that phone without her pass code anyway?"

"I have her pass code." He looked embarrassed. "She let me borrow this phone once when I couldn't pay my own phone bill."

"What's the code?"

Dakota recited a four-digit number and Pete handed the phone to me. "Try it, Lee."

I did. It worked.

"Good. That saves us some trouble. Okay, Berman. How did you get in here?"

"I came back here after you let me go from the station. Everybody had gone to lunch or somewhere. So I hid way back in there, where they used to keep the shoes. I stayed real quiet and looked at everything on Emily's phone. There's nothing there about me. In fact, there's nothing interesting on it at all. Just girl stuff, work stuff and some texts from her boyfriend. Pictures of flowers and cats. It was stupid, I know. I waited until everybody left, then I was going to sneak it back into the drawer, but by then somebody had locked it. Then the school got locked up too and I couldn't get out without setting off the alarm. So I hid again." He sounded close to tears. "I didn't know the police kept old juvie records. I hadn't told anybody about me selling pills, except for Emily and Mrs. Shores, of course."

Pete and I spoke at once. "Mrs. Shores?"

"Sure. I had to tell her so I could get the job as super. She hired me for part-time security guard in those old buildings too. Nice lady."

"Berman," Pete said. "Think carefully. Did you work as security guard at the old diaper laundry last Monday night?"

"Me? No. Another guy works Monday, Tuesday and Wednesday. I stayed home and watched football. Pats/Steelers. The Pats won."

"There was no security guard there on Monday night," I said, almost to myself.

"You can put your hands down, Berman," Pete said. "You know, don't you, that taking that phone from Ms. Barrett's desk was against the law?"

"Are you going to arrest me?"

"You can press charges if you want to, Lee."

"I . . . I'd rather not involve the school."

"You can change your mind later if you want to. Berman, take a seat over there. Put your hands on the desk."

Dakota did as he was told.

"We're going to give you a ride home, Berman." Pete said, holstering his gun and putting Emily's phone into his pocket. "We'll be returning the phone to Dorothy Alden. It's her property and we'll see if she wants to press any charges against you for stealing it." He looked at me. "Lee? Shall we escort Mr. Berman out?"

I turned out the classroom lights and we three walked together down to the front door. I tapped in my exit code, covering the pad with my other hand to prevent prying eyes. Pete's car was close to the entrance. Unlocking it, he opened the rear door and directed Dakota to the passenger seat on the right side, made sure he was properly seat belted, and closed the door. Then—surprisingly—he handed me the keys. "I'll ride in back with Mr. Berman to be sure he behaves himself. You all right with driving this over to Dorothy's?"

"Is that legal?"

"Not exactly. I'll take responsibility. I just feel more comfortable if this one isn't sitting right behind you if I drive, and I have no grounds to cuff him. So," he asked again. "you all right with driving this over to Dorothy's? It's only a couple of blocks."

I didn't even bother to answer the question. Maybe I don't cook or sew, but Pete knows I can drive damn near anything with wheels. So away we went.

# CHAPTER 41

I parked the Crown Vic in a visitor's parking space, and the three of us entered the building, Dakota in the lead. Pete pushed the button beside Emily's name and, once again, Dorothy answered immediately.

"Pete Mondello and Lee here," Pete said, "and we have Dakota Berman with us. We've got your phone and Berman has something he wants to tell you."

Dorothy buzzed us in. "I could have just opened the door, you know," Dakota said. "I have keys to everything."

"Yes," Pete used his very-patient-cop voice. "We know."

We rode the elevator up in relative silence. As soon as we all stepped off on the fourth floor, I saw Dorothy's door open a crack. "Lee?" she called softly.

"Yes. We're here."

"Just wanted to be sure it was you," Dorothy pulled the door open wide. If she was surprised that Dakota was with us, it didn't show in her facial expression. "Come on in. I made some coffee and I have some pound cake. Store bought."

Any kind of food sounded good to me. I thought Pete must be hungry too, though he hadn't mentioned it. We crowded into the small living room, Pete and Dakota sat on the couch, Dorothy and I sat on kitchen stools facing the two men. Emily's phone lay on the counter in front of Dorothy. I sipped strong coffee and hoped my stomach wouldn't gurgle when the sweet pound cake hit it.

"We haven't looked at the contents of the phone yet, Dorothy," Pete told her. "But your young friend here has." He pointed one finger at Dakota. "Tell her what you've done, Berman. She can decide whether or not she wants me to arrest you. Then we'll take a look at what's on that phone."

Dorothy looked confused and who could blame her? Dakota began to talk, first in halting tones, and as he warmed up to his story he seemed in a hurry to finish it. "I'm really sorry, Miss Alden," he said. "I should never have done it, but I was afraid people would think I had something to do with the pills."

"The pills she had in the medicine cabinet? They were prescription pills. From a doctor in Boston. Why would anyone think you had anything to do with that?" Dorothy's brow furrowed. "I don't get it."

"See, I didn't know she had prescription pills," Dakota said. "I was surprised when I heard about it. She'd told me she never took anything but aspirin. Didn't want anything to do with drugs. I was surprised about the wine too." He smiled, a kind of far-away looking smile. "She wasn't much of a drinker either."

"So you'd say that swallowing a bunch of pills and drinking wine while relaxing in a bubble bath was completely out of character for her?" I said.

Dorothy stood up. "She'd never do that!"

"Which? Take pills or drink wine?" Pete wanted to know.

"Neither one." Dorothy almost shouted. "She'd never

take a bubble bath. She was deathly allergic to all kinds of perfumes and detergents and colognes and any of that stuff."

"Are you sure?" Pete stood too.

"Of course I'm sure. I have some of the same allergies, but hers were worse. Neither one of us could even wear makeup."

*Well, that explained that.*

"What would her reaction to something like bubble bath have been?" Pete asked.

"Her face," Dorothy said, touching her own face as she spoke. "Her face would get all blotchy and swollen. Me too, only not as bad as hers."

*Blotchy and swollen.* Pete had used those words when he'd described the autopsy pictures.

"It's the soap. The bubbles," I said. "Pete, did the forensic chemist guy take a sample of the detergent from the laundry?"

"He did. I remembered what you said about what you saw in the . . ." he broke off mid-sentence. "He did."

Another piece of the puzzle slid into place. The white powder I'd seen in the vision must have been the detergent we'd seen in the five-gallon buckets. I was sure of it. "Did they preserve any of the Emily's bath water?"

"I don't believe so. Remember, we were looking at an overdose case. They would have drained the tub when they removed the body."

At Dorothy's stricken expression, Pete apologized. "I'm sorry. This is painful for you. Do you want me to arrest this one?" He jerked his head toward Dakota who had slid down deeper into the couch cushions, as though he was trying to make himself smaller. "For stealing your property?"

"Dakota? Oh, no. He's really a good kid. Emily liked him and so do I. He's sorry, aren't you?"

The big blue eyes brightened. "I really am sorry, Miss Alden. But Detective Mondello, I think I might know something important about this. I mean I didn't *know* it was important. It's just a thing I do. I don't like to waste stuff. Emily understood that. She didn't like waste either. She even saved the edges of rice paper I cut off my tombstone pictures. Used it for writing paper."

And *that explains that!*

Pete interrupted. "Get to the point, man," he said. "What do you know that's important?"

"I've think I've got that bottle the bubble bath powder was in."

"What?" Pete glowered. "You removed something from the crime scene?"

"It wasn't a crime scene then," Dorothy reminded him. "You just said so."

Pete, still glowering, faced Dakota. "You removed something from the death scene?"

Dakota shook his head. "Of course not. I got it from the Dumpster out back. I know when it was too. It was in the morning of the day Emily's Mom called when she couldn't reach Emily."

"Are you in the habit of taking things out of the trash?" Pete asked, sounding incredulous. I knew how Pete felt about that sort of thing. He sounded the same way when I told him that the cute shabby chic footstool I have in my kitchen was a treasure I grabbed one trash day from right in front of a neighbor's house on Winter Street.

"Sure. That's mostly how I furnished my apartment."

"It's true," I said. "Shannon told us that too."

Pete sat on the couch again. "Tell me about the bubble bath powder."

"I almost missed it," Dakota said with a smile. "It was in a paper bag with a broken glass. A wineglass. I could tell by the stem on it. Ooops. I probably should have saved that too, huh?" The smile disappeared. "I didn't know anything had happened to Emily."

"Do you still have the powder? You haven't used it have you?"

"No. There was only a tiny bit left but it was in a nice bottle so I put it in my bathroom. Looks good on the shelf."

"I'll have to ask you to turn that bottle over to me, Berman."

"Is it evidence or something? I don't think it's any good for fingerprints. I washed it off real good." He wrinkled his nose again. "It came out of a Dumpster you know."

Pete stood. "Let's go down to your place and get it right now. Do you always look inside paper bags in Dumpsters?" I could tell that Pete was starting to lose patience.

"Of course not. It could have been garbage. No. I was curious because I saw Mrs. Shores throw it in there."

Pete sat down again. "Mrs. Shores?"

"Sure. You knew Mrs. Shores followed Emily home from her house that night, didn't you? Dorothy knew it. Mrs. Shores was worried because Emily had been drinking."

"Yes, we knew that."

"She'd been drinking all right. I was surprised about that. She was staggering when she got out of her car. Mrs. Shores was practically holding her up when they walked across the parking lot." Dakota scratched his head. "Really surprised me."

"Where were you to see all this?' Pete asked.

"Oh, I was on the balcony next door." He jerked his thumb in the direction of the wall dividing the apartments. "That was before the new tenants moved in. Hot night. My place is so stuffy. I was sitting out there, enjoying the breeze and the moonlight and all when I saw them both drive up."

"Mrs. Shores walked to the building with Emily?"

"Yeah. Brought her up in the elevator too. I heard them laughing in the hall. I guessed they'd both been drinking by the sound of it."

"Didn't you tell all this to the police?"

"No. They only talked to me about finding Emily's body. And when was the last time I'd talked to her and if I knew what time she'd come home that night. I told them I saw her car come in around eleven. That was true. I guess they thought I saw it from my windows, which I could have. I didn't tell them I was in a vacant apartment. I'm not supposed to do that, you know."

"Did you ever tell Mrs. Shores you saw her with Emily that night?"

"Heck no. She owns the darn building. I didn't want her to know I was in that apartment. That I painted on the balcony sometimes." He looked down at his hands. "She found out about that though when she saw the picture with my easel on the balcony. She was pissed."

When the sound of Patsy Cline singing about walking after midnight came from next door we all stopped talking and looked at each other. "I see what you mean about the thin walls," Pete said. "Good choice of music at least."

Dakota wrinkled his nose, but was wise enough not to comment.

"Dakota," I said. "Were you inside the apartment next door when you heard Emily and Mrs. Shores getting off the elevator?"

"Sure. I ducked inside so they wouldn't see me on the balcony."

"So you could have heard what was going on in *this* apartment if you'd wanted to listen, couldn't you?"

Dakota's face colored slightly and Pete picked up my line of questioning. "*Did* you want to listen, Berman?"

I knew darn well he'd listened. People who peek in other people's windows aren't above listening through other people's walls.

Dakota gave the same answer he'd given when Pete had asked earlier if he'd peeked into Emily's window. "Maybe," he said.

# CHAPTER 42

"None of that," Pete said. "Did you or didn't you?"

"Oh dear," Dorothy said. "If you heard anything that might help us figure out what happened that night you have to tell us. Even if it doesn't seem important."

"You won't tell Mrs. Shores? I don't want to lose my jobs."

"We won't tell Mrs. Shores a single word," Pete promised. "What did you hear?"

Dakota wiped one hand across his forehead and took a couple of deep breaths. "I could tell they were in the bedroom because I know the layout of every apartment in here. Emily didn't say much. It was mostly Mrs. Shores doing the talking. She sounded really nice. Like a mother talking to a kid, you know?"

"Can you tell us what she said?" Pete urged. "Try to remember her words as well as you can."

Dakota bowed his head for a moment. "She said something like 'Come on honey.'" His voice slipped into a high falsetto. "'Have some more of this nice wine. It'll relax you. Then I'll help you get undressed and draw a nice hot bath for you.' Then Emily said something like 'That's nice,' or 'thank you.' Polite words, you know? Emily was always very polite."

I saw Dorothy nod agreement. "Yes," she whispered. "That's Emily."

Dakota continued. "I heard the water running so that drowned out some words. Then they were both in the bathroom and Mrs. Shores must have been helping Emily into the tub because I heard a splashing sound. Emily said something but it was like the words were blurry. Like she was drunk or maybe stoned."

Pete spoke softly. "What did she say?"

"I think she said 'no soap.'"

"My grandfather used to say that," I remembered. "It means something like 'no way.' Or 'no dice.'"

"Did you see Mrs. Shores leave?" Pete asked. "Or hear the elevator go down?"

"Sure. I couldn't go back to my place until she was gone. I heard her say, 'Good night dear. Sleep well.' Then I heard some doors closing in there. The elevator went down and everything was quiet. I waited awhile, then I ducked out onto the balcony again so I could see if her car was gone. It was, so I went home."

The blue eyes were wide and clear and innocent.

Pete accompanied Dakota down to his apartment and came back with a brown plastic Walmart bag which I assumed contained the bubble bath bottle.

"Guess we'll have to go back to the station, Lee. Too late to do anything with this at the police lab tonight, but I'd like them to get started on it first thing in the morning."

"What are you going to do about Dakota?"

"Nothing I can do. You two don't want to press charges about the phone—not that I blame you—and he hasn't actually broken any other laws. He answered the questions the police asked about Emily. Remember it wasn't a criminal investigation then. Officially, it isn't one now. I warned him not to leave town and not to talk about what was discussed here. Anyway he's scared enough about his two jobs to keep quiet."

"Shall we see what's on this now?" Dorothy asked, picking up Emily's phone.

"Let's do it," Pete said.

Dorothy spoke the four-digit pass code aloud and handed the instrument back to Pete.

The first thing we learned from it was the fact that James Dowgin had texted Emily several times on the night she died. Texted her repeatedly, desperately. All the messages said the same thing: "Emily. Don't go. I'm on my way. Wait for me."

"By then she must have already gone to the party at the Shoreses'," I said.

"The party that was supposed to be for her," Dorothy added, "and if she actually drank too much while she was there that might explain how she accidently dropped her phone between the seats in the VW. So she never knew what James tried to tell her."

Other than the messages from James, Dakota Berman had been right about the other information preserved on the phone. It was pretty ordinary stuff about work and clothes and food, along with pictures—including a cute one of a white cat peeking out from among the plants on her balcony.

After Pete and I had eaten the last two pieces of pound cake, we excused ourselves and said good night to Dorothy, with a warning to be sure to lock her doors, including the French doors leading to the balcony. With Pete once more in the driver's seat, we headed back to the police station.

"It seems that the Shoreses keep turning up, doesn't it Pete?" I said. "I mean not just because they own the apartment building, but Emily, Dakota and James all worked for them. Too many coincidences?"

"Right," Pete agreed. "I'll be very interested in the reports we'll get from the evidence we collected at the laundry." He gave a wave of one hand. "But of course they own that place too, so there's no reason that Happy and Trudy couldn't have left fingerprints all over everything."

"Well, at least we know Happy Shores couldn't have been there Monday night," I said.

"We do? How come?"

"Television," I said. "Didn't you see it? He was at the Patriots game with a bunch of front office bigwigs."

"Missed it," Pete said. "Good observation."

"Thanks. When will you get the results from the things you collected from the laundry tonight?" I asked.

"Probably tomorrow on the prints and the trace evidence. DNA takes a while. I'm hoping for a fast turnaround on the work boots from Emily's closet too. We still haven't come up with any records of the land the army leased in the wild woods. If we can identify the spot where the chemicals are buried, there'll be some real action on all this." He tapped the Walmart bag beside him on the seat. "What do you bet the bubble bath powder matches up with the detergent in the five-gallon buckets?"

"I wouldn't be surprised at all." I thought about it. "But what would that mean? Soap is soap, isn't it? And nobody would use anything dangerous that was going to be next to babies' bottoms, would they?"

*"No soap," Emily had said.*

"Doesn't seem likely, does it?" We pulled into a space

in front of the police department. "So many things about this case don't make sense. Chief wants me to talk to Emily's doctor again, to find out why he prescribed such a heavy duty sedative to a young woman who barely weighed a hundred pounds. The amount of barbiturates in her system was way more than she'd have needed for a good night's sleep." He picked up the bag, and hit the door lock. "Be right back."

Alone again, I closed my eyes and let my mind wander. I agreed with Pete that while not a lot of this made sense, some of it was beginning to. For instance, Emily wouldn't have *willingly* stepped into a tub full of bubble bath, drunk or not, knowing what it would do to her face. I know *I* sure wouldn't have, even if my very nice motherly boss had drawn the bath for me and even if I was the most polite person on earth.

Another question. What were they celebrating at the Shoreses' home that night? And why didn't the other two guests even mention it? Another BIG question. If James Dowgin died at the Wypee-Dypee laundry, why was his body dumped in the Howard Street Cemetery? Was it supposed to be some kind of a warning? Who was the warning for?

I didn't want to think about the answer to that.

# CHAPTER 43

It had been a long, exhausting day. It was late when we left the police station and headed home—both of us tired and still hungry. Pete parked in his usual spot next to the garage and I found myself scanning the side fence, looking for Frankie as we walked to the back door. No white cat. No lights on in Aunt Ibby's part of the house either. O'Ryan waited for us inside the hall and we all climbed the stairs as quietly as we could.

I heated up a can of tomato soup and Pete made grilled cheese sandwiches which we ate in the near silence that sometimes happens when your concentration is totally on food. O'Ryan was asleep on his windowsill and Pete and I fell into bed without any further discussion of the day's happenings and without even looking at the late news on TV.

Pete left early the next morning, anxious to get the results of the various tests that were in the works so O'Ryan and I were alone in the kitchen when I found out where the missing number six laundry cart had gone. There it was on the *Good Morning Salem* show. It was muddy and torn and some of the wheels were gone but the numeral on the end was plainly visible. Seems some kids had found it in the woods. They'd managed to drag it over to the nearest playground and were taking turns filling it with their pals and riding downhill in it. No one objected until one of them fell out and broke his collarbone. Then it made the news. According to the reporter no one knew where the cart had come from, but I figured it wouldn't be long before they found out.

I called Pete. He'd seen it too. "We've already picked it up. CSI has it, although those kids must have destroyed any evidence that could have been on it. Oh, well. Chief's sending a detective over to talk to the Shoreses' this morning," he said, "and we found traces of milkweed on those boots. I've got a botanist from the college going over to the wild woods to check that out. Woke up a judge to get permission to go in there. That might narrow down the location of Charlie Putnam's toxic waste dump. Making some progress, babe."

I was impressed, as I always am by the department's efficiency. "How much of all this does my class need to know?" I wondered. "They're involved with some of it for sure and I don't know how much information I should share with them—to keep them safe from—from whatever—whoever. . . ."

"I understand. I've briefed the twins on what we have so far. We have reason to believe the Shoreses—or someone connected to them—may be involved in James Dowgin's death. Possibly in Emily Alden's death too. But hell, we still don't know exactly what either one died from. They were both in water, but neither one drowned. Emily could have died because of the combination of barbiturates and alcohol. And Dowgin? He had a nasty bump on his head—enough to knock him out, but not enough to kill him. We need more."

I understood the frustration in his voice. Cops need hard facts. Real truths. They can't accuse people of crimes because of visions in mirrors or messages from cats. "I'm sure you'll figure it all out," I said. "I'm going downstairs to catch Aunt Ibby up on everything, then I'll go to school and just play it by ear? Sound okay?"

"Okay. Be careful Lee. I love you."

"I will. Love you too," I said.

I was out of morning kitty kibble, so O'Ryan followed me down the front stairs to Aunt Ibby's then posed pitifully in front of her pantry door.

"Poor, starving cat," she said, filling his red bowl with fish, milk bottle, cheese and steak shaped–cat food morsels. "And I thought when I went to bed last night that you and Pete must have been starving too. Did you eventually get some dinner?"

"Eventually." I gave her a fast rundown of all that had happened since I'd seen her last. I caught her up too on what Pete had told me about the kids and the laundry cart and the milkweed in the wild woods.

"I'll bet I know right where that is," she said. "Years ago the garden club planted a nice patch of milkweed in there to try to attract monarch butterflies. For years they'd come there on their annual migration, then after a while it seemed as though there weren't so many of them."

"Did it work?"

"Oh, yes. They came back." She frowned. "But I suppose they'll leave again once the mall is built. If it's built."

"The butterflies along with the bees and the fireflies," I said. "Progress. Maybe you should call Pete and tell him where to look. Everything is so overgrown in the woods it might take even a botanist a while to find a patch of milkweed."

"I will," she said. "Look at the time. You go along to

school. You don't want to be late. Bring an umbrella. Wanda says that tropical storm is heading our way and it's getting stronger."

I took her advice, driving carefully through rain that seemed to come in intermittent bands, varying from pounding to pitter-pat. It was during a brief stretch of the latter that I arrived at the Tabby and ran between the drops to the diner door. Dorothy and Hilda had arrived just ahead of me and were stashing umbrellas under the seats. The others were already seated—Therese comfortably dry because she lived upstairs in the school dorm, Shannon, hair damp and red rain boots shiny wet. The twins were in their preferred spot at the counter, both holding newspapers, but clearly keeping watchful eyes on us. I added my umbrella to the others, hung my jacket on a peg and sat down. Dorothy slid in beside me, Hilda on the opposite end of the booth, and we ordered our breakfasts.

"Dorothy," I asked as my coffee and corn muffin arrived, "Do you happen to have any photos of your sister? I've wondered what she looked like."

"I have an old high school picture in my wallet. Emily hated having her picture taken. She'd always stick out her tongue or hide her face. She was so pretty, but never believed she was." Dorothy reached for her purse, opening a worn leather wallet. "Here she is." She passed the wallet to me.

The young girl was lovely. A shy smile, wide-set eyes, and a strong resemblance to her half sister. The image bore little resemblance to the person I'd seen in my girl-in-a-bathtub vision, but looked very much like the girl-listening-through-a-wall.

"Sorry I don't have anything recent," Dorothy said. "This is the only good one I've ever had."

Shannon spoke so softly, I barely made out her words.

"What did you say, Shannon?"

She looked up. "I don't know if I should say anything, but I know where there's a good picture of that girl."

"Where?" We all spoke at once.

"It's not a photo. It's an oil painting." She pointed at the open wallet. "I'm sure it's her. It's in Dakota's bedroom closet."

Dorothy's gasp was loud enough to draw curious stares from nearby diners.

Both twins looked up from their papers. Ray, carefully reserving his place at the counter by putting his *USA Today* on the stool, approached the booth. "Anything wrong, ladies?"

"I'm not sure. Something the police ought to know about though." Dorothy, Shannon and I tried to explain about Emily's pictures—or lack of them—and the oil painting in Dakota Berman's closet, while Hilda snapped a shot of the girl in Dorothy's wallet. Roger, putting his *Boston Globe* on the stool, joined his brother as our group began to draw curious stares from the other diner patrons.

"I want to see the painting. Now." Dorothy's voice was low, but urgent. "I'm going to go home and make him show it to me. Make him explain."

"If there is such a painting," I said, "and if it actually turns out to be of Emily, it could be important to the investigation. I think it's best to let the police look into it before any of us say anything about it to Dakota. We don't want to frighten him. What if he destroys it?"

"I guess you're right." Dorothy's tone was uncertain. "I'd hate it if he did that."

"What do you say we stop talking about it for now,

finish our breakfasts quietly and go upstairs," Roger spoke calmly, softly. "Lee, would you like me to call Pete?"

"Yes, please." I said. The twins returned to their seats at the counter. All of us in the booth were silent for a long moment. Therese, never at a loss for words, asked when we were going to make the sugar skull cookies. It was a good topic, interesting to all of us, and uninteresting enough to turn away the stares of the curious.

"It looks as though the weather is going to be gloomy, so if none of you have other plans, we may as well do it tonight," I said. "The cookie cutters arrived and I have all the ingredients stashed in my kitchen."

Agreement to the plan was swift and enthusiastic. All of the women would be at my place at seven. The twins demurred, pleading lack of cooking experience. I texted Aunt Ibby, who agreed immediately to supervise the operation. Cookie baking plans in place and breakfasts hastily finished, we gathered coats and umbrellas and adjourned to the classroom and our ongoing study of Television Production.

It didn't take long for Pete to text me. Heading for Berman's place. Thnx for tip.

The idea of the young artist having a portrait of Emily hidden in his closet was a chilling one. I wished I could be with Pete, could hear Dakota's explanation for such a bizarre thing. Instead, I gave a brief introduction to a chapter on staging a set for TV, with special emphasis on using an actual room as background. I reminded the class that our cookie baking video would employ just such techniques and promised a discussion of the chapter when we'd all finished reading.

It was difficult for me to stay focused on the announced topic, and I made a special effort to avoid even a random glance toward the shoe behind my desk, fearing that an unbidden vision would completely shatter any concentration I'd managed to muster.

When the reading was finished and the time for discussion arrived, I felt pretty good about my ability to stay on task. Hilda, who was the only one among us who'd interacted with the Shoreses when her parents had sold and bought a house through them, had a good concept of how my kitchen should look. "It's just like staging a house for sale," she said. "Minimize. Mrs. Shores told us to take all the personal stuff out. No pictures on the refrigerator. Hardly any stuff on the walls. The customer should be able to visualize their own things in the space." I thought about Emily Alden. She was surely a minimalist. No pictures. No personal things.

"You mean I have to take down my Kit Kat clock?" I asked, halfway kidding, halfway serious.

Opinion on that was divided. We tabled the idea. Therese put on a rerun of an old *Cool Weather Cooking with Wanda the Weather Girl* program so we could see how a studio kitchen looked. Minimalist indeed. Plain white appliances with a bowl of fruit on the counter. But of course, Wanda was pretty darned decorative by herself. That took us up to noon when the lunchtime bell rang. At the same moment, my phone buzzed and Pete's name showed on the caller ID.

"You off for lunch?" he asked.

"I am."

"Pick you up in five?"

"Sure. Meet you out front."

The rain had let up when Pete's car coasted to a stop in front of the glass doors of the Tabby. He leaned across the seat and pushed the door open. "Hop in. We only have an hour," he said, handing me a familiar brown paper bag and a tall paper cup. "Hamburger with extra pickles, medium fries and a chocolate shake. Okay?"

"Perfect," I said, and it was. "What did you find out from Dakota?"

"A lot. And not just from him. I have reports about the soap. And some more about the boots. What a morning!"

"Can you tell me about it?"

"You know I don't usually share police stuff with you."

"I know. I understand."

"That's not what I meant. This is different. If it wasn't for you and your visions and Dorothy and the others, we'd still be calling Emily Alden's death an accident. And the Dowgin brothers would just be a couple of Steelers fans. So I'm going to tell you what I know so far." He smiled and reached over and helped himself to a couple of my fries. "I'll start with the portrait of Emily. That's the name of it, by the way. That's what Berman calls it. *Portrait of Emily*."

Pete drove toward the Salem Willows Park, a good place to stop and talk anytime, rain or shine, summer or winter. We parked under one of the famous willow trees and Pete turned off the engine. Except for the patter of raindrops on the windshield, all was quiet.

"She never even saw the painting." Pete's tone was sorrowful. "He'd asked her to pose for him and she refused to do it. That's where the peeking in the windows came from. When he was supposed to be painting out on the balcony, he made quick sketches of Emily when she wasn't looking. He did it when she was watching TV or doing the dishes or reading a book. Then over time, he painted the portrait."

"She never even saw it? Is it good?"

"Looked good to me. He hid it because he knew she didn't like pictures of herself. I don't see why. She must have been pretty."

I thought of the smiling, listening girl in my vision. "She was," I said. "Really pretty."

"He's going to give the painting to Dorothy. I think she'll like that."

"I know she will. Tell me the rest. What about the soap?"

"The soap in the bubble bath bottle was, as you'd guessed, the same as the baby diaper detergent."

"But didn't we agree that they wouldn't use harmful stuff on baby bottoms?"

"True. The detergent contains something called benzethonium chloride. It's an antiseptic they use for cleaning cooking equipment, surgical instruments and—no surprise—for disinfecting cloth diapers. It's called a cationic detergent."

"But you believe it killed Emily? How?"

"According to our forensic chemist, in really hot water the body absorbs the detergent through the skin. It can cause convulsions, coma and, finally, death. And the autopsy won't show any trace of cationic detergent at all."

"They killed James Dowgin the same way."

"Looks like it."

"Ingenious," I said, "and horrible. Have you arrested the Shoreses?"

"We picked Happy up this morning for questioning. He's lawyered up. Not talking. Trudy flew to Florida yesterday for some business at the True Shores office down there. A couple of Broward County sheriffs are going over to talk to her"—he looked at his watch—"right about now. So far we haven't charged either Shores. We need something more than a few fingerprints on property they already own. And the only two people who knew about the buried poison are dead."

"Do you think Happy and Trudy might confess? Tell you where Charlie Putnam's toxic bottles are buried?"

"They'll probably deny that they know anything about

it. Word about government trucks and a team of guys in hazmat suits going into the woods looking for milkweed gets around Salem fast though, and about a dozen garden club ladies have called already to tell us where the milkweed butterfly garden is."

"Wow," I said. "Things are moving fast. Where's Billy Dowgin in all this?"

"We've released Billy," Pete said. "He wants to meet you, to apologize for frightening you, making you feel as though you were being stalked."

"Did he tell you why? Why he followed me?"

"He did. James was worried about you because you were asking questions about him. About Emily. He wanted Billy to keep an eye on you until it was safe for him to come out of hiding. When James and Emily took the soil samples, it was just for fun. She was interested and he wanted to show her how it was done. They didn't expect to find anything unusual there. After all, the project had already been approved. When he sent the samples to the lab though, one came back as okay. The other had traces of arsenic trichloride." Pete shook his head. "Bad stuff. James told Mrs. Shores about it. She seemed really grateful. Rewarded him with a big promotion. CEO of the Florida office. True Shores."

"So that's how he wound up down there. Does Billy know why James faked his own death?"

"Mrs. Shores even flew down to Florida and told James that everything had been taken care of and thanked him again. The chemical was just some stuff from the old hardware store, she told him. Something they'd used for rats. The project was still good to go. He believed her since he'd heard no word about any problem at the site. The next day his brakes failed. Fortunately, there are very few hills in Florida so he coasted to the side of the road and found that the brake line was partially cut—just enough so that the fluid would leak out."

"That tipped him off that something was wrong?"

"Not right away. He couldn't believe anyone would do that. Passed it off as a freak accident. But when he was all alone surveying an orange grove, somebody took a shot at him. That convinced him. Emily had just told him that the Shoreses were having a party for her. He tried to warn her not to go. He figured the Shoreses could be lying to him about cleaning up the arsenic in the ground—that they'd found out that she was on the dig with him and that she was in danger too. He faked his drowning and thumbed a ride with a trucker back to Salem. He was too late."

"I'd like to talk to Billy," I decided. "Some neutral place."

"Fair enough. I'll be with you if you want me to." He started the car. "Lunch time is just about up. I'd better get you back to school. I get off at eleven tonight. Want me to come by?"

"Yes, please."

The ride back to Essex Street was quiet. Pete had given me a lot to think about.

# CHAPTER 44

By the end of that afternoon I had even more to think about. Within an hour after I'd come back from lunch, right in the middle of a spirited discussion on creative use of the green screen, there was an urgent text from Pete. Turn on the news!

"Therese," I said. "Can you turn on WICH-TV please?"

The popular Salem-based cable station does hourly ten-minute newscasts, concentrating on local news. The flashing "Breaking News" crawl appeared across the bottom of the screen. A rain-soaked Scott Palmer—using his Very Serious Face and Big Network Voice—stood at the corner of the wild woods road in front of a ROAD CLOSED—ABSOLUTELY NO ADMITTANCE sign. A couple of Boston TV news trucks were in evidence nearby, along with several military vehicles.

"I'm a few hundred yards away from the site of the proposed Wildwood Mall," Scott intoned. "Army engineers arrived on the premises this morning to begin excavation of an area of the property which may have been the site of chemical weapons testing between 1917 and 1920. The

Army Corps of Engineers is in charge of the dig, where it is believed there may still be toxic chemicals buried in the ground. Salem residents are cautioned to avoid the area until further notice. Buildings on the site are unoccupied and no evacuations are necessary."

The camera panned across the eerie scene, and wind-whipped tree branches made a strange humming, crackling sound in the background. In the distance, I saw the blue Wypee-Dypee building, remnants of yellow police line tape fluttering in the wind.

*Will the CSI people be able to continue their work in there with all this going on?*

"The oncoming storm, Penelope, with winds approaching hurricane force, promises to complicate the process, but city officials assure us that every precaution to insure the safety of Salem citizens is being taken," Scott counseled his audience. "All plans for the proposed shopping mall are on hold. Stay tuned to WICH-TV for updates, every hour, on the hour."

The station returned to regular programming—a vintage episode of *Gilligan's Island*—and Therese turned off the monitor. "Wow," she said. "Good thing that groundbreaking for the mall got canceled. It would have been a bummer if the mayor had dug up a shovel full of poison gas."

"I don't think you can put gas in a shovel, can you?" Shannon asked. "It would have to be in something, wouldn't it?"

"Glass bottles," I murmured, remembering the photo of Charlie Putnam. "Lots of glass bottles."

Returning the group to concentrating on the mundane classwork I'd scheduled seemed unlikely, so I let the conversation flow—but with a TV news aspect. "What kind of research do you suppose the TV station staffs are doing right now in preparation for future stories on this?" I asked.

"Where are they going to find it? What kinds of experts will the investigative reporter approach for interviews?" I picked up my colored markers and stood beside the white board. The ideas flowed so quickly that I found it difficult to keep up. The excitement was tangible and their enthusiastic responses made me proud of all of them.

At the end of the school day, Dorothy, Hilda, Shannon and Therese made plans to have dinner together in the diner and to ride together in Hilda's car to the house on Winter Street for our cookie baking project.

There's nothing quite like the cozy comfort of a warm, good-smelling kitchen in the company of friends on a cold, dark and rainy evening. In the interests of TV-appropriate décor, I'd removed clippings, photos and cute magnets from the front of the refrigerator, but allowed Kit Kat to stay in his place on the wall. Aunt Ibby had gathered the necessary ingredients and utensils in assembly-line fashion, and before long, under my aunt's expert direction, the five of us were measuring, sifting, rolling and cutting like pros.

Therese filmed the proceedings as we turned out cookie sheet after cookie sheet of perfectly formed, just-brown-enough-around-the-edges skull-shaped treats and placed them on rows of wire racks to cool. As we worked, there were few comments about the happenings at the wild woods, other than a general consensus that whatever it was didn't look good. The portrait of Emily wasn't mentioned at all. With printouts of Hilda's magazine how-to instructions on giving the blank skulls colorful frosting faces, we prepared to test our artistic skills.

"Should have invited Dakota for the arty part," Dorothy said, carefully spreading a background of sweet white frosting onto a cookie. "He'd be great at this." With a flourish of a pastry tube, she drew two round eyes with red icing, placing a tiny silver candy ball in the center of each one, and passed the cookie over to Hilda who stood ready with a tube full of blue for outlining rows of teeth. Shannon added touches of yellow and I was in charge of green swirls and leaves. Aunt Ibby did pink roses. The process continued, with a minimum of snacking on mistakes, until we'd produced around four dozen of the grinning sweets. The resulting cookies, while maybe not quite as professionally rendered as the magazine pictures, looked pretty darned good.

Therese zoomed in on the twelve best-looking ones, displayed on one of Aunt Ibby's silver trays for the closing shot. "Good job, everybody," she said. "This will attract some attention on WICH-TV for sure."

*And Mr. Doan doesn't have to pay for it. He loves free programming.*

"Now what are we going to do with them?" Shannon asked, licking traces of yellow frosting from her lips. "We can't very well eat them all."

"We should take some to school tomorrow for Ray and Roger," Dorothy said, and Aunt Ibby thought the break room at the library could handle a dozen.

"I'll take a dozen over to the police station," I offered, "and if we each keep a few to nibble on, that'll take care of the whole batch."

"That wind sounds like it's picking up." Hilda cast a worried glance toward the kitchen window, where O'Ryan still lay sprawled out across the sill. "I think maybe we should get going before it gets worse."

The others agreed, and with everyone pitching in, the kitchen cleanup was accomplished in minutes. Before Kit Kat displayed nine o'clock, they'd all left with three plastic-bagged cookies each, while I packed the remaining three dozen into boxes for the library, the twins and the police station.

"That was a job well done," I said to the cat, who blinked in my direction but didn't move. "Come watch TV with me. I want to see what's happening with Happy and Trudy Shores and the big dig at the wild woods."

With a wide, pink-mouthed yawn and a leisurely stretch, O'Ryan left his windowsill perch, trotted ahead of me down the hall to the living room and hopped up onto the wing chair. We caught some of the nine o'clock local news. The same shot I'd seen earlier of the military and media trucks in front of the mall site filled the screen. The voice-over repeated just about the same things Scott had said earlier, while a square in the lower left side of the screen showed an updated track of the storm which seemed to be veering closer to the Massachusetts coast.

"Stay tuned to WICH-TV for full updates of news and weather at eleven," the studio announcer advised. Regular programming resumed with a fishing show, which is one of O'Ryan's favorites.

"I think I'll go downstairs and chat with Aunt Ibby until Pete comes. You just enjoy your show," I told the cat who made no comment, but focused rapt attention on the landing of a giant bluefin tuna.

I found my aunt at her kitchen table working on her laptop, the yellowed pages of Tabitha Trumbull's loose leaf handwritten recipe book spread open before her. I put the box of cookies destined for the library break room on the counter and helped myself to a diet ginger ale from the refrigerator. "Doing another chapter for Tabitha's book?"

"I am," she said. "All that cookie making put me in the mood for it."

"It went well, didn't it? Couldn't have pulled it off without your help."

"I enjoyed it. They're awfully nice girls." She closed the laptop. "I'm sure you know more about what's happening at the mall than you could say in front of them though. Can you share with your old aunt?"

It was a relief to talk about it. I told her about the dreadful stuff that lurked in the ground in the wild woods beneath the milkweed. I described the portrait of Emily and repeated Billy Dowgin's admissions to Pete about stalking me.

"So it looks as though Trudy and Happy are in this mess up to their ears but there's no proof?"

"Looks that way so far," I said, "with Emily and James both dead. But if the army digs up what you and I and are pretty sure is under there, they won't be opening a mall anytime soon."

"Pete will figure it all out. Don't you worry. Listen. Do you hear a cat crying?"

I listened and heard a plaintive "Mew."

"O'Ryan is upstairs watching *Wicked Tuna,"* I told her. "That's not him. Maybe it's Frankie."

"She's probably on the back steps," Aunt Ibby said. "Poor thing hasn't figured out how to use the cat door. Let her in, will you?"

I stepped out into the hall and admitted the wet and bedraggled white cat. The wind had picked up intensity again and I looked around at the swaying trees in our yard. A pale gleam caught my eye. "Aunt Ibby," I said, "There's a light coming from the garage. Looks like one of us might have left our headlights or interior lights on."

"That'll mean a dead battery for somebody in the morning for sure," she said. "We'd better check it." She took a terry cloth dish towel from a drawer and proceeded to wrap it around the shivering cat. "Could you do it, dear? My umbrella is hanging up right out there in the laundry room." She reached for her handbag and handed me her keyring. We each carry keys to both cars, so an extra fob to my car was there right along with her key. "Better start whichever one it is to charge the battery."

I took the umbrella from its hook and picked up a flashlight, turned it on, then hurried down the path to the garage. I was surprised to find that the side door was unlocked. I was sure I'd locked it when I'd put the 'vette away earlier. Aunt Ibby must have forgotten to do it when she'd parked the Buick. I pulled the door closed behind me, collapsed the umbrella and spotted the source of light immediately. The interior lights of *both* cars were on.

It was one of those moments when you know that what you're seeing doesn't make the least bit of sense.

I froze.

# CHAPTER 45

How could both interior lights be on? Was it possible that we'd each forgotten to turn ours off? Possible, but hardly plausible. I pressed a button on my fob and heard the familiar "pop" as the driver's side door unlocked. Slowly I eased my way between the two cars, bending slightly to peer inside, my hand moving along the sweet curve of the Laguna blue beauty. Satisfied that the car was empty, I opened the door, reached across the streamlined instrument panel and watched as the elongated lamps on either side of the rearview mirror faded to the off position. The sudden darkness made me almost sorry I'd turned them off. Using the flashlight, I made my way back to the side door and the switches for the garage overhead light and the Genie garage door opener. If I was going to start two cars, I didn't want to be in a closed space. I pressed the light switch. Nothing happened. The door opener didn't respond either. I fought a rising feeling of panic.

All of the interior lights, front and back, glowed within Aunt Ibby's car. The Buick, facing the rear of the garage, required a regular key, so I had no choice but to walk around to the driver's side door. Timidly, almost on tiptoe,

I approached it, inserted the key in the lock and pulled the heavy door open. My aunt keeps a remote garage door opener resting on the dashboard. I sat in the driver's seat, snatched the remote up and pushed the button. Nothing. I shook the thing. Tapped it against the steering wheel, listening for the familiar creaking sound of the garage double door rolling up and across the ceiling. It didn't happen. But there was a sound. One I hope I never hear again.

It was a crooning, a tearful, sad moan, coming from the woman who opened the passenger door and slid quickly into the seat beside me. I was surprised that such a large woman could move so fast. Trudy Shores held a remote control in her left hand and using it, easily opened the double doors. In her right hand she held a very large gun. Trudy Shores, who was supposed to be in Florida.

"I'm so sorry about this, darling." Tears streaked her face, making rivulets in heavy makeup. "I truly am. I don't want to hurt you but I hope you'll understand." Her tone changed then, and the next words came harshly. "Start the car. Back out of here. Hurry up."

Watching her face, aware of the gun inches from my head, I did as she commanded, and I heard, rather than saw, the garage doors roll shut. Oliver Street is one-way, so I headed toward Bridge Street, windshield wipers barely keeping up with the slashing rain.

Had anyone seen me leave? Aunt Ibby could have heard the car start, but she expected me to charge the battery. She'd think I'd decided to drive it instead of running the engine in the garage. She'd begin to worry after a while though. She'd call me.

Great. My phone was in my apartment with no one to answer it except a TV-watching cat. My handy dandy alarm pendant was there along with it.

"Go left, dear heart," Trudy ordered, her voice all sweetness and light, her gun leveled at my right ear. "You're so pretty. Such a smart girl too." She sighed. Deeply. "If you weren't so smart I wouldn't have to do this. I'm sure you understand."

"Actually, I don't," I said, looking in her direction. "I thought you were in Florida. What do you want?"

Her eyes narrowed. "You haven't figured that out? You seem to know everything else about my business, Miss Nosy! You called my office asking questions. You snooped around in my diaper laundry. You cozied up to Emily's sister. Now I might even have to get rid of her. Your fault. You should have gotten the message when I left the man in the graveyard for you to find." No more sweetness and light—she aimed the gun with both hands. "I never went to Florida. Never got on the plane. Stayed in a little motel on Route One. Now my car is back where it belongs behind my real estate office. I walked over here tonight." She squirmed in her seat. The realization that neither of us had fastened our seat belts flitted through my mind and I almost giggled at the incongruity of that thought.

"I don't understand," I said, fighting to sound conversational, to pretend this was somehow a normal situation. "What do you want?" I repeated.

"Why, it's simple. I want my husband to be happy—like his name. He deserves to have everything he wants. He works so hard. I adore him. Do you know Happy? Have you met him? Don't you think he's wonderful? And so handsome!"

"We haven't met," I said. I drove slowly, carefully. Visibility was terrible. I was mind numbingly scared. What did she want me to say? To do?

"Really? Maybe I'll show you a picture of him before I . . . well, maybe later."

"I saw him on television. At the football game," I offered, voice quavering a little. "He looked good."

"Oh, yes. The game. I gave him the ticket. I didn't want him to be around to see what I had to do that night. You know. To the other nosy one." She gestured with the gun. "Turn here."

Even through the driving rain the sign was visible.

*Howard Street Cemetery.*

I wheeled into the space beside the construction site. The workers hadn't secured everything and pieces of builders' debris tumbled in the wind. A barrel rolled past us and a sheet of plywood banged against the cemetery fence.

"Oh my," Trudy said. "We're in for quite a storm I think."

"Hurricane force winds," I said. "Maybe we should do this another time."

"No, dear. This'll be fine. This way you'll be all wet. Just like the others." I didn't look at her but I could tell she was smiling.

*She's going to kill me. She's going to admit killing Emily and James and then she's going to kill me.*

"What others?" I said. She seemed to want to talk. All I wanted was time.

"I felt terrible about the girl, you know. Sweet little Emily. I loved her like a daughter. I did. And darling James. Such a smart lad. Like you. Too damned smart."

The gun was almost touching my ear. Could I take it away from her? Her finger was on the trigger and she was a lot bigger and, I guessed, probably a lot stronger than I was.

"James got away from me twice, you know. I was glad when I thought the gators got him. Saved me the trouble."

I watched her face. She pouted. "Then he turned up here. Wanted revenge for his little girlfriend, I suppose. I convinced him to meet me at the diaper place on Monday. Offered him a lot of money. I really wanted to tell him what a nice death she had, but I never did get around to doing that." Pouting pursed lips were quickly followed by a bright smile.

"The pills in the wine worked fine. Did I tell you how I got them? I made an appointment with an out-of-town doctor, bought a fake ID with my picture, her name. He wrote the prescription. No questions. She just had a little wine and went to sleep in a lovely bubble bath. She tried to get out of it at first. Stepped on her wineglass and cut her dear little foot. But never mind. I put her right back in the tub. It was beautiful. I wish you could have been there. His wasn't so pretty, but it was quick. I hit him on the head with a hammer the minute he walked into the place. Knocked him out cold with one blow." The crazy smile was back again. "He was heavier than she was, of course, so it wasn't so easy to get him into the nice hot water."

"With the special detergent," I said.

"See? I told you you're a smart one. Anyway it was all James's fault. Showing off like that. Teaching that child how to take soil samples. Did you know that silly little Emily even gave me a library book about poisoned soil? I told her I'd give a little party in her honor. It was James who told me what he'd done though. Thinking I'd be grateful! Not so smart after all." She touched my ear with the gun. "Get out now. Time to go."

"Where are we going?"

"You'll have to walk. I about pulled my shoulder out of the socket shoving him over the fence, all soaking wet like he was. Easier if I just do it and roll you down the little hill. Right?"

*Stay in the car. Keep her talking.*

I heard the words in my head as plainly as I heard her words. I recognized the voice. It was Johnny. My poor dead Johnny. I looked up at the rearview mirror and saw Johnny's eyes.

*It's going to be okay, my love. I'm here. Keep her talking.*

"What were you going to do about the poisoned soil, Trudy?" I stalled. "How were you going to clean it up?"

"Stupid girl!" She yelled the words. "Stupid girl! We're going to cover it up. It will all be under the parking lot. No one needs to know. No one has to get hurt. Happy wants the mall. We've put all of our money into it. He deserves his beautiful mall." The tears had started again, staining her cheeks with black mascara streaks. Her voice dropped to a whisper. "Happy doesn't know what I've done for him. With you gone nobody will know for sure. Anyway, they'll be too afraid for their own lives to say anything after what happens to you tonight."

"Trudy. Mrs. Shores," I said. "It's too late to save the mall. The army corps is already over there, digging for the bottles. Didn't you see the news?"

"You're lying."

"No. I can show you. I'll drive you there. There are trucks and lights and people."

"You're lying," she said again, not sounding so confident.

I stole a look at the mirror again. Johnny was still there.

*Good girl. Keep at it. She's folding.*

"I'll show you. You'll see. It's too late to save the mall. But you can save your husband. The police have already brought him in for questioning."

"No! He didn't do anything. It was me! And James and Emily and you. We're the ones who did wrong."

"Your husband is probably so worried about you. He

must know by now that you didn't go to Florida. He might think you're dead. That poor man!"

"I don't believe you. I don't believe anything you say. Get out." She motioned with the gun. "Open the door and get out. Now."

*Do as she says.*

I did. I turned off the engine and slipped the keys into my pocket. Opening the door, pushing hard against the increasing wind, I struggled to stand as the stinging, almost horizontal deluge tore at my hair and face and clothes. Again, I was surprised at the speed with which the woman moved across the front seat. She was behind me, gun prodding at my back within what seemed like seconds. "Move," she said. "You'll have to climb the wall. The gate is locked at night."

We walked, leaning into the wind, around the corner to where the lawn sloped to its lowest point on Howard Street. It was dark, but there was a street lamp partway up the hill.

*Somebody will see us.*

*What if they do? Just a couple of silly women out for a walk in the rain.*

"You first. I'll shoot you right here if you try anything. Don't doubt me. I'll do it. And I'll get away with it too." She laughed. "I always do. Now. Over the wall with you, sweetheart."

I slipped on the rough granite of the wall, grasping at grass and earth and pulled myself up. I was close to a gravestone, and leaned on it for support. The woman with the gun struggled too, for one brief moment, but not enough to allow me to run, to scream, to distract her some way. She was beside me in a flash.

"Okay. March," she ordered, nodding toward the opposite side of the cemetery. "That way." I knew without asking that we were heading for the place where I'd tripped over James Dowgin's body. I knew in my heart that Trudy Shores intended to leave my soaking wet dead body in the same spot.

We approached the dark looming shape that was the Manning tomb. "Trudy. Mrs. Shores," I said, no longer trying to sound brave. I was terrified and my voice betrayed that terror. "You don't need to do this. Call your husband. He'll understand. He'll come here and get you. He'll take you home where you'll be safe."

"No. I know what I'm doing. All the blame is going to be on that artist kid. The building super I hired. The security guard I used. This is even the gun he carries when he's on duty at the diaper place." The laugh this time was loud and raucous, but lost in the wind. "Everyone knows he stalked the girl, Emily. He was jealous of James, and I made sure his fingerprints were on the cart I used to push James's body down to my car. And his gun is going to kill you in this cemetery, where he's been seen by half the city nearly every day for years!" For a moment, the gun was not prodding my back. "It's a perfect plan. I know what I'm doing. I always know what I'm doing."

*Run, my love. Run!*

I didn't doubt Johnny's voice. I ran. I knew I had to climb the iron fence, and it slowed me down for what seemed like ages. I made it over the top just as a shot rang out. I heard the bullet whiz over my head. It sounded to me like a million angry bees.

I yanked the door of the Buick open and started the engine. I backed out of the lot, tires squealing just in time to see in the glow of my headlights one of the twins (Roger? Ray?), gun drawn, going over the fence I'd just climbed. He looked in my direction and, with his free hand, waved me away.

What to do? What *could* I do? I had no gun, no phone, no way to help him. He was heading right for an armed, crazy woman inside that dark cemetery. Another gunshot rang out. I sped away, turned on my trouble lights, leaned on the good, loud horn of the old Buick.

It didn't take long—even in a pounding rain in near hurricane conditions—for a Salem police cruiser, lights flashing, to catch up with me. I pulled over, rolled down the window and shouted to the approaching officer. "Get help! Gunshots at Howard Street Cemetery."

He walked cautiously toward the car, reflective bands on a black rain jacket making his arm motions appear robotlike. "What's wrong, lady?" His right hand wasn't far from his weapon. I recognized him. A friend of Pete's. He recognized me too. "Geez, Ms. Barrett. You okay?"

I must have sounded hysterical—and perhaps I was, but I managed to convey what was happening. "A woman in the cemetery with a gun . . . shot at me . . . deputy went in after her . . . he's alone . . . get help!"

"We're already on it," he said. "Get out of here."

Then, as the old saying goes, "all hell broke loose." More flashing lights, screeching sirens, a fire truck, an ambulance.

I looked up at the rearview mirror. Johnny wasn't there. I drove carefully, slowly, thoughtfully, through the storm toward Winter Street and home.

# CHAPTER 46

It was well after midnight when Pete, Aunt Ibby, the Temple twins and I sat at Aunt Ibby's kitchen table drinking coffee and eating cookies by candlelight as though nothing out of the ordinary had happened—even though there was a category one hurricane drawing near to the Massachusetts coast, the power was off, we'd been to the emergency room where Ray had been treated for a gunshot wound in his shoulder, we'd just come back from the police station where we'd given our statements, and Trudy Shores was on her way to the morgue.

To hear Ray tell about it (it was he who'd leaped the cemetery fence), it was no big deal. Although the twins had passed on the cookie baking project, they'd decided it would be a good idea to watch the house, "Just in case." Roger had taken the first shift, observing our front door from a discreet distance while we baked and decorated sugar skulls upstairs. Later on, he'd followed Hilda's Jeep until he was sure all four of the women were safely home. Then Ray had driven back here and taken over the stakeout, "Just to be sure." Convinced that all was quiet on the premises after a reasonable amount of time had passed, he'd rounded the block to leave and noticed the lights in the garage. Starting to get out of his car to check, he saw the glow fade, the garage door open, and the Buick back out with two people inside.

"So," he said, "I figured, like anybody would, that the lights had been left on in the Buick and that Lee and her aunt were taking it out to charge the battery. Made sense to me. But the rain was getting worse, so I tailed 'em. Had to stay a good distance back, you know, 'cause Lee knows our car—and what with the storm and all—" He sounded embarrassed. "Well, I kind of lost 'em for a bit just after I passed the cemetery. I doubled back and saw the Buick in the construction site. Heard a shot. Stopped right there in the street, called 911, got out of my car and ran like hell to the cemetery. That's when Lee came barreling out of there. I jumped the fence and caught a bullet." He touched the sling on his right arm gingerly. "That crazy Shores woman shot me."

"You could see her plainly, you said?" Pete asked. "You were sure it was Trudy Shores?"

"There was a flash of lighting," Ray said. "Lit her up like a spotlight was on her. I knew who she was. She was standing under a tree, right next to one of those big tall old tombstones. Had that gun pointed right at me again. Then . . ." He looked down at the table. "Something . . . happened to her."

"Go ahead and tell them what you told me," his brother prompted. "Even if it sounds nutty."

"Okay. But it *does* sound nutty."

"Is this something you didn't include in your report?" Pete pulled out his notebook and pencil. "Something relevant to what happened?" The notebook cover looked wet, and he shook it off. "This is why I use a pencil," he said. "Ink runs on damp pages. Pencil doesn't."

*Good to know.*

"It's nothing that belongs in a report. Don't worry. I've done enough of them. No. This was something weird."

"Just tell it, man," Roger said. "They're not going to laugh at you."

Ray took a deep breath, then blew it out. "Okay. Here it is. She was standing under that tall tree where I took those pictures. Remember? The ones with the big white blob?"

"A white blob?" Aunt Ibby's eyes grew wide. "In the cemetery? What did you think it was?"

"I thought it was nothing," Ray said. "Therese and Hilda tried to tell me it was some kind of a ghost. A spirit."

Pete folded his arms and leaned back in his chair. "Don't tell me you've changed your mind."

"Of course not. No such thing as ghosts."

Roger nodded agreement. "No such thing."

"Anyway," Ray continued, "there was another big flash of lightning. That's when something white whizzed past her and that tall tombstone just tipped over. Fell right across her chest."

Pete wore his skeptical cop face. "So you think this white blob of yours pushed over a heavy tombstone? That the thing didn't simply tip over and crush her chest because it was leaning anyway, it was struck by lightning and the ground under it was completely saturated?"

"Not at all. I know it happened just the way you said. The weird part was it *looked* like the white thing pushed it."

Pete was smiling by then. "The ghost blob?"

Ray smiled back. "Wasn't a blob this time. It looked just like a damned cat."

I sat up straight. "Where's Frankie?" I demanded.

"She's in the living room with O'Ryan," Aunt Ibby said. "Don't worry dear. She's fine. They've been playing together like kittens."

As though on cue, the two cats strolled into the kitchen together, candlelight reflecting in their eyes. They stood next to the kitchen door, nose to nose. O'Ryan backed away and gave a nod of the big yellow head. Frankie nodded back, then turned and went out the cat door.

"They're so cute," my Aunt said. "O'Ryan taught her how to use his door. She's been having such fun, running in and out of it all evening."

# EPILOGUE

Hurricane Penelope barely brushed the North Shore, doing little damage and providing photographers, including some of my students, with some amazing surf pictures. I had to testify about Trudy Shores's confession to the murders of Emily Alden and James Dowgin, and it saddened me to see how hard Happy Shores took the bad news. He closed his Salem office and moved his business to the True Shores operation in Florida.

The police investigation into Emily's and James's poisonings revealed that the warning about skin absorption of the deadly chemical was printed right on the plastic buckets of the diaper detergents. All Trudy had needed to do was use plenty of detergent and extremely hot water to kill her unconscious victims. The chemicals in the soil at the wild woods presented a far more dangerous and complicated problem. The Army Corps of Engineers took over the cleanup project and it was determined that the contamination was not widespread over the entire fifty acres. Even so, it will take a long time and cost a great deal of money to make the place safe. The good news about that is that there are plans to create a county park there instead of a mall. It will be a beautiful new attraction for residents and tourists, birds and bees, fireflies and butterflies.

Our *Dia de los Muertos* celebration was an enormous hit with everyone . . . particularly with the paranormal community who remain fully convinced that the spirit of Giles Corey took revenge on Trudy for desecrating the scene of his death, by crushing her chest just as his had been crushed centuries ago. Naturally Pete, the Temple twins and Chief Whaley pooh-poohed that crazy idea, but Kelsey Roehl and the other ghost tour guides made the most of the story and had a wildly successful Halloween season which extended neatly into November. (By the way, our sugar skull cookie video went viral.)

Dorothy stayed in Salem until the end of the semester, then headed back to Alaska, taking with her the portrait of Emily that Dakota Berman had given to her. Dakota is still painting, and is—with my aunt's assistance—spearheading a drive to repair the broken tombstones in Salem's historic cemeteries. He and Shannon are still an item.

Of course, so are Pete and I.

I've never told anyone about seeing Johnny in the mirror and hearing his voice in the cemetery. Anyway I'm pretty sure I imagined that part because I needed courage at that moment, and Johnny was always so very brave.

One last peculiar thing. At just about the time I went out to the garage to check on the lights, the alarm company received an alert from my pendant—which was in my purse, on my couch, in the room with a TV-watching cat.

After Frankie left through the cat door that strange night, she never came back inside. She hasn't appeared on my fire escape either, although every once in a while, on a moonless night, I think I see her sitting on the fence in our side yard.

But maybe I'm wrong. After all, when all candles be out, all cats be gray.

# ACKNOWLEDGMENTS

Sometimes it seems as though writing is a solitary pursuit, but the business of putting words on paper actually involves many helpers.

The germ of the idea for *Grave Errors* came when fellow writer Richard Erlinger read his article about *Dia de los Muertos* to our regular Saturday morning critique group. Richard's story reminded me of the wonderful historic cemeteries in Salem, the city of my Halloween eve birth. While researching Salem's cemeteries for the book, I contacted Chris Dowgin, author, artist, tour guide and expert on the Witch City's underground who willingly shared a wealth of graveyard lore (and allowed me to borrow his last name for a couple of characters). I corresponded with Kenneth Dyke-Glover, guide on the popular "Sinister Stories of Salem" tour. Kenneth provided details of the legend of the haunted Giles Corey tree in the Howard Street Cemetery and even included a sketch of that infamous site.

My "power group" critiquing partners Laura Kennedy and Rebecca Johnson as always provided valuable feedback along with punctuation, plotting and sometimes much needed praise. Writers' organizations offer sound advice, encouragement and information. Mystery Writers of America (MWA), Sisters in Crime (SinC), Bay Area Professional Writers Guild (BAPWG), Pinellas Writers,

Wordsmiths, Florida Writers Association (FWA) and Writers-Editors Network have all been willing helpers in the creation of my cozy mysteries. Radio personality Patzi Gil, host of *Joy on Paper* and friend of writers everywhere, is a special inspiration as is Dana Cassell at Writers-Editors network.

Naturally a big share of thanks goes to my publisher—Kensington. Editor Esi Sogah, Production Editor Robin Cook, Publicity Manager Morgan Elwell and the amazing artist who does my fabulous covers each add considerable expertise. Together they make each book as good as it can be.

*It takes a literary village. . . .*

Thanks to you all.

RECIPES

# Tabitha Trumbull's Vanilla Bread Pudding

## (adapted by Aunt Ibby)

1 quart of milk
2½ cups firm bread cut into ½-inch pieces
½ cup of sugar, divided into two ¼ cups
4 eggs
½ teaspoon of salt
3 tablespoons butter
2 teaspoons pure vanilla extract
1½ cups thinly sliced peeled apples
½ cup seedless raisins

Scald milk in medium saucepan, stir in bread and set aside. In mixing bowl beat two of the eggs plus two egg yolks, setting aside two whites. Stir in ¼ cup sugar and the salt. Slowly pour in the cooled milk mixture, stirring constantly. Add butter and vanilla extract. Stir in apples and raisins. Turn into 1½ quart buttered casserole and set it in a large baking pan. Pour hot water into the pan within an inch of the top of the casserole. Bake in 350-degree oven about one hour, 15 minutes and remove from oven. With clean bowl and beaters, beat reserved egg whites and remaining ¼ cup of sugar until soft peaks form. Spoon meringue over pudding, spreading well. Return to oven and bake until meringue is light brown—about 15 minutes.

Serves 6 to 8

## Tabitha Trumbull's Cowboy Cookies

(Tabitha's notes didn't explain why they are called "cowboy cookies" and Aunt Ibby's research didn't turn up any clues either.)

2 cups flour
½ teaspoon baking powder
1 teaspoon baking soda
½ teaspoon salt
1 cup shortening (Aunt Ibby uses Crisco)
2 eggs
1 teaspoon pure vanilla extract
1 cup sugar
1 cup brown sugar
1 cup regular oatmeal (Aunt Ibby uses Quaker Oats)
1 package chocolate chips (Aunt Ibby uses Nestlé)

Sift and set aside the first four ingredients. Cream shortening, white and brown sugars and two eggs. Add flour mixture. Add oatmeal, vanilla and chocolate chips. Drop by full teaspoons onto greased cookie sheet, two inches apart. Bake at 350 degrees for about ten minutes or until browned lightly around the edges. Cool for a minute or two on cookie sheet before removing to wire racks.

Makes about 3 dozen cookies

Keep reading for a sneak peek at

**IT TAKES A COVEN**

Coming soon from
Carol J. Perry
And
Kensington Books

Love following Lee's adventures in the Witch City?

Be sure to read

CAUGHT DEAD HANDED

TAILS, YOU LOSE

LOOK BOTH WAYS

MURDER GO ROUND

Available wherever books are sold

# CHAPTER 1

I'd just finished my sample slice of almond cake with vanilla cream filling and vanilla buttercream frosting, and had taken my first bite of chocolate cake with chocolate ganache and chocolate glaze covered in chocolate cookie crumbs when I heard that Megan was dead.

"I can't believe it." Therese Della Monica put down her phone. "I saw her last night and she looked fine." She shrugged. "I mean as fine as anyone can look at a hundred and five."

Bride-to-be Shannon Dumas paused with a forkful of vanilla cake with hazelnut ganache and buttercream frosting halfway to her mouth. "You actually know a woman who's a hundred and five years old? I mean, you *knew* her?"

"We both did," I said. "Therese, does River know?"

"That's who called me." Therese brushed the back of her hand across misty eyes, picked up her camera and once again focused the lens on Shannon. "Megan was the oldest witch in Salem, Shannon. She's sort of famous."

It had been a pleasant spring Saturday. Shannon and I sat in pink ice cream parlor chairs at a round marble topped table in the Pretty Party Bakery. We were tasting wedding cake samples while Therese photographed the occasion for an album celebrating Shannon's upcoming marriage to Salem artist Dakota Berman. I'd accepted Shannon's invitation to be her maid of honor, not fully understanding exactly what duties that honor might entail.

I'm Lee Barrett, née Maralee Kowolski, I'm thirty-two, red-haired, Salem-born, orphaned early, married once and widowed young. My aunt, Isobel Russell, raised me after my parents died and now we share the fine old family home on Winter Street along with our cat, O'Ryan. Therese and Shannon had been my students at the Tabitha Trumbull Academy of the Arts where I teach TV Production. It was because of my class at the Tabby that Shannon and Dakota met and fell in love.

Actually they met in a graveyard, but that's another story.

I was sad about Megan's passing, but she was, after all, more than a century old and blind, so the news wasn't altogether surprising. I'd met Megan through my best friend, River North. River is a witch too, and a member of Megan's coven. I knew she must be upset and I planned to call her just as soon as a decision on the cake was made.

"I don't know what to do, Lee." Shannon held up two forks—vanilla cake on one and chocolate on the other. "Dakota loves chocolate and so do I, but a white wedding cake seems, I don't know, like—more traditional."

"They're all delicious," I said, "so why not have a tiered cake with alternating layers—chocolate and white, with the yummy buttercream frosting on the whole thing? It'll look like a regular white wedding cake with chocolate surprises inside."

"Perfect. That's what we'll do. Thanks, Lee. What would

I do without you?" She popped the last bite of chocolate cake into her mouth and stood. "Want to go pick out invitations now?"

"Maybe later," I said. "I need to call River and check on funeral arrangements for Megan. That okay?"

Therese packed up her camera equipment. "I'm guessing it'll be a big event, even though Megan would have preferred something simple." Her eyes were moist. The young photographer was a novice witch-in-training who'd studied photography at the Tabby, and studied witchcraft with the recently departed Megan. "I loved that old woman," she said. "I just want to sit down and cry, but Megan would tell me to get to work. Come on, Shannon. Let's check out that beginners cooking class." She and Shannon left together, planning some cute shots of Shannon in a chef's hat, holding a wooden spoon.

I was anxious to talk with River and called her as soon as I reached my car, a blue Corvette Stingray—a major and much loved extravagance.

"River, Therese just told me about Megan. What happened? Are you all right?"

"Oh, Lee. She died in her sleep. We're all so sad. Everybody loved her."

"I know. Want to come over to my place and talk about it? There's nobody home but O'Ryan and me. Aunt Ibby's training staff at the library and Pete's working a double shift. I'll leave the downstairs door unlocked for you."

My aunt is a semi-retired reference librarian. She's sixty-something and doesn't look, act or sound it. My police detective boyfriend Pete Mondello knew Megan too. She'd actually helped him solve a tricky case a couple of years back. They'd both be sorry to hear the news. O'Ryan, our big yellow striped cat, had come to live with Aunt Ibby and me after Ariel Constellation, his previous owner—as if anyone can *own* a cat— had been murdered. Ariel was a witch too, and some say O'Ryan was her familiar. (In Salem a witch's familiar is to be respected, and sometimes even feared!)

River agreed to join me in my third floor apartment in the house on Winter Street. She's the late-night host on WICH-TV, the local cable channel. Her wildly popular phone-in show is *Tarot Time with River North*, where she reads the tarot cards for callers in between scary old movies. I once hosted a phone-in psychic show called *Nightshades* in the same time slot on that same station. Though I'd had a number of years of previous successful on-camera experience, *Nightshades* did not turn out well, and that is one huge understatement.

In less than half an hour, River walked through my living room door, with O'Ryan making loving figure eights around her ankles. "Thanks for inviting me over," she said. "The coven has asked me to help plan Megan's funeral and I can't seem to stop crying."

"I'm so sorry. Come on out to the kitchen. Coffee's on. I have some cute little cupcakes too. Shannon and I were at Pretty Party tasting cakes for her wedding."

"Wedding planning is a lot more fun that funeral planning." River picked O'Ryan up and followed me to the kitchen, with the cat snuggling against her shoulder. "This will be the third funeral I've had to go to this month."

"Really? Who else died?"

"Mr. Bagenstose, the banker. Died a couple of weeks ago. They found him in his own back yard under an apple tree. Heart attack, I think."

"Oh, yes. I didn't know him but Aunt Ibby did. She was at the funeral too. I didn't realize he was a friend of yours."

River looked away and, eyes downcast, sat in one of my nineteen seventies Lucite kitchen chairs with O'Ryan in her lap. "Yeah. He was. Kind of."

"Here. Have a chocolate cupcake. It'll make you feel better," I said, firmly believing in the power of chocolate. I put a little cake on each of our plates, poured two mugs of coffee and sat opposite my friend. "You said there were three?"

"Uh-huh. You remember Gloria Tasker? She used to be a waitress at one of the old diners years ago. It was a hit and run. She was riding her bike early in the morning down by Ropes's Point. They never found out who did it. Police said maybe the driver didn't even realize he'd hit somebody."

"I remember her vaguely." I offered River a paper napkin. "Gloria and Mr. Bagenstose were both older than Aunt Ibby and you're younger than I am. I didn't realize you had such elderly friends. Were they Tarot clients?"

Tears coursed down River's cheeks. "No. They were kind of—associates."

"Associates?"

"I guess there's no harm in telling you, as long as you promise not to tell anyone else." O'Ryan licked River's face and she continued. "They were witches."

"Of course I won't tell anyone. That's a very personal thing. I knew Megan was a witch of course, but the banker? The waitress?"

River nodded. "Those two weren't ready to come out of the broom closet yet, but they were witches too—not in my coven, but I saw them sometimes at gatherings."

"Three witches in a month," I said. "Is that pretty unusual?"

"I think so. And Lee," her voice dropped to a thin whisper. "It might be all my fault."

Visit
**Kensing**
to read more from yo
by series, view read

for sneak peeks, chances to win books and prize packs,
and to share your thoughts with other readers.

facebook.com/kensingtonpublishing
twitter.com/kensingtonbooks

*Tell us what you think!*

To share your thoughts, submit a review,
or sign up for our eNewsletters, please visit:
**KensingtonBooks.com/TellUs.**